D I V I D E D

Pony knew her senses were dulled by blood and pain and overwhelming sound. She could not seem to think about the battle that had consumed her with revulsion only moments before. She did not know why Osrick was here, or how Valgar the Beast had appeared out of the confusion to protect her; she could think only of the pain she saw in those gray eyes and the fact that she had caused it.

How could a beast look so? Why did a beast care that the child she carried was not his? They were not questions she could answer. She could not think why she wanted to try.

Val was giving up his weapons. The sword she had so admired clanged on the other Viking steel. The pile of blades looked like a child's game of pick-up sticks. The set of Val's shoulders registered his defeat. His hair was matted to his head with sweat. Blood smeared the chain mail on his right shoulder and stained the leather on his left thigh. Pony wanted to heave her bulk off her horse and run to him. Ah, her bulk! That fact lay between them. She sat up straighter. That and the fact that he was a sworn enemy of her king. That and his killing nature. That and the fact that her daughter might be powerful in her own right some day, if Alfred owned to her. That and the fact that she was of the land invaded, and he was the invader.

Other books by Susan Squires:

BODY ELECTRIC
SACRAMENT
DANEGELD

Danelaw

SUSAN SQUIRES

LEISURE BOOKS NEW YORK CITY

A LEISURE BOOK®

February 2003

Published by

Dorchester Publishing Co., Inc.
276 Fifth Avenue
New York, NY 10001

ISBN 0-8439-5124-9

Printed in the United States of America.

Visit us on the web at www.dorchesterpub.com.

Danelaw

Chapter One

Pony felt the pull of destiny. What she needed was a girl-child. She trudged in front of First Mare, scuffing her soft leather boots in the hard dirt of the trail winding through the green of the Wiltshire downs. Her need scratched at her, just as her flaxen shirt abraded her damp skin in the September afternoon heat. Summer blazed one last time before it faded. Her leggings, bound up with leather straps so she could ride, were not cool enough for walking. She was the last of her kind. It was her obligation to produce her successor. How many times had she heard her mother say those words? She had resisted her obligation for ten long years. But the catastrophe her mother had prophesied was beginning; like the summer, her *gifu,* her Gift, was fading.

Pony ran her hands through her white blonde hair. She would lose the thing she most valued if she did not do the one thing she most feared. It was not fair of the Great Mother to ask it. After the child, would she fade in other ways, as her mother had, until she disappeared entirely?

Pony shuddered as though to shake away her thoughts.

1

She shaded her eyes with her hand from the burning blue sky. Ahead, her own green hill jutted squarely into the sky, branded with the outline of a giant horse cut into the chalk soil. Its white beacon was visible for miles down the Vale. To her left, the mounded earth of Waylan's Barrow hulked over that worthy's ancient bones. She was almost home. Only one obstacle remained. The shepherds. But perhaps they had taken their flock east.

She stopped to adjust the packs over First Mare's dark bay withers. The horse nosed her up and down, breathing on her to exchange the scent of Herd, that they might know they belonged together. She resettled the pack of wool and bowls and seeds, a new metal spade and tanned leather, a welcome exchange for the partnership of Young Dapple.

As she and her horse turned toward home, Pony's fear nipped at her heels. The way to save the Gift was perilous. Her mother had told her a thousand times that she must not let the tumult of letting a man plant his seed disturb her calm. Peace was required to use the Gift.

"Find a man you do not lust after, Epona—though of good stock, strong seed, not simple-minded," she could hear her mother say. *"Lie with him, then send him away. Don't let him cut up your calm. Get his seed. That is his only use."* Where would she find such a man?

Pony sensed the sheep before she heard them. That much of her Gift was left. She resigned herself to running the final gauntlet. The black faces and huge wool coats of a river of sheep swirled across the path below, between her and her home. Hounds yapped at their heels. *Carnivores!* Three coarse shepherds whistled and pointed directions to their dogs.

"Look, brothers," one called. "Our neighbor, Epona. Is it female?"

"It doesn't look female," another responded. "Where is your cyrtle, wench?"

Just keep your peace, Pony admonished herself, even as her mother would have done. The eldest shepherd pushed his way through his eddying flock. His clothes were torn and dirty, like his brothers'. Their father had kept them in line as long as he had been alive. Now, six months after his death, mead and sheep made up these men's lives.

"It has a full pack on that devil horse's back," the eldest sneered.

"Do we want that pack?" The youngest was less coarsely made but wilder than the others.

"What say we see if it is female while we're at it?" The eldest grinned. He sent the hounds out around Pony and her companion. First Mare sidled nervously as the dogs penned her in, staring. The beasts would be upon her in an instant if she tried to run, ripping and tearing with carnivorous jaws.

A shiver of fear traveled Pony's spine. "Out of my way," she said softly.

They laughed. It was a jarring sound, unconnected to the rightness of the world. The eldest stepped forward, towering over her. He breathed rancid butter and onions and mead. He grabbed her arm. She wanted to shriek in distaste, to struggle against that iron grip. Instead, she inhaled once and closed her eyes, willing calm into her center, begging her Gift to gather its waning strength. She put her heartbeat away, the better to hear.

When she opened her eyes, all was clear. The brothers' laughter provided only the bass in a chorus of sounds: sheep bleated, hounds barked, a jay called somewhere. Insects hummed and clicked, wool rasped against wool, cloven hooves thudded in the turf, water slid by stones in the distant stream. First Mare breathed. The hairs of her tail swished through the air. The world sang and Pony listened. Her soul vibrated with the will of the Great Mother.

Into this quivering tension that stretched between her and her surroundings, she sent a suggestion. Swirls of wool and black faces engulfed the brothers, shoving, bleating.

The eldest spun, shouting. "What? Damned sheep!" He lost his balance and went down. Pony could hear his grunts as cloven hooves found his softer parts. She was the still center of the crowding beasts, untouched. The ovine river swept the other brothers to the side of the path and then parted, revealing the little trail, just like that story about the Red Sea the Christian priest had once told her. The shepherds' hounds barked and circled to no avail. Her thoughts could not reach them, they were carnivores, but the sheep could hear her.

Pony and First Mare moved up the path as another brother went down among the sheep hooves. "Ill-begotten bitch!" the eldest yelled.

The tension of alignment dissipated, leaving Pony feeling small and alone, as she always did when the Gift was put away for use another day. She hoped there would be other days. The old dread and depression sucked the blue out of the sky. Pony didn't look back. She and First Mare were still two miles from home.

"And are we to trust one such as he with the honor of holding lands for the Danes?" The words snapped into the sparks that rose from the fire around which the *jarls* squatted.

Val, known as Valgar the Beast, raised his chin. This challenge had been inevitable from the moment he had decided to return from the exile he had chosen on the banks of the Volga. It came from a hot-headed youth, Harald, his the lightest beard among the leaders of the Danelaw. Val's fingers ached for the handle of Bloodletter, but Danes wore no swords when they sat in council. He carried only his bone flute stuck in his boot. That was not likely to convince his fellows of his worthiness. The fact that a warrior was known to play like a scald was yet another sign he was unworthy to lead the fierce Danes. He turned his face to the signposts he had followed across half the world: stars that wheeled above, uncaring in their black bed.

Guthrum, *konnungr* of all this land under Danish law—the Danelaw—was silent. His army occupied the whole eastern half of this great isle, but it was not enough. He wanted it all. His beard was gray, his eyes old with experience as well as years. He could not speak for Valgar. His choice was made; he would appear weak if he defended it.

Val glanced around the circle at faces hardened by battle and sea winds, made harder still by the flicker of the flames lighting them, and pressed his own lips together. Their knowledge of his shame was written in their eyes. His own words could not be raised in his defense. He understood their distrust. Why should they feel differently about him than he did about himself?

Guthrum's eldest son, Ragnor, second in command, was left to say: "Has he not fought beside us these many days? Is his sword not strong for the Danelaw?" No one would mention the tales of his prowess, his nerveless cruelty, filtering back from the east. Those deeds were not inspired by loyalty for his countrymen, but sold to the czars of Garthariki.

Did Ragnor not know the reason why Guthrum had chosen Val? It was not for his sword arm. Around the circle, eyes narrowed, considering Harald's challenge. Val knew why he had been chosen. Pushing the borders of the Danelaw into Wessex was not a matter for the blade alone. The Saxon thegns had seen already the way it would go. Alfred, the young king of Wessex, could not protect them. Guthrum's Danes had defeated their armies many times in the last year, pushing inexorably westward. Those Saxon eorls with Frankish lands had already decamped across the narrow sea channel. The others had bowed to the inevitable. Now the Danes had a task much harder than just fighting their way across the island: As their numbers stretched and thinned, they would have to control what they had won. With organization and with leadership, they would bring the "law" of the Danes to barbarians who did not understand the way of it.

"He speaks their language better than any of us," the one called Egill said. "He could speak it almost from the first. And he has ruled in Barbary, where he was foreign to the people yet bent them to his will. He knows our way ahead."

Egill understood. The *jarl's* hard blue eyes examined Val. A scar running down the line of his jaw gleamed in the firelight. Egill was practical. His men fought for him like demons. Guthrum, wily fox that he was, trusted him as much as one like Guthrum could trust any man. Egill pressed Ragnor from behind for his position as second to Guthrum, even though Ragnor claimed the position as Guthrum's son.

"*Ja*, how *is* that?" Harald asked. "How does he know the words of our enemies? And he wears his hair long in back, as they do, like women."

"The better to seem their natural leader," Egill said. "He is crafty, this one."

Ah, Val thought, Egill did not yet trust him, though the man saw his fitness for the job ahead. And he was right. Val had not shaved the nape of his neck when he returned from the steppes, as other Danes did; nor did he braid plaits as they did in the longer locks hanging around their faces. His hair waved down his back and around his face, free, longer than the Saxons wore theirs, but not so much as to seem strange. He had worked to learn their language from the day he landed. He had planned exactly how he would make himself indispensable to Guthrum. He had counted on the *konnungr* to see his value, even if the others did not.

Val followed Guthrum's gaze around the circle. The others laid their lot not yet with Harald, but they did not share Guthrum's faith in him. Guthrum was silent. He did not command their agreement. He would wait until most had consented or rejected Val. His rule was based on loyalty, not fear. That was the way of the Danelaw.

And that love of loyalty was just Val's problem. How could these *jarls* trust one who had committed the ultimate betrayal? Val twisted the leather strips that wrapped his wrists, his gut twisting too. He should never have left Garthariki. On the shores of the Volga it was natural to be hated and feared for the mercenary he was. Here he found that his own people distrusted him even more.

"First *Jarl*," he barked into the crackling of the fire and the pointed silence around the circle. He stood. "Test me." He would prove his worthiness with blood. Who would

Guthrum send against him in that honored tradition? Not Harald. Harald didn't have a chance in the battle test. It would honor Val too much to send Ragnor. Val wagered it would be Egill. They were both strong in battle. Egill was rangier, his shoulders and arms not quite so thickly muscled as Val's, but he was taller, well over six feet. He would have the advantage of reach.

The silence stretched. Val was left to stand awkwardly in the circle, his offer unaccepted. He clenched his fists, refusing to look at Guthrum. Would the *konnungr* humiliate him by refusing a test, when Val was his own choice to hold the Downland?

Finally, Guthrum eased himself to standing, feet apart. He nodded his grizzled head slowly. "I will test you, Valgar, son of Thorvald." He bent to pick a brand from the fire.

Val blinked against the pain that flickered somewhere inside him every time his lineage was named. Why would Guthrum remind every *jarl* around the circle of his shame?

"Let *me* test his worth," Harald shouted, leaping to his feet.

Guthrum nodded, arms folded. "You shall be the one."

Val jerked his gaze to Guthrum's face. Muttering broke out around the circle. It was no honor to cleave a stripling. But the king signaled the *jarls* to widen their circle, then beckoned to Val and Harald. Val set his jaw. This would win him no acceptance. Was he reduced to returning to the shores of the Volga? His life had been empty there. Would it be worth living in some other exile? Perhaps he would press from island to island across the great North Sea until he lost himself in new lands. Bleak ice landscapes would mirror his heart.

Val and Harald moved to stand before their *konnungr*. He could smell nervous sweat on the younger man, feel his excitement. This was, no doubt, his first test of honor. And his last. Harald had the same hair as Val's youngest brother, Erik, like yellow silk from the lands east of the steppes—and the thought made Val realize he might fail this test from his own cowardice. He had never had the stomach for killing the weak, though he was known as the Beast. Not that Harald was weak, he told himself sternly. He would not let it be like the other times. Ragnor went to get their swords.

"Ho, Ragnor," Guthrum called. "We have all we need."

Val eyed Guthrum warily. The king swung up the burning brand. "Roll up the sleeve on your shield arm, Valgar," he commanded.

Val and Harald both stared at the blazing wood. Val's eyes flicked to Guthrum's impassive face. So, it was not a test of combat. Guthrum handed the brand to Harald as Val bared his right forearm.

"This may test courage," Ragnor protested, "but not loyalty."

"As much as trial by battle," Guthrum grunted. "We ask: is Valgar capable of betrayal?" He glared out at the circle. "If Valgar passes the test, he is loyal. If he does not, then Harald is right, and Valgar is capable of betrayal."

The *jarls* nodded, murmuring assent, but surprise flashed across some faces. Testing through pain had been replaced by trials of combat long ago.

Val's stomach clenched. Harald grasped the torch held out to him in a hand that shook slightly. His eyes would not meet Val's. Val held out his right fist. At least it would not be his sword arm charred to a stump. Would any follow a Dane with one hand? The light curling hairs on his thick forearm gleamed in the torchlight over the taut cords of muscle.

Guthrum clasped both their wrists. "You hold the torch, Harald. Press your arm into the flame, Valgar. He who flinches first will tell us the truth of the matter."

Val's breath came hard. It should be the leader who called halt and declared the test over, not the one who held the torch. What cared Harald to stop the test? Val's arm was forfeit, sure. If the burn festered, he was a dead man. If he lived, he was a cripple. He jerked up his hand, his biceps bunching. The *jarls* were intent, masking their surprise at Guthrum's rules. The circle thickened with other men, even

8

with serving women, all drawn to the drama of pain and courage.

Harald's eyes were big. Beads of sweat stood among the sparse hairs of his upper lip as he thrust out the burning brand, its flame licking upward.

Val steadied his breathing, willing himself to the courage demanded. He thought of the time he was wounded and left for dead in the snows above Novograd. He must go away from himself now, just as he had then, to hoard strength. He laid his forearm slowly into the flame.

The sear of pain that shot through Val's flesh shocked his brain. He had counted on that. Around the circle, men gasped. Harald's torch flickered with his shaking hand. Val saw his own arm redden as the flame licked at him. He stared at the flame, willing his arm steadfast. *Rock. Your arm is rock.* The pain ate into his mind, raw, searing. He pressed his lips together. *Rock feels no pain.* His biceps trembled with the effort of keeping his arm in the fire. He saw his skin begin to bubble. He gazed into Harald's eyes. Fear sprouted there. Harald knew he could burn Val's arm into a blackened stump. Sweat beaded Harald's forehead. Val's sweat dripped into his eyes. He wanted to howl like an animal. More than anything he wanted to jerk his arm away and run screaming from the circle. But he did not. That way lay only terrible isolation, exile from his people, the shame of knowing he had defiled his family's name; that no woman would wed him, no man call him friend. His forearm slowly blackened. *Like rocks blacken in fire,* he told himself. *Rocks. I am rock,* he sang to himself, *rock, rock, rock.* A tune beat in his head. The music carried him away from here and now. Harald began to moan. Did he himself not owe this pain, Val wondered, in retribution for his deeds of long ago? He smelled cooked meat and knew that it was his own flesh. He heard his grunts of pain. *Odin, let me not faint,* he prayed in time to the tune crescendoing in his head.

Harald jerked the brand away with a cry. Val held his

arm steady, so all might see that he would have held it there forever.

"What is this?" Harald shrieked. "Should *Danir* do such a deed to *Danir*?"

Slowly, Val gathered in his shaking arm and cradled it against his chest. "It is done," he gasped. Was his shield arm forfeit? Would his life fester away as well?

"It is done," Guthrum agreed. "Valgar holds the Downs while we press south to clutch the remnants of Alfred's forces in our vise." He turned to the others.

"It is done," the hard voices of the circle agreed.

Harald cast the torch from him and staggered away. Guthrum motioned Ragnor to go after him. The young warrior had learned a lesson today in the ruthless kinds of courage that might be demanded of a Dane gone *vikingr*. Val had been ruthless with his enemies and the enemies of those who paid him countless times. Why else was he named Valgar the Beast? He cradled his arm against his leather jerkin. He was more Valgar the Beast than Valgar Thorvaldsson. In some strange way, his father had made the first name more appropriate.

The circle dissolved into the night. No one came forward to give Val a kind word. They still did not trust him. Guthrum clapped him on a shoulder hunched against the pain. "Tomorrow you start for the Downs." The old gray eyes examined Val's face as though he looked for more answers than the test provided.

"I will hold the Downland for you and for the Danelaw," Val said. His voice was steady, loud in his own ears. "I am *Danir*." He could say no more than that.

Guthrum nodded and strode toward his tent, pitched in the common ground of the village.

Val's knees went weak. He had gotten what he wanted. He would hold the Downs for the Danelaw, no matter the price. Then would these dogs know the meaning of loyalty. Then would his history finally be wiped clean.

* * *

Pony rose from her seat by the fire in the small hut. Something inside her was fluttery. She tried to still her heartbeat so she could listen, but all she could hear was skipping beats and blood throbbing in her temples. Outside, one of her Herd gave a shrieking whinny, calling her. It was White Stallion. She tossed back her mane of white blonde hair and groped for calm. *Breathe in,* she commanded herself. *Smooth your brow. Breathe out. Relax your shoulders.*

There it was! How had she not heard it? Once she would have heard it clearly without trying. Now, White Stallion had to tell her when to listen. She dared not let dread and disappointment poison her stillness. She put them away for later examination. Now, she just listened. She heard fear, of course. That was the way of prey. Wariness echoed around her from a thousand sources. There was more. She moved silently to the open doorway and peered into the last shadows of twilight. The downs sloped away in dusky green ahead of her. Night had already claimed her woods beyond the pasturelands to the south, where Herd moved restlessly. Was it they who called her? Again she pressed the thump of her heart away. This time it faded obediently. Warning. She heard a warning.

Slowly she glided out into the gloaming. No wind, only the last of the summer's heat making her shift cling to her damply. Clouds massing on the horizon threatened heat lightning. It was not her Herd that called her, though they had heard the warning too. White Stallion wheeled, looking for wolves. Pony blurred her eyes to erase the Herd's concern and pushed away the sounds of their hooves and their distant whinnies. She must listen more intently. She stood still.

Ahhhhhh. She sucked air into her lungs. The danger was not to her, not to Herd, but to . . . to one who had traded his freedom for the partnership she promised him. Young Black. Bonds of trust were broken. The covenant was violated. Pony's throat closed around bile. Rising anger choked off her listening. She shook her head as though she could shake her anger away. There were things she must yet know.

11

Her mother would have remained calm. Her mother would also have heard the warning immediately. Pony cursed her lack of control and wondered for one of uncounted times why she was not more like her mother had been.

The full moon peeked over the wood in an orange crescent too huge to be real. She breathed in the scent of ripe grass cooling toward the dew, the acrid smoke from the fire inside her hut, the aroma of oat cakes on her hearth, and faintly, the musky scent of Herd. She willed away emotion as her mother had taught. Breath stilled, heart quieted. Calm.

The stag stepped out of the trees, his great head weighted with the forked antlers that branched there, his eyes liquid wariness. *There you are, my pretty,* Pony thought, not moving, not breathing, serene. *Tell me. Tell me.*

He did. He told her everything. When he was done, he dipped his nose to touch the long grass at the edge of the wood, then lifted his head and sprang back into the trees. He disappeared instantly. He had risked much to come here with his tale, got from a doe who got it from an ox she grazed with, who got it from a horse who pulled a cart to Chippenham.

Pony breathed. She knew what she had to do. She turned slowly to the steep, green-clad hill looming behind her hut. The moon limned the chalk outline of the great horse into a white accusation. She was her mother's daughter, and her mother's mother's daughter, and the child of a thousand mothers before her. She lived under the white chalk horse on the downs. It was her covenant, her Gift, her obligation that was violated here. She must take back her own. There would be tumult ahead. It would be hard to be serene enough to listen. But if she tempted the Goddess to possess her, she might win through. She had no choice.

The moon had shrunk to a cold white sliver. Thunderclouds building in the west had begun to move—she and Herd might not stay ahead of the rain tonight. She did not discard her nightshift in favor of her buff leather breeches and flaxen shirt. Together with her hair streaming around

12

her, it would make her look ghostly in the moonlight. She counted on that, and on Herd. She owned no weapon. But she had a talisman of the old religion, a shining black glass pebble strung through with a leather thong tied around her neck. Let the Goddess be with her tonight.

She strode down to the pastureland in front of her wood. Herd was perhaps thirty. They lifted their heads at her approach, ears pricked toward her. Dark bay and chestnut that would gleam red if there were sun, whitening gray and dapples, roan and dun, they made a moving tapestry bleached by the moonlight. The great whitish stallion squealed into the night. The mares and younger horses, the foals, all wheeled in the dewy grass. Pony clicked her tongue to them and they rounded as one to encircle her. She smiled, letting the quiet creep into her bones again. They knew what news the stag had brought. Now they needed only to know what they must do. If she were quiet enough, they could hear her plans; she could tell them. Her eyes blurred, her breath stilled. She put away the beat of her heart and closed her eyes.

When she opened them, sixty large, liquid eyes regarded her. What they would do was dangerous. The wind blowing up ahead of the deluge ruffled manes and tails. The mares with spring foals moved to the back with their young; they would stay behind tonight. First Mare stepped forward. Pony smiled at her. The horse was delicate, not large, not showing her strength or the stamina Pony knew she had. The brown dapples of her haunches and belly edged into black on legs and mane and tail. Pony nodded. First Mare tossed her head and whinnied.

Pony tied up her shift, then placed both hands on the mare's back. With one hop first for spring, she vaulted astride. The horse sidled, settling Pony's weight. Now would begin the Language of Touch, the song of weight and balance that bound First Mare to Pony and bound Pony back again. Pony pushed her weight into her heels and turned her shoulders to look behind her, shifting the pressure of her hips. First Mare wheeled in the direction Pony

13

looked. Pony leaned back slightly and scraped First Mare's sides with her calves. She felt First Mare rise into the canter and sat into the rhythm, opening her hips into the mare's back with each stride. She did not have to look to see whether the others followed. Together they thundered out across the downs, spurning the great road off to their right, into the coming rain. They were one: a score of horses and one human girl jostling each other as hooves thudded in the soft earth of the downland. Power surged among and between them. Together they belonged to the Goddess. Possess us! Pony sang silently. And the Goddess flowed through her veins. Her blood chorused with the souls around her and the great soul that cascaded from the moon, and the white chalk horse behind them. They were a single being, Herd.

First light found them near the town of Chippenham, soaked with the showers. The song of the Goddess was an eerie melody inside her, not a shrieking chorus. Still, she could hear it, and Herd through that. Pony's shift clung damply to her breasts. Her wild white hair hung in wet strings around her face. Her bare legs and those of the horses were splashed with mud. They passed huts on the outskirts of the town. Pony saw Christian early risers cross themselves when they saw Herd. Everyone knew Pony, even as far as Chippenham. They knew her as She Who Lived Under the Sign of the White Horse, as her mothers had been known before her. Pony spared them no attention. She was for Osrick.

Herd thundered through the mired streets, past wooden buildings, thatched roofs, animal pens, the stalls of woodworkers, smiths and weavers, crowded markets with vegetables and the carcasses of slaughtered animals. The stench threatened to gag Pony. How could these people eat meat? The aroma of flesh mingled with the close smell of too many humans gathered together, and it stifled thought. The unwelcome tumult of revulsion grasped at Pony's serenity. People shouted after Herd, grabbing children out of its path. Herd thundered on. Soon, now. Pony could see the huge hall standing behind its palisades on the rise ahead, shouldering above the litter of the town. That was where she would find Osrick and Young Black.

Through the open gates of the palisade, into the yard of the great hall galloped Herd—Pony and First Mare in the lead. Pony listened, pushing down the tumult of the town, the fear of what Herd must do. Lowing came from a small barn off to her right. Oxen. She could hear the scratching of hens, the grunt of pigs, the snort of horses. All knew her name. Several men shushed slop into the sty. They looked up in shock. Pony sat back on First Mare. Herd swirled to a stop, milling and stamping in the yard. Pony scanned the outbuildings. The chickens cackled, full of the knowledge of where Young Black was imprisoned. Once she would have heard him on her own. Now she needed help.

Pony urged First Mare around behind the hall. The horses whinnied to draw her attention. There were six or seven in the pen. A young stallion, almost black, half-reared in salute. Pony saw the bloody welts across his hindquarters, evidence of the broken covenant. Her heart contracted. Herd milled nervously. No time for guilt, she told herself. She took a breath and held it. Then she smiled.

Herd surged toward the pen. The horses inside backed away. Twenty chests and flanks pressed against the poles. Squeals filled the air. The pen wall leaned and creaked with strain. A crack of wood sounded; the gate broke asunder. Shouts behind them seemed distant. Pony and First Mare spun. Pony beckoned to the captives. Herd swirled slowly into retreat. The voices of the men multiplied, angry now. The captives flowed through the broken wood of the pen into Herd. Together they trotted out from behind the hall. The fringe of Herd took down the sty, freeing the pigs, who grunted their thanks. A rat-a-tat of hind hooves against the cracking barn door was answered by the grateful lowing of the oxen. An ox shouldered into the daylight.

Osrick stepped from the great hall, his shirt hanging outside his breeches, his black hair shot through with gray and disheveled with sleep. Pony would have recognized his hard features anywhere: flat brown eyes, a body hard with fighting for what he wanted. His face was marked by the ravages of pustules when he was young. His chin jutted pugnaciously under his beard. He carried a sword that looked as if it had been forged in his hand. Two other men stepped out behind him, armed with swords as well. Pony shivered.

"You!" Osrick accused. He knew Pony well. She was the only human for two score miles about who did not call him lord. "You dare to steal my property?"

Herd sidled nervously around her. The edge of Osrick's sword glinted in the early sun. Pony clenched her jaw. Fear or not, she would prevail. "I did not promise Young Black to you."

"The farmer could not pay his debt to me," Osrick shouted, his lean cheeks flushed.

"My covenants cannot be traded," Pony hissed. "They are made with those who learn the Language of Touch. I would never make a covenant with you."

"You sell your horses," Osrick sneered. The point of his sword tipped up, menacing. Herd snorted and First Mare sidled, mincing. "The one you sold him to owed me his tax. Not a bargain, devil that the horse is, but I will break him."

"You will never have the chance."

The two men behind Osrick fumbled with their swords, glancing nervously at Herd, swelled now to nearly thirty stamping beasts. The pigs cried out that several men were flanking them. There was no way free but through Osrick. Pony pushed down fear. Fear killed the quiet. She let her face relax. She took a breath. White Stallion heard her. He squealed and looped out to the right, followed close on by Dun Mare and Young Dapple. Osrick turned to meet what he thought was an attack. Herd sprang to the left, haunches under themselves. Thirty horses leapt into a gallop. Osrick slashed low at White Stallion, who leaned back on his haunches, hooves flailing. Old Dun Mare and Young Dapple lunged in, strong, square teeth bared. Osrick gave ground. His men cried out and shrank away, just for an instant.

It was enough. Herd galloped past Osrick on the left,

following First Mare in an equine stream down the hill and into the town. White Stallion and his seconds whirled and followed. Osrick's shouts were tiny in Ponys ears; the swell of triumph shut out listening. She didn't care. Herd was meant to run, a force of nature loosed upon the town.

Then they were out on the downs, tails streaming, their newest members bucking as they ran in celebration. Pony fingered the black glass pebble at her throat. *Gift of my mothers, you are vindicated today.* The wind on her face was already warming with the day. Osrick was not fit for the magic of the Language of Touch. He did not matter. The covenant was redeemed.

Chapter Two

Osrick bellowed in rage as the cacophony of hooves and whinnies streamed from the fortress down into the town. He whirled to the horse pens only to find them broken, their occupants scattered. He would never catch the she-devil now.

He gritted his teeth in frustration. He would not have caught her, even had a horse been to hand. Her herd protected her, and the horses were fast. "God damn her to hell!" His men backed up around him, wary of his rage.

Only the young priest stood his ground. "God has no reason to damn her," he said mildly, at Osrick's elbow. "He uses parts of the Old Religion when they benefit his cause."

Osrick turned to the face so like his own, yet unlike. The eyes were brown, true, but they were filled with ideas and feelings Osrick despised. "Be careful, Elbert," he threatened. "I suffer you to remain because you teach men to be content with what they have and hope for more only in the afterlife. Should you cease to be useful, you shall not find me so lenient."

"That does not surprise me, Father. I only hope *you* are surprised one day."

Osrick snorted. "The world has long ceased to surprise me, boy." He turned back to watch the horses disappear in the distance with the witch who commanded them. "I shall not let this challenge go unmet. She will pay for flouting me today."

"Not wise, Father." The young priest put his cowl up over his tonsured head. "The people believe in her as much or more than they believe in Christ our Savior." He began walking away.

"Because she has trained a few horses?" Osrick called out after him, snorting.

"Because her gods are older than mine, if no wiser." The cleric walked out the gates.

"You are a coward," Osrick yelled. "Other priests would not let her blaspheme so!"

But then he turned and cursed. The boy was probably right. No use to challenge an authority not based on physical might but on belief. How did one win a battle like that?

He paused, the answer coming to him: One used her instead, just as Osrick himself had used his son when he saw the battle to mold him into a warrior was lost before it was begun. His son a priest! Who would have thought it? He brushed his hands and headed into the hall to finish breakfast. But if he could not use Epona, he would see her in hell.

Pony leapt off First Mare's back and patted her neck. First Mare turned to breathe on her, up and down her torso, her velvet nose again sharing the scent of Herd. Pony scratched the horse's forehead and breathed softly back. She might share a relationship with the whole herd, but her covenant was with First Mare. She looked around as the horses ambled down to the little stream to drink, or allowed themselves to be distracted by the grass to graze. She called to Young Black. He trotted up, excited by his escape in spite of all the miles they had covered since. She touched his haunches to promise she would clean his wounds.

He could not stay long with Herd. She would have to find another man to partner with him. Herd would not accept two stallions. As the young males came into their own she found them partners, before the fights with White Stallion could break out. Someday she must allow one horse to challenge him, when he grew too old to lead. All things had their time in the sun, her mother had always told her; then they were required to move on. Pony clenched herself against the hurt, the rebellion that rose in her breast. She sucked in a breath, remembering the Day, the Dread Day it happened. But rebellion was no use. Her mother was right. The law of the herd was certain proof. She surveyed the horses grazing across the green of the down. The Dread Day for White Stallion was not yet.

The horse understood the current problem. He would allow Young Black to join Herd, at least for now. And First Mare would keep Young Black from challenging his elders: she was the disciplinarian. Pony stroked Young Black's shiny coat, his fine arched neck newly heavy with adult muscles. "I'm sorry," she whispered. "We will do better next time." The stallion's next rider would be wiser.

Pony wandered among her companions, stroking, patting, their warm hair tickling her palms. The scent of wet horse dissipated as the sun dried the beasts. Her calm quiet had returned. The grass gave off a fecund smell as it surrendered its dew to the sun. Osrick's perfidy was only a rock in the river of her life. Pony swirled around it, the ripples it caused soon forgotten. The mares with foals nudged closer, wanting to know about Herd's adventure. They stood patiently to let their foals suckle while Pony stroked them. These mares fulfilled their destiny to provide Herd with its foals so naturally. To accept a stallion caused no tumult in their souls.

Pony turned toward her hut. Why was she not more like these mares? The very thought of allowing anyone like Osrick or these brutish shepherds to touch her revolted her senses. Yet there was no peace in refusing the call either. The need to conceive her girl-child was more urgent with each passing day. It was the will of the Goddess that tugged at her constantly, fueled by the knowledge that her Gift sputtered and faded. She ran her hand through her hair. It was wild from her ride. What was the way forward?

Pony ducked into her small house, shooing hens from the door. They clucked in outrage and scurried away. Her gaze swept the room, taking in the oatcakes cold on the stones of her firebox, the dusty loom she never used, her storage shelf above the bedbox stacked with baskets of dried berries and grain. When a mare was ready, she welcomed a stallion. Pony herself was simply not ready. It was right to delay. It made her feel sad inside to be so caught between the fears and needs. It had been like that for so long. She closed her eyes and nodded to herself. She just needed sleep. Closing the wicker shutters, she lowered herself into the furs of the bedbox.

But when would she be ready? An image of her mother rose in her mind, admonishing. Behind her mother, in echoing shimmers, stood all her mother's mothers, the long line of women who had lived beneath the white chalk sign of the horse, frowning down at her. Each day she waited, she betrayed their trust. They pressed her to complete the destiny dictated by the Great Mother of them all. *Let me be, Mother!* Pony begged, pushing down the memory of her mother like so many others of the woman. *I will not end as you did!*

Pony shrieked, waving her arms above her head and charged the carcass of what was once Chestnut Mare. Herd galloped up the hill toward the chalk incision of a horse, its fear cascading over Pony. "Get away from her!" she screamed. One wolf straightened from where it tugged at the bloody haunch, and snarled at her. The other two continued to rip at the meat. Pony stopped. What could one eleven-year-old do against the most feared of carnivores? She let go one more anguished cry, filled now as much with despair as with outrage. "Chestnut Mare!"

The wolves had known that Chestnut Mare was the weakest. Burns from the fire in the wood had hobbled her.

She could not run with the others. Pony had heard her fear, her pain even inside the little cabin. Now Pony watched helplessly, transfixed by the desecration of the horse. Sobs tore at her. Her mother came to stand behind her. Pony could feel her there, so strong, so distant. If Pony had heard Chestnut Mare's distress, her mother must have heard it even more clearly. Her mother's gift was twice her own.

"Epona, where is your quiet?" Her mother's voice was devoid of emotion.

Pony could only shake her head and watch the snarling pack grow until seven feeding wolves almost hid Chestnut Mare's lurching body, drenched with blood.

Her mother took her firmly by the shoulders and turned her away from the carcass to stare into her blue, blue eyes. "Carnivores are evil—men and beast alike. They are not of the Great Mother. They will always do what their nature commands. You cannot change that, and you cannot let them disturb your peace. After the carnivores will come the carrion eaters, more foul yet. They are not of us." She started the chant: "Our way is quiet. We follow the Mother." She shook Pony, causing Pony's tears to spill. Pony knew what was required. She shut out the snarling behind her, the snapping of jaws. Could her mother truly expect her to achieve inner peace here, now? Yes. Her mother always expected more than she could give.

"Our way is quiet," Pony managed to whisper, swallowing the thickness in her throat.

Her mother raised her brows, demanding.

"We follow the mother." The words threatened to choke Pony.

"Hers is the way," they said together. "Our destiny is to be alone." That was all Pony knew.

But her mother continued. "Men are the enemy. They cut up your peace. Carnivores are evil." Pony could not tell whether that was part of the Goddess's chant or an addition of her mother's. She looked up. Her mother breathed so regularly. Distance drifted into her eyes, the same distance that had been coming more and more frequently.

Pony wanted to bury her head in her mother's cyrtle and sob out her grief for her friend's horrible death, her hatred of the carnivores who did it. The snapping sounds, the tearing behind her threatened all sanity. But her mother would never allow that. Servants of the Horse Goddess did not need hugs. They did not sob. They were calm. They were quiet. They connected with their Gift.

Her mother turned her face down toward Pony, but the distance still lurked in her eyes.

"Go into the hut, Epona. Practice your Gift. Your Gift must be nurtured much more diligently if you are to pass it to your girl-child before you pass on. I fear you will never be as proficient as I am." She sighed then and drifted away, ignoring the carcass, ignoring the carnivores. "But we must work with what we have."

She left Pony standing there, unable to find the peace she herself seemed to have so naturally. Pony knew that her kind was meant to live apart, alone. In truth, she had never felt so alone as at this moment. But that did not seem to protect her from the ravages of emotion. Her eyes darted back to the snarling pack. It would take them an hour or more to clean the carcass of her friend. The remains would attract scavengers, feeders on rot, to the meadow. Herd would stay down by the Barrow until the bones were cleaned. How long would that be? She turned back toward the hut, the scene of destruction behind her shrieking in her mind.

"Hallooo!"

Pony started at the sound. Who could be here now? Someone wanting her gift of partnership, no doubt. Pony rose and peered out the door to see a golden-haired young man striding up from the stream to her right. She had never seen him before. One would remember that face. His brow was smooth and high, his face open and guileless as he smiled in greeting and raised his arm. He was dressed simply and his clothes were travel-worn, but a fine broadsword hung at his side. His boots were tooled leather, though scuffed and muddy. She glanced behind him and saw a band of perhaps forty men, some mounted, some on foot, half a mile away on the downs. Her heart stuttered. What were so many men doing so near her hut?

He saw her glance and held up both his hands, shaking his head. "Worry not!" he called as he approached. "We mean you no harm."

Behind Pony, the horses wheeled away toward the wood to her left. Only White Stallion and First Mare stood their ground, ears pricked, nostrils pulsing to sift the air. Pony trembled, uncertain. She could race to First Mare and vault astride in an instant, she told herself, and be away in a moment more. She wiped palms suddenly slick with sweat on her flaxen shirt.

The beautiful man smiled as he drew near, his eyes reassuringly merry. He was little older than she was herself. His gaze took in her nightshift knotted up around her thighs, the flowing white blond hair that was the mark of her family line. He stopped about ten feet from her, expecting a greeting. Pony breathed herself calm and poised in the doorway, ready for flight. When she said nothing, he bowed. "My name is Alfred," he said.

Still she said nothing, but waited for him to state what he wanted.

He cocked his head and raised his brows in surprise. "Alfred," he repeated. Then, he cleared his throat. "King of Wessex, third and most powerful of the Seven Kingdoms."

"Where is Wessex?" she asked, since he seemed to expect something of her.

"Well . . . here." Alfred looked around. His golden curls caught the morning light.

Pony accepted that. She waited.

"What do you think of being visited by your king?" Alfred asked. He put his fists on his hips.

"I think you do not look like a king," Pony answered. "You have no crown."

Alfred folded his arms across his chest and looked around at his men in the distance, as though for support. "You don't wear crowns all the time, even if you're a king." He glanced back at Pony, who waited. "Things are a little difficult now," he admitted. "What with the damned Vikings winning battles. The eorls have seemed to lose heart recently." He looked down at his boots.

"Why do they lose heart?" Pony asked.

"Well . . . it might have had something to do with my older brother being killed." Alfred chewed his lip. "He was more experienced than I am as a soldier. Now they seem content to change masters as long as they keep what they have." He sighed. "That is why we are here."

At last. Pony waited in the doorway.

Alfred shifted his weight from foot to foot. The silence stretched. "We . . . we need horses," he finally stuttered. "I know I can win through. It is my destiny."

Pony chuckled.

"Why do you laugh?" Alfred bristled.

"I see only two score men," she apologized. One should not laugh at another's destiny.

"I am regrouping with my forces to the south," the young king explained earnestly. "But if I am to muster a fighting force we need horses. We commandeered whatever sorry beasts we could from the locals, but they are not enough. I was told you might provide horses, at a price."

"I may, or I may not," Pony answered. He was sincere. He thought he had a destiny. That, she should understand. He meant to pay her. Yet somehow she thought he was concealing something of his purpose in coming here. And she had been wrong about men before. She waited.

"We *can* pay," Alfred said, growing resentful.

The fact that she was not sure of him galled him. "Do you know the price for partnering with my herd?" she asked.

He seemed relieved. "State it."

Pony stood aside and gestured inside her small timbered house. "Come in, and we will discuss how you may be worthy of my horses."

* * *

Val cradled his right arm against his belly. The suppurations from his burn leaked through the dirty bandage onto his leather jerkin. For the first week he had left the burn untended, but when it started to blacken, Harald had insisted on rubbing it with rendered lard and bandaging it. Every movement now sent shocks of pain through him. The strain of holding his face impassive against the constant, grinding agony made Val's breath come shallow and fast.

Behind him, his weary fellow *Danir* stretched out in a line of leather and metal, their helmets glinting in the red light of the setting sun. With the ten men he had left to hold ford of the great river and those he had left at the village yesterday, there were perhaps fifty left to follow, hardly enough to challenge the next target. Val wanted the town belonging to the Saxon eorl called Osrick. He had learned of it in the last village. Osrick's keep would make a good seat of power, the place from which he would govern the Downland. But fifty men were not enough to capture it. And Val was himself weakened. Once he had been sure of his ability to make Guthrum marvel at his deeds; now he was not sure of anything.

He must not let his men see him waver in his saddle. They must not lose what little faith they had in him, got from Guthrum secondhand. Fever had crept into his body through his blackened forearm. It alternately chattered his teeth and bathed him in sweat. If his mission to hold the Downland for Guthrum failed, he was as good as dead in his own eyes. His head swam. He must call a halt for the night before he fell from the saddle. He glanced ahead to the line of willows curving across the grassland.

He raised a hand and turned to Harald, riding directly behind him. Guthrum had sent the stripling along with Val. He had sent Svenn and Sigurd, his acolyte, as well. Svenn was a leader in his own right. Did Guthrum think to hedge his bet? It would compromise the mission to have them at each other's throats, but if Val failed to win the hearts of his followers, Svenn would be there to step in. "We camp at the stream." Val put his remaining strength into his voice.

"The Saxons must wait another day for their fate." Harald's eyes were anxious. Couldn't he see Val was in no shape to take revenge on anyone? "Ride ahead, boy—and you, Svenn. See that there are no Saxons hereabouts."

Harald nodded crisply and cantered off, along with Svenn. Val turned his horse Slepnir toward the willows. A flat area bare of trees in a broad curve of the stream would hold their number and make an enemy cross open ground to attack them. He swung his leg over Slepnir's back and thudded to the ground, hoping no one saw that his knees gave under him before he could straighten. Perhaps some rest would strengthen him for tomorrow. First, he owed his horse a rubbing down for his long service today; only then could he himself rest and eat.

As he curried Slepnir with a handful of willow shoots, his men made camp around him. They were *Danir* on the move and they traveled without fanfare or accoutrement. A blanket, some jerked meat, skins to fill with water from the stream, their weapons and their shields: these were enough. Val wondered for the hundredth time why Guthrum would choose him to hold the downs, then cripple him. Why make it hard to do the job he set? Val could not fathom it, no matter which way he turned it in his mind. He saw Svenn's calculating eyes. The man waited for a misstep.

Men stood around him to listen. Val leaned on Slepnir's warm flank and looked about. Normally he was the first to sense danger. There it was: the movement of many animals and bleating. A flock of sheep trotted over the rise to the south, along with three surly-looking Saxon shepherds and a grinning Harald on horseback.

"Mutton for dinner, anyone?" the young Dane called.

Val's lips curved into a smile. Keep the men busy slaughtering a few ewes and roasting a good dinner; they would not notice whether he took early to his blanket.

The shadows lengthened outside the hut. Pony rose and stirred her fire.

"My head runs with a thousand plans," the young king

was saying. His limbs were stretched out from the stool. He leaned against one of the beams that supported the roof of her small hut. His cheeks glowed with life. His eyes were the bluest Pony had ever seen, except for her own in the mirror of her stream. His delicate lips were a promise that he was more than a warrior. "The people need something to bind them into peace with one another. All this fighting, all these years—it takes our time, our blood, our strength to fight each other. Cent against Wessex, Anglia against Mercia. And what do we gain? The chance to fight again? Fighting against the Viking evil brought us together once—but it was all for naught. Edmund lost everything to the Vikings at Thetford, and our sad retreat began. It had to happen; I know that. It is part of our destiny. I just don't know where it will end. And now we do not even stand together against the Vikings."

Pony took down a wooden bowl, a sealed pot of milled oats and one of her precious eggs, and set about making a fresh batch of oatcakes for her dinner.

Alfred sat forward suddenly. "If we could just get to peace, there would be time for everything. I have been translating the Bible into Saxon, you know. If people could hear the words of our Lord in their own language, it would be more real to them. The priests at least should read—and the eorls. How else can we learn from our fathers?"

Pony smiled at his intensity and stirred her oats. He must know she did not worship Jesu.

He laughed. "You think I am crazy, just like my men. But if I was king in a time of peace, I could build faestens all along our coast, so these Viking thieves could not run their ships up our rivers. Or . . ." He paused. His eyes gleamed. "Why not build a navy of our own? What a shock that would give them!"

Pony tried to make her mouth be serious. "Are you never quiet?"

Alfred grinned. "I cannot sleep more than four or five hours a night," he confessed. "There is too much to do, too many plans to be made."

"I must have heard them all this afternoon." Pony patted her cakes into shape.

"Oh, no." Alfred shook his head. "You have not heard the half. Why, I have not yet mentioned my ideas on how to construct huge churches so the roof will not collapse. Or the adjustments I want to make to the wergild owed for injuring a man. . . . We need a system, so it isn't just the local thegn who sets the cost. That is one thing the Danes have. They call it 'law.' The idea of rules even a thegn cannot break is attractive to people. It is one reason they embrace our enemies." His face darkened. "We must borrow that and turn it to our advantage."

"No. You did not mention those ideas." Pony laid cakes on the flat stones around her fire.

"And there is another idea." Alfred stared into the flames. "A dream only."

She waited. She understood dreams.

"When we are rid of the evil of the Danelaw, we will not go back to a world where the Seven Kingdoms fight among themselves. We will have one kingdom. I will call it Angleland, after we Angles and Saxons who settled it."

"What about those here before the Angles and Saxons?" Pony asked. Alfred started. "Trevellyan's people to the west, and before that, *my* people." He hadn't asked about her in all the afternoon, not even her name.

"I heard at my mother's knee about you," he said slowly. "I was born in Wantage, not four leagues from here. But everyone has heard of you, even in Winchester. Did you know that?"

Something in his manner, in the tentative tone of his voice, told her that this was near to the other purpose in his coming that he wouldn't speak of earlier. Pony waited.

"I heard that you talk to animals. They can tell you things that happen leagues away."

"It is not a matter of talking. You must listen."

He did not understand. But he did not pause to think about it, either. He had his own purpose. "They say you're the last of the old magicians of the Celts. I've read about them. Druids. You are the last Druid priestess in the land. Is that true?"

"You speak of Trevellyan's people, who once ruled here. But I am from the first of peoples, before Trevellyan. I have my Gift from my mother and all the mothers before her. And my duty is to the Great Mother of us all."

"They had a horse goddess you know, the Celts." Alfred drew up his knees and leaned his elbows on them. "Guess her name."

Pony smiled and shook her head. He was so sure of himself.

"Epona," he said simply. "Or sometimes Rhiannon, or Macha, depending upon where people lived. I've read the Latin accounts of her."

"Epona?" Pony drew her brows together. "But that's my name."

Alfred nodded. "She was the mother of all the Celtic gods, the Great Fecund Mare."

Pony was startled. These Druids followed the Great Mother Goddess and her horses?

"Do you practice rituals?" Alfred asked.

"What do you mean?"

"Oh, you know: sacrificing things, praying . . ." His tone was casual, but his eyes were not.

"I don't believe in sacrifices." She paused, but he wanted more. She took a breath. "I touch the horses. I listen." She looked over to him to see if he understood. He did not. "They speak through the Language of Touch. Those who want my horses must learn the Language of Touch. Only then will you know the equine soul. They will go where you go, and you will go with them. You will be one. It is a covenant between you." It was the most she had said to anyone in years.

"That sounds like a ritual to me." He paused, thinking of how to approach his subject. "You know, Druid priestesses were supposed to be the mortal incarnations of the Goddess." His eyes lighted from within. He wanted to say more. But he bit his lip and was still.

His holding back made her nervous. "What would you say and cannot?"

"Nothing." He raised his head. "You know, your gift could change the world."

Pony shook her head. She did not want to change the world. Her duty was to connect to it, not change it. "It is a small Gift. I hear animals, at least the ones who do not eat meat."

"I knew one who had gifts once," Alfred said. His voice was a murmur in the growing gloom. His face was lit by the flicker of the fire. "She could heal people. She called the elements, even the earth itself, to do her bidding."

"She sounds like the priestess you speak of, not me." Pony sat back on her heels.

The man's eyes turned inward, remembering. "Most called her a witch. But I know she was a saint. Her gift was from Jesu, surely. Did he not raise Lazarus from the dead? It was she who healed me when I was burned and would have died. She prophesied that I would be called Alfred the Great, that I would rule all the island, and the island would one day rule the world."

So that was why he was so sure of himself. He clung to a prophecy. Perhaps he *was* a king.

He sighed. "But she also gave the Danes the victory that made the Danelaw. She brought down Edmund's fortress and set the Vikings loose upon the island, curse that they are. Now the Danelaw is expanding until there may be nothing left for me to rule. It is all very confusing."

"Did she serve the Goddess?" Why had her mother not told her she was named for this Druid horse goddess? Something was wrong here. Pony's mother had told her only about the Great Mother. The Great Mother did not belong to these Druids, yet she and all her mothers were named for their horse goddess. Or was it the other way around? She was not what this fledgling king thought she was, the last Druid priestess. Trevellyan ruled the wild Celts who had retreated to the western mountains and south to the rocky edges of the island in Cornwall. He was half-legend himself. But her kind was older than his kind, older than any Druid, any Celt; they had been in this land since it had been thrust from the sea. It was the one thing she was sure of.

Alfred shook his head. "She told me she was not sure who or what she served. She would tell you she brought down Edmund's faesten for love, not for the future of the world." He took a breath and straightened up. "She lives in the Danelaw now, in the great fenland to the north and east. And the man she sacrificed this island for is Viking. Who can tell the right of things?"

Pony thought about that. Could you serve a goddess and not know it? Did this witch serve some force that would carve the future, yet was not sure how or why? They had much in common, she and this witch or saint.

"Have you never heard the story of the Bible?" Alfred asked, head cocked.

"I have heard."

"And yet you do not serve Jesus through his one true church. Why not?"

Pony shifted from foot to foot. These Christians could be most insistent. She usually tried to listen politely, but it always ended in them wanting to dunk her in some pond or river. She had resolved long ago to never let water close over her head, else she would have let them do it. It didn't seem to matter to the Great Mother whether she was dunked, and it mattered so very much to the Christians. Perhaps it would have made their priests accept her better. It would not have affected what she believed. But she couldn't do it, not with what had happened to her mother. Still, she had to answer her king. "I did not see that women were important in your church."

Alfred sat up straight. "The mother of Jesus is the most important of the saints."

Pony smiled. "But she is not his equal. No women are his priests." She shook her head. "Mary is there to lure unwise women. No, the Christ Cult is no place for those who understand that the world is fertile. Fertility is the first principle. And that is the province of women."

Alfred rubbed his chin. "The Bible values the weak. Is that not appealing to a woman?"

"Why would that appeal to me?" Pony asked, puzzled.

"I must think on this. The Christians must make room for those who hold the old religions. Perhaps . . . I must think on this," he finished and fell silent.

"I still say," he continued, after a bit, "that you could use your powers to change the world, not just stay here in the Downs where there is so little scope for your gift."

Pony shuddered. "We have always lived here, my mothers and I. How would people know where to find me if I did not live here? Here is part of who I am."

Alfred smiled. "Perhaps your destiny has not yet been revealed to you, as mine was to me. Show me the Language of Touch," he said simply. "Show me your horses."

Pony stared at him—still, listening. Then she nodded and rose. She strode out her door into the deepening twilight without looking back. He would follow. She went down to the meadow with swinging strides. The shapes of the horses loomed out of the gloaming, the whites and grays eerie. Young Black was but a darker shadow in the distance. Heads came up from their grazing. Ears pricked in her direction. She stopped still in the middle of the meadow and breathed. First Mare trotted out of the looming shapes and nickered softly, halting ten feet from Pony to sift the wind. She smelled Alfred.

He is an acolyte, she thought calmly in the deepening dusk. *Help me show him how to partner.* First Mare stepped delicately forward, nose brushing the grass. Pony took two running steps and pressed both hands to First Mare's withers, then vaulted onto her back. Instantly, they were off at a canter, Pony's arms outstretched. No bridle sullied First Mare's mouth. They wheeled and stopped to look at Alfred. He stood at the edge of the meadow. The moon rose behind her stark hill, limned with its ghostly chalk figure. The other horses spun away and ranged themselves behind her in an attentive line, a silent chorus to the demonstration.

Pony stroked First Mare's neck with her palm and received a nicker in return. She pressed her calves to the horse's flanks and they thundered down on Alfred. His eyes widened in surprise that turned to fear. He stood his ground, though. At the last minute she veered to the left, then touched her leg to First Mare's left side. The horse rocked back, spun tightly, Alfred the quivering pole at the center of a series of circles. Pony shifted her weight to the inside, widening the circles slowly with her inside hip.

When at last they reared together and stood square, facing Alfred, Pony could see that his face was white. She cocked her head and raised her brows, smiling.

"Uh, the Language of Touch?" he stuttered, and flushed with relief.

She nodded.

"Can I learn it?"

"Come tomorrow."

"I don't have long," he warned.

"Be a good student then," she recommended.

He gasped a shaky laugh. "Very well, Epona. I will make you rich for this."

"I do not want money. I will give you a list of my needs." Pony slid from First Mare's back. *Thank you, good friend.* First Mare shook her whole body and whirled back to the herd.

"Epona," Alfred began behind her, astonishment in his voice. "You *are* a priestess, whether you know it or not. You are the goddess Epona."

She turned and they walked together back to her little thatched house as the darkness closed in. As they reached the door, she expected him to go back to his men down at the stream. She could see the lights of their fires, hear the dim mutterings of male voices, and sometimes the louder crack of laughter in the distance. But he did not.

He touched her shoulder. "Epona," he whispered. "Have you ever heard the legend that the incarnation of a goddess is the only one who can anoint a king? The Celts believed it."

She turned toward him. His face, so filled with his ideas, glowed in the light from her small fire. She shook her head.

He seemed to lose his way. He sighed, his eyes roving over her, then shrugged. "Making love to the incarnation of a goddess is the only way to confirm a king according to many of the old religions." He looked apologetic for what he was proposing.

He *was* proposing; she could see it in his eyes. The rush of realization shooshed through her like a March wind off the downs. Was he the answer to her prayers? She didn't lust after him, though he was pretty. But who could say he was not well made? Would her mother not call a king good stock? He was a man with a destiny and he needed to fulfill it. So did she. Here was the man who could give her a girl-child. "What does your Jesus think of that?" she asked.

He looked sheepish. "Not much, probably." His mouth twisted and he chewed a lip. "But it does not hurt to appease all the gods you can find, does it?"

"I understand why you offer yourself," she said slowly. "Why do you think I will agree?"

He nodded. Here he was surer. "Because you need a purpose, Epona, and I can give you one." His voice was lit with ambition, just as his face was lit by her fire. "Join me. Use your gift to help us win back the Danelaw. Help me make the Seven Kingdoms whole again."

"I am not a fighter." She shook her head and turned into her house.

"We need horses. My men would learn the Language of Touch," he hastened to add, trailing after her into the tiny hut, smoky with her fire. "Your horses could tell you about the Danes. They could be the ultimate network of sentries. . . ." Already he was planning.

She laughed softly. "That is not why I will agree."

He said nothing for a moment, almost holding his breath. "But you will agree?"

She nodded. Fear circled in her belly. She was going to

do it. She was about to embrace her destiny, and all the danger that implied. She would do what her mothers asked of her.

He breathed in deeply. "My men will see that you have chosen me. It will increase their faith in me, in our destiny. In that way alone you will have served the greater good."

"I do not do this thing to serve the greater good." She wondered what would happen next.

Alfred glanced outside. "There must be witnesses to this ritual, else my purpose fails."

Pony backed up a step and then another. The corner of the bedbox prodded her knee. "I'll not bed you on some blanket in a circle of your men," she said breathlessly. "Do not think it."

Alfred reached out his hands, palms up. He made soothing, shushing noises. "No, no, Epona. I would never ask that." He glanced outside again. "Only, there is a little priest. His name is Asser. He served my father and my brother and now me. He could stand outside. . . ."

Pony looked at him askance. "This is not a good idea." Then a wary thought intruded. "Why do you tell me? Why did you not just ask him to stand outside?"

"Because you might sense him." Did that mean he would have lied if he could?

He was wrong. She could not hear people. But she nodded, still unsure of what to do.

"Come in, Asser." Alfred held out a hand, not looking at the door.

Pony was shocked to see a small tonsured head poke around the frame. She felt betrayed. Alfred had known what he wanted from her all along. And it was more than horses.

The priest was nearly as short as she was. The lines in his face and the gray shooting through his beard said he was older than Alfred by some twenty summers. He had sad eyes. She could imagine them upcast to his God. She would wager he had calluses on his knees. He nodded to her and pressed his palms together in the age-old gesture of respect. "You *planned* this?" Pony asked. It felt like a betrayal.

36

Alfred thinned his lips, and lifted his brows. "I could only hope."

"Your hope is dying quickly. . . ." Could she stop him if he pressed her?

"You agreed for a reason," he protested. "Is that reason gone?"

Pony's eyes went to his face. It was open, guileless. His blue eyes crinkled in a smile, warm, human as genuine smiles always were. He was right. She still needed a girl-child. He did not profess his love for her. He was the perfect gift from the Great Mother. He would not want to stay with her, yet would father a strong girl-child. He was a king. Who could be better? So, the reason was still there. Could she refuse the Great Mother's gift?

She took a breath and held it. As the air escaped, her calm reentered. She had decided. "The reason is still there."

Alfred nodded to the priest, who bowed his head and backed from the room. Soon there was quiet. As though guessing her thought Alfred whispered, "We will forget him soon enough."

Pony was not as sure. She was not as sure of anything anymore.

Alfred glanced to the bedbox, suddenly not sure either. He clenched his jaw and managed a nervous smile. "I have never made love to a goddess before."

Pony shook her head. "I have never bred at all. I would not expect much."

Alfred laughed and took her hand. "You are a very practical goddess."

Part of that was true. This was a practical solution to her problem. The Great Mother had sent her a king to give her a girl-child. *Thank you, Mother.* She squeezed Alfred's hand and drew him to the bed. They sat, a little awkwardly. Alfred smoothed back her hair.

"You look every inch the goddess."

"You say that because you want me to be a goddess." Pony hoped he knew what to do. She longed for it to be as simple as what passed between stallion and mare. Even if it was the first time, horses were born knowing what to do. She was not born knowing anything at all.

Alfred grew serious. Maybe he did know what to do. He lifted her shift over her head, leaving her naked. "Oh, Epona." His voice was thick in his throat. She watched his hand touch her shoulder so she did not have to look into his blue eyes; the burning there frightened her. *Calm,* she thought. *Like stallions and mares, no fear, no entanglement, no tumult that further destroys your Gift. Just let it happen.* Her breathing slowed. Would the Great Mother bless the union with her presence? Would her spirit consume Pony tonight? She did not feel it yet. She watched Alfred caress her, cup her breasts and lift them. Her mother always said she had generous breasts, the better to suckle a daughter. Alfred pulled at the leather laces to his jerkin, his fingers frantic. That made her want to laugh. But she bent to pull off her soft leather boots. She peeped up to see Alfred's body, white and lean, a stripling just thickening into manhood. He had good haunches, well muscled, like Young Black. His chest was almost hairless, the nipples pink and puckered though the room was warm. He stared at her as he continued to fumble with his clothes. What did he see? The incarnation of a goddess? Or just a strange girl who talked to horses? He wanted her to anoint him. How exactly did one do that? And what of the priest outside the door?

Again she stilled the questions. *Calm.* They were naked just like a stallion and a mare. He enveloped her in his arms and kissed her hair. She could smell the scent that was a signature in the animal world as she pressed into his chest. He turned up her chin and kissed her. His mouth was soft. His tongue caressed her lips, then poked inside her mouth. How surprising! Like the little nips a stallion gives the mare along her neck, just to see if she is ready. She pulled back a little, then leaned in and touched his tongue with hers, to encourage him. He grinned into her mouth and pulled her close. He kissed her hungrily. She ran her hands over his shoulders, through his hair. Something strange was happening in her loins. Her breasts pressed into his chest. She was feeling swollen down there. Blood pumped in her ears. He drew her in to sit on his lap. Her thigh brushed his erection. He was ready to service her, that was certain. Could she take all that inside her? A mare took something even larger when she was ready.

Pony was ready. Alfred drew her down onto the furs and rolled on top of her. His weight was not unbearable. Just as a mare was built to stand a stallion's weight, so was Epona built to stand Alfred's. He kissed her frantically now, his hands clutched in her hair. She opened her legs to him and he eased himself in. To her surprise, she was wet. Was this it, then? He pushed hard once. Her virginity tore away in a sear of momentary pain, and his whole length was inside her. She gasped. She had fulfilled her promise to her mother. *Give me a girl-child,* she commanded silently as Alfred slid in and out. She bucked in rhythm to his thrusts, instinctively luring him deeper inside her. Their breathing turned to gasps. Somewhere inside she felt a threat of something coming toward her, frightening. Before the threat could be fulfilled, Alfred stopped and arched above her. She felt his seed squirt inside her belly. She lay still, accepting all of it, trying to quiet her heaving breasts so that nothing would disturb the moment of conception.

He collapsed on top of her, sweating. Pony smiled as her heart returned slowly to its regular rhythm. Not so bad. Not bad at all. The Great Mother had not consumed her, as she did at Samhain. This was just as with a stallion and a mare. Her mother had been right. It was a small price to pay to make the urgent tugging of the Mother Goddess go away. She felt Alfred withdraw. He rolled off. Ah, but he could not take back what he had given her; she had just fulfilled her destiny.

Pony jerked upright at a charred smell. It was only her oatcakes, forgotten on the stone, blackened and wafting smoke. She glanced to the door to see two heads disappear, one from each side. There had been more than one witness to her breeding. Alfred had been careful. She should be angry, but she wasn't. What matter? Each had gotten what they wanted tonight.

Alfred raised his head. "What is it?" he murmured, his eyes heavy and sated.

Pony stood and slipped into her shift. "Only my cakes burning." She scooped them into a bowl. Alfred sank back into her furs. His cheeks were ruddy with their rutting. She had fulfilled her destiny. Why did she not feel whole? She clenched her eyes shut. Because there might be more to come, a slow diminishing over the years after she had conceived her girl-child, until there was nothing left but the Dread Day. Emptiness sat in Pony's middle. That was what had happened to her mother. Perhaps the girl-child pushed out everything else until there was room only for your own Day. Perhaps the Day was her true destiny.

Chapter Three

The smell of juicy, well-cooked mutton still hung in the air, along with the acrid smoke from the fires. Val was pulled from a heavy sleep by the pain in his arm. He shifted against the saddle that acted for a pillow, trying to get comfortable. The night was warm, so he had not pulled his blanket around him. Now he was chilled with the dew. It was the black heart of the night, before dawn lightened the sky. Around him, lumps of men sighed or snored. In the background, sheep stirred, horses breathed and shuffled at their hobbles. The shepherds had been bound together so they might not call down their fellows against the *Danir*. They would be released in the morning. The *Danir* would have need of shepherds and their flocks if they were to rule here.

Val laid his arm out straight beside his thigh, since it screamed so. That was no better. He had seen the swollen infection in the burn. He knew what lay before him. He rolled to his good side and pulled the blanket over his shoulder, trying to still himself. The sentry's steps crackled in the leaves as he paced the perimeter. As they died away, Val heard low voices somewhere off to the left. They were speaking in Saxon. He caught perhaps every third word.

"At least Alfred paid . . . ewe he . . . feed his men," a voice hissed.

Val strained to hear. Payment? Alfred? Had the King of Wessex been through here?

"Tomorrow we tell them, all friendly-like, about the horse girl. The thieving whoreson bastards will head up to the hill, sure."

"And run smack into Alfred and his men," the third voice whispered gleefully.

"Shush." The crunch of the sentry's feet silenced the voices.

Val pretended to stir in his sleep and confirmed through slitted eyes that it was the three shepherds, bunched together inside the circle of *Danir,* who spoke. He never expected he would be so fortunate as to encounter the King of Wessex in the downland. Alfred's men were close, and these Saxon louts could lead the *Danir* to them. Glory and honor would be Val's as he gutted the leader of all the Saxons, or led him in chains to kneel at Guthrum's feet.

The fever running through his veins burned up, giving him strength. Even if it was false strength, he could use it. He struggled to his knees and pushed down the pain radiating from his arm. It must be done before the dawn could wake the Saxon camp. He grabbed Bloodletter.

"Up, bold brother *Danir,*" he called into the stillness of the camp. Men snorted into wakefulness. Steel slithered from scabbards. "The prize is near. We must seize it by the neck."

Harald was first to stand, blinking, sword in hand. "What is to do?"

Val stood over the huddled shepherds. "Alfred, King of Saxons, is encamped not far from here." He lowered Bloodletter slowly toward the quivering three. "These know where. We follow their word path to glory, or their blood will slake our weapons' thirst."

Men stood now in a circle, some crouched and wary,

some yet rubbing sleep from their eyes. The circle deepened
as others rose, until all fifty Danes had eyes only for Val
and the Saxon shepherds. Val lifted the chin of the shepherd
whose face was most lined with sullen resentment. "*Hwaer
beon* Alfred?" He shook his head, disgusted. "Where is Alfred?"

The shepherd shrugged after a moment. "What do I care
if you know? He is camped under the White Horse. He
wants horses from the bitch priestess." He pointed east.

"*Hu manig?*" Val growled, and wondered how uneven
the odds would have to be before he would abandon his
attack.

The shepherd guessed the meaning of the Danish words.
"Twenty. Maybe twenty-five."

Val nodded, eyes slitted in satisfaction, and sheathed
Bloodletter.

"Kill the woman and take her horses, too," one of the
younger shepherds added.

Val began shouting orders, even as he donned his jerkin
and chain mail. The camp disintegrated as blankets were
rolled, horses saddled. The several fires were kicked apart
hastily. Harald untied Slepnir from the other horses. Val
whistled and the horse trotted over. He heaved his saddle
onto Slepnir's back with his good arm. *Thor, give me
strength. You have brought a chance for honor. Let me be
equal to your challenge.* He steadied himself and breathed
in. Twenty-five Saxons to their fifty? The work of a moment. Unless the shepherd lied.

Val stopped hauling on the girth. The fever made him
careless. "Svenn," he called. The older man presented himself, gray locks nearly covering an angry scar that wound
across his forehead. "Go on ahead," Val said, his voice low.
"Confirm numbers and position."

Svenn nodded and pulled himself into his saddle, motioning to Sigurd to come with him. Val watched them depart. Svenn was the most experienced warrior among his
men. He might wait to take Val's place, but he could be
trusted to work for the good of the Danelaw.

43

Val led Slepnir about the camp, encouraging stragglers. They must attack before the advantages of darkness and surprise were lost.

When Pony woke, Alfred was bringing wood in for the fire. It was not yet dawn. The man had told her he never slept. She tried to feel the child growing inside her, but there was only an emptiness Alfred could not fill with his seed. The young king knelt beside the stones she used for a firebox and blew into the coals. Sparks shivered into the darkness. A small flame licked hungrily at the new wood. Alfred rocked back and looked at her, speculating. "Will you come to meet my men when it is light? I want you with me to announce your gift of horses."

Pony nodded. What he really wanted was to have his men see that she had *anointed* him that night. It did not matter. If he had used her, she had used him in her turn. At least he seemed to have no idea of staying. He was for battle in search of his destiny. Battle? She turned on him. "The horses will not be used in battle."

Alfred started at her tone. "We ride our horses between battles—"

"But in the battle itself?" Pony hissed, leaning over the edge of the bedbox.

"They are . . . are in the rear, unless we need them to . . . to pull the battering ram, or . . ."

"My horses are not used in battle. Your men must pull the cart."

Alfred smiled a smile that lit his face and nodded.

"If you use them in battle, they will away to me," Pony said flatly. Alfred's smile would not be a dismissal of her order.

Alfred nodded again, serious this time. "You could see that I treat them right yourself, Epona. You could come with me. What a pair we would make! The leader of a new land and the last practitioner of the old ways. We would be unstoppable. You would provide the people comfort while

44

I bent the old ways into Jesu's path. We would push and pull the people into their future."

Pony stared at him, startled at the torrent of words. She had been relieved to think he would not stay and bring tumult into her life. Now he wanted her to go with him? That was worse. She shook her head. "I am here, under the sign of the horse."

"These are troubled times. Your gift must serve the greater good."

A distant shout floated through the wicker shutters of the hut, followed by a shower of staccato voices and the faint squeal of a horse. Alfred sprang to his feet and reached for his sword. He dashed out the door, still strapping it on. "Vikings," he cried. "*Yfel feond*! They dare to follow even the old roads. Stay here," he shouted as he ran down the rise in front of the hut.

Pony hurried to her horses. *Into the wood! Follow me!* She had heard about the Vikings. They were the carnivores of the human world, fighting and devouring all. They were the antithesis of what she was. If Vikings were about, no one was safe—not her horses, not her, not her daughter.

Val swung Bloodletter in a wide arc to keep the two Saxons in front of him. His right hand gripped the leather handle of his round shield. He couldn't feel his hand anymore, he only felt the pain of his burn as his bandages scraped against the wood. *Thor, let my strength hold*! Axes and swords, ghostly in the waxing light, rose and fell. Saxon screams and Dane split the dawn. Svenn had counted thirty-five, not twenty-five. That still made odds enough. Val and his fifty had plunged into the groggy camp a moment after the sentry's alarm. It was his last. Several Saxons fell before they could lurch from their blankets. But these were not callow youths like their king. They fought like Hel's legions when they realized their danger. Val's plan had been to push the Saxons up against the river and ring them in where they could be gutted in a seething mass or picked off as they tried to make it through the fast-running water.

Now three of them had Harald cut off from his fellows to Val's right. He should leave Harald to his fate. Let the Valkyrie take him. There was honor in that. Val dared not let his penchant for defending the weak draw him from his push to the river. Curse the boy. Curse his father's seed, his mother's milk! Val stepped right, and hated himself for it.

Val put his shoulder into a Saxon shield and staggered toward Harald. Fear was etched into the boy's face. The dark smears at his shoulder must be blood. The world was clear to Val, perhaps too clear. Movement slowed. He saw a Saxon arm come up, sword hanging over Harald. He could smell the dew in the grass around him, the acrid stink of fear and sweat. Val's chain mail clanked against his body. Sweat ran down his neck from under his helmet. He could not feel his forearm at all. He seemed to drift just above the ground, sword arm held low. He cocked his weapon upward, like a Danish member raised in anticipation of a wench, and thrust it up into the small of that Saxon back just as the sword descended. Harald's mouth grew round, but no sound issued forth. Around him the clanking and the shouts dimmed in Val's ears. He jerked his blade back and swung it right into another Saxon belly, then floated toward the third. He shouted. He could feel the sound tremble in his throat even though he could not hear it. The last Saxon swung his ax. Val met it with his shield. The blow shuddered up his arm. The ax cleaved his shield, its blade entangled in the wood. Val jerked his shield back and the ax came with it. The Saxon's face suffused with rage as Bloodletter found his throat. Val swung round as blackness floated in around him. *No*, he protested to no one in particular. His limbs felt as though they moved through water. He was about to fall, to fail, to falter in his purpose. His dream of acceptance faded. No! It was his own fault, just like before. He was his own worst enemy.

Val tried to push the blackness back. Harald still stood, Saxons in disarray at his feet. Then Harald seemed to recede within the thickening circle of darkness until the darkness ate him.

* * *

The sun was high when he woke. It flickered through a green curtain. Val blinked, wondering what world this was. Was he underwater, in Fafnir's land, with all this light and waving green? He remembered feeling as though he dragged his body through water to fight. . . . whom? He shook his head and squinted around. He wasn't surrounded with water but by waving willow fronds. He was propped against a tree trunk in the shade, his chain mail, his shield and helmet, along with Bloodletter, piled carefully at his side. The throb of his arm told him he was alive, but it was curiously dull. Sounds came to him through the curtain; clattering, groans, low voices. He struggled to his feet, leaning on Bloodletter, and pushed through the shady curtain of privacy into the glare of the sun.

The familiar detritus of battle confronted him. His men washed each other's injuries and stitched themselves. Bandages were rinsed in the stream and reused on fresher wounds. Saxon dead were already piled at one end of the clearing, ready for burning. They numbered perhaps fifteen. Val wondered if the gods had smiled on him and Alfred was among them. Graves were being dug for the five fallen Danes, that each might be laid with his weapons ready as befitted a warrior. Their souls already feasted in Valhalla. Val's gaze returned to the Saxons stacked like cordwood. A full score had escaped. He sagged against Bloodletter. He had let the Saxons escape their fate. His men were disappointed, too. He could see it in their eyes. Val noted dully that several glanced to Svenn, first among them the hothead Sigurd. He had shaken their faith in him. They searched for another leader. And all because of his cursed impulse to interfere with the fate the Norns had woven for Harald.

The young warrior hurried over. Svenn strolled up behind him, followed like a shadow by Sigurd. "They crossed the river," Harald said, "when that young whoreson king came running down from that hill over there. He rallied them."

Val tried to get his breath. Had his strategy been faulty?

The *Danir* should have been able to cut the Saxons into thongs of leather when they were pinned against the river.

"Ja." Svenn answered the unasked question. "It should have worked. But they did not turn and fight. Alfred grabbed our strings of horses while we were busy hacking at each other and took them across the river. He yelled to them, and they all just turned tail and waded across the river as fast as they could go. They were galloping away before you could blink."

"We did not have enough horses left to go after them." Harald flushed to the roots of his blond hair. Val glanced around frantically. A score of horses grazed at the end of their tethers. Slepnir was among them. Val breathed again. At least he had not lost Slepnir. They had been together since the steppes. But a score of horses would not mount his band.

Val sighed. "He may be young, but he is a crafty son of Loki." Val turned toward the hill that Harald had indicated, leaning heavily on his sword. Odin, but he felt weak! How could he lead in such a state? Svenn would be glad to take the leadership. The hill loomed behind the willows that lined the stream, jutting up in a green-gloved gesture of defiance. Carved into its side, visible for miles in daylight, was the white outline of a crudely drawn horse. "What was he doing there, our Saxon boy-king?" Val wondered aloud.

"The shepherds said he was getting horses from the 'bitch priestess,' " Harald mused.

"We need horses now," Val muttered. "We will go to this hag."

"You need food," Svenn admonished. "Not to chase an old woman who chants spells."

"I must fulfill my vow to Guthrum," Val barked with as much strength as he could muster. He would not cede his place to Svenn just yet. "For that I require horses."

Pony had climbed to the crumbling faesten built by the ancient ones atop the peak of her hill to view the battle from a distance. She had left Herd safely dispersed in the wood.

She saw it all, until the Saxons disappeared into the blue and green haze of September on the downs.

Alfred was gone. She needn't fear him pestering her to come with him now; she could get back to normal as soon as the Vikings moved on. As her shadow shortened toward noon, the Vikings predators poked around her hut. Stories of torture, blood-eagles, rape spread before these harbingers of chaos like drops of blood in water—but they would soon be gone.

When she could see no more of them, she returned to her hut and threw open the wicker shutters to the afternoon light. She washed in the water she'd brought up from the stream last night, then put on her buff leather leggings made from wolf hide and her soft boots. The boot leather was worn and supple. Winding their narrow strips up her legs, she tied them at her waist, then pulled a clean white flaxen shirt over her head, leaving it loose around her hips. Today was a day for working in her garden. The new spade from Young Dapple's partnership would be most helpful.

She put an oatcake in the small pouch she wore tied at her hip and walked out into the day, plaiting her white blond hair. Things were right again. She didn't feel any different, now that the seed was planted. That was good. She dreaded becoming as heavy with child as the farmers' wives. How did one ride with that great belly bouncing before you, destroying all your precious balance? Perhaps that was what made getting with child the beginning of the end. Perhaps you just got more and more distant from your Gift, from life, until . . .

It was time to recall Herd. Perhaps she should take them to graze down by the old barrow surrounded with oak trees they called Waylan's, just until the smell of the pyres was gone. She went still and put out her thoughts. The horses cantered out of the wood, led by First Mare and White Stallion. As they returned to Pony, White Stallion shrieked a whinny. Herd stopped about a hundred yards away. They stood, sifting the air, ears swiveling.

Pony glanced wildly around. What did they sense? There,

coming out of the trees down to her right, were three men, clothed in metal and hardened leather. Vikings! They had hidden in the trees until she returned. Her heart thudded. The scourge of the North, the carnivores of the race of men, coming up from her stream! Could she escape? But First Mare was too far away, and wary of coming closer. The Vikings were almost upon her. She was trapped. She would never outrun them on foot!

What would her mother do? Would she let her heart thud in terror? Pony stilled her breathing. What if they . . . ? No. Think not those thoughts. She let her mother's spirit infuse her, her mother's calm, her distance. She drew herself up. She knew what she was. Great Mother would protect her. First, she must protect Herd. She whirled and sent her thoughts out, raised her arms. But Herd did not hear her. They only stood, ears swiveling. Pony turned back toward the intruders.

A great sword clanked at the leader's side. He cradled one arm against his belly. The hand was swollen. He was a big man. One of his fellows was taller, but the leader gave the impression of immense strength. His heavy shoulders dripped chain mail over a sleeveless leather jerkin. Its links made a chorus of tiny clinking. His leathers, bound over his massive thighs, were dark with use and sweat. His boots were hardened leather to protect his shins in battle. Only slowly did she raise her eyes to his face. His light brown hair was thick and waved over his shoulders. It stuck to his forehead where he had sweated into a helmet. His face was . . . decisive, the nose prominent and straight. The chin was strong under a short beard. His cheekbones cut finely upward. He was quite close now. But she had no thought of running. She wanted to see his eyes at close range. They were gray. Alfred's eyes were clearer, more arresting. These eyes, held . . . what? Pain? Pain from his injured arm was etched in the lines between his brows. But it was not that pain that sat in his eyes; it was older, deeper. Resolution was there as well. Not Alfred's resolution shining out of every pore like an oil lamp under a basket—more like a hard acorn, tiny and bitter. Osrick's eyes were bitter, too. But this man's eyes were different than Osrick's. Maybe because the pain tempered the bitterness somehow. As though he were sorry for the bitterness but could not help it. Pony recognized his pain in an instant. It was as if a light shone on him alone.

The Viking devil stopped, flanked by his companions. Pony had no eyes for them. She stared up at him from her five feet to his six, dwarfed by his immense frame. His eyes roved past her to the horses. They came back to rest on her face.

Pony shook herself. *He is like a snake that holds his prey with his gaze before he strikes,* she thought. *He has bewitched me.* She felt a tugging at her mind. She blinked, as if to prove she could, then she looked up at him, mustering calm.

Silence stretched. Then the Viking too blinked. "Greetings," he said slowly, in heavily accented Saxon. "Is the old woman of *hestr . . .* of horses here?"

A polite Viking? He must think to trick her. She shook her head.

His eyes jerked from her face after long moments. "Those horses." He pointed with his good hand to Herd. The hand was strong and large. The palm was wrapped with leather strips that his sword might not slip on his sweat. She was close enough to see the calluses from sword and leather. "Who has them?"

She cocked her head at him. *I am my mother.* "I do." Her voice was strong. Strength was something these barbarians would understand. It might be her only protection.

He looked down at her in surprise. "You are the bitch priestess?"

He had got her direction from the shepherds. Only they called her that. She nodded.

"We need horses. Will they ride?"

She lifted her chin. "They obey me. They carry only men I choose."

The Viking's eyes darkened. He was feverish, his forehead damp with sweat not from his helmet, but from the fires inside him stoked by the rot she saw in his arm. "I wager you let Alfred ride."

She started. But he didn't mean what she had first thought. She nodded, her silence resentful. She would have given Alfred her horses. He was willing to learn the Language of Touch. He was not a barbarian Viking who wanted to steal her precious friends.

The two other Vikings whispered their barbaric tongue in their leader's ears. A graying warrior with a scar winding over his forehead and a stripling youth whose beard was not yet full. The big leader nodded and snaked his good arm around Pony's waist. He threw her over his shoulder.

She gasped in outrage as much as fear. What did he want with her? She kicked and pounded on his back, but he had one massive arm around her backside and seemed impervious. He turned and strode down toward the stream, where three horses grazed under the willows, invisible from her hut. The others followed, laughing at her fear. She was so angry, she could hardly think what to do. All her peace was gone. Could he just take her like this? What of Herd? *Herd!*

She went still. Lifting her head, she looked up toward the meadow. White Stallion shrieked in challenge and reared, hooves flailing. The rest whirled in confusion. Pony needed her Gift now. Let it be there, somewhere inside her. She breathed in and let the air out slowly. There was no room for fear or anger with what she had to do. She stared straight at them, banishing all other thought, weaving her connection to them. *Go.* She thought about the great forest to the south, felt the hard thrust of trunks, the cool of shade on her skin. *Go.* First Mare stood her ground. White Stallion let his great weight plunge to earth, and he pawed the ground.

Go! Pony thought, with all the certainty, all the concentration she could muster. Herd shuffled, indecisive. The meadow grass waved in the morning breeze. Foals glanced anxiously to their dams. *Go! Go now!* But they didn't. Could they not hear her at all? As the Viking strode down to the stream, First Mare made the decision for Herd. She trotted slowly after Pony and her captors.

Chapter Four

Val felt the girl go still, her weight settle into his shoulder. She knew when she was bested. When first he saw her, he feared she had bewitched him. The white of her hair, the fineness of her skin, her eyes so blue-purple they were the color of the finest lapis lazuli from the lands around the azure sea, held him transfixed. She was tiny and young, not at all what he expected of a priestess, but in her purple eyes he saw . . . peace. Purpose. She seemed sure of herself. She seemed sure of who he was as well. He saw her decide about him.

He shifted her weight on his shoulder, just to let her know he was in control. She did not know him. And he had no intention of letting Alfred circle back and steal even more mounts for his armies. This woman apparently had control of her horses. They followed now, no doubt at her behest. He could feel their hooves beating in his chest as they hit the turf. What tie did this girl have to these horses that they followed her? The stupid shepherds thought she had uncanny powers. They said the gods protected her. It did not matter. In taking her, he'd get the horses, too.

But there was something else here. Alfred had been at her hut when he came down to steal Val's men's mounts, so the shepherds said. Had he been trading for horses, or asking for the favor of this girl's gods? One did not trade for horses in the middle of the night. The girl had given Alfred more than horses. He had bedded her. Of course he had. Who would not, if given half a chance? But that meant taking her deprived Alfred in two ways. Alfred might have prevailed this day, but Val had both his woman and her horses. He felt her breasts against his back through his mail shirt. Her slight form was easy enough to carry, even depleted as he was, but he was suddenly aware of her thighs under the crook of his arm, his biceps pressing against her leather breeches. Good women, even Saxon women, wore cyrtles over their shifts and brooches at their shoulders, a cloak in winter perhaps. He should have known she was a daughter of Loki, the Trickster, just from her leather breeches. He glanced behind and saw her white blond hair swinging against his hips, its braiding half undone. A brief image of her naked body writhing in pleasure under the Saxon king shuddered through him. The heat of his fever was making him weak. He must to Slepnir and away from here. He was for the fortress of this Osrick, and hoped he had men enough and strength enough to take it.

No! Pony thought at her Herd. Why did they disobey? Could they not understand? But it was plain that First Mare meant not to abandon her. White Stallion had no choice but to come along. That meant all were on the move. Epona let her head drop, her hair swing in rhythm to the stride of the giant devil who held her captive. The heat of his body seemed to boil up and engulf her wherever she touched him, though their flesh was separated by metal, flax and leather. The bulge of his biceps across her thighs captured her attention, in spite of the tumult, the fear, or *because* of the tumult. She willed herself to calm again. Where was her mother's still center now? Images of her body drawn and quartered, her throat slit, burnt at a stake, flashed through her. Or rape might be her lot. *Mothers save me!*

She heaved in a breath, her breasts pressing against the devil's back. *Calm. Else how can you listen? How can you know the truth of the world? Limp. No resistance. Go with him until you see your way. That is the way of the plant-eater. Run, or submit until you can run again.*

The giant Viking called out in that guttural tongue that sounded so barbaric. She craned around his waist to see other Vikings mounding up raw loam into small barrows in the clearing by the stream. All around her smoke, rife with the smell of burning meat, drifted from the pyres until Pony wanted to gag. *Think of something besides cooked meat.* There were five barrows. They were burying their dead.

Vikings greeted the party returning, but Pony heard reservation in their voices. All was not well in the Viking camp. Did they not trust their large leader? Did they not want her brought into their midst? Pony's heart thumped in alarm. Perhaps they thought she was a witch who could do them harm. Herd fidgeted some hundred yards away, lurking in the willows.

Breathe. Calm.

The Viking said something to his fellows as he dumped her on the turf still wet with dew. Pony went small and clutched her knees to her breasts, letting the curtain of her hair shield her from their eyes. Could they know she carried Alfred's child? No. Only Alfred and the two witnesses knew, at least until she swelled. Pony wasn't sure how long that was for humans. In horses it took many months. Pony peered through her curtain to see Vikings shouldering packs, saddling the horses they had left. Several glanced her way. She didn't like their looks. Some looked fearful of her. They must have been listening to the shepherds' tales about her. But others had a sly and covetous expression; they looked like wolves eyeing a rabbit. She didn't like to think what they might want.

The big Viking argued with the beardless youth in front of a great chestnut stallion whose coat caught the sun and shattered its light into a thousand copper shards. The giant Viking's good hand unconsciously slipped to the horse's great neck and smoothed its palm across the arching muscle there. He shook his head, sure his order was law and surprised to find argument. Pony had eyes only for that hand stroking the gleaming copper coat, and the great liquid brown eye that half-closed as the stallion nosed the Viking's backside and breathed his scent across the man's leather breeches. Ahhh. Partners. Could Viking carnivores be partners?

The younger Viking pointed to the leader's swollen arm and then stood, legs apart and arms folded across his chest, his protest concluded. The leader closed his eyes and pressed his lips together in disgust, then turned and mounted his stallion. Pony realized they had been arguing about who would ride. When he was settled, pale and grim, in his saddle, the leader pointed to her. The young Viking dragged her over to the the great chestnut horse. She steadied herself with a hand at the stallion's shoulder and breathed deeply. The warmth of the coppery hide melted into her hand. She felt the familiar, swimming feeling, buoyed by the current that arced between them, beast to beast, body to body, soul to soul. Ahhhh. The horse served the barbarian willingly, not as drudge but partner.

Pony's focus snapped. A hand clutched her forearm and pulled her up. The barbarian bent his toe up and pushed his heel down. "Step there," he ordered in Saxon. She swung herself up in front of him, turning her body so she could lift her leg over the chestnut's neck. The Viking settled her against him, her back against his chest, her thighs captured by his, her backside pressed into the joining of his legs. Burning red suffused her cheeks without her permission. Her captor grasped the reins in his good hand and wrapped that arm around her waist. She noticed a hollow bone tube sticking out of a loop in his saddle. Surprised, she realized it was a flute. Was it his?

"What is your horse's name?" she asked to distract herself from what pressed against her rump.

"Slepnir." The other Vikings shouldered packs and fell in line behind them. Several of those who rode were wounded. Herd moved restlessly in the trees. The Viking's voice rumbled in his chest. His breath was hot in her hair. "Slepnir strides the heavens of Odin with eight strong legs."

"Slepnir," she whispered, feeling the horse's broad back between her thighs, feeling other thighs spread across his back. "His spirit is strong." She looked down at where the Viking's swollen arm lay across his thigh. He wouldn't be able to keep it down for long. It would start to throb. As if in answer to her speculation, he raised it gingerly and held it out. She heard his breath hiss as the arm jostled against her. His hand was swollen and a little gray.

Good, she thought. He was weakening. Soon he wouldn't be able to hold her. She would await her chance to escape. Perhaps when they next stopped to rest. She would call to Herd and leap onto First Mare's back, and then none could catch her, not even this fine stallion. Not if he carried a heavy Viking, hot with fever and like to lose his arm.

Forty *Danir* to take Osrick's hold at Chippenham. Not enough to pry the Saxon out if he holed up inside. Yet there would be no reinforcements: Guthrum had made that clear before Val left Anglia. Val's vision wavered. They followed the great road north of the stream. It was made by the ones from the south, called Romans, gone now. Raised above the surrounding land, its surface was still paved with square-cut stones, though in places dirt covered them. Val had seen their roads in Valland as well, though not along the River Dieppe or the Volga in the great eastern realm of Garthariki. This one, called Ridge Way, snaked from the settlement called Londinium first west and then southwest, an artery of conquest for the *Danir*. If you rode as far as it went, then took the road that crossed westward, it would lead to Chippenham.

Well enough that it was easy, since Val sank slowly into the delirium of his fever. Sometimes he thought it was the girl's fault that he burned so. Holding her was a trial. And

58

how could his errant sex find the strength to stiffen when he was faltering? It was his shame that he rode while most of his men walked. But Harald had been adamant and worse, right. Twenty miles to Chippenham. Twenty miles to ride, and a fight at the end he doubted they could win.

He had failed to vanquish Alfred today. He'd been busy saving Harald instead of pushing his foes to the river. What kind of warrior was he? Fifteen years he'd spent exiled as a mercenary to the czars just because he could not put loyalty to his cause above the needs of a person. He didn't even *like* Harald. He must get the better of this side of himself or it would get the better of him. Assuming, of course, he lived.

Thirty horses from the girl's herd followed them all the way to Chippenham. Only at the first huts did the animals peel off to avoid the confining spaces of the village that surrounded the Saxon palisades and spread out around the fortress like the skirts of a maid. Val and his men bore down on the compound, which topped the hill to the south. There was no point in subterfuge. He wondered whether Osrick and his men waited in ambush, or whether they counted on the fortress to protect them. Osrick would have received word that Danes now controlled everything south and west of the River Thames. There was a chance the Saxons had abandoned their position. If not, Val could expect a fight— but with how many warriors he did not know. Likely more than his own.

The dirt streets were deserted, though villagers peered from shuttered houses and lurked in smithies and stables and tiny shops. The fortress was a fairly small affair, little more than palings made of logs sharpened and bound together. The massive gates were open. No sentries manned the catwalks behind the walls. Val peered inside. No movement teased his senses. Why would the gates be open? Was it a trap? He saw what looked to be a large central wooden hall and a series of outbuildings and animal pens around a large yard.

Val felt the girl's back arch straight against him, alert, as they stopped in front of the open gates. She felt the danger, too. It was almost palpable, hanging in the heat and the heavy air of late afternoon. Behind him, the tension of his battle-hardened troops was a protective shield against what might come. He knew their swords were out, their axes raised. He did not pull Bloodletter. If the Saxons were in there, let them have a chance to surrender. The snorting of the horses, the shuffling sound of their sidling movements as they sensed their riders' wariness, seemed small against the silence that issued from the fortress. "Stay here," Val barked to those behind him, his voice echoing in the silence. "See that you are not flanked." He urged Slepnir toward the open gates as his troop deployed themselves outward in a phalanx.

Slepnir passed through the towering gates, and Val halted. "Halloa," he shouted in Saxon. "I, Valgar, trusted of Guthrum, *Konnungr* of the Danelaw, seek Osrick, Eorl of the Downs."

Silence bounced back the echoes of his call. Slepnir nodded his head nervously. Val held him in place with the pressure of his legs. Let his waning strength not fail him now.

In the open doorway of the great hall, a shadow moved. Val tensed. A man ducked his head and walked out into the sunlight. He stopped and straightened, examining Val through slitted eyes. He was very tall, lean even under his leather jerkin and chain mail. His face was all planes and angles, his eyes dark holes that offered no expression, his lips thin and supple. His head was covered with a conical metal helmet. A bronze protector almost concealed a hawk nose. A giant sword with a hilt bejeweled and inlaid hung at his side, but it remained undrawn.

"I am Osrick." The newcomer's voice was raw.

Val nodded. "I am come to take the Downland for Guthrum. Do you yield?" He tried to keep his voice steady, his eyes focused on the eorl. He dared not let his weakness show.

The eyes of the Saxon widened; no doubt he was surprised that Val spoke his tongue as well as he did. Then those eyes moved from Val's face to the girl in front of him. "Does the witch serve you?" Osrick's voice held a sneer. Val felt the girl tremble against him. His vision seemed to shimmer at the edges.

"If I wish." Val let his eyes rake the hall behind the man, searching for the source of the fear he felt in the girl. Where was the danger? Or was it simply her hatred of this man?

Osrick gave a mirthless laugh. "She deserves a barbarian master."

Val had no wish for conversation. If this man had been deserted by his men he must yield. If not, let him call them down and the battle begin. "Do . . . you . . . yield?"

Osrick cocked his head, speculating. Then his thin lips narrowed into an almost invisible line. He shook his head in disgust. "I yield." The words were spit out like milk that had turned.

Val let his eyes glance to each side. "Your men?"

"Most are gone." He turned his head. "Come out, my rabble."

Movement could be seen inside the hall behind him. Grim-faced warriors walked into the light. There were perhaps fifteen. Some were not quite steady on their feet. They had been surprised at their revelry. Those sober or disloyal enough had abandoned the faesten. Val turned to Osrick. The man could not hold his troops together: That said something about him.

"You will need help to rule this cursed land. The peasants are sulky and withhold their taxes. Though you speak Saxon a little, still you need a strong second in command. You will move on to conquer other towns. You need someone to hold this town for you."

"That is you?" Val asked, his voice carefully neutral.

"It could be."

Val didn't like his mouth. Such a mouth was used to sneering or lying. "Lay down sword and ax." He gestured to the ragged line of Saxons.

They filed forward and tossed their weapons with distaste into a clanking pile. Val motioned Svenn to bring his men inside the gates, to segregate the Saxons and encourage them to give up their smaller dirks and hidden weapons.

He turned back to Osrick. "Let us talk." He swung the girl off his saddle. Tipping to the side that he might let her to the ground, he felt the darkness close in. Hastily, he righted himself and waited for the pattern jumping before his eyes to recede before he swung his own leg over and dropped to his feet. He grabbed the girl's arm as she inched away. "You come inside."

Pony jerked her arm away and tried to muster some dignity as she walked into the hall behind Osrick, the Viking named Valgar striding behind her. Between the two of them, there was not much to choose. Both the barbarian Viking who had stolen her and the dissolute Saxon thegn were cruel. Caught between two evils, how could she maintain her mother's calm? Her heart fluttered in her breast. Her hands shook. This would never do. Calm was the only weapon she had against them. She sucked in air and let it out slowly. Inside the darkened hall small fires crackled in fireboxes at each end. Women servants murmured as they crouched in a corner. The hall smelled of the oil in lamps, needed even though the building's wicker shutters were open to the late afternoon sun, their channels of light cutting the dimness. The place reeked of mead and piss and male sweat. It needed a good airing.

As her eyes became accustomed to the dark, she saw huge tapestries on the walls, wooden benches and trestle tables made from heavy planks. At one end of the room sat an ornately carved chair, almost a throne. The firebox was fitted with a spit for roasting meat, and a metal hook upon which hung a blackened pot. Osrick lived in squalid luxury. Valgar dragged Pony with him to one of the trestle tables. The Viking gestured to Osrick to sit and pulled off his own helmet, not so different from the Saxon's. His hair was plastered to his head with sweat. It was the fever. She had been wishing all day that the fever would kill him before he could ravish her. Yet now, as she looked between him and Osrick, she was not so sure she wanted him dead.

Valgar came to the point. "What can you offer, Osrick, that I could not take myself?"

"I know where you can squeeze more silver from the town, which farmers have a richer harvest this year, which shepherds have the biggest flocks. The Elders do my bidding. They have seen what disobedience brings. I mete out justice and they know it. I will keep them in line." Osrick gave a thin smile that made Pony shudder. She saw him eye Valgar's injured arm.

"The people, they hold back?" Valgar asked. Sweat gleamed on his face. The lines around his mouth spoke of the effort he was making to sit and talk.

Osrick laughed. "When do they not? You must squeeze to get what they can give."

"What do you give in return?" The Viking's eyes were hard behind his pain.

Osrick peered at him. "Why, protection from bandits. I submit their portion to the king, punish criminals."

"Ahh." The Viking nodded. "What kind of crimes?"

"Stealing." Osrick shrugged. "We cut off hands for that. I set the wergild for taking a life, or maiming. The criminal pays the family of the victim; and me, of course." Osrick grinned and folded his hands on the table in front of him. "I could be very useful to you."

Valgar only nodded, his mouth set in a grim line.

Osrick turned hard eyes on Pony. "She stole a horse from me. She should be punished."

"What punishment would you make?" The Viking's deep voice rumbled. Pony held her breath. Was this Osrick's opportunity to be revenged on her?

The Saxon thegn's eyes narrowed. Suddenly he laughed. "Perhaps she should escape having those lovely hands cut off—they could be put to better purpose. But I might lash her, just to make sure she was diligent in pleasing me." His eyes roved Pony in ways that made her skin crawl.

The Viking looked at her. "Did you steal?"

Pony felt tears of anger start to her eyes. "I gave Young Black to a farmer who made a covenant with me and with the horse. Osrick took him from the farmer. He made no covenant. I set Young Black free to run with Herd, where he was safe from Osrick's whip." She choked. "Only I can make a partnership. The crime is his."

The Viking stood. He pulled her up with him and drew her in against his burning side. He was not entirely steady on his feet. "I see your value," he said to Osrick.

The Saxon grinned. "Then we are agreed."

"Do you know the word *law*?" the Viking asked. His voice was light, inviting.

"*Law*? No. What is it?" Osrick leaned back, confident.

"It is a Danish word. You will grow to know it well." Valgar's voice was filled with the steel of a sword. "*Law* sets the tithe. *Law* says a *jarl* does not 'squeeze' his people. *Law* says the punishment for crimes. The *jarl* cannot 'take his share of wergild,' or another's horse."

Osrick looked puzzled. He sat forward slowly. "A thegn takes what he will. Why else be thegn?" The words clanked onto the table between them.

"You are *jarl* that your strong arm may serve your people, to judge with law, to see the land heavy with harvest." Valgar's voice was ragged, but there was no mistaking his meaning.

Osrick's eyes narrowed. "You sound like my father. He never took what he might have. I vowed I would not follow his way." Pony could feel the Viking stiffen.

"Nor am I like my father," he barked. "But I follow *law*."

Osrick glanced to the open doorway. Vikings crisscrossed the yard. The confiscated pile of Saxon weapons was clearly visible. Pony could see him realize that his choices were few. "If you would have it thus." He nodded. How that must gall him! "Your *law* will be thegn here."

Don't believe him, Pony wanted to shout. *He lulls you into thinking he is with you!*

Valgar grunted. "Order women to bring food. My men are hungry."

Osrick rose and dipped his head again. Pony saw his jaw working. "Of course."

Pony pulled at the scratchy hemp that bound both her arms to the ornately carved chair so big it looked like a throne. Her wrist was raw with pulling, but she was bound as tightly as ever and the chair was much too heavy to drag with her, even should she find opportunity to escape. Valgar had tied the knots himself and they were tight. More, he had fended off what she could tell were several offers for her from his men. One had held back her head by her hair and stroked her cheek, not caring that she spit at him. What he cared about was the snaking sound of steel behind him as the big Viking drew his sword. The man had lifted hands in the air, pretending to laugh as at a joke. By that action, Valgar had claimed her. Pony was half-grateful and half-chilled. What did he want? Did he wait only to take her to his bed? Herd was far away, out on the downs around the town. It could not help her.

She pulled at the knots again, but that would only make her wrists bleed. She must be patient until she could run. Like her horses, that was her only defense.

Pony looked around at the great feasting hall. Her throne was at one end of the great room, no doubt Osrick's favorite chair. Smoke hung in the rafters above. She was sweltering. In the blaze behind her, what was left of a pig turned on a spit. She was glad she didn't have to look at the carcass. Doors to shadowy rooms opened off the main hall, and at the other end a stairway ascended to rooms above. The chamber echoed with Viking guffaws as they ranted in their barbaric tongue. They were singing sagas of their homeland.

The Saxons were left outside the hall under guard, except for Osrick, who sat among the Vikings, toasting songs he could not understand with a smile that looked like it was killing him. His discomfort gave Pony joy. He thought the barbarians might still kill him. Let him stew in his own juices.

The smell of meat and smoke and sweating men was almost overpowering. Pony refused the plate of food a Saxon serving woman offered, for the juices of the meat had spoiled even the roasted parsnips and the summer beans. The mere sight of the bleeding haunch sickened her. "Do you not care what devil you serve?" she whispered as she refused the plate. The serving woman eagerly took Pony's portion and snorted in derision. Osrick had no doubt been as cruel a master of humans as he was of horses. That made his retainers not overly particular.

Again and again, Pony found her eyes drawn to the Viking leader who sat off to her left. Just because she was curious about when he would actually fall over, she told herself. She wasn't sure how he had made it here, let alone directed the taking of the faesten. He had put off his chain mail, even his leather jerkin, and now sat in his flaxen shirt, his arm cradled on his lap. She could see the bulk of his shoulders, the light hairs on his chest where his shirt fell open. Stained bandages bound his wound. No blood, though. She would have thought there would be blood. His gray eyes shone with fever. He would not last long. The other Vikings glanced toward him surreptitiously. They must wonder when he would fail, too.

Osrick was more open in his speculation. His avaricious eyes never left Valgar. What did he think to do? Even if the Viking fell, Osrick's men were still outnumbered. Valgar surprised them all by pushing himself to stand. The muscles of his thighs bunched under his leggings, but his back was straight and his bass voice booming as he called to his fellows.

"Danir!" Heads around the hall snapped his way. Their eyes grew wary as he called out what she thought might be orders. His mouth was a line—whether against the pain of his arm or in opposition to his men she could not determine. Oaths were muttered into greasy beards all around. Hard eyes glanced about to other hard sets of eyes. They did not agree with what was being said, and they were looking about for support. She noticed especially the older man with the scar who had come with Valgar to her hut that morning.

Men called him Svenn. Many glanced toward him, but he stared straight ahead, his face stony.

When he was done speaking, Valgar lifted his head and challenged the room. None met his eyes. The scarred one, Svenn, nodded without words and turned to shake out a woolen blanket from a stack. Valgar eased himself onto his bench and slumped against the wall. His eyes closed as though the strength it had taken to hold his men's will had sapped him. The scarred one lay down on his blanket. As if that were a signal, the other Vikings spread blankets around the room and laid themselves to rest. Several eyed Pony hungrily. She simply stared back at them, knowing her calm would make them uncertain. That and the memory of the sound of slithering steel. She glanced toward the Viking who had claimed her. He would be no threat to her tonight. But that meant he could not protect her either.

He opened one eye, even as she looked at him. "Osrick, go with Harald to your men outside." He motioned to the young blond, whose name must be Harald. "Tell the guards not to bar the gates tonight." He repeated the Saxon words in his own Viking tongue. Did he want Osrick to know the gates would not be barred? Heads snapped up around the room. Harald did not question the orders, but bowed so low in front of Osrick that it must be mocking. He gestured toward the door. Osrick snarled an epithet Pony couldn't hear and shoved past.

The hall quieted. Pony squirmed, wishing her seat were not so ornately carved. Between the knobs in her back and the hemp at her wrists, she would not get any sleep. By the time the big Viking died, or descended so far into fever that his men no longer heeded him, she had best be gone. She twisted in her ropes and sighed. She must wait and be calm to hear her opportunity.

She pretended sleep when the young Viking returned. Through her lashes, she saw he carried a bundle of clean white cloth. He shook Valgar to consciousness. The Viking leader came to himself, groggy and slurring his words, as though from mead. The younger man tried a voice of authority, but the leader only shook his head. Others raised their faces from their blankets, eyes turning toward the pair. Was the young one challenging her captor? The young Viking lowered his head. He said something, low, not pleading really, but not challenging anymore. The hardened leader looked at him, then closed his eyes. Pony could sense some internal struggle. What was passing here? The young Viking knew he had won. He reached down and hauled Valgar up by his good arm, pulled it over his shoulder and staggered with him through a door. He was back in moments and headed straight for Pony, brandishing a short knife. Pony sat up in alarm, but he only cut the hemp that bound her, grabbed one of the lamps and pulled her to her feet and through the door.

In the new room, Harald's light pushed back the darkness. It revealed Valgar seated on a bench, the Viking leader slumped across a trestle table, his injured arm laid out before him. The room was only a thatched lean-to against the great hall. The full moon outside its single open window showed Pony a broad back standing guard. A bedbox lined with furs was in the corner, a small firebox glowing with coals and two stools, too—this had been a private living quarters.

Valgar's face was curtained by thick hair as his head sagged on his shoulders. The young Harald pushed Pony to the table and gave her some order she could not understand, gesturing at his leader's bandaged arm. What did he think—she was some kind of witch, that she could heal wounds? Perhaps she could banish boils, too. She shook her head. "I am no healer." The one called Harald got even more determined. He shut the door and pushed her onto a stool. "Mother taught me to care for Herd," she protested. "Not men."

Valgar raised his head. "He saw marks on your horses. Burns," he rasped.

Pony's eyes jerked to the seeping and greasy bandage. Was that why there was no blood?

The stripling held the big man's wrist and, drawing his

knife, cut the stained cloth. His victim clenched against the pain as the bandage raked his arm. The lad pulled the wrap gently apart. A sickly sweet smell of rot suffused the room. Pony suppressed a gasp. The fleshy part of Valgar's forearm was bubbled and buckled in a patch as big as her palm. At the center, a blackened core looked like hidden evil churning to the surface. The burn must have penetrated to the muscle. The flesh oozed with animal grease and with a weeping liquid of its own. Even on top of the forearm the skin was reddened, the hair gone.

Pony turned shocked eyes to the younger Viking, who raised his brows. He was asking for help. Valgar looked up at her steadily, asking nothing. She wondered if he had ever asked for help. She sucked in a breath. The boy was right: She knew burns. He must have seen the scars on Dun Mare. The south grove had burned when Pony was ten, the summer before her mother's Dread Day. Three horses died. Their screams of terror still rang in her ears. She and her mother had tended burned legs and seared hide for weeks afterward. Yes, she knew burns.

She stood slowly. Saying nothing to either man, she stared at the mottled flesh. Harald nodded encouragement. No wonder the big Viking's arm festered. Animal fat and bandages kept the rot inside. It was the same with horses. You had to scrape away the dead flesh; then the wound might knit. The burn would seep, and you had to clean it again and again. In the end, if you were lucky, the edges grew together with grainy flesh until all that was left was a pink scar.

She stared at the arm, swollen with poison, the hand pale because the blood could not make its way through burnt flesh. Was it too late? Maybe they would have to hack it off. She shot a horrified glance at its owner. "If you want me to bind your stump, I will not do it."

"Svenn waits for that," the Viking said, but Harald shook his head violently. Valgar looked up at him. "Harald thinks to save it."

"If we wait too long, you'll die." She grunted. And dead

69

or with a stump, he was no protection from the barbarians in the hall. It seemed a choice of numbers. She would try to save the Viking's arm. She picked up the bundled cloth.

"*Ja,*" Harald muttered. "*Gut konu.*"

She ignored his air of victory, tearing off a piece of cloth and holding it out. "Tell him I need it soaked in water," she ordered Valgar. "*Clean* water." He issued curt instructions, almost embarrassed, then turned his face away. *I was right,* Pony thought, *he has never asked for help.* Harald nodded eagerly and trotted out the door.

Pony hated hurting her horses even to heal them. Her eyes strayed to the Viking's bubbled flesh. She would have to hurt this man. She didn't want a struggle. If she could prepare them, her horses bore her ministrations stoically. "I must hurt you," she warned, her voice calm. "Whoever tended this did not know burns." He nodded and braced his elbow against the table. Cords of muscle moved across his jaw under his beard. His gray eyes hardened. He was a man who had been hurt before. Good; he would not be surprised. She ripped the sleeve of his damp shirt to the shoulder, then lifted his swollen hand. A small grunt passed through his clenched teeth, but his arm was steady. She tossed away the bandages, heavy and wet, then laid his arm on the clean cloth.

While she waited for Harald, she would get the healing blood moving through his arm. She took his injured hand in hers. It was swollen yet cool to the touch. Still, she could only think of summer heat as she stroked it. The heat came not from him but from inside her. "This . . . this will get the blood flowing," she muttered to explain her action.

She squeezed and kneaded his fingers, his knuckles. Her own hands tingled with the friction. She kept her gaze fixed. His hand. This was a hand that killed, a carnivore's hand. It was finer than she would have thought a barbarian should have. It bore the grime of riding and eating and tying knots. She would mend that later. Her thumbs moved over the mound of flesh under his thumb. That felt worse. She concentrated on her movement until she was rewarded with a slight pinkening of his flesh. Someone would have to do this many times a day. It could not be her.

His breathing was ragged as she moved up to his biceps. Blood must flow into his forearm as well as through to his hand. She gripped his massive upper arm with both hands. Heat jolted through her. She held her breath and pushed her thumbs into the muscle, which was relaxed now, hiding its strength. With circular motions she worked her way up to the Viking's heavy shoulder, the flesh hot against her palms. His strength was borne of holding up a shield that weighed four stone, of manning a great oar when the wind was not a friend of ships, of cutting trees to use as battering rams on Saxon faestens, of killing with a heavy sword. She shuddered. These men were monsters just as her mother had warned. But fear or revulsion was not what made her shiver. It had something to do with the skin underneath her fingers, smooth and soft, lightly tanned—this man did not always wear his tunic and his mail. Or maybe it was the soft bulk of his muscle, oiled with a sheen of sweat. Pony's breath came shallowly, her eyes drawn to the Viking's face against her better judgment. Shock filled his gray eyes, or maybe fear. Her hands circled on his flesh even while his eyes held hers, fever bright. She was aware of his chest, heaving against the coarse flax of his damp shirt. She was close enough to feel his breath.

Harald clattered into the room behind her. Pony jerked her hands back as though stung by a wasp. She grabbed the wet cloth impatiently and motioned the youth to hold his captain's wrist. The lard must go, and the dead flesh beneath. She chanced a glance to her patient's gray eyes.

He shrugged as though it wouldn't matter. "Do it."

"Have the other man put a knife in the fire." She hardly heard him translate. Instead, she held her breath and used the cloth to wipe salve away. She could feel Valgar mastering his shudders. His breath rasped in and out. "Shush, now," Pony soothed in a singsong as she worked. "Quiet." She attacked the blackest part and rubbed away the flesh that was putrefying. He held his arm as though it were a

71

rock or a tree, incapable of pain. She glanced to his face. His forehead creased and his mouth turned down. His lips were cracked and dry from fever. What full lips he had—strange for such a hard man. He pressed them into a thin line. She should be grateful for his courage, but the toll it was taking on him was echoed in some smaller way inside Pony. To witness pain was only half a step from feeling it.

Valgar's flesh began to bleed. Which was good. Pony scraped again. Blood arced across the table. "Knife," she shouted. Somehow it appeared, dull red and fading to black, in her hand. She pressed the tip, flat, onto the spurting vessel. Flesh sizzled, but the spurting stopped. She handed the knife back without a glance. She did not look at her patient's face either, but scraped again. The knife was once more needed to cauterize a vessel. When at last the wound was red, all blackened flesh removed, Pony sat back, limp.

Harald held out more cloth. Pony crumpled a small bit and packed it into Valgar's gaping wound, then bound it lightly with a strip and tied it off. Harald grinned at Pony, as though to say they would save Valgar whether he would or no. Pony was not so sure. The burn was severe. It had been left long to fester. Fever burned in him.

"Lie down," she said, pointing, and went to get more of the white cloth. Harald helped him do as she asked. He looked disgusted with himself. Pony laid a cloth across the big man's chest, then set his arm gently over it. She sat back on her haunches and put her fists on her hips, nodding in satisfaction as she surveyed her work. "Now you can heal, if you will." His brow was beaded with sweat. His chest heaved. But he was a fighter. Maybe he would heal.

Harald touched her shoulder and said something. "He asks if you know herbs," Valgar muttered.

"Tomorrow we will get thornberry for the burn, and mint for pain, vervain for fever."

Valgar translated. "Harald orders you to show him in the morning." He was fading.

"He should ask, not order," she responded calmly. "Have him get me a blanket."

"*You* should ask, not order," he gasped. Was there humor there, behind the glazed eyes?

Harald went to do as he was bid, leaving the door open. Pony got up and closed it against the snoring and smell of his countrymen. Somewhere outside, she knew Osrick was plotting. When she turned, Valgar had faded into uneasy sleep. *Don't die,* she thought, and wondered if she meant it.

Chapter Five

An aching somewhere tugged at Val's mind. It was an enemy, that aching. It throbbed with the beat of his heart and grew until it seemed like a beast tearing at his flesh. Thor's Hammer protect us! Where was Bloodletter? He must gut the beast before he lost his mind.

His eyelids creaked open on darkness broken only by dim checkered light seeping through wicker shutters closed against the moon. He blinked to full awareness. No beast tore at him. A foreign thing, a slab of meat, lay across his chest. The throbbing pain radiated from it. Was that his arm? It seemed a thing apart. He willed his breathing quiet.

"Are you well?" A female voice lilted from the darkness. A pale face haloed with white foam loomed to his right. Not Valkyrie. It spoke Saxon. It was Alfred's horse-girl.

"Ja," he lied, straightening. He must have been writhing on his bed. Had he cried out? He hoped his men had not heard. The girl laid a cool hand on his forehead as if to soothe him—but you couldn't call that touch soothing. He sucked in air through cracked lips, remembered her rubbing

his arm. That had almost been worse torment than his burn. Her fingers brushed his lips. He shivered, though the room was hot. The girl rose and was gone. Where?

When she knelt beside him again, she slid a hand under the wet hair at his neck and lifted his head. "Drink," she said. Pressing a leather mead sack to his lips, she squirted cool honey liquor into his mouth and throat. He gulped convulsively. "Slow," she murmured, but she gave him more and more. He would have drank forever, but she pulled it away at last and laid his head down. "Better?"

"Ja," he answered. The mead soothed him if her touch had not. He could not see much of his arm in the dim checkered light of the moon. "I will lose the arm, *ja?*" It would be Svenn who challenged him after the amputation. Val could stand down, but he would not. He would fight, one-armed. If Svenn gave him time to heal before the challenge . . . Perhaps he could strap his shield to the stump.

"It may heal." The girl's calm voice interrupted his plans. "Your heart is strong." She laid a hand on his chest. His heart thumped against it. "Believe in your strength."

Before he could focus on anything but his heart and her palm, she took the arm on his chest that might be his, but might not, and began to knead the hand. She had done that before. Or had he dreamed it: her thumbs pressing into the fleshy pad beneath his thumb, circling in his palm? Her touch seemed like some vision born of fever or passion. She pulled on his fingers, rubbed his knuckles. He could not speak. He could feel only the tingling in his hand, the pressure of her thumbs. No one had ever touched him like that. He mourned when she laid his arm once more across his abdomen. Then she turned her attention to his upper arm. The hands on his biceps were small but strong, with calluses born of work and short nails. She rubbed Val's shoulder, the tender place in the crook of his elbow. He was so bewildered he could not think whether to pull away or hope she never stopped.

"What is it you do?" he finally choked.

"Blood helps you heal. You will do this yourself when you are better."

Better? "The muscle is gone." He couldn't help the bleakness in his voice. Could he even hold a shield? Perhaps better to have the arm be amputated and be done with it. But then, without his fighting skill to give him a place, he would be outcast in these faraway lands. What life was left?

"Animals are wonderful things. Flesh fills in. Scars knit wounds. I have known a body to heal damage I could not bear to look at." The eyes he knew to be purple were only dark pools. "I know what you fear, Valgar," she said. But she did not know the half of it. True, he could not think of losing his warrior's prowess. But there were other things to fear. She did not know about the rages that could grip him, or the pity he could not refuse. His nature would do him in, if his burn did not. "I think you will fight again," she whispered.

Did she believe what she said? Her voice was so sure. But he knew nothing about her, not enough to know if she lied. "What is your name?" he asked. It was a start.

She said nothing for a long moment, looked around as though coming to her senses. Her hands stopped their strange, demanding caress. "I do not tell my name to Vikings who take me from my home and hold me prisoner." Her voice cracked as she drew back and disappeared. The loss of her touch startled, nauseated him.

Was she his prisoner, or he hers? Alone with her in a dark room, his weakness and rotting arm made him helpless. Had Harald searched her for weapons? He might find a knife in his throat when she returned. Or perhaps her strong thumbs would press into his windpipe until life fled. He shifted to face the danger. Pain ripped up his arm.

Her dim shape lay on a blanket in the corner of the room. *Breathe, fierce warrior,* he chided himself. *If she had wanted to kill you, she would have done it in your sleep these hours past.* As he stared at her back, curled on a blanket in the dark, he wondered why she had not.

* * *

76

Pony rolled herself in her blanket as though it would protect her from barbarians, or from herself. Why had she let herself be talked into helping a Viking? Why had she promised him he would fight again? Had she taken to helping carnivores? She had to get out of this hall that stank of Osrick and his captors, and find Herd. She belonged under the sign of the White Horse. How could she be ripped from her Vale now, just when she had fulfilled her destiny? She *must* escape.

She could not escape tonight, though. Not with a guard posted outside the wicker shutter and two score bestial Vikings snoring just beyond the door. Outside, the rustle of a raccoon or an opossum in the undergrowth beyond the clearing competed with the singing of cicadas for her attention. Snakes slithered through grass. Owls announced their hunting prowess with soft hooting. The animal world went about its business, not caring that Pony was a prisoner. Hunger tightened her belly. She would starve if she couldn't escape. All these Vikings cared for seemed to be meat. The hall reeked of it. She could hear the Viking breathe behind her. He was awake, listening to her breathe, too. She should have let the monster suffer and die. Too late. She had done what she had done. She pulled the blanket around her shoulders and let her resentment grow. How hateful he was to sling her over his shoulder and take her away from all she knew.

Alfred was no better: telling her that she should use her Gift for the good of the world. He wanted to use it for himself. What did he know of her? She *did* use her Gift for the good of the world. She was the last of the Ones who joined the human world to the natural one. It was she who connected men to animals and through them to the Great Mother herself. What if men lost that connection entirely? What would happen to the world then? Her final duty was to produce One who could continue that connection after she was gone. Generations of her mothers had fulfilled their destiny beneath the sign of the White Horse. Was their destiny something to be despised?

She rubbed her belly, remembering that her duty was now fulfilled. It should have comforted her. But the child meant that she was one step closer to her own Dread Day. Somehow she had thought that when she finally answered her call, all her questions would be silenced; she would be fulfilled along with her duty. Not so. She was more chaotic inside than ever. It was this Viking's fault, taking her away from where she belonged, for who knew what dire purpose.

She wanted to be angry with him. She wanted to feel the relief that she had found a man to father her child. But she was so tired. So much had happened today. And she could not risk those emotions. Anger made tumult. Where was her calm? Her mother would disapprove.

Seeking to regain her peace, Pony tried to sleep.

She stood in icy water as always. It was black and translucent, each wavelet crescented with a gleam reflecting the grim moon above. The raft was not strong enough to hold Pony and her mother; its water-worn boards lashed together with leather strips lurched along just under the surface as Pony tried to pole it toward a shore she couldn't see. Her mother lay in the tiny lapping waves, her skin as translucent as the moonlit water. Her cyrtle spread soddenly around her. The woman was so ill, she was thinning right before Pony's eyes. Her bones made their presence felt beneath the skin, her eyes clouded, going pale, as white as her skin. She was depending on Pony to get her to shore.

Pony pushed the pole down, trying to move them forward, but there was no bottom to this lake, no edges. Her pole thrust down into nothing: no grip, no purchase. The glassy water tugged it out of her grasp. The pole sank beneath the surface, its form barely visible in the black, transparent water, until it disappeared entirely. Frantic, Pony turned and knelt beside her mother.

The woman's lips were drawn back, her skin now parchment stretched across the bony points of her cheeks. "Pony," she whispered. "You are my only hope." Her face was so calm, so perfectly calm, but her hand stretched out.

78

The leaky little raft sank on one side. Pony tried to grab her mother, but the raft only tilted more. Her mother was sliding into the black, cold water. The more Pony reached out, the more quickly her mother slipped away, until only her hand was above the water. Pony could still see her face: calm, eyes wide, drifting downward through the glassy blackness, until she was gone. Pony couldn't scream, though screams hovered somewhere in her chest. Tears flooded down her cheeks and joined the lake. She would never scream again. . . .

Pony groaned and rolled to her knees. It was morning. Her hips hurt from sleeping on the wooden floor. Tentative dawn light had replaced that of the moon in streaming through the shutters. Men shouted outside. Boots crunched on hard packed earth. She glanced to the Viking. He stirred.

A knock sounded at the door. It was the second. The first had wakened them. Harald pressed into the room, a steaming wooden bowl in each hand. He was cheerful and grinning, but he peered with concern at Valgar over his smile. Pony got to her feet. Harald greeted her with busy words and went to look at Valgar's arm. She peeked over his shoulder, then pushed the young man aside to undo his leader's bandage. Already the seeping liquid from Valgar's burn was drying into yellow crust around the packing of the wound. For better or worse, she had started the process of healing.

She pulled out the packing. It would bleed no more. Now she would let it be open to the air, at least until she could devise a poultice. She raised her eyes to Valgar's face. His gaze met hers, studying. His eyes were still shiny, but they had not the muddled glaze of last night. He still had fever, but he was better. Pony felt a chill slither up her neck. Was he well enough to fulfill his claim on her? She had traded the evil of thirty for the evil of one man-beast, a dreaded carnivore. The bargain did not yet content her.

He grunted as he sat up. He meant to be up and about.

"No kidnapping, no riding today," she chided. "You must stay quiet, rest and eat."

He shook his head. "Much to do. I must . . ."

"Not if you want to keep your arm." Pony put her fists on her hips. She could be master here for a little longer if she used his fear against him. Harald set the bowls he'd brought on the table. Behind him the older man with the scar, the one who had come with Harald and Valgar yesterday to her hut, poked his head through the door, frowning.

"Svenn," Harald greeted. Svenn measured Valgar. His eyes held a look of regret and relief both at once. He barked barbarian words. Pony heard the word *Osrick*. Valgar shrugged and responded carelessly. Pony lifted her brows.

"They have surprise that Osrick and his men escaped," Valgar explained.

Pony breathed once, fast. She could not regret that they were gone, though it left her in barbarian company. She turned, curious. "You let them go. You left the gates open."

Valgar nodded, casting a glance at Svenn. "Should I slaughter them? They have friends or women in the village who would resent that." His countenance darkened. "Yet such ones could not stay. They are poison to *law.*"

Pony searched his face. This one was cleverer than he looked. "I must into the woods to gather thornberry leaves for a poultice," she said. Circling the steaming bowls Harald brought, she saw they were full of porridge made of oats. Excellent. She dipped a spoon into one.

"You will stay," Valgar insisted. "If I am prisoner here, you will join me."

Pony stopped in mid-scoop. He knew she meant to escape. She shrugged. Then, with as much venom as she could muster, she cursed: "May your arm rot."

Svenn handed him the other bowl. It was a gesture of goodwill, yet the man's eyes were watchful. They darted from Valgar to Pony and back again. He, like the other barbarians, waited for his leader to falter. Pony suddenly wanted to take back her curse.

* * *

The still afternoon air was even heavier inside the lean-to. It hung in her lungs and drew rivulets of sweat from her hair, and Pony rolled her head to gaze out the open wicker shutters. The leather jerkin covering the broad shoulders of the guard who stood just outside had not moved in an hour. How could he stand there in the heat? She could hear insects buzzing in the grass; the tick of the guard's fingernails against his lance as he drummed to pass the time; and Valgar's breathing, where he lay watching her just as he had for most of the day. Her enforced inaction, the tiny room, her fellow prisoner's steady gaze—everything made her want to scream. She'd been made to run with Herd, to live under the sign of the White Horse, not to sit here, her backside going numb, waiting for . . . what? What *was* she waiting for? But screaming was no good. Along with the freedom of Herd, she also required calm. What difference if she sat here without moving, or danced in the moonlight of Samhain night? The truth of her life would not change anytime soon.

She turned her head and met Valgar's stare. "Why do you keep me here?"

"That you may not give your horses to our enemies." His voice was a rumble in the barrel of his chest. She had never heard a man's voice so deep. He was not like Alfred at all.

"All Saxons are your enemies, not just our king," she said, taunting. He did not have to know she had not known who her king was until yesterday. "*I* am your enemy." Nor did he have to know that she did not consider herself a Saxon.

"Do you heal enemies?" he asked, his gaze roving over her face.

She squirmed against the wood of the wall. Why had she done it? Was it only that she could not stand to see a creature in pain? He was asking who she was again, in some sense, as much as when he asked her name. And he had not told her anything about who he was. She lifted her chin. "How do you speak Saxon? Where did you chance to speak the words?"

81

He rolled his head on the furs and gave a weary chuckle. "Not speak. You must listen. If you listen well, you hear the pattern. You pick up the words."

He knew the secret of listening! Was that how he'd partnered with his chestnut horse?

"The others think I am a traitor to Guthrum because I know your tongue." The hollow in his throat gleamed with sweat. The heat in his body reached out across the room, animalistic and tantalizing. How could that be? She was of the prey, he of the predators. "To hold a land, you must speak to its people. Guthrum knows." He began to fidget. His gray eyes darted to the ceiling, plans and problems storming there.

"You translate for your men. They do not speak our language."

"*Ja.*" he sighed. "They will learn only to woo a wench or trade a horse."

His words gave Pony a start. "Those are not soldier things to do."

He searched her face. "We are too few to be just soldiers. We must hold the land by living." As though that thought pushed him, he lurched up. He grunted. "I cannot waste more time."

It was no use to tell him he should rest. At least she would sweat alone in the close air of this little room. Or maybe he would take her with him. Yes! Then she might find a chance for escape. "Good," she said firmly. "We go."

He shook his head . . . then seemed to think better of it. Pursing his full lips together, he nodded. Giving a smile that held a secret, he said, "*Ja.* You come."

Val sat astride Slepnir with the girl in front of him. He did not trust his strength. Bracing the palm of his bad hand against his thigh to keep his wound from touching anything, he held the reins in the hand that circled her waist.

The girl tugged at the hemp that bound his good wrist to hers, as though in protest, then quieted as he had never seen another do. What was this calm that sometimes seemed to

82

emanate from her like tiny smooth ripples in clear water? It was soothing, this calm, but unnerving, too, as if she went somewhere far away where the world did not matter, where even she herself did not matter. Of course, she was not always calm. He smiled grimly, remembering her anger when he had roped them together, ruining her plans of escape. It had taken her an act of will not to shout at him. He liked being able to get inside her calm.

Pointing Slepnir to the hall at the crossroads, Val felt better. But that meant he was even more aware of her rounded backside pressed into him, her shoulders against his chest. Heat rose in him and pooled in his groin. He wished he had this girl's calm. His thoughts flitted to last night, her hands on his biceps, his shoulder. Had she touched Alfred so? He cleared a throat suddenly tight. What was he doing? He had no time for wenching when his future depended on consolidating his power in the Downs. He was not even sure why he had brought her. Harald could have been set to guard her.

He did not like to think of Harald watching her, though. The boy sought her out at every opportunity. He was becoming most annoying. His sudden concern for Val's welfare was unseemly. Val understood it: guilt. Oh, Val knew guilt well. He himself had fueled that guilt by saving Harald's life, perhaps even at the cost of taking Alfred and his men. If anyone should atone, it should have been Val himself for once again letting his feelings subvert his duty.

Val felt the familiar heaviness descend into his entrails. He pressed his calves against Slepnir's flanks, walked the horse down a narrow path of rutted, hard-packed earth one could hardly call a street. This would be a mire in winter, but it was lined with busy huts and stalls now. Lath poles arched against the summer sky. Two young boys worked treadles to make stool legs and bowls. An ironmonger sweated in front of his coals, held a knife blade against the sun. The sullen glow of the metal darkened as it cooled, like the knife the Saxon wench had used to cauterize Val's flesh. Another stall held horn goods; combs from antlers, carefully

83

carved drinking horns inlaid with worked metal. At a separate hut, an old woman stirred a steaming cauldron while her daughter hawked pots of ointment and salve. The pair were surrounded by the noises of a place of men: shouts, laughter, the clang of the hammer, the squeak of the treadles. Chippenham might be small and mean compared to the great cities of the East, but it was a busy hub of local commerce. It smelled like a place of men as well, Val noted: smoke from fires, the sour smell of cheese being made, late summer sweat, the tang of steaming herbs and behind all, the subtle stench of the wicker privies. Val preferred the open country. Yet it did not matter what he wanted; his job was here.

Slepnír made his way through a flock of complaining goats, urged on by their goatherd and the jangle of the leader's bell. Val rode without guard, Slepnir and the horse-girl his only escort. People stopped their work as the trio approached. He caught their glances, their whispers and nudges. *Viking!* He could see the wariness—if not outright fear—in their eyes. And always they glanced to the horse-girl. When their heads nodded in deference, Val was sure it was not to him. Still, he nodded and greeted them. They made much show of ignoring him. At least none of these Saxons had fallen on him with axes. Yet.

Val had told his men how it would be. With Osrick and his troops gone, the town was a whirlpool with nothing at its center. They had been subject so long to their thegn's rule, just or unjust, they mourned the loss of direction without knowing how to replace it. They were powerless to stop whatever the Vikings intended, so they waited.

Val bade Slepnir halt in front of a hall larger than the huts and stalls around it. A Saxon servant in the fortress had said Osrick collected taxes here and sat in judgment. On the wall next to the door two pieces of wood were nailed, crossed. The building was apparently the center of the *Kristr*-cult, as well as the assembly hall. Here Val would find whoever spoke for the ceorls of the village.

Something moved in the dark through the open door. Val

sat patiently on Slepnir's broad back and waited. They would come to him. A gray head ducked out into the late afternoon light, peering up at him and the girl. The head was followed by four others. A man perhaps half the age of his companions brought up the rear, head bent to reveal its tonsured crown. He was dressed not in breeches and a jerkin but a woolen robe. He was their priest. His acquiescence would be important. He could foment rebellion in the hearts of any who saw him as a guide to their afterlife.

Val nodded as they ranged themselves before him. "I am Valgar." He did not give his lineage as other *Danir* did. "I come for Guthrum, who rules the Danelaw."

"Aye," the most-lined, most-decrepit of the men muttered. One of his eyes was sealed shut, probably over an empty eye socket. His white hair thinned over a pink pate. "We have been expecting you, or another like you."

Val nodded. The priest said nothing, merely watched.

"We did not expect you to speak the civilized tongue," the eldest continued. He peered at the girl with his one good eye. "Or that you would bring the servant of the Horse Goddess with you." This provoked fierce muttering among his peers. The eldest bowed his head in deference.

They knew the girl. What did he mean, *horse goddess?* The shepherds called her a bitch priestess, but they did not mention a horse goddess. Did these barbarians worship a horse goddess as well as *Kristr?* Was the girl an offense to the priest? They competed for worship in some way. Perhaps bringing her had not been wise.

"I see she does not come willingly." The old man pointed one clawed hand at the rope that bound Val and his captive together. "Epona, Mistress of Horses, do you support this barbarian?"

So that was her name! *Epona.*

"I am his prisoner, as you see, that I may not aid our king against them." The girl's words were bitter as she raised her hand to display her bonds. The elders muttered to each other.

The priest said, "Yet he has captured her. It is a sign of his potency."

Val glanced toward the priest. In that face there was no disapproval of the villagers' belief in gods other than his own and no fear of the *Danir,* only speculation. The girl was a powerful symbol to these people. He glanced at her white halo of hair. She would give him power in their eyes. He would use such good fortune.

"I am more powerful than your *jarl* . . . your eorl," he corrected.

"And therefore more like to steal from us," one of the elders said.

Val ignored that. Now was not the time to argue. He needed information they would be loath to give; best get it before they planned a lie. "Your thegn did not fight for you, for this place." They looked disgusted. Val eyed the priest. His brown eyes were as opaque as his robe.

"If treachery does not carry the day, Osrick must run like the coward he is," an elder said.

"He is nearby, regrouping." Val said it in consolation. Then he listened.

"Osrick?" the eldest asked derisively. He had no respect for his thegn, no love. None of them did, it was obvious. "He is long gone." They did not say they were glad. But they were not sorry either.

"Jesu works in mysterious ways," the priest intoned.

He was trying to take credit for Osrick's departure. This might work out yet. Val called out loudly, "I wish to speak to your. . . ." His Saxon deserted him. He used the Norse word: ". . . *thing.*"

"*Thing?* What is this word?" the eldest asked in a querulous voice.

"A meeting," Val stuttered. "Of Elders." This was not the way to look commanding.

"Council," the eldest said firmly. "Not *thing.*"

"I would speak to your council," Val began again, his voice clear, ringing out for all to hear. "This night I will say the *law* for all to know."

"Law?" The eldest glanced at his fellows. "I do not know that word, either."

"The way of it between Saxon and Dane," Val explained. "How we live now."

"Taxes," muttered one man.

"What acts are punished," another offered.

"Ja," Val agreed, glad they understood. "What are punished."

"Why get bad news?" the one who seemed to be fixated on taxes growled.

But the oldest Saxon nodded grimly. "We will assemble at dusk, Viking."

Val acknowledged the nod. He only hoped he had strength to stand in front of the Saxon council at sunset. Turning Slepnir back toward the palisades of the fortress, he heard a breath sigh out behind him. It was the priest—likely amazed to have encountered *Danir* without being skewered.

Val's arm throbbed. He lifted it, trying to ease the swelling in his hand. He shifted in the saddle and adjusted the girl against him. *Epona.* "So you are named Epona." Her hair smelled of sunlight and grass drying into autumn.

"Aye," she said, resentment soaking her voice. "It is one of my names."

"They named you 'servant of the horse goddess,' also. Who is this horse goddess?" Val tapped Slepnir's sides lightly to keep the horse picking his way among vendors, livestock and carts. Epona did not answer. "I thought Saxons worshipped Woden and Thor, not so different from our own gods. Or they worship Jesu and his mother."

"Saxons have not always ruled this land." The girl's voice was flat, as though she did not care, but Val felt a tightness in her that said she found this conversation distressing.

He was quiet for a moment. "So, the horse goddess was defeated by new gods?"

"No." The word cracked like a broken stick. "Nor did she defeat the Mother Goddess before her. The Mother became the Horse Goddess, became Jesu. She informs the world

87

still." Epona pointed toward the last stall in the street where mother and daughter apothecaries stirred their pots of herbs. "Get thornberry leaves there," she ordered, "since you won't let me gather them."

He bridled at her orders. But the throbbing in his arm reminded him that the limb was still very much in danger. Epona might be the difference between losing the arm and keeping it. He tapped Slepnir's right side and the great chestnut sidled up to the women's wooden table. The herbalist's daughter stood staring at him, clearly holding her breath. The mother had stopped stirring her cauldron. "Thornberry leaves?" Val asked, careful with the strange words. Both women nodded vigorously. The young girl, her face besmirched with soot, her brown eyes bigger for the blue underlining smudges of too much work and too little sleep, held up a small pot covered with hemp cloth and tied with twine.

"And vervain," Epona added. "And some mint."

Val nodded. "How much?" he asked. The girl chose two other little pots as well.

The women looked to each other and back at him. "For you, Viking, a gift," the old one cackled. Her voice was hoarse with the smoke of a thousand fires of years of simmering herbs.

Val could feel eyes dart his way. Noise subsided. Movement stopped. The street waited for him to demand his first tribute. "How much, old woman?" he repeated.

The crone was silent, trying to find the trap. He could see it in her darting eyes. She was afraid to name a price. Val looked around and pointed with his bad arm to a man frozen in front of a display of wooden bowls at the next stall. "How much if *he* buys them?"

The old woman's eyes fixed on his burn. She scuttled forward and took the small pots from her daughter. Val could practically hear her joints creak with age. "Salve for burns, child," she croaked. Her long yellowed nails clutched a sheaf of leaves tied with twine and a sprig of mint. "For him, two coppers or a wooden spoon, perhaps cloth for a headscarf."

Val nodded. He reached for the leather pouch that hung at his belt, but his swollen fingers would not do his bidding. A valiant display of fairness was about to become a humiliating example of his weakness. Clenching his lips together, he whispered into Epona's halo of hair. "Take two coppers from my purse." How he hated asking her for help.

He expected disgust, a taut refusal at the least—especially as he realized he had not really asked at all, but ordered. For a long moment she gave no sign. Her head was bent, but her shoulders were straight and uncompromising. She might have been looking at the burn on his arm. He almost jumped when she grabbed his leather purse and jerked open its ties. Her fingers clutched coins: Dane, Saxon, even some old silver pieces with laurel wreaths on one side he had got from the lands around the sunny sea. She picked out two coppers from the gleaming array.

"Here, old mother," she said, and tossed them onto the herbalist's wooden table.

The woman smiled. Four visible teeth jutted at odd angles from her gums. Her daughter scooped up the coins. The old woman grimaced in surprised satisfaction as her daughter went around the table to offer up the jar and the leaves. "May your arm grow pink with new skin," she croaked.

Epona took the purchases and nodded curtly. She poured coins through funneled fingers back into Val's pouch and jerked the ties tight. Val heard the whispers he sought around him. They had not expected a barbarian to pay for what he wanted. Epona looked straight ahead as he nudged Slepnir up the hill back toward Osrick's hall.

The *Danir* had created a perimeter around the palisades. Several men patrolled the line. Others slept, in their turn, or tended to their weapons or their horses. They were not happy about Val's orders last night forbidding pillage or taking of Saxon women. Sigurd, especially, whispered in bitterness. Val could see him muttering to his fellows. He stared at Val, then turned to Svenn to pointedly share a laugh. His men's glowering glances told him they obeyed only because he was Guthrum's appointed. *Let that be enough,* he thought. As Val and Epona approached, Harald came out to greet them.

Val made to lift Epona off Slepnir, but she swung her leg over the horse's neck and sprang to the ground. Val hauled himself over the cantle. Exhaustion washed through him. His knees half-buckled as he met the packed earth. How would he make it through the meeting tonight? He leaned against Slepnir. "How goes it, Harald?" he managed, throwing the boy the reins.

"It goes." The young man's face betrayed nothing. If it came to Svenn against Val, he knew which side Sigurd would take, but which would Harald be on? Two days ago he would have been for Svenn. Now, Val was not so sure. Harald's misplaced sense of gratitude went against the boy's own best interest. The deed Harald valued was a grave miscalculation for a true leader. Val was not worthy of such loyalty.

Slepnir swung his haunches out, shuddering. Val almost fell, righted only by the tug of the hemp at his wrist. He staggered about to see Epona straining against the rope. Her eyes were held by something far away, her body taut and quivering. Slepnir let out a whinny. Val's eyes followed Epona's gaze beyond the village and down the hill. Rolling downland was checkered with sunlight, alternating patches of a green so brilliant it hurt the eyes and sullen shadow. There thirty horses grazed, knee-high in grass, heads bent, moving peacefully. Only a great white horse and a smaller bay circled the herd, ears pricked to detect danger.

Slepnir shrieked another whinny. "Whoa, boy," Val heard Harald say. Epona's shoulders relaxed. Val saw that puzzling sense of calm move over her body. She turned, purple eyes glowing, her lips softened in an unconscious smile. Behind Val, Slepnir half-reared and tugged at the reins. Harald's efforts at soothing were for naught. The stallion's great brown eyes showed white as they rolled, and he dragged Harald along as he skittered backward. Twelve hundred pounds of horseflesh rioting on hard hooves frightened more than Harald: Several *Danir* who had come to help stepped back with big eyes. Val reached to grab the reins. Harald was no match for the big horse.

The rope at Val's wrist went slack. Epona moved past him. She held out her hand. That uncanny pool of calm moved with her, rippling out over Val, who dropped his hand; to Harald, who quit tugging on the reins; to Slepnir, whose liquid eyes went soft. Val saw the horse sigh out his anxiety and drop his head into her hand, reins dragging on the ground. He blew into her palm.

"Yes," she breathed. "You want to be with them. But you and White Stallion would not agree on that point." She moved her hands up Slepnir's velvet muzzle to slip off his bridle. She handed it to Harald without looking. "What do you want with saddles?" she asked as he ran his nose up and down her thigh, snuffing and blowing on her leggings. She ran her hands over his copper shoulder and pulled at the buckle of his girth. A single push and the saddle fell to the ground. "Better?" she asked. Val felt sure the stallion would wheel and gallop away. There was nothing to stop him. His panic to escape could erupt again at any moment. But the horse lipped Epona's neck instead. "Harald will take you to your dinner—will you not, Harald?"

The boy hovered, not understanding. "Take him to the barn. Feed him," Val translated.

Harald nodded, eyes big. But he didn't know exactly how to do as he'd been asked.

"Go." Epona gestured and nodded. "He will follow."

Harald started off around the corner of the building, glancing back to find Slepnir striding placidly behind. How had she done that? Val wondered. Slepnir did not tolerate strangers. Why did he respond so to Epona? And what of her aura of sureness? Val had never seen anything like it.

Epona tugged on the rope between them, her eyebrows raised. "Might you offer me food while I apply the herbs to your arm?" Her eyes roved over him. The calm seeped away from her. He could feel it go. He nodded. Her eyes drifted

91

past his shoulder to her horses. It occurred to him that he had no idea how to finish what he had started here. He couldn't keep her roped to his wrist forever. But the minute he let that rope go she would be down to her herd and away to the hill with the white chalk horse. He might retrieve her and she might escape again in some endless children's game of tag and run, but there was no way to keep her by him short of a rope. His only other choices were to kill her or let her give her horses to Alfred. His thoughts skittered over what else she might like to give to Alfred. Svenn would have killed her. Val could not think of bloodying her white hair, her almost translucent skin. He trudged into the darkness of the hall, pulling her behind him. He had been stupid to start a game he could not win.

Chapter Six

Herd was near! Pony sucked in a last breath of life from the outdoors and ducked into the dark, close air of the great hall behind Valgar. Now only let the Viking relax his guard for an instant and she would be away, vaulting onto First Mare's back, streaming away home.

The channels of late afternoon sunlight in the hall swam with motes of dust and buttery color. Still, the dark wood, the dimness that gathered under the high ceiling, and the comparative closeness of the air, made it unpleasant when compared with the meadows where Herd grazed. The hall smelled of sweat and dimly of cooked meat. Which reminded Pony she was hungry, though not for that. She had other needs as well.

She jerked on her bonds, forcing Valgar to turn around. He looked haggard. She had told him to stay quiet this afternoon, but he had run off to play thegn to Chippenham. She had to admit he had surprised her, though; and she was not alone. Paying for the thornberry, talking to the elders—why? Barbarians just took what they wanted. Didn't they?

But as long as he was tied to her wrist, he had to pay at least a little attention to what *she* wanted. "I need to use the privy," she said bluntly. Let him cope with that or let her go.

He nodded. Was that a gleam of humor in his eyes? He gestured magnanimously to a door at the head of the hall, but he made no move to untie her. She huffed past, moving quickly. Let him keep up if he could.

He did. *Because his legs are longer,* she thought bitterly. On horseback, she was Valgar's equal and more. They pushed out into the streaming light of the rear yard. It was here she and Herd had freed Young Black, what, two days ago? It seemed forever. The pen was now filled with Viking mounts. Their thoughts were only for the bale of hay a Viking heaved over the fence: she could hear them. Was it because she had done her duty that she could hear? Had her girl-child renewed her Gift? Harald was just leading Slepnir into the barn. Several Vikings turned buckets of slop into the wooden troughs of the pig sties. Cackling chickens skittered about, and a young woman cast grain as they flocked toward her in a rustle of feathers.

The privies were head-high wicker enclosures set well back from the hall next to the far wall of the palisades. Behind the palisades the hill continued, covered with trees, ash and maple as well as oak. Pony picked the nearest privy and trod forcefully toward it. Last night Harald had taken her and stood at a discreet distance while she did her business. Valgar showed no signs of such discretion. She wondered if he meant to join her inside.

She did not need to open the door to smell the stench. Valgar turned his back and leaned against the wicker. He was going to stand right there while she relieved herself! She jerked open the door and pulled it shut against the rope. He obligingly braced his foot against it to keep it closed. Struggling one-handed with the leather that bound her leggings, she fumed. She could not *bear* to be tied to this Viking predator. She must escape. Would he post guards again tonight? She did not doubt it. Would he keep her bound to him with rope? Unendurable!

Another uncomfortable thought occurred: When she took Herd home, he would know right where to find her. She simply wanted things to go back to the way they were before he came. But would they?

Finished, she redressed and tied the leather thongs tight about her waist, then let her shirt fall over them. The flax was dirty and stained with sweat. She had no fresh clothes and no way to clean. At home, she brushed her several pair of leather leggings and aired them frequently. Her cloth shirts and cyrtles were washed on the stones of the river when she bathed.

She pushed open the privy door. "What will you do when I want a bath?"

Valgar was not disconcerted. Instead an appraising gleam entered his gray eyes. They were like the clouds that swept overhead today, shot with light and subtle colors, gold and slate.

He grinned. "Let us find out. We bathe on Thorsdays. Is not the morrow Thorsday? It is said that Saxon women want we *Danir* because we bathe and your men do not."

"Said by whom?" Pony snapped. "Viking beasts, no doubt." Her hand twitched with a desire to slap the grin from his face. But in a contest of strength she would never win. Horses taught you that. Speculating, she lifted her chin and looked him in the eye. Perhaps men were like horses, and strength was not the key to . . . "I want food, and I don't want it spoiled with meat," she snapped, breaking the hold of his gleaming gray eyes and turning toward the hall. She did not wait to see if he followed. "Unless you think to starve me."

"I ordered the best portion for you." She could hear the frown in his voice.

"If you call the portion with all the vegetables swimming in blood the best one, I got that," Pony agreed. "I would rather starve." He put his hand flat on the door to keep her from opening it. Maybe she had gone too far. She turned to face him. He was too close. She had spent two days too close to this man. Sweat gleamed on his face. The damp waves of his thick hair practically brushed her cheek. He smelled of man and leather and horsehide.

"Say what food you do want," he said through his teeth. "I do not starve my—"

"Your what? Your prisoners, barbarian?"

His eyes searched her face, at a loss for words. Slowly he took his hand from the door.

Pony yanked the door open. The hall had grown dimmer as the afternoon faded. Valgar stepped ahead of her, spewing orders in his barbaric tongue to a half dozen Vikings. Then he half-dragged her to the little lean-to room and collapsed on the bedbox with a groan, his eyes closing. She was left standing with nowhere to sit.

Her eyes roved over him. His leggings were wrapped tightly around his thighs. She had never noticed how heavily muscled men's legs were. Not that she had been around many men, not up close. Really, only Alfred. Alfred's thighs were not so overlaid with thick slabs of muscle as this Viking's seemed. They matched his barbarian arms, of course, and his shoulders. She had touched the bare skin of his arm last night. Her hand reached out toward the thigh before she could stop it. She caught her breath. What was that throbbing? She jerked back, wondering if he had seen her. But a glance at his face showed his thick lashes were still closed. The lines around his mouth said he was in pain, even if he would not admit it.

She perched on the edge of his bedbox and covered her confusion by taking the hand of his injured arm. She rubbed it as she had last night to make the blood flow. The lashes on his cheek fluttered. The heat of friction between his hand and hers seemed to have crept into her loins somehow. Enough of this! She unbound his wound and grabbed a cloth. Again she wiped the bloody fluid that seeped beneath the yellow crust. Then she fumbled at the pouch at his waist, her knuckles brushing the leather of his breeches, and found the thornberry and the mint. She crushed the leaves, packed the wound, and bound the whole into place with a light bandage.

"The mint should cut the pain," she muttered. "It will feel numb."

The Viking opened his eyes. "You eat no meat?" he rumbled. His voice was intimate in her ears. She shook her head. One corner of his mouth lifted, though his eyes were as hot as the afternoon. "It is not a wonder you are small."

A Saxon woman in a drab brown cyrtle poked her head in the door. "Do you want food?"

"Get her plants to eat, whatever she wants," Valgar muttered.

"And some mead," Pony added. She would put the vervain in his mead to break his fever.

The servant disappeared. Pony turned back to the Viking, refusing to meet his eyes. Perhaps his fever was catching. "I will show you how to get the blood flowing." She took his good hand and placed it on his biceps. "Rub here and down to your elbow, thus. And grip with your hand. You must move or it will die." The damp skin of his hand was distressing. It was not just the physical presence of him. It was something more. It was the way he'd talked to the villagers—were those the words of a man-predator? She jerked away as the gray-haired Saxon returned with mead in rough wooden cups and a bowl of steaming food. Pony's eyes lit at the smell of browned parsnips and cabbage stew.

"No meat?" she asked warily.

The woman raised her brows but shook her head as she withdrew. Pony poured some vervain from its container into one of the mead bowls. She turned to Valgar. "You, sit up and drink."

Valgar took his doctored wine, his eyes watchful. He sniffed at it.

"Mothers!" Pony swore in disgust. "If the thornberry was not poisoned, this is not like to be." She grabbed her wooden plate and spoon. The Viking downed his mead at a single gulp, almost defiant. Pony turned to her steaming dinner and ate standing. Parsnips had never tasted as good.

And cabbage? A gift of the Great Mother. It was only when her plate was empty that she realized Valgar was staring at her. She swallowed the last bite.

"You want your horses," he said after a moment.

"Of course. I want my life back."

He looked away. "No. You will give horses to Alfred."

"I will not give my horses to Alfred." It might be a lie. But she was sick of the lot of them. She wanted only to return to the life she had led, her horses her own.

His eyes searched her face. He was unsure of her. But he could not keep her tied to his wrist forever.

"How long can you keep me? What can you gain?"

His eyes flitted over her face. "I do not believe you, priestess of horses. I think you have lain with this Alfred, and that you are under his spell. You would give him whatever he asked."

She was shocked, not only that he guessed she had lain with Alfred, but that she seemed not to be able to dissemble with him. Blood rose to her cheeks. She knew it was a betrayal of her asseverations.

He had seen that the town elders set store by the fact that she followed him, willing or no.

"So be it." He judged her. She saw it in his eyes before he sank back into the furs of his bedbox. The fever still consumed him.

"Eghhhhhh!" she snorted. The man was impossible, a demented beast. How could you talk to such a rapacious beast, a man who ate the land, took it from its rightful owners? Seething, she stood over him as he closed his eyes. She refused to sit again on the bedbox. She wanted to be nowhere near him. Cross-legged, she sank to the plank floor. But soon she was chewing her lip. Was he worse than Osrick? That was who he'd taken the land from, not from the elders. The people of the downland had not been free. It was yet to be proven who was the worse man, the viler predator. She hated the fact that there might be degrees.

* * *

Osrick hailed the sentries around the five campfires. Five—not many for the camp of a king. He set his lips in a line. His choices were few. He had no Frankish lands across the channel to give him silver and power in lieu of his land in Wessex. He would have no power or influence under the cursed Viking law the barbarian had spouted. He had spent the time since his father was killed in battle with Northumbria squeezing the downland in an iron grip. His only chance to get his land back was to throw his lot in with Alfred.

It was not much of a chance. The other eorls and thegns were all abandoning the boy sovereign: that was clear from the fact that there were only five campfires. Still, in some way that was an advantage in itself. As one of the few to stand by Alfred, would not his influence be greater? If he could get his way, perhaps he might receive for his loyalty more land and more power than he had just relinquished. Alfred was young. Osrick smiled grimly. The situation had possibilities. A callow king, with himself as a cunning second. Osrick's mind clicked over. Eorlred might be brought to their cause—and even Borogand, who he had no Frankish lands.

For a moment, the image of the white-haired witch floated into his thoughts. She had already befuddled the Viking; Osrick could see it in the devil's eyes. His teeth ground together. Between the Viking and the bitch priestess, they had locked him away from all he owned. He must cast his lot with Wessex now.

The first sentry answered his hail, sword drawn. He could hear the rustle of men rising around the campfires, the slither of swords unsheathed.

"We are Alfred's friends," Osrick called into the night. *Friends* might be an exaggeration. He should have called himself an ally. Still, Alfred might want a friend more than an ally. A hopeless position was a hard burden for one who owned little more than a score of years . . .

The king stood into the light of the fire as Osrick approached. There was no mistaking him, gleaming hair, eyes that burned blue with passion. Osrick was taken aback. Alfred's faith in himself shone in every pore. Did he want a king with faith in himself?

"Osrick." He introduced himself and dropped to one knee. "The servant of your cause."

"Rise, Osrick, and welcome," Alfred said in that voice full of surety. "Are you come to join our fight against the Viking hordes?"

"I am, King. I regret that I bring only a force of forty." His desertees had rejoined him now that he was exiled, too.

"Every forty is welcome, as are you." The young man smiled at him. It was like the sun rising. "Come sit at the fire. Bring your men. We have naught but what we hunt, but you may share our little."

Osrick walked into the light and reached for Alfred's outstretched hand. His lot was cast.

Val stood at the head of a procession of his men at the council, and Pony stood at his side. How irritating he was! The rope was gone. The Viking had given her that much. But only because he knew that with a dozen of his men surrounding her there was no way she could escape.

He looked stronger, too. The vervain had broken his fever, and removing the rotted flesh had improved his burn. Still he had stretched himself to come tonight. He was determined. She would give him that. Glancing up, she watched the tall men duck inside the door. Valgar had a pleasing countenance—that could not be denied. In profile his nose was straight, his cheekbones pronounced. His beard did not hide the cleft in his chin or the curve of his lips. She had seen him grimace with those lips, but given their freedom they were soft. Did a murderer and rapist have such lips?

She tore her gaze away and surveyed the hall. Ten old men sat on benches and wooden platforms at one end. The Chippenham priest sat at the front. He would play a crucial role. Craftsmen and farmers from the countryside crowded the perimeters. Behind her, ten Vikings, including Svenn and Harald, stood fingering their swords. Pony hoped a massacre could be avoided. Valgar had brought her as insurance, an extra proof of his dominion. Was that all she was destined to be—a prize for Alfred or this Viking?

Valgar nodded to the old men. His hands hung at his sides as though he did not need a sword to show his mastery. Still, the sword was there, swinging in its leather binding. "I am Valgar, *jarl* of this land by word of Guthrum, King of Danes. Good night," he said, formally.

Pony wondered if he knew he had begun badly. The elders glanced at each other. The eldest finally nodded. "The night belongs to you, Viking. What would you?"

Valgar gestured. "I will speak the *law*," he said, then hesitated. His command of Saxon would be taxed tonight. "The way between Saxon and Dane, now that we come to this land."

The Saxons glowered and muttered under their breath, but the old one wriggled widened lips around toothless gums and said, "Proceed."

Valgar did. "Taxes. Farmer says how many ploughlands he tills. His portion is thus totaled."

"What is a ploughland?" one asked querulously.

Valgar's brow creased in thought. "The land a team of oxes . . . oxen plough in one day."

Around the circle of men, Pony heard farmers muttering as they calculated their holdings in this new way. Their frowns told their anxiety about how much would be required of them.

Valgar knew what they wanted to hear. "A tenth portion, I take for the common good."

Silence fell. "You speak not aright, Viking," the oldest finally said. "You mean half?"

Valgar looked worried. He glanced to Pony. "I mean . . ." He searched for words. "One part in ten parts?" Pony nodded when he looked her way and held up his fingers. She smiled inwardly. He had no idea that they would have been glad had he only taken half the product of their fields. Osrick had taken more. Valgar pressed on, expecting protest.

"In return, strong Danish arms will slay any who come against you. We dig wells if you need water, build halls if you need halls. I hear the complaints of one against the other, that there is no killing for revenge."

The elders bent their heads together. They were plainly stunned. The crowd behind them rustled, wondering if the Viking leader understood what he said and if his word was to be trusted.

"What of the craftsmen?" one asked, raising his head from the circle.

"They give one part in ten of what they make."

The eldest pounded his staff upon the ground. "How will you decide complaints?"

"The *law* decides."

"This does not tell us. If one man kills another, how do you decide the wergild?"

"*Law* decides," Valgar said again. "Not me. Price is the same, always. Price for stealing, same." Valgar queried Pony in a low voice. "What is the word for a woman with no man?"

"Widow, if the man is dead," she replied.

He shook his head impatiently. "No husband, ever."

"You mean a virgin?"

He nodded. "The price for taking a virgin is the same," he said to the crowd.

"Except if it's a Viking who takes her," someone in the crowd guffawed. General grunts of bitter assent rose around the hall. Viking hands moved to their swords. They might not understand the words, but they understood the tone.

"Same *for Dane or Saxon*," Valgar insisted, raising his voice. "*Same.* That is my pledge."

Several of the elders looked to the priest. "So are we judged by Him who judges all," the cleric finally said, examining Valgar. It was assent.

The eldest stood, back hunched with age. He leaned upon a stick as gnarled as his countenance. "We have no choice, Viking, unless we want to fight." He gestured toward the

102

restless men behind Valgar. "You knew we would not fight." He stumped up to stand before his would-be lord. "Why did you come tonight? Why do you pledge this?"

"We live together easy or hard," Valgar's bass voice filled the room. "I want easy."

The eldest stared the huge Viking up and down, though his head did not even reach the silver oval that pinned the other man's cloak. Valgar bore the scrutiny without flinching, without speaking. When the elder finished he turned his gaze to Pony, who felt the questions in the man's eyes and was suddenly conscious no rope tied her. That alone would give the Viking stature. The elder turned to Valgar. "What you propose is fair, Viking."

Pony saw Valgar draw a breath. This was what he had wanted. The eldest stumped away; he thought it was done. But Valgar's voice boomed out again. "Same for both means more," he said. The eldest turned, surprised. "Dane can take land if no Saxon owns it. Dane can take Saxon wife if she agrees." There was a silence. "Land can pass to widow from Saxon or Dane." He glanced to Pony for reassurance on the language. She nodded, but she was puzzled. *Danir* women could be landholders? It was shocking. "*All* is the same."

Protest coursed around the room. One Viking drew his sword some inches from its leather scabbard. Valgar's hand cut through the air at his hip and the sword was sheathed. But the Vikings looked uncomfortable. They could not understand what was passing here.

"Women do not own land," a voice in the crowd called.

"After this day they do. It is *law*." Val said it quietly but he sounded very certain.

The eldest pressed his lips together and glanced to the priest. Pony saw the cleric give an imperceptible shrug. The old man cocked his head at Valgar. His eyes crinkled ever so slightly, though his mouth betrayed nothing. "This will be a longer road than I thought, Viking."

Valgar nodded, his own eyes gleaming in the light from the torches on the walls. "If you make a *Council*, I will join it. We will talk more."

"And what of you?" The elder turned to Pony. "Will you join our council, Priestess?"

Pony shook her head in shock. "I am not—"

Valgar cut her off. "*Ja*," he said. "That is wise. She will come. So will you, Priest."

The priest glanced to Pony, his distaste obvious. He would not like her word to be considered equal to his own. After all, he believed he spoke for the only god.

Pony swallowed, bitter. The fact that Valgar could compel her gave him stature. The last thing she wanted was to spend her evenings watching a barbarian spar verbally with old men in butchered Saxon. And yet . . . she could not help but wonder, along with the elder, why Valgar bothered. Why not just kill a few of them and thus demonstrate to the others the advantage of obedience? That was the way of the predator. Osrick would have done that. Why try to explain this *law*? Did he know that a tenth-portion tax was a miracle to these people? That they expected nothing in return, let alone the pledge he gave? It might lure them to listen to his *law*.

Then there was the fact that he hadn't killed the priest. Barbarians *always* killed the priests. Christians felt a loyalty to those men, which made clerics natural leaders against invaders. But Valgar had instead invited the priest to join his council. Maybe he *could* be master here. . . .

Pony was surprised the eldest wanted her at the council. She had seen his distaste at the idea that women could own land, and she was shocked herself. Why had Valgar insisted she be a part of this? Perhaps it was as Alfred said: She was known as a symbol of the old religions—though no one knew precisely which ones. They wanted the blessing of the old gods as well as the new.

Valgar nodded to the elders, each in turn, then turned on his heel. His ten Danes turned with him and strode from the hall. Valgar grabbed Pony's hand in a firm clasp just slightly more civilized than the rope that had bound her to him this afternoon, and led her from the hall. The feel of his damp palm in hers made her shiver.

In the warm night outside, the Danes parted on the path so he could stride ahead, Pony still in tow. Once through his men, Valgar dropped her hand as though it was a burning coal. "Thank you," he growled, his face obscured by the moonless night. "For your words."

She said nothing. She could hardly believe she had heard him thank her.

"My men need words, too. You will teach them." He did not ask.

"I will not!" she snapped back. "You keep me from my horses. Why would I teach your barbarians Saxon?" Her thoughts gained momentum as though she ran downhill. "Will you kill me if I refuse like the predator you are?" Inside, she knew he wouldn't kill her. He wanted the good will of the villagers. But she wanted to hear him say it.

He strode on in silence. She could feel him seething. Then his shoulders sagged. "If I let you go to your horses, you will go from here."

"Yes," she admitted.

He grabbed her hand again. His hot palm pressed hers. The ten Vikings still strode behind them, but he drew her closer. She tried to squirm away. "Listen," he almost whispered.

She went still. He had issued the one command she must obey. How many times had her mother said that to her? She walked for a moment in silence. But it was hard to listen. The moist palm she clasped made her own palm sweat. Or had she begun to perspire as he had in this warm gasp of dying summer? The press of flesh to hers made listening hard. She concentrated more intently. Insects in the night. The call of a nightingale, the shuffle of feet, the clink of swords and chain mail, the breathing of men, the murmur of argument in the hall behind them: all seeped into her consciousness. She could hear his breathing, the shush of leather as his leggings brushed her.

"You can go to your horses when the ten behind me have simple words. Is that enough?" His voice was part of the night. It was as though the darkness bargained with her.

She nodded.

"Then we are agreed." Could he see her acceptance in the dark? Or did he just assume?

"Yes," she whispered. "I pray they learn fast." But would a barbarian keep his word?

Chapter Seven

Osrick hunched over the fire. It was the third night in Alfred's camp. A little priest called Asser who Alfred apparently took everywhere with him turned the spit with a haunch of venison from the deer they had shot yesterday. They were moving fast to the southwest. Tomorrow they should come to Borogand's faesten. Borogand was a powerful eorl. If Alfred's faith in his destiny did not convince Borogand to lend his hundreds to their cause, he and Osrick would have private conversation about what lay ahead under Viking rule.

Alfred paced by the fire, working off the endless energy he seemed to possess. "If we get there tomorrow, then if we are off the next, we should reach Edward in . . . three days, or maybe four." He was speaking to himself as much as to Osrick and the others.

"My king," Osrick said quietly. "You forget the time it takes to raise the army. He will have only a few soldiers in the faesten, even as I did. He must send to the farthest field and river for the farmers and craftsmen and fishers to take up arms. That will take weeks."

Alfred made a strangled sound deep in his throat as he whirled and paced back toward the fire. "How many times I have wished for a standing army."

Osrick closed his eyes and sighed. "Then who would till the fields and tend the cattle, lord? If no one tills because they wait to fight, soon there is nothing to eat."

"Your point is made." Alfred stopped and rubbed his chin. "But what if you alternated—half serve and half till? You could have a standing army then, not so large but ready instantly when danger threatens. No Viking could surprise you. Indeed, they might get a surprise themselves. And I want ships, Osrick, to defend the southern shores . . ."

The man was off again on his wild scheming. "The problem of delay?" Osrick prompted. "Why should we not go from ally to ally quickly, and while we are off to the next, each raises their army to meet us at a place of your choosing on an appointed day? That would save time."

Men around the fire muttered their approval of the plan. "Excellent," Alfred assented. Osrick agreed. Soon he would have the king dependent upon his advice. The young monarch clapped him on the back. "Now where shall we meet the Danish hordes?"

"My humble suggestion, my king, is to meet them at Chippenham, or just south. There is a plain for fighting. Their force there is small." Osrick felt the flutter in his stomach.

Alfred smiled. "You would take back your lands from the Viking."

"And the bitch priestess." Osrick had not meant the words to come out so raw.

Alfred crouched beside him eagerly. "A white-haired girl? Epona?"

Osrick nodded, wary. "Aye, that's the one."

"Does he have her? No doubt she stands as a symbol of his power." Alfred stared into the fire. "She is important to me in the same way."

"We must kill her as the symbol of his power." A thrill of pleasure cycled through Osrick.

"No, no," the king protested. "If we find her, no one must

kill her. She has anointed me as king by lying with me, witnessed by Asser, here, and Ralf." The priest and another man nodded.

"What matter if you had her before the Viking?"

"Because I am a Christian, and well known for being so," Alfred explained, as to a child. "There are those in the land who, though Our Lord Jesu's words are on their lips, still hold to the old gods in their heart. It is those hearts I require, if I am to win through from such a start." He gestured into the night, where fifteen fires warmed their small troop of perhaps a hundred men. "I must convince the people that I am born to lead them. To do that, I need their faith in Jesu *and* that part of them that howls to the moon on Samhain. With witnesses that the incarnation of the Horse Goddess has chosen me as king, and with her by my side to prove her choice, I will have won both. More, I will bend the Old Religions to the will of the One True God." He shook his head and spoke louder, knowing those directly around him would carry his words to others, whispered lips to ears. "No, I need Epona alive. She belongs by my side."

Osrick pushed down the grinding in his belly. He wanted Alfred to mobilize the people of Wessex against the Viking hordes as much as anyone. But the youth would have to do it without the bitch priestess. He would see to that.

Pony shook her head at the assembled men. "Words. You learn Saxon words." She wanted to scream with impatience. They repeated it back to her, their deep bass voices rumbling in counterpoint to her soprano. It had been a long morning in the darkened hall. Outside the bright midday air had a bite that signaled autumn. Harald had gazed longingly out the nearest window for the last hour. Svenn sat stoically, but she could see him seethe with rancor at being required to learn Saxon at all, let alone from a woman, herself a conquered Saxon. Did they not know she hated teaching as much as they did learning? Yet it was her way back to her horses if Valgar kept his word, and she would bear it, whether they would or no. She had learned more of

109

Norse than they had of Saxon, she was sure. She could understand much of what was said around her now. It had been as Valgar said; listening, understanding the position and the pattern of the words, knowing what people might be trying to say in the situation, all this helped you to learn. Listening was something she was very good at. Those words she didn't understand, she asked him at table in the evening or in the small room at night. He still tied her to the post that held up the lean-to's roof, but it was a perfunctory gesture. He had not touched her, not once. She had grown to trust that he would not. That was good. Her hand moved to her belly. She must protect her girl-child at all costs.

"Is it Thorsday?" Harald asked, sitting up, as two Vikings carried a barrel past the door.

"*Ja, ja,*" circled excitedly about the room. "Thorsday." They shoved up to standing, muttering. A bench fell over. The room filled with broad shoulders, leather and silver arm rings.

Harald bowed in apology. "Sorry, Epona. Sorry. No werds. Water now." Behind him several huge men sidled out the door. Harald bowed again, backing up even as he spoke.

The room was empty before she had a chance to protest. What did they mean *water?* She strode to the door. The common area of the faesten was a beehive. Men pulled off their clothing even as they laughed and called insults to each other. Barrelhalves, perhaps ten, were set round a central fire, where cauldrons simmered. Half-naked men hauled water from the well and passed full buckets to their comrades. Two others careered in through the open gates, a full half-barrel sloshing on a makeshift wheelbarrow, laughing and sweating as they pushed it up the hill from the river. Mead sacks squirted into open mouths. Half-naked men were quickly turning fully naked. Pony had never seen such a sight—muscled thighs and rounded buttocks, the rippling contours of backs that swung a sword, the swell of biceps, the fleeting glimpses of their most male parts, a jumble of masculine bodies in the midday sun.

Pony wasn't sure whether to be horrified or fascinated. She had seen but two naked men in her life, one being Alfred and the other an aging farmer glimpsed at the river, and here were what seemed like half a hundred of them. She stood in the doorway, wondering what this was about, her eyes casting around for a single body, a specific head of waving hair.

There he was, his back turned toward her, on the far right of the crowd that dumped water into several barrels. He stood barefoot, his hands working at the laces of his breeches. Pony's breath caught as he turned. He was laughing. She had never seen him laugh. It made his eyes crinkle, his features soften. She hardly recognized the grim-faced barbarian who had captured her. His laugh was a rumble half again as deep as the voices around him. He rubbed his beard and pretended to sniff under his arms. "Do we need this?" she heard him shout in *Danish*.

An answering roar of laughter circled round the fire. "*Ja*, two weeks and more."

Harald heaved a cauldron from the coals at the fire's edge and poured its steaming contents into a barrel. Pony could not tear her gaze from Valgar's thumbs sliding his breeches over his hips. She let her eyes wander over the heavy muscles of his chest and shoulders, remembered rubbing his upper arm. The memory of touching him went from her mind to a place between her thighs as though shot by a bow. The ribbed muscles of his belly, the ridge of muscle over his hips that held the girdle of his loins, all drew her down toward the thatch of light brown hair between his legs. Her mother said a man's member was silly if it was not primed for breeding. But Valgar's was unconscious, natural, different from Alfred's earnest erection. She would not call it silly. She only wondered that men's upright stance left them so vulnerable. A horse wore his male parts sucked up where they were protected.

Valgar stepped into the steaming barrel. Svenn tossed him a bar of soap. Valgar caught it with his bad hand. His burn had healed well in the last fortnight. Pony still repacked it once a day, but it would draw together, leaving only a depression. He worked his arm, that he might increase the other muscles around the ones he had lost. Soaking in the barrel, he tore at the bandage with his teeth.

Pony stopped, then jerked into a run as she realized Valgar's intention. He must not wash his burn, not yet. He settled himself more into the bath as she raced across the hard-packed earth. "Valgar," she called, pushing at bare hips to make her way through the crowd. "No soap!"

All at once she stood next to him. Harald poured a bucket of water over his head. Valgar looked up, startled. The other men stepped back. The quiet was sudden. Valgar's streaming hair dripped water onto his shoulders. His skin gleamed wetly in the light. Pony was most aware of his body only half-hidden in the shadows of the water. His gray eyes met hers. Slowly, they lit with a smile. Pony found she wasn't breathing. She cleared her throat. "Uh, you—do not wash the burn with soap." How small her voice sounded. "That would dry it."

He jerked his arm upright and laid his elbow on the edge of the barrel. "I understand," he said.

She nodded curtly, feeling as though she were marooned on some remote island rather than standing in an empty circle surrounded by naked Vikings. She tore her eyes from Valgar's and stumbled back to the main hall. A tide of raucous laughter followed her.

Once in the hall, she refused to look out the window. Yet there was nothing for her to do. No one wanted teaching; they were all at their baths. The women were busy cleaning the Vikings' clothing. At last Pony wandered outside and volunteered to help, if only to keep herself from standing at the window. She was glad she did. One of the younger women, Una, offered her a shift and cyrtle so that she might clean her own clothes. Pony had never been so grateful in her life. She was more than tired of her leggings and her shirt. She took the clothing and was just about to say her thank you, when Una's eyes shifted to something behind her and went wide.

Pony whirled to find Valgar, his long hair damp and waving, clean breeches on under a dark leather jerkin, freshly brushed. He smelled of strong soap and perhaps pine. Someone had dumped the needles in the bathwater, no doubt. The Viking nodded to Una, then pointed to where two freshly scrubbed men hauled a sloshing barrel. "Will you bathe? It is Thorsday."

Pony clutched her fresh clothing to her chest. "I do not care for a bath as a public event." She cursed the blush she could feel rising up her neck. What a fool she had made of herself, rushing up among all those naked men to Valgar's bath.

"We can make it private." His voice was coaxing.

"Absolutely—absolutely not!" she snapped. "I did not mean that. I meant—I meant I would rather have a quiet stream or a pond to bathe in. Where . . . where nobody is, I mean."

He shook his head, laughing again in the way that transformed him. "Words. Wrong words. I did not mean that, also. Come." He took her arm. "I will show you."

Una giggled behind Pony. Valgar's grip was firm. She could not let him drag her away in front of everyone, so she pointedly shrugged her arm out of his grasp. He let her go, but slid his hand down into hers and drew her along behind him.

As they rounded into the hall, the two Vikings with the wheelbarrow were unloading their sloshing barrel of water into the L-shaped corner formed from the hall and the line of lean-to rooms that jutted out from it. Harald was stretching a rope between two eaves. He grinned at her and Valgar. "We should build a sweating house, with plenty of baths," he proposed. Another Viking brought a steaming cauldron around the corner. The splash as he poured it into the other men's barrel was joined by a hiss of steam.

"*Ja,*" Valgar agreed. "By that pond to the west, it may be."

"No, no," Harald insisted as he flung a blanket over the

113

rope. "No protection. Better inside the faesten." Pony smiled to note that he used the Saxon word.

"Why will we need protection? Saxons will use the sweating house also."

That made Harald think. He finally shrugged and turned to Pony. "Bath," he said slowly. "I learn the word. Thorsday is bath day." He grinned.

"Better than a stream," Valgar said to Pony as he held the blanket aside. "Water is hot."

Pony eyed the blanket. It looked a very tenuous barrier to all the Vikings carnivores about. She would have preferred a good, stout door with a bar.

Valgar watched her hesitate. "I guard you." He laughed. "You need the bath."

Pony gasped, then reddened, knowing well that he was right. Saxons did not bathe regularly, but she did. She had got into the habit of it with Herd, who enjoyed a refreshing swim in the river followed by a rub-down with fragrant herbs. It was a favorite afternoon activity in the Vale. She stalked into the makeshift room past Valgar, her heart clenching. She missed Herd.

Inside the little triangular area, the wall of blanket did not quite extend from corner to corner. Valgar peered in at her, grinning. He saluted and pulled from his boot the long flute she had seen stuck in Slepnir's saddle. He turned and sat cross-legged in one easy motion, his back across the gaping blanket. Pony hesitated. Could she trust him not to look? The heat from the steaming water wafted over her. A hot bath would be a luxury.

Valgar put his flute to his lips and began to play. From his general exuberance today she would have expected a gay melody. But it wasn't. It had odd, unexpected notes in it that made Pony feel sad. The swell and softness alternated in a mesmerizing pattern. Pony felt her anxiety melt. She stacked her clean clothes on the grass growing in the corner, and slipped out of her dirty ones. Hurried along by the threat that the wonderful steaming water would cool, the notes of the flute caressing her back, she stepped into the barrel.

The water was so hot it made her shiver. She sank down into it, ecstasy on the edge of pain. A bar of soap floated in the water. She immersed herself, hair floating around her, then soaped her whole body and her hair. The music tantalized, relaxed her. Its notes were indistinguishable in their gentle caress from the slick soapiness she was rubbing over her arms and breasts, around her neck, over her face, between her legs. The music did not command that she listen as much as insinuate itself into her soul and her body. She ducked her head under the water again to rinse the soap away and came up gasping as the final notes echoed.

Silence stretched as she stared at Valgar's leather-jerkined back through the gap on the blanket. He still held the flute to his lips as though unsure his song was over, his silver arm rings hugging his bare biceps. He lowered his arms. His head sagged between his shoulders. "Do you want more hot water?" he called.

"No," she breathed. "What music was that?"

"I do not know. The music I wanted to play to you."

"Does the song come from foreign lands?" That might explain its effect on her.

"No." He shook his head. "But songs from other places are in it."

"Do others know it?" she pressed. She had to know more about this music.

"No." He chuckled, his back still turned. "Like a saga sung by a scald, it may be repeated, but each telling will be different. That is like my songs."

Such magic had poured from his flute before? "Do the songs come from your gods?"

He shrugged. "If you listen, you hear notes, like they were always there."

The listening again. He listened to language and music. She listened to animals and earth. Was what they did so different? "The music you hear is wonderful." It was too little to say and too much. She rose from the water, which was cooling fast now. The linen towel Harald had left was enough to blot her dripping body. She squeezed water from her hair and stepped from the tub. "Do all Vikings hear such music? I have never heard anyone play like that."

"No. I am the only one." He sounded very alone. She understood that.

She pulled on the shift and buckled the leather straps at the wrists. In spite of the linen toweling, it clung to her damply. The cyrtle was palest yellow. She would have to tie the straps over her shoulders. She had no brooches. "It is a *gifu*," she told him. "Accept that it is given to you."

He barked a laugh. "The gods exact quite a price for such a slender gift."

She pulled the blanket aside. *"Thonc to thu,"* she said. "For the bath, for the music."

He stared at her, a small smile growing. *"Ja*, the bath *es gut*." He slipped out of Saxon as though distracted. Unfolding himself, he stood over her. From a pocket inside his breeches he took two small oval brooches and held them out to her.

She was blushing again—whether from the fact that he was telling her she had needed the bath or from the gift, she could not be sure. The small oval brooches were silver, not bronze, and deeply etched with animals whose twining bodies were like ribbons, whose eyes were small red stones. She shook her head. "I cannot take those."

"How else hold your cyrtle?" he asked. "Dane design is not pleasing?"

"No . . . no, they are very nice. I, uh . . . like the dragon's eyes." He reached for the awkwardly tied straps at her shoulders. His strong fingers worked the knots. "Are they dragons?"

He nodded. The first knot came loose. He fastened the brooch. His knuckles seemed to send shocks through her shoulders. "Or water beasts. They wait for travelers."

"I am not sure I want such beasts to hold up my cyrtle," she said. But all she could feel was the warmth of his large hands in the hollow below her collarbone.

"They will protect you." He was working on the other

strap, but his eyes had strayed to hers. How had she ever thought they were cool gray? They boiled like the sea in a storm.

Una came around the side of the hall and hailed her. "Epona!"

Both she and Valgar started like guilty children. He focused his attention on the brooch.

"I will see that your clothing is cleaned." The Saxon woman looked them both over before she stooped to pick up Pony's clothing. "There is so much . . . bathing. You will catch your death."

Valgar turned. "What is your name?" he asked.

At that moment Harald, too, returned to see how Pony fared. He came around the corner and stopped dead when he saw the threesome.

"Una," the Saxon girl answered, suddenly gone shy.

"Well, Una." Valgar glanced to Harald. "Bathing makes us smell better than Saxons."

The girl managed to glance at the red-haired Harald, his body damp now as well. She curtsied, then backed away. "So much bathing. Does it not wear one away?"

"Ask him." Valgar turned to his man. "Although, Harald, you will have to work harder to study her words if you are to tell her anything." This last was in Dane.

The young man flushed to the roots of his hair. Pony was not the only one to blush today. Una backed up until she finally turned and hurried away. Valgar's rumbling chuckle echoed after her.

When he turned back, Pony knew she could not let his eyes resume their boil. "So, Viking, it is time to scrape your burn and see if new flesh grows beneath the crust." She strode past him and around to the front of the hall, knowing he would follow. Not an ideal escape from the heat she had been feeling after her bath; she would have to touch him, and he smelled of soap and pines. But at least the pain would keep him from feeling amorous.

* * *

She was nearly finished carefully rubbing the yellow crust away from Valgar's arm. Pony had soaked the burn in oil to soften the cracking surface, and the flaming pink skin beneath at the edges spoke to the fact that he was healing. Valgar said it had been a little more than a fortnight since the burn had occurred, but already the healing was well along. The muscle beneath the worst of it had drawn together. The scarring would be worst there. Still, Pony could not but be pleased with his progress. More crust would develop in the next days to protect the new pink skin. When that was next removed, perhaps in another week, he would be marked but able to hold a shield. She focused on the wound to distract herself from the sound of Valgar's ragged breathing and the scent of pine and soap.

Noise brought her head up with a jerk, and Valgar's as well: a woman shrieked. Valgar got to his feet, hand on his sword, and swung out into the main hall in spite of Pony's protests. She followed breathlessly as the shrieking continued, first muffled and then clear again. Valgar was flying. By the time she caught him, she was not alone; there were half a dozen Vikings trailing along. They came upon one of their fellows; she thought it was Sigurd, loyal to Svenn. His hand was clapped across a woman's mouth, her cyrtle up around her hips, and he kneeling astride her. She writhed under him, and he was drunk or clumsy, for he couldn't stop her screaming. He hung over her, the side pieces of his long hair curtaining his face. Hers was blotched and streaked with tears.

"Sigurd!" Valgar shouted. He jerked the younger man's shoulder. "What is this?" Pony's command of Danish words was good enough to understand. The rage in Valgar's voice was clear. "Get up!" he shouted, hauling on the man's jerkin. "Did I not forbid rape?"

Sigurd was drunk. "She doesn't matter. A servant girl, no more." His words slurred.

Valgar took a single step forward and drove his fist into the man's belly. Sigurd went sailing backward, grunting as he landed. Valgar went after him, enraged. "You would make us hated?" he shouted. "I will show you hate." Sigurd struggled up and Valgar hit him again. The other Vikings ranged themselves in a circle about the two combatants, shouting encouragement. No one looked like they wanted to interfere.

Pony squirmed into the circle between leather-clad hips. She looked up and saw Svenn. A wary expression on his face gave way to a small smile. She looked to see what made him smile. Valgar braced his feet and drove his fist upward into Sigurd's belly. The man grunted and staggered, but Valgar braced him upright only to hit him again. The sobbing of the forgotten girl provided a rhythmic counterpoint to the grunts and smacking sounds. There was no reason. Sigurd seemed battered.

"Valgar," Pony shouted. "Stop!"

It must have been her higher female voice that penetrated the wall of masculine shouts to Valgar's ears. He stopped a kick on its way to Sigurd's belly and shook his head. Sigurd groaned and rolled into a ball to protect himself.

Valgar shook as he crouched over his foe. Pony should be running as fast as she could from such a beast, but she found herself stepping into the circle. "Valgar," she whispered as she neared his elbow. He turned on her, his gray eyes swimming with some hatred she could not understand. It frightened her. He had gone to some place she could not reach. Still she had to try. She reached out a tentative hand and touched his good forearm. "Valgar?" she repeated.

His chest heaved. As she watched, the brimming emotion drained from his eyes. He straightened slowly. "This man," he gasped in Danish, "has disobeyed a direct command. I forbade rape." He looked around the circle as his breathing slowed. "There was a purpose in commanding thus. Guthrum needs to rule this land. We are too few to keep it if it is not given—at least in some sense. It will never be given to those who cannot live as neighbors. If we take from Saxons, they cannot give. If they cannot give, we cannot rule. Would you deny Guthrum the island he craves?" Valgar glared at the circle. Pony did not understand all the words, but she sensed the intent. "There will be battles. We must win them. But we only win the island if we rule fairly and live beside our neighbors in good faith."

Pony looked up at Svenn and saw him frowning. She glanced around the circle. The other Vikings looked thoughtful. Some nodded. Some crossed their arms, considering. Svenn's narrowed eyes told her he was evaluating Valgar's effect on the men. He did not like what he saw.

Valgar turned to Sigurd, who was barely conscious, his face bleeding and unrecognizable, his arms cradling what must be broken ribs. Valgar shook his head and looked away. His voice was so low, Pony could barely hear it. "You are outcast, Sigurd. Find your way in other lands and think what it means to be loyal to your king, your fellows, your task."

"You are soft, Valgar," Svenn grunted. "If he has broken your command, why not kill him or cut off his hands?"

Valgar turned. His eyes were dark gray like clouds at night. "Soft? I condemn him to a fate only he can master. If he does not, he will die inside each day until he prays his body follows." Pony had never seen anything so terrible as the look in Valgar's eyes. Where was the laughter of this afternoon? Where was the sweetness she had seen?

The Viking leader drew himself up. "Do you challenge me, Svenn?" he asked. The quiet in his voice was as frightening as his uncontrollable anger.

Svenn studied those gray eyes, the grim mouth. Pony saw him decide that the time was not yet right for such action. He dipped his head. "You are Guthrum's chosen." That was not an endorsement, just acquiescence.

"Be gone by nightfall," Valgar breathed. Pony knew he meant Sigurd, thought he did not look at him. Blood and mud covered the younger man's face, and Pony wondered if it would ever be whole again. Valgar moved to the Saxon girl, now whimpering, big-eyed, outside the circle of Vikings. "Go seek your women."

As Pony looked around, several women hovered in the background, including Una. The besieged girl scrambled up and clutched her skirts about her as she ran to their protection. Svenn and Harald hauled Sigurd up between them.

Valgar strode off toward the hall. Pony exchanged glances with Harald, whose face told her he had never seen Valgar like this either. He and Svenn carried the broken Sigurd off toward the barn. Pony pushed down her revulsion and whirled to go after Valgar, but the door to the little lean-to room they shared slammed shut. He was not seeking company.

This was her chance, of course. He was not watching her. Escape might be possible. The other Vikings in the yard milled and whispered. They were paying no attention. Svenn had taken Harald by the arm and was talking earnestly with him. Did they plot against Valgar? It mattered not to her. What mattered was that no one would notice if she slipped away. Through the open gates the pasture below the hill where Herd would be grazing beckoned. She should be glad to escape the bestial rage she had witnessed.

Why did she hesitate? Was it the waves of pain emanating from that slammed door in the corner? What did she care that some ruthless Viking predator was upset? And why? He had demanded that his men not do things that came naturally for barbarians carnivores. When they did them, he became some kind of raging animal. Then he seemed ashamed. She didn't understand any of it. She gazed out the open gate of the faesten for a long moment before she turned back to the darkness of the hall.

She pushed into the small lean-to room—none of the rooms had locks. He had thrown himself on the furs of the bedbox. One arm was cast over his face. It was the one with the burn. He must have heard her, but he made no sign.

"I haven't finished with your arm," she said into the stillness.

"Later," he muttered.

"No," she said deliberately. "I tend it now or it will fester."

He heaved himself up from the bedbox. "What matter if it festers?" he shouted at her.

She knew he shouted at himself. "Why do you shout?" she asked, in the reverberating silence.

His eyes searched her face, then he glanced down at his boots. "I almost killed that young fool," he said, his voice so low she could hardly hear him. "I was *berserkr*." He looked to see if she understood. "Man becomes animal, wolf or bear. It is the same with me, always."

Pony didn't understand this *berserkr*. But she understood how anger could frighten him. She smiled. "Always?" she asked.

He stared at her. His breathing slowed. At last he tore his eyes away and shook his head. "Always when I fight for the . . . weaker one." He glanced up. "Is that the right word?"

She nodded and, with her calmness, asked him to continue.

"Crimes against the weaker one remind me . . ." He cleared his throat. "They make me too angry. It is not a good thing to see inside you."

"No. I would be afraid, too." He was afraid of being what he was. That, she could understand. "There are other things to fear. Just as bad."

He glanced up at her again. She could see the question in his eyes. She swallowed, wondering if she could explain. "The other side of anger is calm. I know calm. It is what allows me to listen to animals, to the earth. It is my . . . connection."

"Why is that a thing to fear?" The dim light of day's end made the small room intimate.

She chuckled, but it was forced. "With too much calm, you do not care. Not about yourself. Not about your child. Not about anything. It is a kind of death." She couldn't speak of her mother's ultimate calm. "Be grateful for your anger. It shows you are alive." She grabbed his hand. Even the danger of touching him was better than more talking. Why did she feel the need to comfort someone who had just demonstrated so clearly the violence of his nature? Was it because his rage pained him as much as it pained her? "Now let me finish what I started."

Chapter Eight

Val woke to sunlight through the wicker shutters. There was a brisker feel to the morning air. It had been a month since the Vikings had come to Chippenham. Harvest was over. The village had been aclatter all week with farmers bringing produce, women grinding grain. He sat up in his bedbox and flexed his left hand. The flesh in his forearm had filled in slowly. He would hold a shield again. Already his arm was gaining strength. He glanced down at the pink flesh like a newborn babe left too long in the bath, its waving scar tissue tender, almost wrinkled-looking. Epona had given him back his arm.

He glanced around the empty room as he did every morning, as though she might be lurking there. In a way she was. This room would be scarred forever with her presence—as his arm was scarred. He grunted and pulled on his deerhide boots. He had been right to give her a sleeping room of her own. It mattered not that two were required to guard it lest she slip away; her presence in his own sleeping quarters had become . . . impossible.

It was Thorsday. He suppressed a smile. Bath day. The woman and her daughter who made salves down in the village also made soap. Even from across the room, he could smell the Frankish lavender in the bar he had bought from them yesterday. Hot water would release its scent even more strongly. Epona would like that.

Val laced his breeches. Best not to think on such. He had no time for women. This one was useful only as a symbol of power. The villagers respected her. She had been a voice of reason at the meetings of the council. But he reminded himself—constantly, as he had to—that she was Alfred's creature. His promise that she might go to her horses when his men had learned Saxon had been made to keep her from running. He hoped he did not have to honor it. For as long as she stayed, willing or no, the Saxons would bear him a grudging respect. And while she would not give him her horses, at least they were not for Alfred while she was here.

He had sent men down to the common area to capture some of the beasts where they grazed. But she had somehow warned them, and they were away before his men even came close. He had seen her with Slepnir. She had a way with animals. What was she? Priestess? The incarnation of a horse? And to whose gods did she pray?

He pushed thoughts of Epona aside and pulled a jerkin over his head. It was not good when a woman filled your thoughts. Women were weak. Protecting the weak led to *berserkr* madness and betrayal. Who knew that better than he? A familiar tightness cinched his chest.

It was time to break his fast. He pushed through the wooden door. But before he joined the others already stirring in the hall beyond, he turned back and grabbed his flute from the table. He stuck it in his boot and took the bar of soap, too. It was bath day. Epona liked music with her bath.

Later that day Val wrung out his long hair, soapy water dripping into the mud around the barrels. The air was still warm enough to bathe outside in the compound by the grainery. Several of his men dressed nearby. He was among the last to bathe. Where could Epona be? He dressed quickly, his stomach tight and fluttery—as it had been all morning.

He strode to the main doors of the great hall and peered into the dimness. She wasn't there. He marched over the rough board floor and wrenched open the door to her sleeping chamber, but it, too, was empty of her. Again, at the hall door, he surveyed the compound. Might she be already at her bath? He stalked around the corner of the hall to where was constructed the makeshift shelter for her bath each week. Harald was there, kissing the Saxon girl, Una. She giggled and pushed him away. Val was surprised to hear him murmuring Saxon endearments. He had not thought the young man so apt a student. Yet while his own command to learn was not sufficient inducement, Una was, as he had always suspected.

"Well, another violation."

Una gasped. Val jerked around to see Svenn staring over his shoulder at the pair. Other Danes were coming in behind him. "What are you doing here?" Val grunted.

"You seemed upset. We came to help, to see if there were enemies to be repelled." He gestured at Harald. "Instead we find a second among us disobeying your order against rapine. What is your will, *jarl*? Will it be banishment again?" Svenn was so careful to suppress his sneer that its absence proclaimed his disgust all the more. He was challenging Valgar openly for the first time.

Val stood easy, his muscles relaxed and ready, as he surveyed the Danes ranging themselves behind the others. Now was the moment Svenn had awaited. Now Val must act. He shrugged. "Banishment? First we must know if there was a crime." He turned to the reddening pair behind him and spoke in Saxon. "Are Harald's kisses unwelcome, Una? Rape is forbidden here." Harald hung on her words, his eyes hungry for her answer. She stepped closer to Harald for protection. Val let the smallest of smiles cross his features. Una's cheeks went from pink to scarlet. She stared at the dirt as she shook her head. Harald's face lit.

"What?" Svenn barked. "What did you ask her?"

Val turned to the Danes. He saw quite clearly which of them had been diligent at their studies. They grinned or nudged their companions knowingly. "What, Svenn?" he asked in Danish. "Have you not attended to Epona's lessons? Harald has." He chuckled. "His efforts serve him well." Chuckles broke out behind Svenn, who glowered at the offenders.

"Harald, you demonstrate the rewards of practice," Val said. He did not take his eyes off Svenn.

The other Danes groaned and laughed and punched each other's shoulders. Val glanced over to see Harald sweeping Una into his arms, her own stealing around his neck as he kissed her. Val nodded. "No banishment. This is not rape." He strode past Svenn, who glared at his fellows. "Svenn, your mistake." Svenn had spent the capital of their trust; his hold was broken in their laughter. Svenn and his machination receded in importance. "Harald, go see her father before this goes any further," Val called back.

He ran his hands through his hair to push it back from his face. Now where could Epona be? She liked bathing. Why was she not at the accustomed place? He stopped and surveyed the compound, fists on hips. No sign of her. Of a sudden, he knew. He headed back behind the farthest hall, to the highest ground inside the fortress.

She sat with her knees clutched to her chest in the browning grass almost under the palisades, seeming so small, so fragile, crouched there. She did not see him. Her gaze was saved for some far point up beyond the lower walls. As he neared, she recognized his approach, but she did not move and did not speak. He glanced up, and saw what he knew he would see. In the far distance, her herd was clearly visible.

He cleared his throat. "The hot water is almost gone." His voice was rough in his own ears. "Best get some while you may."

She looked at him. Her eyes were stark windows on a mourning she had no wish to hide. Grief reached out from her and into his soul. She shook her head. Her eyes returned to the freedom out beyond the palisades, the freedom where her horses ran. He rubbed his hand across his mouth and through his beard. How long had it been since he had brought her here? More than a month. Guilt infused him.

"Harald is courting Una," he announced.

"I know," she responded. But she did not look at him.

"His Saxon is improving."

Now he had her attention. He was glad to see the spark of speculation in her eyes flash into hope. He cleared his throat. "The . . . the others have not learned enough to fulfill your obligation." Her face fell and her eyes filled.

"But," he went on hastily, "perhaps enough for a brief visit to your horses." She searched his face. He bit his lip, suddenly unsure of himself. "Will you ride out with me?"

"Are you going to tie us together?" she asked. Derision soaked the question.

That had been his plan. He coughed. "No. Not if you promise to return with me. If you promise, we can go after your bath. If you keep your promise this time, we can go again."

She eyed him up and down. "And if I don't keep my promise, then I am free."

He tried not to let his smile show in his eyes. She was right, of course. "But if you are free, then I must hunt you."

She pursed her lips, then rose in one fluid motion. "Bath first, then we ride."

Slepnir's glowing, coppery shoulders felt natural under her thighs. How wonderful to sit astride a horse again! That joy was confused by the feel of Valgar's thighs touching hers, his belly and chest against her back. Which felt decidedly unnatural. The layers of clothing between them were nothing; she could feel his heat as though they were naked. She tried to hear Slepnir. Her Gift had been returning—perhaps a little bit, now and then—since bedding Alfred and fulfilling her destiny. At least she hoped it was returning. But under the assault of her senses by Valgar, she could not be sure. The lavender soap he had given her was pervasive, and the smell of his own body clean from his bath lurked just beneath it. The notes of his flute still haunted her. He had played for her as she soaped herself in that steaming water, banishing the quiet she needed.

He seemed uncomfortable as well, tried to move his hips back in the saddle as though he could escape her touch. But he couldn't. His arms surrounded her to hold the reins. She pressed into his crotch to fit both their bodies in the saddle. Something unfamiliar pressed at her spine.

Pony tried to concentrate on the late afternoon light, the tang of autumn in the air, the blond stubble of the wheat fields around them, the torn clouds strewn across the sky. It was no use. "How far?" she asked to break the spell cast by his body.

"Not far. Just across the field." His voice rasped in her ears. He pulled Slepnir up and vaulted off. She turned, surprised, as he flung the reins over Slepnir's head. "I . . . I will walk," he said. "We dare not frighten your herd." He strode ahead so she could not see his face.

What she could see was bad enough: the long, waving hair, so thick, shining in the late sun, the broad back. He had a sleeveless jerkin on that left his massive arms bare. Silver armbands bound his muscles, bunching and fluid under his skin. Her muscles didn't look like that, though she thought herself strong. Predator and prey, that was their difference. Her fascination with that seemed a betrayal of her mother. Confusion over her destiny circled inside her.

A whinny pierced the clear air. Herd! Across a small stream lined with cattails, thirty pair of ears caught the wind. Thirty heads swung in her direction. First Mare trotted almost to the edge of the stream and stopped, wary. White Stallion shrieked again.

Pony flung herself off Slepnir and ran forward, stumbling on the clotted earth of the field. She splashed through the cold of the shallow stream. The horses wheeled as one and cantered off only to circle back to her. First Mare trotted up, nickering. Pony stood still, hands out, palm up, welcoming. The mare shook her head and chuffed into Pony's palm.

"My mare," Pony whispered softly, tears rising to her eyes as she breathed over the horse's nose in return. She moved into First Mare's warm chest, stroking the soft hide of her neck. First Mare blew into Pony's neck and fumbled at her flaxen shirt with equine lips. The other horses pushed up, poking with their noses. White Stallion shouldered his way to the front and nudged her with his head.

"I know, I know," she whispered. "I could not help being gone."

She had returned to where she belonged. She was a part of Herd. Their concern, their chastisement, their relief all washed over her in comforting waves. She touched them each in turn, moving among them, greeting them. Several ground their teeth at her in greeting, announcing that they were plant eaters. She clicked her back teeth together in acknowledgment. Kind to kind, she signaled them. She pushed through to the back of Herd where the mares with young gathered for protection. "How you've grown," she whispered to the foals, who sidled up to their mothers. She went still and allowed them to approach her in their own time. The kind eyes of the mares encouraged them. Nickering greetings were exchanged before they spun away, pushed into motion by the bursting life in their young bodies.

At last she came to Young Black, hanging back, out of White Stallion's way, unchallenging. He stood still, serious. She let her stillness radiate as she approached him. He curled to watch her as she stroked his haunch, now healed, where Osrick's whip had gouged him. She breathed her regret. He nuzzled her arm.

The other horses faded out. The day disappeared from her awareness. She had attention only for the liquid eyes of Young Black. Descending. That was what she felt. She was falling into the black liquid of his eyes just as in her dream of her mother's death. Tumbling into blackness, she let go; the waters closed over her . . .

. . . the day trembled into stark outlines once again. Pony looked around. The blue sky hurt her eyes. The bodies of the horses were outlined too clearly against the brown of the field. She blinked against the reality of it and gasped for breath. Valgar! The Viking stood with Slepnir just this side of the stream. She must tell him what she had learned from Young Black. Valgar was in danger. Osrick had an army massing to the south, ready to wreak his revenge on the Vikings who'd taken Chippenham from him. Young Black had the news from sheep driven up from the south. His hatred of Osrick made him eager to hear it, eager to tell.

Pony stumbled toward Valgar. First Mare fell in beside her. White Stallion flanked her other side. The others trotted behind. They were Herd. Valgar's expression tightened as she approached. *Why?* Slepnir sidled nervously. That she could understand. Those who had been subjugated by man often felt uncomfortable in the presence of a herd. Maybe Valgar did, too.

I can't tell him about Osrick. The realization struck her as though her mother slapped her cheek. It wasn't just Osrick who was massing an army to the south. He must have joined Alfred. It was her king who raised a force to throw out the foreigners—barbarians like the one who stood before her, glowering. Young Black would not have focused on Alfred; he cared only for the hated Osrick. Alfred was the leader of her kind—like White Stallion, in some way—and Osrick was her kind, hated though he was. Valgar was not. She could not betray her kind, any more than she could betray Herd. Her stomach knotted. Her step slowed.

Slepnir reared, pulling his reins against Valgar's strength. White Stallion shrieked. "Down boy, whoa there," Valgar soothed in Danish. Slepnir would not be soothed. He and White Stallion plunged and reared, eager to challenge each other.

"White Stallion," Pony tried. "He is no threat to you." White Stallion thought differently, though. He reared and churned his hooves at Slepnir. Pony pushed down the alarm that surged in her and concentrated on calm. Though White Stallion plunged beside her, she closed her eyes.

When she opened them, both stallions brought their

hooves down, but their muscles quivered and their ears pricked forward at each other as they snorted and danced for several long minutes. At last they quieted. "That's better, you two," she whispered.

She turned to find Valgar looking queerly at her. She shrugged. What could she say? They were stallions, though she would not have thought that White Stallion would find Slepnir more of a threat to his leadership of Herd than Young Black. Slepnir wore a bridle, after all.

Before Valgar could stop her, Pony turned to First Mare, gave one hop and vaulted onto her back. Ahh, sweet connection! No saddle between them to muffle the Language of Touch, only First Mare's warm back against her crotch and thighs. She stretched her arms above her and threw her head back in ecstasy. First Mare sidled through Herd. The wind combed through Pony's hair and pinched her cheeks. The sun of coming autumn melted her to the horse under her. She leaned forward as First Mare reared at the edge of Herd, then cantered across the sloping pasture of the Downs. She held her arms out to the wind, in perfect balance with First Mare's stride. Behind them, Pony could feel Herd wheel and follow. Laughter gurgled up from her core and burst into the blue afternoon. She turned her shoulders to the left, shifted her weight into her right hip, and First Mare circled left. Then Pony leaned slightly forward. First Mare increased her speed. Pony brought her arms down and wrapped her fingers in the flapping mane before her. Together, she and her horse thundered down on the tiny figures of Valgar and his chestnut stallion, Herd's hooves thumping in her chest until she was filled. She waited until she was close enough to see Valgar's eyes widen, then she sat back and closed her knees. First Mare sat back on her haunches to skid to a stop. Valgar took hasty steps backward.

Weak with laughter, Pony fell forward to embrace First Mare's neck as the horse snorted and pawed in front of Slepnir and Valgar. Slepnir stood his ground. Pony's gasping laughter turned to tears. She sucked in air as she sat up and tried to get control. She brushed at her cheeks.

"It has been too long," she said to cover her lapse into what must seem madness.

Valgar glanced at the milling horses behind her and nodded, his eyes uncertain.

Pony touched First Mare's sides with her calves before he could protest, and trotted off. Herd was content to graze as First Mare and Pony cantered in lazy circles or walked along the stream. An hour passed before Pony saw that Valgar sat with his back to an elm tree. Slepnir grazed beside him. Pony sighed. She walked to him and vaulted off First Mare's back.

"Thank you, friend," she murmured into First Mare's warm muzzle. Then she slapped the powerful haunches and sent her friend back to her companions. She turned to Valgar. "I will go back now." She should resent the fact that she must return to captivity. She *did* resent it. But the resentment was dimmed by the animal joy of having been with Herd for an hour.

Valgar looked at her for a long moment. "We will come again," he growled, grabbing Slepnir's reins. They turned toward the faesten perched on the hill above.

"Tomorrow?" Pony tried to keep the eagerness from her voice. After all, it should not fall to him to allow her to Herd, or not allow. She should be free to come and go.

He nodded curtly. "Mayhap."

Pony glanced at his face but could not read it. Suddenly, she remembered what she had learned from Young Black. Soon Valgar would not be able to refuse her. He would be dead. And what of her and Herd? If they were caught here when the coming battle crashed around them, death for some or all would surely follow. She hung her head and stared at her feet moving one in front of the other through the stubble of the field. Danger seeped out of the earth into the soles of her feet. For the sake of Herd, she must break her vow to Valgar. His threat of hunting her down if she escaped meant nothing if he was dead by Alfred's hand or by Osrick's. She must escape. But when? Too soon and Valgar would come after her. Too late and she was caught in the coming cataclysm. The faesten looming above her had regained in a moment all the fear it had once held for her. She glanced to Valgar, silent by her side. His wooden flute was stuck in his boot. That flute accused her. Soon it would be silenced forever. How dare it look so vulnerable peeking from that boot?

Smoke hung under the rafters of the assembly hall, which was crowded as usual. Its smell, and the close odor of many men, were not banished by the cedar boughs hung all around. Perhaps it was the secret that Pony carried in her breast, unsaid, that took her breath and kept her from eating, or from looking Valgar in the face.

The new council consisted of seven elders, Valgar, Pony and the priest. They sat near a fire built at one end of the hall against the chill of the October night. They had met several times. The priest appeared to be surprised that his opinions were valued by the barbarian chief and that his head was not yet spiked on a lance above the gates of the faesten. The elders were puzzled by Valgar's *law* and the fact that he himself did not break it. All in all, the council had been a surprising experience for everyone involved. Pony even found herself, once, enjoying the fusion of people she saw occur. But no more. Osrick would be back soon to disband the council. And Valgar would be dead.

It had been more than a week since she had heard Young Black's news. She fidgeted on the bench. She was too close to the fire. How much longer should she stay in Chippenham? How could she escape so that Valgar would not be after her and Herd until it was too late? That was the only thing that made her fidget. It was. It could be naught else.

The first supplicant approached the benches near the fire. He was a callow youth, his beard not fledged. As he pushed his way through the crowd, another burlier man, full-bearded and flushed-faced, also stood.

The oldest councilman nodded. "What is your supplication, Cynewulf?"

"My uncle is dead," the Saxon complained. "I am equal in rights of his possessions to Aethel. Yet Aethel has moved his family into my uncle's house and shares neither acres nor beasts with me. I am here to claim my right."

His rival puffed out a massive chest like some angry bird.

"I know this case. Neither of their fathers live," the eldest explained. "The dead man had no issue from his loins." Heads nodded along the bench. Beards were stroked.

Valgar leaned forward. "Is there a widow?" The muttering stopped.

"Yes. Emma. I claim her as well," the youth, Cynewulf, piped up.

His adversary Aethel growled, "He can have the wife, I have one of my own." This one was used to getting his way. Pony wanted to shock him, but she could not say so.

Valgar stood, and suddenly Aethel did not seem so large. "Let the widow Emma come forward." His voice boomed. Muttering and shuffling near the far door resulted in a small woman in an ocher cyrtle being spit into the center of the throng. Her red-rimmed eyes darted about. She was not as old as Pony would have imagined.

"Come, woman." Valgar's voice softened. "Were you put out of your husband's hall?"

She nodded. "I stay with a daughter, Eorl."

Valgar's lips hardened. His eyes swept over the bench of elders. "This woman is the rightful owner of the dead man's lands, his beasts, his house and his possessions. They are hers to dispose of for her lifetime and to grant to whom she will upon her death."

A gasp circled around the room. "That is the richest pastureland west of Wantage."

"A woman?" another hissed.

"She can hold land. So says the *law.*" Valgar's voice was implacable.

"Not my *law,*" Aethel barked. "What right have you?" But when Valgar's hand went to his sword, he checked himself. He was a farmer, not a warrior, and no match for a Viking.

To everyone's surprise, Valgar sat. "No right, except to defend the *law*. The council will decide." He glanced along the bench, his eyes touching each face. "You choose for *law*, or you choose for what you knew before. I will defend what you decide. But if you decide against this *law*, you decide against all *law*. I am freed from it as well as you."

The elders looked uneasy and thoughtful in turn. Pony suppressed a smile and glanced at the priest. He would not like it that a woman could hold land. The thought gave Pony courage. She was from a line of her mothers. "I choose *law*. The widow owns the land."

The oldest thumped his staff on the wood floor. *"Law."*

The word shushed down the line until it reached the priest. He was obviously torn. "There is no precedence in scripture," he muttered. "Yet could not the Mother of our Savior own us all and welcomely?" He looked up from his hands and nodded.

"Fools!" Aethel shouted, looking as though he might burst.

Cynewulf looked only petulant. He had no less than what he came with.

The bigger man got himself under control. "I will not challenge you, barbarian. Your word will not stand for long. Alfred and Osrick will grind your neck into the mud before a fortnight passes. And I will take what is mine when they do." He spun and pushed his way to the door.

There, it was said! Pony was half relieved that her secret was no more. Now let the gods decide the outcome of the coming battle. Valgar was warned. He stood and took the widow's hand. Did he not note the import of what had been said? To him was it but an idle threat?

"The land is yours. Take a husband if it pleases you. The land goes to him only if you will it so. Else it passes to your kin or whom you choose."

The widow looked to him with questioning eyes.

"If you know not how to work the land, to hire ceorls or

135

bargain for beasts, I will send someone to you." He glanced to Svenn. "I know just the man, if he would learn some Saxon."

Svenn cast a covetous eye over the young widow. Valgar was wise to give his rival a stake in the land, Pony realized. Men who had something to lose did not fight except to defend it.

"I always helped my Ralf," Emma said, tears welling. "I know enough."

Valgar looked out over the sea of faces. "Enough for this night." The oldest Saxon thumped his staff and nodded. People shuffled to the door among much muttering. Svenn glanced to Valgar, then strode after the young widow. Harald led the way outside.

Pony stood, swaying. Did Valgar not know that he had just been told his fate?

"You led the way tonight." His voice was soft at her elbow. "You made your choice."

Yes. She had chosen *law*. She had chosen the female line. But she had also chosen *his* way, *his* custom. She searched his face. Did he not know how it would be when a massive force of Saxons descended on Chippenham and its few Viking conquerors? There would be a massacre.

He lifted his brows. Pony broke the spell that held her and hurried forward. The night outside the stifling hall was autumn cool. It hit her flushed cheeks like a breaking fever. The other Vikings headed up the hill, their torches flickering in the blackness. Saxons scuttled for their homes. All this would be trampled under the feet of Alfred's warriors, and Valgar did not notice that he had been warned. She trotted until she was at his side.

"What worries you?" he asked after a moment, awkward.

What did worry her? That her people would conquer at a cost she could not bear? That Valgar would be drawn and quartered and his limbless torso dragged through the dirt of Chippenham? Should it worry her that Osrick would be back in control, hating her and Herd as he did? Or worse, that all she should want she did not? She cleared her throat.

"Did you not hear Aethel? His threat, I mean."

"A coward's last defense." He chuckled. "No more."

She grabbed his arm in the dark and pulled him around to face her. "No, it *is* more." His face loomed over her in the crisp darkness. The stars behind him flickered as though unsure themselves. "I know it for true," she breathed, then rushed on before she could remember where lay her duty to her people. "There is a force massing south of here, ready to sweep back over the downs. You will be crushed." There! She had said it. The truth would not fester in her unsaid.

"You listen to a bitter man?" he asked, searching her face, still not believing.

"I listen to Herd," she replied. "Young Black had it of sheep who had it of mules who drew carts that carried supplies." She sucked in the night. "I have known for more than a week."

She could see in his eyes that he believed her, and that he knew her reticence was some kind of betrayal. Speaking now was torn from her against her will. He stood frozen, glancing up behind her as though the darkness might even now hold hordes of Saxon warriors ready to shout their battle challenge. Then he grabbed her hand and dragged her, running, up the path to overtake his men.

"Into the fortress," he yelled as he and Pony pushed among them, through them. He did not stop until they burst into the great hall. He shouted orders in Danish as she stumbled to a halt.

"Olaf, find Svenn. Bring him here, no matter what excuse he gives. Gimli, prepare to shut the gates tonight. Harald, you have the fastest horse. You must for Thanet Island east and south. Tell Guthrum Alfred has an army massing and is like to march on Chippenham. He must send succor if he wants to hold what we have gained."

Harald stared at him open-mouthed. "You cannot ask Guthrum for aid. He presses the north. We must hold the Downs ourselves."

"We are at our last resort. Only his troops stand between us and Valhalla. If we die, the Downs are lost. It is his choice. So, go, man!" Valgar shouted. Harald found his legs and lunged for the door. "We hold council here in half an hour," Valgar called after him. The men burst into questioning cacophony, but he waved them away. "Woman, prepare a pack of food for a day's ride and be quick," he called to a Saxon turning a pot on the fire. Then he made his way to his own small room, dragging Pony with him.

She was breathless by the time he slammed the door and turned on her. Fear welled in her throat. She would say he was mad, but his orders had an air of sanity. He was surely instead angry that she had kept such a secret for a week. Did he not realize what telling him had cost her?

"You must go now," he said. "Can you find your way to your horses in the dark?"

"What? You want me to go?" He had kept her against her will for six weeks or more—anger began to shut out listening—now he just let her go?

"Whether Guthrum brings his army to our aid or no, this will be a place of blood and death. You do not belong here." He jutted his chin. His eyes were churning something, she could not tell what. "Give horses to Alfred as you choose if he wins out."

She studied his face. Did he send her away as punishment for keeping her secret? Anger shushed out with her breath and was gone. No. If he wanted to punish her, he would keep her here with him as Alfred and Osrick descended, screaming for his head. There was something else at work, but she did not know what. She nodded.

Grabbing a cloak, he thrust it into her arms. "Get food from the women."

His gray eyes locked with hers. There she saw echoed her own realization that this might be the last time she would see him. They stood, her clutching the cloak to her breast, his breathing hard. Behind the realization in his eyes something floated. Regret? She closed her eyes against it and pushed past into the hall, through chaos. A woman pressed a bundle into her arms. Then she was into the night, down to the gates and out to freedom. She sucked in evening air and began to run. Herd called.

Chapter Nine

Pony's turmoil pushed her to her feet. *Yfel Denesc hornungsunu!* Why could she not stop thinking of him? She let out a growl and strode to the door of her hut, unable to share the peace that settled over the downs as twilight stole the color from hills and sky. She ran her hands through her hair and shook her head as if that would clear it. It was his fault.

It was more than a week since she had returned to the Vale of the White Horse. Now, when everything should be perfect, when she had fulfilled her maternal destiny, when she had escaped the clutches of the *Dene*, when a life where her Gift could flourish in peace was hers; now nothing made sense. She didn't feel fulfilled. The turmoil inside her had been growing ever since she left Chippenham. The images of what would happen when Osrick and Alfred caught the small band of Vikings in the faesten would not be banished. Visions of barbarians spitted on stakes, drawn and quartered, whipped to death, tormented her. Would Alfred stop Osrick's brutality? She didn't know the king well enough to know. And if Valgar's leader had sent a great army to meet Alfred, it only meant more carnage, more suffering. If the *Danes* won, the Vikings would surely possess the entire island.

A little voice inside her said such would be no tragedy. Was not Valgar a fair and just eorl? More fair, more just than Osrick, certainly. Predator he might be—but who was worse? And Alfred was untried, unknown. Who was to say that Saxon lords were better than Viking ones? She cursed her traitorous soul. What should she care who won? She only cared who lived. And what she wanted was for the Viking to live.

No, she did not, she told herself firmly. She only wanted peace enough to hear her horses, peace enough to raise her girl-child. Nothing else mattered. Of course, she wanted her Gift. That was hard. Only yesterday she had tried to summon First Mare for a ride, hoping to clear her head of all this worry over the battle taking place some seven leagues across the downs. But First Mare had not heard her at all; she just continued to graze in the meadow down by Waylan's Barrow with the others, as though Pony didn't exist.

It was that *yfel* Viking's fault. He would not stay out of her head and give her peace. She had thought that getting herself with child would stop the deterioration of her Gift. But her breeding state apparently could not overcome the thoughts of Vikings and battles that kept her from communicating with First Mare.

Pony ran her hands yet again through her hair, clutching it in handfuls as her thoughts ran round and round. She couldn't stand this! "I want calm!" she shrieked into the dusk.

Across the pasture, First Mare raised her head and pricked her ears in surprise. White Stallion neighed a warning. The mares with foals wheeled to the rear.

Great Mother! They thought she was an enemy carnivore.

Pony covered her mouth with her hands. What was she becoming?

Enough! Pony whirled into her hut, lit only by the dim

coals of its firebox. She grabbed her cloak and stuffed some carrots and parsnips into her pack, along with some fennel-seed cakes. She kicked the coals apart and strode out into the deepening dusk. She should be heading up the Vale to-ward Wantage to put as much distance as she could be-tween herself and the battle that consumed her thoughts—but it was too late for that.

There was but one way to stop this chaos in her mind. She would to Chippenham, to see what had happened there and who remained. Then she would live with what she found. She must banish this Viking from her head, one way or another; and to do that, she would chance the world again.

Val surveyed the burning fortress, leaning on his sword. His limbs would barely hold him upright. Silhouettes of men heaving buckets of water onto the burning walls hardly seemed connected to the shouts and exhortations drifting through the smoke. Their efforts were not enough. The fire would have its way with the palisades.

"Leave off!" he shouted. He pointed to the walls of the hall standing nearest the ravenous flames. "Put your water there!" It at least might be saved.

He turned his back. The fortress was lost. Smoke filled his lungs and fogged the detritus of battle, half-concealing the rent bodies, the overturned carts, the groaning survi-vors. One could hardly tell the time of day. The sun was red and the world dark.

A party of warriors made their way up from the stream where the heaviest fighting had been. The raven pennant, black bird on yellow field, fluttered on a staff above them. *Guthrum.* His *konnungr* had come to reinforce his small troop in battle. Alfred had brought a thousand men. Val could not have been expected to defend against that kind of force. Still, he had been too weak to hold the Downs. Did Guthrum hold that against him?

Val waited. The day was theirs, yet his heart was not glad. Another battle, one of how many in his life? Battles did not

141

seem to matter. It was good that he had sent Epona away. She might have been killed in the slaughter, or burned in the fortress. That he had sent her away surprised him. He should have kept her as a hostage to bargain with in case they were defeated. Had she not bedded this Alfred?

The thought churned his gut as it always did. Alfred might have offered much in the balance for her. Val had half-expected to see her riding next to the golden-haired king on her bay mare. It had not been wise to free her, that she might give her horses to her king. But in her case, he was never wise. He raked his hands across his beard. What a fool he was! He would have put protecting her life above the interests of the *Danir*, of Guthrum, had she stayed. That way lay *berserkr* rage, the loss of all he wanted; the trust of his fellows, the order of belonging, a life that was more than empty battles. He scanned the smoky sky. Hel take her and the way she crept into his thoughts! He had been wise to defend himself against her by sending her away. He pushed aside the flickering thought that defending himself was not why he had done it. Could he live in a world where she did not exist somewhere?

Harald stumbled to his leader's side. He was sweating and bloodied, with whose blood Val could not tell.

"You live?" Val grunted.

"The gods have erred once more."

Val looked away to the horizon, to where the raven pennant made its way up the rise. It was time to set this one free from his guilt. Val understood the danger that lurked in actions taken for the wrong reasons. Harald might have been killed today, he'd fought with such abandon, always staying at Val's side. He had saved Val from a Saxon sword more than once and had the favor returned. "We are even, *fraendi.*" Val flexed his shield arm. It had served him well enough today, in spite of the burn.

From the corner of his eye, he saw Harald shake his head, his mouth quivering at the corners. "No, in truth, I think you owe me one or two at this point."

Val grunted again, suppressing his own grin. Harald had

become a friend. " 'Til the next battle, then."

Guthrum's form was a ghost in the drifting smoke, his grizzled hair an echo of the gray air. He emerged slowly, his bodyguard around him, grim and bloodied. "Valgar, son of Thorvald, your way was blood bright today," the Viking chief called.

Val flinched at his father's name. "My sword but sang your song, *Konnungr*."

Guthrum glanced around, taking in the burning fortress, the corpses scattered by the hundreds across the gentle slopes of the downs. "The trap you set has won the day."

It had been Val's strategy to position Guthrum's reinforcements north of the hill that rose beyond the meadow where Epona's herd once grazed. Alfred had swept down upon the fortress from the south, thinking his way clear. Guthrum's surprise thousands had closed them in against the fortress. As they'd turned to fight Guthrum, Val and his men opened the gates and poured out to harry the Saxons from behind. "Valkyrie took many strong hearts to Valhalla this day."

"There is but one body I see not on the field."

Val nodded. Alfred had escaped. "That one lives to fight again. Osrick, too."

"Then must I hunt him down," Guthrum vowed. He turned to Egill, who was joining the group with a small band of his best-trusted men. He had left his son, Ragnor, to hold Jorvik in the north, for he knew he must keep his son and his trusted second separated by miles of river and fen until he was ready to make a clear choice between them. "Parcel out three hundreds of our Danes to stay with Valgar. The rest, with me, are for Alfred—wherever he may hide himself."

"Let me go with you, *Konnungr*," Val growled. "Blood-letter wants the Saxon's neck."

Guthrum stepped forward. He clapped Val on the shoulder. "It is a job not worth you, Valgar. With my hundreds, dispose of the bodies here. Put this place right. Then push our strength west unto the sea and keep what we have won, lest it be taken by yet another army."

It was not what Val wanted. He did not want to stay even another hour. If he stayed, he would be tempted to ride east toward the strange horse cut into the hill. He nodded to his wily old leader brusquely. "I wish your sword will hunt like the eagle—sharp-eyed—my *Konnungr.*"

Egill nodded along with Guthrum. "We will miss your own sharp eyes and warrior cunning," the man said. It surprised Val. Egill's praise was hard-won. If Egill succeeded Guthrum over Ragnor, Val could expect a place at his side. That was good to know.

The pair of leaders turned, but before they could melt back into the smoke Guthrum stopped. "I hear there was a woman here, one with powers she could give to Alfred."

Svenn had told Guthrum that Val let Epona go. He nodded in assent. "I sent her away."

Guthrum raised wild gray brows.

"Osrick wants her dead. Dead she does us no good. If the Saxons won. . . ." The excuse was lame.

Guthrum's eyes were opaque. He dipped his head to the side, as though considering, then shrugged. With one more searching glance at Val, he strode off into the smoke.

Val took a breath and marshaled his strength. There was much to be done here to restore Chippenham to peace if he was to be away and fight battles for his king. He shouted to the *Danir* at the fortress walls to leave their buckets and gather what they could of what was left. At least he would not have time to think about Epona for a while.

It was late afternoon when Pony left Herd in the wood about a league from Chippenham. They had followed her without her asking. Good thing, since she was not sure her Gift would ever allow her to ask them again. It had taken her many hours to pick her way across the leagues with Herd in tow. All the day Pony felt her insides churning with the prospect of encountering all the death ahead—one death, perhaps, in particular. Her nerves were stretched as tight as a bowstring. Now she realized she could not take Herd up through the town to the faesten, bold as you please, until she knew how things stood. Smoke from a great fire had been visible all morning. Straggling bands of Saxons had become a steady stream on the main road as people fled the battle. She rode First Mare up to the edge of the stone road to ask news. None could give her aught but speculation. Some swore Alfred was come to save them and had won the day. Others scoffed and said the barbarians held the faesten against all comers. All anyone was sure of was that Chippenham was no place to be. And that was just where she was going.

Pony cursed herself and returned to Herd. She led them ever closer to the carnage until they came to the wood just outside the faesten. She tried to muster enough calm to tell White Stallion he should keep his charges in the trees. Her heart was thumping so the message was lost. Her Gift was unequal to the task she set it. Herd showed no signs of following. She wasn't sure whether it was the smoke in the air or the faint scent of blood or her commands that repelled them to seek safety in the trees.

She and First Mare went on alone. Pony took deep breaths to calm herself until the smoke made her choke and sputter. First Mare sneezed and snorted, too. The scent of blood grew stronger. They almost tripped over the first body. Pony gasped. First Mare whinnied and shied to the right. The body lay twisted, one arm hacked off. The earth was blackened with blood. The warrior's wild-eyed fear was frozen on his face. It might have been Val.

In the next minutes she saw many bodies. Some wore oval brooches that proclaimed them Dane, some the figured armbands that bespoke Saxony. Both sides wore conical helmets, chain mail for those who could afford it, leather greaves, steel slippery with darkening gore. Pony's eyes widened at each new desecration of the life that the Fecund Mother had struggled to bring forth from her womb; the woman in her hated such waste.

At last her eyes glazed and her mind numbed. She was a

plant-eater not a carnivore. Who could comprehend so great a violation of the rightness of the world? Even First Mare ceased to snort and sidle. Yet Pony examined each face, in case it was the one she sought. She dreaded seeing gray eyes staring blankly up at her, or his cleft chin, his gleaming hair muddied and worse. But she *had* to know what happened to him.

Pony was surprised when she came to the stream. She had not thought she was so near the faesten. She peered into the smoke ahead. Just there had Valgar stood with Slepnir during her reunion with Herd. First Mare splashed through the stream, washed through with rivulets of spiraling red. They picked their way up the slope. The first live figure she had seen loomed ahead. It clanked with many suits of chain mail gathered from the dead, many swords. Pony and First Mare froze in front of the apparition. He gasped as he noticed them and clanked to stillness, too. One of the victors. Saxon or Dane—which to hope for?

"Epona? Is it you?" The words were Dane.

"Harald!" She vaulted off First Mare's back. "It is I," she said in Danish.

He let the weapons he carried clatter to the ground and clasped her arms. "You are returned."

"Does Valgar live?" She choked.

"*Ja.*" Harald nodded, his face streaked with blood from a scalp wound. "The clever bastard won the battle for Guthrum, Thor take him. Though Alfred has escaped to fight another day."

Pony's knees gave way. Harald held her up. "Let me take you to him." He switched to Saxon and grinned. "He will blame me if you die now when he sent you away to save you." Pony looked up at him, trying to focus on what he had just said. Valgar had meant to save her by sending her away? Harald's words clicked. He *had* meant to save her. What did that mean? What did she want it to mean?

They found Valgar inside the assembly hall, facing the commanders of his new forces. His face was smudged with soot, his hair matted with sweat and dirt. His chain mail glistened red with blood Pony could only hope was not all his own. She could see a slash on his thigh through his leather breeches, and a rent in his chain mail over his ribs. What was she thinking? That it was better that he had killed than he had been injured? She shuddered.

"Separate the bodies into Saxon and Dane," he was ordering in that booming bass that made her shiver. "Erik, your men will dig the pits."

Blood pounded in Pony's head. The hall blackened at the edges. Someone answered Valgar. She could hear no words at all, only the singing of her blood and a strange lassitude that crept into her bones. Curse him, Great Mother, that the mere sight of him could rob her of her senses! She reached blindly for Harald and he steadied her. Slowly the blackness faded and she found that Valgar had turned to look at her, along with the men behind him.

She had no idea what she expected to see in his eyes when they met, but she had not considered horror a possibility. She could not mistake it. Exhaustion, yes, but also horror.

"Look what I have found among the dead," Harald called.

"Why did you come?" he choked. He seemed stunned. He did not switch to Saxon.

"I come to see if Saxon wins or *Dene*," she managed in a mixture of their two tongues.

"Good," Svenn pronounced. "Now we take her horses."

"Yes. We had such luck catching them the last time," Harald noted dryly. "Besides, she came with just her mare as far as I could see."

Valgar looked down at his hands. Pony followed his gaze to see that they were trembling. He must be fatigued, indeed, from fighting. He looked up. "Well, now you know who won." He had recovered himself enough to switch to Saxon. He turned back to his men.

Did he not care that she had crossed leagues—that she had witnessed unthinkable destruction of man and animal— just to see if he lived? He had once kept her at his side by tying her with rope. Now he cared not whether she stayed or went? Anger welled in Pony. Valgar said something to the assembled men, but she was listening only to her anger. How could he dismiss her thus—he, who was a predator, who violated every belief she held dear? Yet she had thought only of him! She had wanted only to know that he lived. What a fool she had been!

"Yes, now I know barbarians have defeated the one truly good man in the kingdom," she called. Her voice rang with bitterness. "But I trust he will prevail in the end."

Valgar did not turn. "Harald, take her to where the women tend the wounded. She may make herself useful until she chooses to go."

Harald stared first at his *jarl* and then at Pony, then back to Valgar. He lifted his brows. "Come, lady priestess," he said. "Let me take you and your horse to water, at least."

Valgar turned back to his men. "I have ordered that any Saxons wounded though not unto death be brought to this hall. The priest you shall have the tending of them."

Pony heard the low roar of *Denesc* protest behind her. Valgar's voice rose above it. "Any who swear allegiance to Guthrum may go home when they are able to their farms or their trade."

Pony stalked into the night behind Harald, her anger at Valgar only fueled by his generosity to her people. What business was it of a carnivore to be generous? How could he be both predator and a fair administrator? It made no sense. Osrick—now, Osrick was the kind of predator she recognized: taking, always taking, like wolves tore at Chestnut Mare's body. The image washed over her and made her shudder.

"He may regret this night," Harald muttered.

Harald did not seem surprised at Valgar's order.

"You knew of this?"

"*Ja.*" He nodded, shaking his head. "Leaving Saxons alive, even wounded . . . it is a danger. It is not the way of *Danir*. Svenn is angry."

"I wager he is," she agreed, disgusted. "By this act of

mercy, your Valgar binds them to his cause more surely than he bound me with rope. Danes would not have fared thus at Osrick's hands, and these people know it."

Harald glanced at her, surprised. "They are not of the Danelaw. They know not loyalty."

Pony let her breath out in a bitter huff. Mayhap the predator had found a more effective way of mesmerizing his prey. "He has made them of the Danelaw now," she said. "He just showed them the way to loyalty."

Chapter Ten

Osrick threw the lance with all the strength his shaking limbs could muster. "Damn your God, Alfred, that he sided with the Viking horde!" The lance shuddered into a tree trunk. The murmur of men's voices ceased, leaving only the noises of a wood at night.

They were camped under the huge beeches and oaks in Savernake forest, but they would not be safe here for long. Danish scouting parties searched for stragglers even now. This was the end of all Osrick's aspirations, soon to be the end of his life. He had tried to lead this stripling king. He had mustered an army against impossible odds. All for naught. He rounded on Alfred, who sat calmly on a stone near a tiny campfire; the priest, Asser, crouched next to him. Alfred examined a piece of dried venison. How Osrick wanted to wipe away that calm assurance! Did the boy not know the entire island was lost to barbarians?

Alfred glanced at the priest and stood. "Asser," he asked, "did God side with the Vikings?" His voice carried across the dozen other small fires that licked at the darkness, to be heard by the smudged and bloody faces bunched around.

"No, lord." The priest's voice was as strong as his king's.

"You see, Osrick? An *official* opinion." Alfred stared at him.

Osrick glanced away. *Fools!* he thought. *Can't you see what happened here?* Alfred was not so different than his own stupid son. How much faith they put in God's attention to the details of their lives.

The young king turned to his half-seen troops. Though his words were a response to Osrick, he spoke to them all. "God is testing us to see if we will keep faith with him and with our cause."

Osrick scoffed. "He tests us thoroughly when we are reduced thus." He gestured to the scrawny fires, the jerked venison that was their only sustenance.

"As he tested Job, Osrick," Alfred replied. He gave Alfred one of his blinding smiles and turned it across the camp. "And did not Job prevail? So will we. In future times, they will see us as a miracle. How did we sink so low and yet come back to rule all the island? 'Tis no miracle unless we saw the darkness firsthand, and yet made our way to the light."

He turned to Osrick. "Ah, my friend, you doubt. I see it in your eyes. Yet there is one certain proof that we will prevail. Who among you does not know the story of the saint who lives in the fens, she who brought the faesten down at Thetford with heaving earth?" A murmur of assent circled the camp. "She foretold that I would be crowned king of all the island. Her vision of my future is your guarantee of victory." He clapped Osrick on the back and drew him to walk among the fires, touching the shoulder of one warrior, nodding to another, beaming sureness over all. "We will go south where my power is strongest, near my capital at Winchester, and get up a resistance."

"With winter coming on, the eorls will not like to move," Osrick objected.

"Then we will find a safe haven and bide our time, my friend." Alfred laughed. "Those who have left for Frankish lands have left behind men who may treat with us. We will find them and set our plans in their ears."

"Like shrews and hares we hide?" Osrick asked. "Where?"

"I know not yet where." Alfred took a piece of jerky offered by one of his men and gave a smile of thanks. "But our job is to keep alive in the next days—like shrews and hares if we must."

Osrick bit back a retort. He was not a man who liked to think of himself as a shrew or a hare, for all that it seemed not to bother his king.

Alfred held up the piece of jerky, grinning. "We live today," he shouted. "And we will live to see this island ruled again by Saxons in a single peaceful kingdom where a man can earn his bread and listen to the word of Jesu. Are we alive?" he challenged.

A roar went up from many throats. "Aye," they shouted.

"Will you see my destiny with me?"

"Aye, aye," echoed into the trees.

Alfred smiled on them.

Osrick grimaced. "Aye," he muttered. What choice had he? He had cast his lot with this man, for good or ill—and it looked to be very ill at this moment. He was not skilled at biding his time, but he had better learn.

Three days later, Pony was still in Chippenham. She'd told herself that she had not returned to her Vale because she was needed here. But while she had bound up wounds and filled mead sacks at the barrel; helped to feed those who could not feed themselves; stirred cauldrons of gruel or soaked poultices in herbs, which women with greater skills than hers could use on the wounded—still her heart had found no ease.

She stepped out of Osrick's great hall and drew her sleeve across her forehead. Behind her echoed the moans of the injured. Ahead, more wounded stretched out in the common area. Her eyes searched between the buildings and injured bodies for one familiar figure. She had not spoken to him or he to her since she returned, though she had seen him often enough and heard him making plans. He was putting Chippenham back together.

He was not in the yard. Pony's gaze moved out beyond the still-smoldering stumps of the wooden palisades to where men and horses hauled new timber to reconstruct the walls. Valgar's broad shoulders strewn with light brown waving hair were nowhere to be seen.

Pony let her gaze drift farther to the busy slopes beyond, where men dug graves all along the north face. The women wrapped linen around bodies dressed in their best armor. Men lowered those bodies into the earth and laid their weapons by their sides. These were the Viking dead.

Farther down the hill, on a crescent of land formed by the folding of the stream upon itself, there was another smoldering heap—this one of charred Saxon bones. The fire had been burning since the night of Pony's arrival. The enemy dead had been stripped of everything of value and laid on the conflagration, their souls to ascend with the sparks in the night, or float as ashes into the first breeze of morning. Piles of silver armbands, leather boots and greaves, chain mail, bronze conical helmets were stacked to one side. Val burnt the Saxon bodies without ceremony, so that all would know the price of challenging his rule. Yet he treated the living with generosity, seeing to the village needs, apportioning supplies, employing the villagers at pay for the rebuilding as well as marshalling his Danes' strong backs to the work.

Suddenly the bodies, the smell of rotting flesh and acrid smoke; all poisoned the bright autumn morning. Pony felt compelled to flee lest she go mad—no matter that her gut whispered, *Not yet*. Pony strode behind the hall to the large pen where First Mare dipped her nose into a trough of water. The horse's ears swiveled nervously. She did not like the smell of rotting flesh either. At Pony's approach, the beast lifted its head and trotted to the railing. Pony opened the gate, and First Mare pushed through the other horses to step into the yard. Pony vaulted onto her back, and felt health and life seep again into her own soul through her palms.

"Come, pretty partner," she whispered. And together they picked their way among the wounded, out through what once were gates, across the earth pitted with graves, down past the horrid pyre of mangled, blackened bones and fluttering ashen souls on the breeze. Splashing through the stream, Pony headed for the forest where she had left Herd.

Slepnir overtook them. He and his rider must have been upstream of the pyre, and they'd angled to catch up. Pony's heart had to be pressed down severely, to keep it from leaping into her mouth. What cared she if Valgar accosted her? He could not prevent her leaving as long as she was mounted on her fleet mare. Feeling him bearing down on her, she imagined his face—but she refused to look, refused to hurry.

He did not hail her, so Pony glanced over only when his steed merged strides with hers. His face was set and grim, his soft full lips pressed into a line. He still did not speak. She turned back toward her goal. Let him follow if he wanted—what did she care? Her breathing was ragged, and she hated herself for it. Well, ragged or not, Valgar would not turn her from her purpose. She trained her eyes on the edge of the forest. He cleared his throat once or twice, but otherwise he was silent. She saw his fists clenching and unclenching on Slepnir's reins. He wore leather strips wound around both wrists now. His forearm had healed as much as it would.

The memory of his flesh under her hands, rubbing the blood into his arm, assaulted her in places she did not expect. Pony sighed. The silence stretched. She dared not let her thoughts wander as they would. 'Twas not the way to calm. "I . . . I could not bear the blood and the smoke anymore," she said finally.

"Nor I." His voice was low; the two lone words seemed torn from him.

Shapes moved out of the trees ahead. Pony could not help

but smile. It started in her heart and curled her lips whether she would or no. *Herd.*

"Do you . . . do you take your *hestr*—horses home?" he asked.

"I don't know," she answered, truthfully. "I only know I must be gone from here."

Herd approached, White Stallion in the lead. Pony let her gaze rest on Valgar for the first time. He took a big breath and let it out slowly. His flute was stuck in his boot. There was a leather sack tied to Slepnir's saddle. "I, too, wanted a few hours away," he said. He looked up at the sky, stretching his neck. The strong muscles there bunched. His hair cascaded down his back and swung slightly with the rhythm of Slepnir's walk.

"Soil is good here."

She said nothing.

"Like your Vale. You could grow more than horses there."

"Why would I want to?" Valgar's face screwed into a wry grin—did he laugh at himself? He shook his head as though surrendering to something. "Will you ride with me?"

Herd was upon them now, milling. White Stallion nudged First Mare, who was in heat, but she bared her teeth at him. Pony laughed. First Mare was not ready for a stallion yet: Pony understood. Still, she longed to be so sure. She was *not* sure. Not when she was anywhere near Valgar. He was a predator. He was male. Yet he surprised her, with his music, with his smile. He judged fairly. And more, she . . . liked him. She had never really known a male. The three shepherds? Osrick? The farmer who had taken Young Black? Another thought occurred. She knew this Viking Valgar better than she knew even Alfred, the father of her girl-child. She looked at him from under her lashes and made a small decision. She said to Valgar, "We are Herd today. It is you who may ride with us, if they allow it." For protection the mares with foals circled into the center of the group. The swirl of horse colors, soft nickers, thudding hooves and blowing was everywhere.

Slepnir sidled, unused to being Herd. "Easy, boy," Valgar soothed. His voice was to Pony like the rumble of rocks coming down the hill, when you could not hear them yet but only feel them in your chest. Pony thought his voice might sooth the lightning, or even the rushing cataract.

Herd, accepting them, moved off to the east at an easy pace. Valgar didn't speak, and neither did Pony. But the tension that had pushed them apart through the past days melted away. Chippenham loomed off to their left, then faded behind. First Mare and Slepnir led the way. White Stallion circling in the back, protecting Herd's rear. Pony felt the soul of the group fluttering in the morning sun—it sang along with the insects in the grass, the gurgle of the stream, the breeze caressing willow leaves. She could hear everything. It was the spirit of the Great Mother as she had not felt it in weeks. As she listened, power swelled inside Pony. She felt relief, and tears welled in her eyes. The Gift was back. She heard contentment as Herd wandered through the high brown grass of autumn. She heard hares, frozen as the horses passed; and starlings' outrage. She heard . . . *a warning.* She reached over and grasped Slepnir's bridle. He halted.

"What do you?" Valgar asked. He looked impatient.

"Wait here," she ordered.

He pulled back, skeptical of taking orders, but then a poisonous adder slithered across their path and disappeared into the grasses. Slepnir reared in panic. First Mare sidled away. Pony quieted her.

"How did you know?" Valgar asked as he fought his mount back to all four feet

Pony laughed. "You would not like the answer if I told you." The joy of knowing the Great Mother could still speak to her was overwhelming. Hadn't her mother always told her the Gift would return when she conceived? Why had she doubted?

"Like it or not, chance me to hear it."

She shrugged. "A hare warned me of the snake. It is the Gift of the Great Mother . . . when the Gift is working."

Valgar calmed Slepnir and stared at her. His eyes roved

Pony as though he had never seen her before; then he looked around himself, as though unsure where he was, or perhaps looking for a place to run. "Who *are* you?" he whispered.

Pony looked down at First Mare's shoulders, the muscles undulating under the shiny coat. Valgar was afraid of her. He had not truly understood that she was different until this moment. It was more than being a good horsewoman: he saw that now. "My king thinks I am a Druid." Herd seethed around them, walking, grazing, snorting. Perhaps Valgar would believe what Alfred did.

He gathered himself, stilled his roving eyes. "And who are Druids?"

"Priests." She shrugged. "The priest caste of the people who were here before the Saxons. They are still here, mostly to the west. A man called Trevellyan is their leader, so people say. Druids find their strength in trees, not horses, though. Especially oaks. They wore white, like the mistletoe berry that was their symbol."

Valgar pushed Slepnir closer. He looked intrigued. "Mistletoe. I have seen Saxons kiss under mistletoe. Is that why?"

"It invokes the protection of the Druids' gods. It is a small thing, a holdover from former times." Pony ran her hand along First Mare's shiny neck, feeling the warmth of the horse give her strength. That strength had been there forever, far longer than the Druids. "Alfred sees in my white-gold hair that I am like them."

"Do *you* see that?" Valgar asked. His voice was serious.

Pony shrugged. She glanced over at him. His horse walked confidently among Herd, which was unusual. Most horses who bent their wills to man were uneasy in the presence of Herd. Just as Slepnir's rider was tense now. She looked into Valgar's gray eyes. His lips were softer set than she had seen them. Pony shook her head, then jerked her eyes from his face to the horizon. The downs rolled out to the west and south into a flat plan that stretched, she'd heard, all the way to Sarum, past the great forest to the east. The bite in the air said that autumn was hard upon them. It must be near Samhain! Had she so forgot her mother's teachings that she could lose the seasons, too?

"So, what are you?" Valgar asked, unaware of her thoughts. "The village says you are the horse goddess, Epona . . . that Alfred wants you because the Goddess chooses the king. I never believed that." His voice said he was not so sure now.

"I am not a goddess," she assured him. But what was she? Her Gift was unreliable, her destiny fulfilled yet unfulfilling. Alfred wanted her to help his cause. Her mother wanted her to have a girl-child. She herself knew no more than this Viking did about what she was or what she was meant to do. Tears filled her eyes. Pony's knee brushed the Viking's as First Mare and Slepnir wandered together. Valgar's horse nosed First Mare, who bared her teeth and flattened her ears. Pony took a breath. Why did she so want to tell this man how deep her confusion truly was? "I am not even Epona," she confided. "It is the name of all who live under the White Horse. We are *all* Epona."

He looked unmoved. "But you name yourself Epona. That is what counts. Many share my name, too."

"I call myself Pony as my mother did," Pony corrected. "Though I will never have the Gift as she did. I cannot keep myself calm enough to listen for long. Not like she could."

He examined her, but his thoughts focused inward. "Mayhap it is best you are not like your mother. I want to believe that I am not like my father," Valgar said, his voice breaking. "That at least is my hope, Pony." Her name sounded like a rumbling caress upon her cheek when it left his lips. She was glad she had told him the name by which she thought of herself. He was not finished, though. He swallowed. "I deny my father's name. I say not: Valgar, son of Thorvald. To me, I am only Val."

"Val," she repeated slowly. He had a secret name as well. Then confusion rose again. "But I *want* to be like my Mother," Pony whispered. Didn't she?

"And what is your mother like?" Pony found herself frustrated. Despite her answers, still Valgar pressed her to tell him what she was, who she was. Why? What did he want?

158

Had she not told him her secret name was Pony? She did not *know* what she was. She had never really known her mother. The early autumn afternoon flowed around her, charged with lighting she could feel but not see. Her heart thumped as though she danced under the moon at Samhain. Something called to her that she did not recognize. How could she tell him what she didn't know? She wanted to gallop away from his questions, from his soft mouth and serious eyes. But something stayed her. He wanted answers, but so did she.

Wait! A solution. There was a place that, more than any other, was rooted at the center of all she was, she and her mothers before her. One place held all her history, her soul. She jerked back to him as the problem of how to tell him was solved. And perhaps the problem of finding out herself. "Do you have courage, Val?" she asked.

"Some." His voice was rough.

The thumping in her heart turned from fear to anticipation. It cried out for galloping, for dancing, for Samhain. Pony grinned. "Follow if you dare," she cried.

"Where," he asked.

She tapped First Mare's sides with her calves and leaned forward. The horse leapt ahead across the downs. "To the center of the world," she called back as she and First Mare melted into each other. The rhythm of hooves in the soft chalk earth exalted her. "But you must keep up!"

Valgar followed Pony, as did Herd. "I ride the eight-legged horse of the Gods," he shouted as he caught up and passed her, the strong haunches of his chestnut stallion pushing him ahead.

But First Mare was fast and not burdened by saddle or bridle; she lengthened easily and matched Slepnir's strides. Pony wound her hands in the horse's flapping black mane, one with her mount. "Big is not fast," she laughed.

Together she and Valgar and their steeds streamed across the downs to the southwest, Herd in their wake, to the place where her mother had first shown her who she was. She could not explain it to him; he must see. Then perhaps she would remember, too.

Chapter Eleven

The afternoon was almost gone when the stones appeared in the distance. Several canted at strange angles; others stood straight and black against the sky, holding up lintels as big as themselves. Pony was glad Valgar did not ask her what they were. It was a time for silence and he knew it. The horses trotted, their gallop gone.

As they approached, the stones loomed larger, their impossible weight shouting that they were cut by some unknown god and lifted, with some magic long forgotten, into place. Pony doubted Valgar even noticed the two barrow mounds they passed, one on each side of the surrounding flat plain—the great stone circle alone held his gaze. The sun was waning, but it cast its final rays across the towering monuments, limning them in incandescence.

Valgar dismounted and cast his reins over Slepnir's head. His face turned up to the giant stones. He wandered into the center of the circle, to the holy place, as the sun died. Pony dismounted and followed. First Mare dipped her head to graze. Valgar pulled the bridle off Slepnir. Both horses

160

wandered away, unimpressed with their surroundings, seeking more succulent tufts of grass.

"Who built them?" Valgar asked quietly.

Pony pointed outward to a lump on the horizon, then turned, her arm still outstretched, to indicate the tens of other barrows in a giant circle, miles wide, all around the stones. "They did."

Valgar turned with her. She saw the speculation on his face. He cast his eyes up to the immense stones around him. "Not without help from the gods."

She walked out to the circle and pressed her palm against the cold stone, too flat for nature, too huge for men. She could feel the power humming in them. It vibrated through her palm into the place between her breasts. "Perhaps."

"Not Druids?"

She smiled and shook her head. "Long before the Druids."

"This is who you are?" The stones seemed to swallow his voice.

She turned. Twilight fell quickly this time of year. Already the barrows receded into dusk. Soon these stones, too, would only be dark smudges against the stars. She saw Valgar look around, realize they were far from Chippenham and the safety of his Viking brethren. She nodded. "So my mother taught me. She never named our people. I call them the People of the Stones."

"These stones are from your gods. Can you not name your gods?"

She shrugged, shaking her head. "You think there are many. Well, you give them many names perhaps. But in the end, there is only the Great Mother who gave birth to all. She gave me my Gift. I hear her creatures. These are her stones. Her trees shade me. Her snow falls in winter. Does she sometimes call herself Alfred's Jesu? Slepnir's master, Odin? If it pleases her."

"How do you call on her?" he asked, wandering nearer.

The hard lines of his face were softened by the dusk. "I do not call. I listen."

He nodded slowly. He'd moved so close she could feel the heat from his body as the dusk chill shook her into a shudder. "We should go back," she murmured.

"Too late. Horses are tired." He looked up. "The night will be dry. If we make fire . . ."

He was right. And she did not want to return to the crowded faesten or the streets of Chippenham. Here, among the stones, she felt who she was. She was a creature of the Great Mother, just like the ones who'd built this circle.

Pony peered about her for the pile of wood. It would be next to the largest stones and the lintel they pushed up against the night sky. She pointed. "Use that."

Valgar grunted and strode off. A moment later he emerged from the gloaming with an armload of faggots. "Someone left wood."

"I did. I gathered it on the morning after Beltane, against my future need."

"You come here often." It wasn't a question. It rumbled out of the darkness, where she could just make Valgar out.

"At Beltane in May and Samhain." She looked up at the darkening sky. She'd lost track of the moon in the chaos of battle. Her heart fluttered. Was it the tug of the Great Mother she felt? It must be growing close to Samhain.

Val knelt in the exact center of the circle. Did he know it was the most sacred point? "What do you do here?" he asked. With twigs broken from larger sticks and branches, he began to lay a fire. At least they wouldn't freeze tonight.

"I listen to the Great Mother." That was true, in essence.

Pony gathered dried grass from about a stone plinth that had fallen inward. She clutched her cloak around her as a mist began to rise. The earth was cooling. Val took the grass she offered and stuffed his cone of twigs with it. Next he produced a flint and striker from his pouch. The clicking of his stones showered bright sparks over his construction, lighting first the dried grass and then the twigs.

The fire lit his face from below, masking it in shadow, and Pony suddenly realized she knew no more who Valgar was than he knew about her. All she knew was the pull he seemed to exert on her and that he had been to foreign lands. She had been no farther from her White Horse than this stone circle or Chippenham. What made a man leave his home for the ends of the earth? How did he stay connected to who he was? She knelt beside him, staring into the fire as he added a larger log, and then another. Its warmth was welcome in the autumn night. First Mare and Slepnir wandered nearer. She could feel Herd, in the darkness just outside the circle. Their soft nickering, the almost imperceptible thuds of their hooves joined the other night sounds.

"You have a place to listen to your gods. That is an anchor. It must feel good," Valgar said.

The crackle of the fire almost covered the sounds of the horses ripping grasses at the root, the grinding of their teeth, the rhythm of insect songs. He was right—here she felt whole. "Do you not have such a place?"

He shook his head. "Not for many years."

She decided it was time to ask. "Why did you come to this island? For plunder?" That wasn't why, else he would have stripped the Saxon ceorls of all they had, instead of trying to rule the new land fairly.

The Viking gave a small shrug, as if to shake off thought. "My people were here."

"Your people were in your own country, too," Pony pointed out.

A line appeared between his brows. "I will never go there." His voice was tight.

Could she continue, despite his obvious reticence? In the night, in the circle, she could ask anything. "No wish to return to your home?"

He lifted his brows as though gathering himself, and the pain snapped in his eyes like the reflected fire. He sucked in air. "My people do not want me there." The tumult inside him wouldn't be contained. He stood, looking down at her. "I am outcast, criminal. I broke faith with my people and their law. Is that what you would know?" His voice was hoarse, halting, as though each word was torn from him. It was hard for Pony to watch, frightening even.

So she lent him some of her mother's calm. She called it up from where it pooled inside her chest, behind her eyes, and let it shine out in a quiet smile. She didn't ask him what he had done; she just let her eyes go soft. He glared down at her, unseeing, filled with other times, other pain. Pony's heart almost faltered under the weight of that pain. Still, she managed the smile she hoped reassured him. After a moment he heaved a shuddering breath. He blinked twice and focused on her again. The line between his brows relaxed. Pony's smile grew. He looked at her in speculation, as though he suspected what she had done. Finally, he shrugged and breathed a disgusted chuckle. "I spent long years in the steppes far to the east." He poked at the fire with a stick.

"What are steppes?" she asked.

"Flat, almost desert. Hills that jut." He knelt. "Like this." He made a cutting motion with his hand. "Barren," he said. "Only grasses sometimes."

"What did you do there?" She tried to imagine a land like that, so different than the soft green downs she knew with their sheep and cattle, oats and wheat and rivers.

"Fight. I know fighting." Bitterness edged into his voice.

"For what?"

He looked at her askance. He didn't understand.

"Why did you fight?" she explained.

"Their *kunnungr* paid good silver." His armbands glinted red in the light from the fire as Valgar settled himself. "They called him *czar* after the *kunnungr* called Caesar to the south. I led his guard."

"Did so many want to kill him?"

Val chuckled. He prodded the fire until it loosed a fountain of sparks. "Many. Sometimes me. He was bad. It took much silver to keep his *Russ* guard. *Russ* was their name for *Danir*."

Pony looked with new eyes at the lines in his face—from blood and fighting far from his home for people he didn't care about? "How many years?"

He looked out at the stones around them. "Ten. Maybe more. Until I am dry inside." He touched his chest. "What is left? Only fighting. I am outcast, but I am a good fighter. I thought they might let me fight for the *Danir* if I came to where they needed me. Here."

He was wrong. He was good at other things than fighting. She had seen that in Chippenham. He was valuable to the Danes as an administrator. He must know that. Why else did Guthrum trust an outcast? But he did not want to admit that, at least to her. "So you could not go home. Do you not want to stop fighting?"

"Want?" He looked at her, brows drawn together. "I want cattle and land and a warm hearth. I want that to-morrow will be like today."

She nodded. That was what she wanted, too. She didn't need to ask whether he thought it was possible, though. Neither did.

"That is why Danes have *law*," he continued after a moment. "*Law* tells how things will be." The horses snorted. "And loyalty to his *jarl* earns a man his place. Loyalty and law. They are all."

Was it like being true to your Gift? Perhaps Val's kind of loyalty was like obeying Pony's mother's commands. Was it obeying your destiny? That she could understand. She put a hand over her belly to feel the quickening there. Wasn't she, too, trying to find her place?

Valgar rose, breaking the mood of shared confidences, and went to draw the saddle from Slepnir. He also brought back the thick woven blanket that, when doubled, protected the horse from saddle sores. Air buffeted the flames as he shook it out upon the ground and motioned Pony onto it. She drew her cloak around her. Val took his wooden flute from his boot and threw down his saddle so that she might lean her back against it.

Pony sat and drew up her knees. Val sat beside her. The blanket was small enough that their shoulders touched. Tightness fluttered in her belly. Was it the child within her calling? Or was it the Viking's touch? He had caused

165

strange feelings in her of late. She began to tremble. Behind her, First Mare's whinny pierced the darkness. Pony looked around. The stones seemed to pulse with energy. *Great Mother*, she thought; she knew this feeling. She'd had it twice a year for as long as she could remember at the exact moment the seasons changed direction.

The rust-red rim of the moon rose between the barrows to the east. Pony's eyes widened as it broke the horizon. Full. Samhain. Samhain was tonight! The rhythm of the seasons, the force of the moon, the weight of millennia pulled her to her feet. She stood, shaking. She wasn't ready! She had done no preparation, no ritual. But she had been called here tonight—that was why she had felt compelled to come. The moon shoved itself above the horizon, even as she watched. She could not escape. Least of all here in the very center of the circle of stones. Samhain, the churning inside her would not be denied.

She sagged and straightened, sagged again. *Not here, in front of the Viking.* Pony did not want him to see this much of who she was. Already he was looking at her strangely. Yet in some frightening way, she *did* want him to see. Something inside her had known this was Samhain, even if only at the deepest level of her soul. And she had wanted to be here with him. Why else this wild ride to the center of the world? She knew, on some level, that he was a carnivore. She should not be sharing this with him. Yet she was; she would; and that was what the Mother wanted, else they would not be together here as the moon rose on Samhain night.

Her head dipped and circled. The old, familiar throbbing bubbled up inside her. No wonder she had mistaken its beginning for the feelings Valgar had stirred in her. The call of Samhain boiled inside until her vision blurred. Pennants of fire seemed to lick the moon orange. The crackle of the flame grew louder, but behind it she could hear the rustling of her acolytes outside the circle. Herd had been joined by countless others. They had come, to watch, to join, to worship the moon and the change of the season tonight.

"Pony." Val's voice boomed in her ears, though she knew it was but a whisper. She could hear the whole world tonight. "Are you well?"

"No," she breathed. "Or yes." He was about to see everything and somehow that was right. She pulled the pin from her cloak. It fell to the blanket with a thundering crash. "Have you ever seen a dance to the moon on Samhain night?"

She did not see his reaction. She was transfixed by her heart throbbing in her chest as the moon broke free from the earth and lifted into the sky. A black lightning bolt of antlers moved in front of the ruddy orb. They were coming. Her shoulders swayed. Eyes closing, she tore at the laces that bound her leather leggings.

"Pony?" Val's voice thrust into her ears above the rustles around the circle.

"I am well," she breathed. "It is . . . my night. I didn't know." She pulled at the crisscrossed leather straps, scraped off one soft boot on the heel of the other. Her blood burned. She could feel the throbbing in her veins, pulsing in her breasts, flushing her cheeks. "Ahh . . ." she cried, lifting her face to the moon even as her leggings slid to the ground. The night air on her naked legs did not cool her. She burned with Samhain, and nothing could put out that fire except the dance. Her feet moved on the woolen blanket. Each woven nub caressed the calluses of her heels. Only her shirt remained.

She could contain the spirit of the Goddess no longer. It sprayed out through her up-flung hands. Eyes still closed, her hips began to sway of their own accord. The blades of grass thrust through her toes as she whirled out from the blanket. The weight of her hair swung wide around her. Flaxen cloth brushed her nipples, making lightning course down to her loins. What was that feeling? She had danced on Samhain night many times, yet the feel of lightning in her loins reminded her of touching Val more than these wild dances with her mother.

Thought drained away. There was only the dance. She

stood on the balls of her feet and tiptoed through the grass, the moon drawing her arms in an undulating circle. Hundreds of animals, male and female, rustled around her, their eyes upon her. She heard them all. The world was full to overflowing with their spirits.

First Mare and Slepnir watched, ears quivering. The moon rose exactly between the two large plinths at the east portal of the circle. Pony whirled and danced with the spirit of the world and the animals inside it. Here was the one time when no calm was possible, needed or required of her, and all the tumult in her breast trembled in shuddering concert with the world's turning season.

Into her whirling madness came a note, clear, pure, followed by another, long and low, then a trill of notes. She turned and saw Val, as from a great distance, and he was staring at her, flute to his lips. She swung around and snapped her head back, and the notes followed her, rising, arching toward the moon. Her breath heaved in her chest; her vision trembled with the power of the Goddess. She bent and skipped to the side, and the Viking's flute skipped with her, pushing her, pulling with notes so right, they seemed to drip from the moon itself. Val's eyes shone in the night as he stared at her, unblinking, and played. Pony dipped and swung her hair, feeling the notes sparkling at his fingertips, showering over her. Wilder she danced, and wilder. The notes fluttered into the night. The flax cloth rubbing at her nipples became a painful barrier to the moon and the music and the rustling presence of the animals in the darkness beyond the circle. Pony pulled it over her head with one movement, swung it out into the darkness and whirled, arms above her head, laughing with the music.

Val played without thinking, eyes only for the white figure capering naked against the bloodred moon with such grace, in such perfect syncopation with the notes wrenched from his pipe. He was dimly aware that animals, large and small, stood outside the circle of strange, huge stones; they throbbed with the music and the moon just as Epona did, just as he himself did. The pulsing in his chest was echoed by a throb in the entire earth. His fingers danced furiously over the holes in his flute, trying to match Pony's whirling pace—and he did, perfectly.

He gasped for breath, heart pounding, loins pulsing. As the song echoed into the dark, his member hardened. He was male, and alive—so alive he hurt with it! He knew he would never remember these notes, given to him as they were by the confluence of her lithe white body, her mane of incandescent hair, the red moon paling as it rose over the stones and the heartbeats of the animals around them. He was drawn into a world conjoined, belonging together. He and his notes belonged in it. The night could not do without him: he was part of it and the moon, part of Pony and her dance. Those two things pulled the world into autumn. The spirit of the world, or of Odin and Freya, or of Pony's horse goddess, coursed in the air and the earth and the stones and the moon and the beasts and his music. He belonged.

Pony leapt and came down like an arrow shuddering in the ground, her face raised in a shriek at the moon. She trembled and was still just as the last note from the Viking flute faded away. Lowering her head slowly, she felt energy pulse through her heaving chest and down toward a deeper core of her. Val stared, transfixed. She half-expected horror in his eyes, but she saw only the showering sparks of the fire reflected and amplified. Around her the animals stirred. Was it time for them to go? The night air seared her nose, her lungs. She should be feeling lost, bereft of power, now the dance was done: That was always the way of it.

But the season wasn't finished. Its call still pulsed inside her. What was happening? Was her dance not done? Pony shook her head and found herself distracted by a pair of hares off to her left, heaped together. Their frantic movement told an old story. Her eyes drifted up. Slepnir, glowing red in the firelight, nipped First Mare's neck. Pony's mount arched her neck under the stallion's delicate nibbling and lifted her tail in an elaborate sweep. *First Mare!*

Pony jerked her head around the stone circle. Everywhere animals were pairing off, the spirit of the moon infusing them. Her own loins ached as though they would break. Slowly, against her will, Pony's gaze was drawn back to Val. He stood. Fire still gleamed in his eyes, though he was silhouetted by the flames. Pony felt that fire jolt through her veins, pool in her center and build for release. Before she could stop herself, she moved toward him, reaching out. That he was carnivore seemed not to matter. The goddess drove her to comprehend the moon through human flesh.

Val's cloak fell to the blanket. His twisted silver armbands clenched his biceps. Pony wanted to do that. He ripped at the lacing of his vest, and her hands met the flesh of his chest and smoothed the leather off. Val's fingers worked the ties of his breeches. Pony moved him backward toward the blankets and the piles of their clothing. The moon was growing colder, but the fire burned hot. Somehow it had got into her veins.

She touched the swell of Val's chest, pressed her thumbs against his nipples. His skin was feverish in spite of the night. He looked like he might bare his teeth and growl at any moment. But, it did not matter. The Mother drew her on. She pressed herself against him, breasts to his belly, it produced not growls, but groans from both of them. Pony's thighs felt slick. She pushed him and he pulled her with him as he fell.

She shoved herself up with her hands on his shoulders and just looked at his body, but almost completely bare. It was a fine body. Strong. Val's erect member trembled in anticipation. So did Pony. She laid herself along his length as his boots came off. His groaning became more desperate, more needful. The two of them were naked, flesh to flesh at the navel of the circle. Her hair brushed his shoulders. She knew what she wanted, what the Goddess wanted. And she wanted it, too. With Val. It had always been him she wanted. He had always called to her in a language she had not recognized, but the Goddess knew firsthand.

A tiny thought intruded. What if she damaged the girl-child she carried? But all around her stags mounted their does, shrews rolled in ecstasy, birds batted their wings to hold their place on their mates. The Goddess demanded, and Pony wanted to answer more than she had ever wanted anything in her life. She parted her knees and knelt across Val's hips, the swollen shaft lying along his belly nesting into that spot between her legs. The thick juice she exuded allowed her to slide along it.

Val moaned and gripped her upper arms. "Pony," he whispered with all the longing, all the melting heat she felt herself.

She grinned. Did her eyes glow as his did? Was it the moon that lit them or the passion that boiled inside them both? She rubbed herself along his shaft again. It did not relieve the ache inside her, but rather intensified it, as though she might split herself, or he might split her. He drew her forward, pressing her to him, and rolled her over. She spread her knees, longing for him to pierce her; arched herself, inviting him to bury himself in her; wanted to swallow his member with her body.

He lay between her legs, his erection pushing at her but not entering. He bent his lips to hers, his thick hair curtaining their faces. Those soft lips brushed hers once, then pressed more hungrily. His tongue penetrated her mouth, licking her own tongue, then exploring her with thrusting urgency. She returned the action. His breath was hot. The curling, light hairs of his chest, pressing against her breasts, made her faint. She pulled back and examined his face; the lashes that brushed his cheeks, the lips that curved. She knew that curve now as she knew First Mare's liquid eyes. Had she always known it? How had she not recognized him when first he came to her hut beneath the sign of the horse? He was carnivore and she was prey, but tonight they were part of some whole spirit the Mother claimed for her own. Pony arched into him.

The silken knob of his member pressed harder and slipped inside her. She opened to him and he eased in farther, then out a little. He pressed again, and she crushed herself against his careful thrust. If he was looking for the breaking of her maidenhead, it would never come. So she thrust up and took him all, the whole length of him, inside her.

Their mutual groan of satisfaction exchanged their breath. They writhed together, trying to get closer. There *was* no closer. They were animals copulating at the direction of the Goddess, under her moon in the navel of the world. As Val slid in and out, Pony found the rhythm of his thrusting. It was the rhythm of the seasons, the phases of the moon, the flow of her menstrual cycle, the tides of the sea, the ebb of the rivers. She matched it, was one with it, riding that rhythm toward the center of the earth, where all was dark and all would be revealed. Over Val's shoulder the moon crested the great lintel of the eastern portal stones. *I am yours, Goddess. Fill me.*

She was about to burst. Val quickened, and Pony began to grunt, reaching for the energy, straining toward fullness. He slowed for three strokes, careful, not fully entering her. *No, don't stop,* she thought, frantic. Then, when he thrust into her again, banging against her fully, faster and faster, she wanted to shout in affirmation. *"Yes!"* Before she could, the Goddess answered. The end washed over her in shrieking, head-shaking waves. She bucked against Val as he stilled and arched. She slid him in and out until he groaned and she felt a jerking inside her, and she pulsed against him, starting the waves again in echoes of her first ecstasy.

He breathed in uneven gasps of air, then melted against her, falling to the side and cradling her tenderly into his shoulder. "Pony," he whispered. "Pony." His lips touched her hair.

"Val," she sighed as the energy washed out of her. She felt heavy, so tired she could not think what had happened, what would happen next. Lazily, she turned her head. In the darkness beyond the fire she saw Slepnir still mounting First Mare, his own back arched across hers as she braced her hind legs apart to hold his weight.

First Mare, she thought sleepily. *We both felt the Goddess tonight.*

She watched the moon shrink to a shard of ice as it rose in the sky. Valgar had drawn the cloaks up over them, and Slepnir's blanket kept the damp of the earth away. The coals of the dying fire still spread a glowing warmth over her right side.

What she had done tonight felt right. Samhain had demanded it. How strange that was! Pony trembled. The ecstasy of Samhain always transformed her, but never had she felt that need for another in her loins, never had the fire inside her demanded mating. How different than her time with Alfred! Had she brought on this aberration by failing to prepare herself with bathing and with oils for the dance, or was it because she had brought a man into the navel of the world? Or was it Val that made everything different?

She watched the moon course from the eastern portal stones to the western ones. Val's breath was soothing in her ear. Still, a creeping foreboding nibbled at the edge of her brain. *Why* had the Great Mother wanted this night to happen? She had already answered the mother's call and done what was required with Alfred. Was the frenzy of last night required, too?

These thoughts were disturbing, but Val's arm across her belly and his sex, quiescent against her thigh, were comforting. They spoke of something primitive and elemental, like the animals who had disappeared now that it was over. First Mare and Slepnir grazed quietly off beyond the circle, their frenzy gone, too.

Why had First Mare yielded to the Viking stallion when she had resisted the leader of her own herd for years? Pony didn't know. But she did know she didn't want the night to end. She wanted to stay with the Viking predator forever. Yet the moon coursed relentlessly across the heavens. It looked cruel, so small and cold, as it did.

The sun was warm on their backs when Val stirred beside her, and Pony squinted against the light. All trace of Samhain was gone. She was just Pony once again. Val was just a Viking marauder fighting against her rightful king, carnivore if man ever was one. He was the antithesis of what her mother's claimed she was. But at least she had her destiny ahead. Pony's hand moved over her belly. She was breeding. She had filled her mother's command.

Why did the prospect not hold more satisfaction?

Val lifted his head, his eyes full of sleepy contentment, his face inches from her own. *"Gothr morginn,"* he whispered.

His arm about her waist under the cloak suddenly seemed heavy, physical. She could feel the hairs on his thigh against her flesh. The thigh was hot. The very rumble of his voice into the brisk air almost erased the sounds of early insects and the cooing of the mourning doves in the distance. His breath brushed her cheek. She seemed to flush everywhere. *No,* she thought. *That feeling belongs to Samhain, and Samhain has passed.*

Val's gray eyes darkened, not in anger but with that something she had seen before and could not name. She thought she knew now what the look meant. She felt his member swell against her thigh. And now she knew that the wetness between her legs meant she was ready for him. Her heart thumped against her ribs, drowning out all sound. She felt like First Mare last night, unable to resist Slepnir. Except now was not last night, and she still could not resist Val.

He brushed his lips across her neck. Pony shuddered along her whole body. But the gooseflesh that ran down her left arm and leg could not distract her from her fascination with the way Val's wavy hair dropped over his muscled shoulder when he bent to kiss her, or the way that muscle bunched and rippled under his silken skin. "Pony," he breathed into her ear, and his breath seeped into her soul, tempting her, luring her on toward something she had not known until last night.

She rolled into him, her nipples brushing his chest, then pressing into the curling hairs of their own accord. His thigh captured hers. The feel of its thick muscles clenching against her was a sweet threat. Her breath shuddered in and out as his arm enfolded her. He was fully erect. His member pressed against her belly and she pressed back. A roaring in her ears blotted out the world's sound. "Val," she might have murmured.

One of his rare smiles lit his face with tenderness. It was so strange to see his features changed as if by magic into those of someone who looked forward expecting wondrous events, not backward at pain and hard experience. Did predators look like that? Could she have been mistaken about him? She lifted her lips to his, just brushing them, wondering where she found the strength not to clutch at him, or scream for him to take her immediately. His lips sought hers again, and this time he tilted his head and explored her mouth more fully. When his tongue slipped inside and ran around her lips she was shocked and delighted. She returned the gesture and felt him tremble under her hands on his back. He thrust his tongue against her teeth, urging them to part. His groans of need were drawn into her lungs with each gasping breath. But his hands moved over her body with great deliberation. His callused palms, hardened from battle, roved from her back to her backside, pressing her against him.

She touched his erection, eager to pull him inside her. Gently, he shook his head. "I want this not like last night," he whispered softly.

"Why?" she asked, taken aback.

"There is another Language of Touch," was all he would say. Instead, he pressed her hip away, her left thigh still his prisoner, so that her knees were opened as she rolled to her back, naked to the morning air. She felt exposed, her most private parts available for use. But it did not feel wrong or bad. Her private parts should be used, must be used, again and again, often, now.

Val seemed in no hurry, though. His hand explored her body, cupped her breast, ran over the ridges of her ribs, lingered over her hipbone before descending to stroke her thighs. Then he did a most surprising thing. He touched her wetness and rubbed it up and down with his middle two fingers. Pony was suffused with tingling. Her world drew down to a single point between her legs. She spread her knees wider, opening herself even farther to him as sensation flooded in. She arched her pelvis against his hand, making his soft caresses serve the demands that were growing in her. She could not think, couldn't hear, could do aught but long for release. Her body was a tumultuous cacophony of sensation.

"Pony, my Pony," he whispered in her ear. It sounded far away. Then his mouth was suckling her nipples. The sweet drawing of his lips pushed her over some edge she had not known was ahead of her and she cried out, bucking against Val's hand as her body jerked with contractions so powerful she thought there might be some spirit inside her fighting to get out. On and on the sensation beat across her in waves, until she clenched her face and shrieked. At the apex of her shriek she jerked away from Val's hand.

"You are the death of me," she whispered, shaking her head violently from side to side, as though to shake the fit from her body. At last her breath gave out, and her head lolled back. Her senses started creeping back.

The first sensation to assault her was the hard rod of Val's erection throbbing against her thigh. His need was not yet assuaged. Languid as she was, she could not deny him his own release, since she knew firsthand how demanding his body must be. It would like to drive him mad if he got no release. Or perhaps it would drive him mad to get it. She was mad, for certain. A surge of life seemed to pool within her, not in spite of her release, but because of it. She pulled at his shoulder, smiling, urging him atop her. He crawled between her open thighs, holding the weight of his torso off her with his elbows.

Pony's hands moved around to the swell of his buttocks. His member pushed at her, begging entrance. Staring into his gray eyes dark with need, she pressed him into her, gasping as she did. She was lifted from the cloaks as he took her in his arms, then he pulled out and thrust inside her again.

She could see him try to restrain himself. He stroked in and out once more, slowly. But his need had been denied too long in favor of her own. A moment later he clutched her to his chest and she matched his frantic movements. Soon he groaned and arched, stilled against her loins. She could clearly feel the odd pulsing as he loosed his seed inside her.

For just a time, she was sorry that Alfred's seed had already lodged there. This was the man who should have fathered her child. This was the momentous feeling worthy of someone fulfilling her destiny. The warmth she felt toward Val was more than she had ever felt for anyone, even her mother. Predator though he was, she belonged with him. She knew that in her loins, in her belly, in her heart.

He collapsed against her, bathing her neck in kisses. "I know not what powers your goddess gives you," he said. "I am not strong enough to stand against them. I am yours."

A chill shuddered through Pony. Did he think to stay with her? She had not been able to think at all while he was driving her mad with desire. In fact, she had not even been able to hear normal sounds about her, let alone achieve the calmness needed for her Gift. Now he was saying that he wanted to remain with her. And she had thought longingly of staying with him!

This could not be! She could not just cast off her destiny. Staying with Val meant giving up the solitude, calm, her Gift. And she had been considering just that! She could hear her mother's voice, admonishing, shocked at her actions. By the Mothers, *she* herself was shocked.

Pony pushed at his shoulders and struggled to sit up. Of a sudden, she had never felt so naked. She had made some terrible mistake here, lured by the time and the place. But *she* had brought *him* here. Looking back on the last month she saw that Val had become more and more a focus for her thoughts, even when they were apart. And he was man, and carnivore. What had she been thinking?

The pulsing she felt at her throat still shut out sounds around her. Panic surged up from her stomach. Had she already betrayed her Gift?

"I must go," she mumbled, clutching her cloak around her. The pulsing she felt at her throat still shut out sounds around her. She hardly saw the pain in the gray eyes that stared solemnly at her. She scrambled after clothes and boots scattered from last night's frenzy. *What about this morning's frenzy?* Her mind screamed at her. *There is no Samhain to excuse what happened here!*

First Mare! she called silently, pulling on her shirt. The horse continued cropping grass quietly, standing beside Slepnir in the dew. Pony heaved a ragged breath. Her friend could not hear her. Not with her call silenced by a thumping heart and the sweat between her breasts.

"Come, friend," she said aloud, her spirit falling. This was Val's fault. *He is a carnivore*, she wanted to shriek, *and you have given him your soul!* The voice inside her head sounded like her mother's. What had happened here was not for her!

Val rolled to where he could watch her. She knew he would realize she meant to leave him, and she dreaded that he would say a word to hold her back. But there was only silence. It pressed on her. She tied the laces on her leggings. She must away from here before she weakened and stayed forever. Her destiny was all she had. She pulled on her boots awkwardly and whistled. First Mare raised her head and ambled over. Pony spared a glance into the hard silence around her. The betrayal in Val's gray eyes slapped her. She turned away from the blow. Vaulting onto the bay mare's back, Pony then dragged her cloak over her lap and spun the animal toward the Vale. She dared not look back. In Val's hurt eyes lay betrayal of the Great Mother, abandonment of all her mother taught her, and of Pony's destiny itself. There could be no question of what was more important. She and First Mare cantered northeast, between the weighty sentinels of the standing stones. Herd streamed in their wake.

* * *

As Pony headed toward the White Chalk Horse, the chaotic feelings that had sent her cantering away faded—and with them all certainty. If she went back to her hut, Valgar would just come and find her. She couldn't allow that. Not after this morning, when she had proved she was not steadfast to her destiny. Even now the feeling of fulfillment in her body tugged her back toward him. Their lovemaking was a lure away from her mother's teaching and her destiny. Valgar was a carnivore, for the Mother's sake! But she had lain with him after she had fulfilled her duty to produce a girl child—and all her calm was shattered now. It had not been like with Alfred. It had been soul-wrenching. Not just because it was Samhain, but the next morning as well. She shuddered, but was afraid it was in remembered fulfillment rather than horror.

She slowed First Mare to a walk, and Herd followed her lead. Confusion surged inside her. Her mother's destiny suddenly did not seem enough, especially when that destiny ended the way it was meant to end. Was there no other way? What was her destiny? Just to stay in the Vale and talk to her horses? To dance on Samhain night and mark the seasons? That was what her mother had believed. Alfred's words echoed in her head: "These are troubled times. Your Gift must serve the greater good." Even Val bent himself to the greater good of his people—was he not concerned with loyalty and *law* above all else? So where was Pony meant to be? Had her mother been wrong all those years in her teachings?

The way home grew long. What did it matter? Her Gift seemed to have disappeared entirely, since even First Mare couldn't hear her. Some hope that it was Val who'd dimmed her Gift flickered inside her. If she was away from him. . . . If the coming of her child brought back her power . . . Her mother had not lost the Gift upon conceiving. Her powers had slowly waned until the Dread Day. Perhaps it could be the same for Pony.

She was stiff by the time she saw the chalk horse rampant in white upon her hill. Her hut seemed so small below it.

Her destiny seemed small here as well. She heaved herself from First Mare's back in her own dooryard. Herd wandered down to the meadow and the stream. The blank face of windows and her hut's open door were not welcoming. This was no longer sanctuary. What would her mother advise? No question. "Your destiny is to pass the Gift to a girl-child under the White Chalk Horse," her mother would have said.

But to what point? Why was the Gift passed down through the centuries? What good had it done her mother but to advance the coming of the Day? Who could want that? The Fecund Mother? Why? Questions whirled in Pony's brain until she trembled with fatigue. Her stomach clenched against the bile in her throat. The feeling of rebellion that rose within her was surprising, uncomfortable, unwanted.

Her mother had been wrong. The answer could not be just to pass the Gift and drift until the Day came to gobble you up like a greedy shadow gobbled light. Her mother hadn't lived in these times, or been challenged by Vikings and kings to be other than she was. To embrace one's destiny dumbly was not a virtue. One must embrace it with full thought and confidence. One had to be sure.

Pony realized she had been unsure of her destiny for a long time. Why else had she waited so long to breed a girl-child? Why, once she had done so, had her doubts not quieted?

Why had she almost sacrificed everything, rutting like a mare in heat with a Viking? Her rebellion knew no bounds. She didn't want to drift away from life until she reached the Dread Day. Her mother had embraced that Day, created it. But that was not for Pony. Yet what would take its place? Helping Alfred to *his* destiny? And how could she help him if her Gift was lost? What if it did not come back, even when she had banished all thought of clutching Val between her legs until she lost herself in ecstasy? What if the Gift was gone for good?

There must be a way to find sureness of her destiny, to

get her Gift back. What she needed was someone to tell her how. Alfred had that. The witch or saint, whoever she was in the fenland to the north and east, had told him his destiny. That was how he was sure. She needed that, too.

Pony walked slowly into her hut. What to do?

Perhaps she could get sureness in the same place Alfred had got his. . . . Could she not herself journey to this witch in the fenland and get her to speak of the future? Yes! But it would be a long way. She had never been outside the Vale of the White Horse, except to Chippenham and to journey to the Standing Stones. She would have to take Herd with her, lest they fall prey to the likes of Osrick, or even the Vikings or Alfred. Finding them forage would make slow going. Winter would be coming on by the time she got there. *If* she could find the place, *if* the old woman existed, and had not died by now. The prospect of leaving all she knew and venturing into strange territory made her palms sweat. But the certainty that she would try was all Pony had. She was for the north and the wet fens.

Chapter Twelve

Pony sat on First Mare's back securely in the middle of the grazing Herd. It would rain soon, and they might as well stop for the day. They had covered little ground; but, if Pony wanted to be dry, an abandoned barn on the rise ahead, its ribs outlined against the coming storm, offered some protection.

She listened for signals of danger from the plant eaters in the fields ahead with little hope. Her Gift had been faint and sporadic. She heard nothing. A hawk circling on the updraft of lowering sky captured her attention. *What?* she asked. She stared up at the bird, and it cocked its head and swooped low. A tremor ran through Pony's shoulders and down her spine. Tears made the green and gray and brown of the world melt and run together. She felt the stab of an impression, visceral, churning. Her eyes seemed to dart here and there, though she knew what was happening. A faint squeak of fear thrilled her. Triumph welled and surged like life and strength in her veins as she dove—

Pony jerked her eyes away as the hawk dropped like a

stone to the stubble of the field, claws extended in a horrible attack. The shriek of the shrew's fear echoed in her mind. So, too, did the feel of the fat promise of supper as the shrew struggled in the hawk's claws. The bird flapped off toward the barn. Pony found herself sobbing, both for the death that was her own death careening through her brain and for the surging in her breast of the triumph of the killer that was her as well.

The world shuddered into quiet. Pony could hear nothing but her own blood singing in her ears, her own breath wheezing in her lungs. *What had happened here?* She had just heard a carnivore. She had never heard carnivores before, nor had her mother, or her mother's mothers before her. Her kind didn't. Worse, she had felt what it was to *be* a carnivore. She had known the triumph of killing that shrew. She did not want this. The chaos of killing—was that not like to destroy whatever was left of the Gift entirely?

First Mare curled her neck around to touch her nose to Pony's foot, wondering what was wrong. Pony got hold of her breathing and patted the horse's shoulder with a reassurance she didn't feel. She pointed First Mare toward the derelict barn. "I don't know whether the barn is safe. But that hawk considers it an excellent source of mice."

That night in the part of the barn that still had a roof, huddled with the mares and foals of Herd, she had a hard time finding comfort.

Val trudged along, leading Slepnir. It had started to rain. The long line of *Danir* wound up out of the valley, the smoking ruin of a fortress below. He rolled his shoulder, trying to ease the muscles in his back where he had taken a blow. Blood leaked from several cuts hastily bandaged, but they were not serious, just annoying. He hoped he had done the right thing in leaving Svenn here in charge of Cirencester.

The man had seen him chewing his lip in uncertainty as Val had prepared to lead the main force on toward the river Severn. "*Ja,*" he had said, confirming Val's thoughts. "I will grow strong here." Then he had half-chuckled. "But to challenge you, I will have to do as good a job as you have done in binding the land—and the Saxon barbarians—to my side."

Val soothed himself that Svenn's ambition would serve Guthrum's cause. Cirencester had been the first of a series of battles that stretched ahead, necessary to give Guthrum the island entire. And they were necessary to give Val the place he wanted among his fellows. He had thought his life would seem less empty when he lived among his people and was accepted by them. But it wasn't true. He was accepted now, if grudgingly. Ever since taking and holding Chippenham most *Danir* did his bidding, trusting his judgment. Even Saxons sought his opinion. He fought for his people, instead of as an outlaw on the steppes of the czars. But he had not lost the hollow feeling in his gut. For a time purple eyes and white hair and a moonlit night had banished it, but he was no longer so foolish. She had left him, just as she'd been sure she was all his heart craved. Why was he surprised? Abandonment was not new to him.

How did men find value in their lives? He looked around at his fellow *Danir*. They lived for adventure. Or to prove their prowess in battle, as though they were only alive when death stalked them. Or to have the satisfaction of possessing a hoard of silver. But these were the *Danir* who had left their homeland. What did the ones who stayed at home treasure? Working the land, feeling the change of the seasons, seeing their seed grow into sons, wedding their daughters with large dowries: were these things what made lives meaningful? Or something else?

It was not the gods. The gods had their own problems, since they knew full well that they would die at Ragnorok. If they thought of men at all, it was to torment them. The only reward that waited for a man was to die honorably in battle and be carried off by the Valkyrie. But to what? To battles every day and feasting every night, until the world was finally destroyed by the Fenris Wolf? Val could think of nothing less inviting than endless warfare.

Many Saxons worshipped *Kristr* now. Mayhaps they had

found meaning where Odin and Thor, Freya and Loki did not provide it. He would know more of this Christ cult. He turned to the priest. Now that Pony had left him . . . His heart clenched. How many times had that name leapt out at him in unsuspecting moments? Less than two days after the miracle in the circle of stones he had raced from Chippenham to obey Guthrum's orders to push west. He'd dared not stay close to her Vale, lest . . . lest he knew not what. Rivulets of rain coursed down his neck. *Get back,* he thought at the name. He sucked in a breath. There—he raised his eyes to the line of *Danir* trudging west at his command—that was better. He continued his thoughts.

Now that Pony had left him, Val had brought the young priest along as an icon; he would show the world he was supported at least by the god of the *Kristr* cult. He motioned the priest forward. The man's robe was soaked, his sparse beard dripping, but he quickened his step to match Val's. When he came abreast, he peered out from his cowled hood with questioning eyes.

Val cleared his throat. "What is your name, Priest?" he asked after a moment.

There was a glint in the young man's blue eyes. "To you I am 'Priest.' "

He was right. They had served on the council, shared the road for days together. Yet Val knew not his name. He was more a function than a man. "I would you were more."

The man nodded but seemed wary. "Father Elbert."

"Young to be a father," Val growled.

"Age is not the issue." Father Elbert's voice was sure of itself.

Sureness. That was what Val wanted for himself. He had been very sure once, in a circle of stones, but that sureness was lost. He meant to replace it if he could. The rain slackened. Blue broke through the clouds to the west. "Were you trained in your religion as a boy?" Mayhap he had known nothing else but this worship of a sacrificed god.

Father Elbert shook his head. "I took my vows when I was more than twenty."

Val nodded, pleased. It meant the priest's course had been considered. "Why?"

Elbert peered at him, then glanced away self-consciously. "I felt the call to serve."

"Your god *called* you?"

"In a way. My people called me. I believe God spoke through them."

"How did your people call?" Sun cast the world into sparkling clarity. All around, the tramp of feet in the mud made squishing sounds among the clank of metal and the idle talk of Val's men.

"They needed hope in the next life, if not in this one. They needed a code to gentle this world. Christ's teachings provided both things, so I vowed to spread his Word."

"You must have had nothing to give up." Val's voice was hard.

"You are right. I renounced nothing I cared for—only my place in my father's house, his land and his possessions after his death."

"And these things were not of value." Val was disappointed but not surprised. If the priest had given up something of value to pursue this idea, then it might be what Val had been seeking all his life.

"Judge for yourself. Osrick is my father."

Val's head snapped around. "Osrick?" The man had given up the riches of a *jarl*?

"The things were not important," the young man assured him. His face was calm, serene.

Val was shocked. And the priest would bear watching. A son of Osrick could be a spy. Of course, so could any Saxon. He was also impressed by young Elbert's choice. A horse came thundering back along the line, its rider waving a raven pennant. "There is a stream and a place to camp not a mile from here," he reported breathlessly.

Val touched his helmet. "Show the vanguard."

The sun reddened where it was setting through the clouds. It made the rain water gleam like drops of blood in the Danes' hair, on their mail, in their horses' manes. Val urged Slepnir ahead, then wheeled, plunging. "We will talk again, Priest Elbert. I would know more of your God."

Pony asked at every opportunity for the direction of the Witch of the Fens. Mostly she got blank stares. A few told of an old evil living in the swamps, a monster who ate children and caused the water to burn. Such tales did not sound promising, but the way the people pointed was ever to the northeast. So Pony and Herd continued. What other choice did they have? The comfort of home was lost to Pony, as was her sureness about her destiny. Only Herd was constant—and Pony's relationship with them was changed by the recurrent fading of her Gift. Now she'd become afraid of even trying to hear them. She'd told herself the hawk had been an aberration—and perhaps it was—but the existence of such an aberration changed everything.

The way was slow. Herd needed many hours of grazing to fuel its travel. It was fast over the distance to be covered in a day, but then it required rest and food. And pasture was sparse as November turned to December. Many high dead weeds were lined below with green fuzz growing from black earth, but such grass was new and hardly worth a mouthful. Grazing became hard work. In search they went more than a day out of their way on several occasions, looking for a place to ford a river. Thus Herd grazed and walked and walked and grazed its circuitous way to the northeast. Pony herself gathered sorrel in the woods to supplement her flatbread, and ate small hard apples she stole from a farmer's field.

The land grew flat, flatter than Pony had thought anything could be, and the sky grew big with racing clouds. Long days of wet were blown away by winds that tangled the flag of her hair and infiltrated the folds of her cloak, chilling her.

At last Pony drew near the town of Ely, just after the passing of the winter solstice. Snow lay on the ground. Ely was the site of a large monastery. Its stone tower rode the fog in the morning sun more than a league away. It would be a good place to ask after the witch. Those who studied religion would surely know the whereabouts of a practitioner of the older arts—one must know the competition, after all.

Pony left Herd grazing in a meadow and climbed with First Mare to stand on one of the old straight roads. A small man with tonsured head and rough brown robe approached. The monastery had come to her.

The man's brown habit was tied at his waist with a simple knotted rope, his fingers worked a string of beads. "Greetings, Brother," Pony called, secure atop First Mare's back. "What is your name?"

He looked up rather shyly from under his lashes. His eyes took in her wild white hair and her horse. Then they strayed to Herd, grazing in the meadow below, and widened. The little monk understood that Herd belonged to her. "Father Alphonse, child," he answered. "And you?"

He was rather unassuming to be a Father. Of course, the Christ cult called men to be fathers, whereas she came from a line of mothers. Were they opposites, or were they halves of the same whole? "My name is Epona. I would ask direction of you."

He smiled—a wonderful, simple smile. It touched his lips, glowed out of his face, lighted his eyes. Pony liked him. "May God grant that I know what you seek to learn."

Pony took a breath. "I seek a witch who lives in the fens. Do you know of her?" She prepared for a sign against the evil eye, or simply a rough refusal.

The little monk looked consternated. "Well . . . yes, depending."

"Depending upon what?" Pony asked, surprised.

"Which witch you were wanting." He shrugged, as though that were an explanation.

"Oh." First Mare sidled under Pony. "How many are there?"

"Well . . . the one that was, and the red-haired one."

"Oh, dear. I know not. I only know she told Alfred of Wessex he would be king."

Father Alphonse nodded, pleased with himself. "Ah, you want Britta; the red-haired one. If you wanted the other one, you would be disappointed—for Britta killed her, I think."

Great Mother! Still, she had come too far to lose courage. "Where is this Britta?"

A wary look came into the little monk's eyes. "Many seek her. Not many succeed. The fens are dangerous, and she does not help all who go to her. What do you want?"

Would he refuse direction if he didn't like her answer? "I would know my destiny," she decided to say.

"Everyone thinks they want to know their destiny." Father Alphonse shook his head sadly. "But it really does not work out well in most cases. And Britta won't throw the bones or read your palm in return for copper pennies, you know."

Pony pressed her lips together. Must she tell this stranger everything in order to find her way? Perhaps she could find someone else to ask. Still, he knew this Britta. And then there was his smile . . . She took a breath and let her shoulders slump as she expelled it. After chewing her lip for a moment she said, "I want to know how to use my Gift to best advantage."

"Ah, I understand, child." Pony doubted and started to explain. "No, no, don't tell me. That is between you and your God." Alphonse fumbled with his beads. "And yet . . . going to Britta could be fire to tinder. I revere her, of course. Who would not? She is a saint. But she frightens me as well."

A saint who kills people? Pony thought. Alfred had said she'd brought a faesten down and killed thousands. She'd killed the other witch, too.

Four other monks in rough brown habits scrambled up onto the raised road and hurried toward the pair. "Oh, dear," Father Alphonse murmured. "I have not much time." He turned to search Pony's face. She could see him form his conclusion. "God put you in my way today." He squared his shoulders. "Britta lives in the village of Stowa, straight north of here some two score miles, in a place called Wicken

Fen. Take the road from Ely until it peters out, then keep to the chalk plateaus, for the bogs are treacherous." He glanced behind him to the approaching monks.

"Father Alphonse," one called, out of breath. "We are so glad to find you."

Pony realized she had held her breath only when it sighed from her lungs. "Thank you," she said.

The little monk was soon surrounded by the others, all of whom surpassed him greatly either in height or in bulk. "Father, Father," one admonished. "Must you come out to the road alone?"

"It is hardly seemly for the head of our order," another exclaimed, bowing his head.

"A road where anyone may accost you." The tallest frowned at Pony and First Mare.

Father Alphonse shrugged in embarrassment at Pony. "The church sometimes gets between its children and their best intentions. Locking ourselves away does not teach us what the people need," he admonished the other monks in a soft voice, but he allowed them to bundle him away. "Today, someone needed to find the Witch of the Fens. And coming after me gives one a break from illuminating manuscripts, does it not?"

The brothers stopped herding him. They had the grace to look abashed.

He glanced around at them. "Ah, well. A walk in the wood with me will clear your eyes and steady your hands." The little monk then, the surprising head of his order, smiled at Pony once more. Seeing the smile, she thought his position was perhaps not so surprising.

Very well, she thought as she turned to the north. The clouds boiled black against the horizon where her destination lay. She clucked to Herd. She would go to this Britta who killed but could tell your destiny. Father Alphonse called her unpredictable. Pony wondered what that meant. It didn't sound good, but she would go to Wicken Fen.

* * *

Val put his feet up on a bench in the hall of the captured town of Bath and lifted a mead horn to his lips. Around him his weary troops celebrated yet another victory with feasting. *Just like Valhalla*, he thought grimly, as a comely Saxon wench snuggled willingly into Harald's lap. The *Danir* had grown accustomed to the stricture against rapine, but there was nothing Val could do if the women hung about Danish necks and kissed Danish ears.

His bones ached. Not the least his hip, where a lance had pierced it. It had been bound, and no ligaments were cut. He could do with some time for healing. He had been lucky. Some of his fellows had not. They had buried nigh on a score after the battle today. He had thought this place undefended since its *jarl* was long gone. But there had been mustered a basic resistance. He should not have let it take him by surprise. He was getting soft.

Soft or not, he must take some days to rest, as must his men. He had already met with the local elders. He was used, now, to their incredulous stares as he told them the terms of conquest. Still, he kept his face stern as he told them they must give one part in ten to the common good and as he iterated his piece about the council and the *law*.

Val drained his horn and banged it against the bench. Once he would have used this time to soothe his soul with the music of his flute. But no more. He had not played since . . . well not in a long time. The flute stuck in his boot accused him. He should abandon it, but he could not, not just yet. Raucous laughter echoed from the corner near the fire. Men cast dice made from carved antler. Others played a game of *hneftafl*. The remains of a feast sat on a giant trestle table at the other end of the room. He leaned against the tapestries that kept the winter at bay. This hall was almost worthy of a *jarl* in *Danmork*.

A girl hurried over with a leather mead sack. Maybe he needed a woman. If he smiled on her, might he not get this one to crawl into his bedbox tonight? Then would it truly be like to a night in Valhalla. But he didn't smile at her. His

191

mouth simply wouldn't obey. The girl had not purple eyes and Valhalla had come to seem stale.

The priest, Elbert, brought a plate filled with roasted trout from the local streams, flatbread, small red berries called currants and some of the root vegetables Pony had liked so. *Pony. No, none of those thoughts,* he admonished himself.

"Where have you been, Elbert, son of Osrick?" His voice was rougher than he intended.

"I have seen the local priest." The younger man sighed, sitting. "You know, it would go well if one or two of your men would agree to be baptized."

"Ah." Val gulped mead, frowning. "The dunking. It is the sign of a choice of gods."

Elbert nodded. "Is it so bad?"

Val snorted. "It is disloyal. The Norse gods can be vengeful if they are ignored."

Elbert looked at his plate. "They need not be ignored."

"That is like serving two *jarls*." Val raised his brows. "Such a man is loyal to neither."

"Hear me," Elbert entreated. "We celebrate the birth of Christ at the winter solstice. Is that not when Danes feast to ward off Fimblevader, the winter that lasts for years and signals that Fenris Wolf will end the world in Ragnorok?"

"You know much," Val observed.

"I listen," the priest said. That got Val's attention. Other conversations about listening drifted into his memory and had to be banished.

"And do you not sacrifice to Freya," Elbert continued, "goddess of crops and Spring, just when we are marking the sacrifice of Christ's body and his risen soul? We call it Easter."

Val nodded. "It is called Oester, too, with us."

"Where do you think we got the name?" Elbert smiled, eyes glinting. "It is much easier to find adherents when the new is not so much changed from the old. We are very practical."

"So you are saying that *Danir* could have this dunking

and yet not ignore their own gods?" Val was thoughtful. It would integrate the peoples more surely than just *law*. The priest was a leader born. And yet, to abandon one's gods—was that not the ultimate disloyalty?

"Not without your sanction," Elbert said seriously. "Else I create rebellion in your midst."

"A man must believe in his religion." Val sat forward. He held out his horn to a passing girl, who squirted mead in it until it frothed at the brim.

"For you. Others are more practical, *Jarl.* They want to take wives. Girls' fathers see your Danes as barbarians too strange to be given daughters in wedlock. And the girls will not wed without their fathers' leave. What better way to prove they are not strange than to convert?"

Val sighed. It would happen just as the priest said, whether he himself agreed or no. Yet without his permission, the converts must rebel. Which would not serve Guthrum's need. If Val embraced the conversion, it would bind people together. And was it his place to judge another's path to loyalty? He could only speak for himself. "Dunk any who want it, with my permission." Elbert nodded with a small smile. Val's eyes did not leave him. He was thinking of that earlier talk. He had a hole in his middle that needed filling, caused by something he didn't want to think about. "You must have believed, son of Osrick. You gave up position, wealth. Now you have nothing, unless you serve your father still."

Elbert sipped his mead. "My father hates me for taking my vows. I thought at first I took them to spite him." He gave a wry smile and stared off into the dim, smoky hall. "You know how it is with young men and their fathers."

Val closed his eyes against the memories of the rebellion that had caused his lifetime of bitterness and exile, the exile that did not seem like to end, though he had rejoined his countrymen. It was of his making as well as theirs. "*Ja*, I know what is between father and son." His voice did not shake. He could not help the weariness, but it did not shake. The men dicing around him had taken on an unreal quality, their game and their conversation a distant burring background to the memories hanging in the air between him and the priest.

The cleric touched the beads that hung about his neck then continued: "After a while, as I studied, I began to see the differences between Christianity and the old faith. I came to believe that one was truer than the other."

Val waited, but the man seemed disinclined to go on. He did not behave like most of these Christian louts who constantly exhorted everyone in sight. It was no wonder that some *Danir* were worn down. Still, what if their conversions were more than simple practicality? Had they found something he had not? The key lay in what each religion thought was worth achieving. What was Valhalla for the *Kristr* cult? He said. "You said your faith held hope in the next life. Of what?"

The priest laughed. "You will be disappointed, raider. The reward is nearness to God."

Val felt confused. "I see not the benefit."

"I did not think you would." Elbert hunched over, rubbing his beard in concentration. "A feeling of wholeness, a connection to the power of the world, a peace we cannot understand: that is the reward. Not just a repetition of our earthly struggles and triumphs."

Val grew thoughtful. Christianity offered something subtler than Valhalla, yet larger. "How do you earn this reward?" he asked. "You follow this code? Speak of it."

"A man must live a good life," the priest said, shrugging his shoulders.

"Good? Does this mean brave, honorable? Does it mean following his king?"

"No, it is more than brave, more than honorable. It means . . ." The priest thought hard. "It means being kind to those weaker."

"Ah, like women." Val nodded.

"Or poor, or sick, or different, or small in spirit." The priest now stared down at the fire in the hearth at the far end of the hall, as though he did not see the flames at all.

Valgar snorted. "This is a religion for weaklings."

"I think in some ways it is only for the strongest among us. I have not the strength enough for it. Only sometimes." Elbert sighed and smiled, his eyes focusing once more on Val's face. He raised his mead horn to Val, who clanked his own against it in turn. "To the strong," he toasted.

"To the strong," Val muttered thoughtfully and drained his horn.

Chapter Thirteen

The road to Wicken Fen became precarious, just as Father Alphonse promised. Herd stretched out in single file along the hard lime paths that raised above the reeds and stagnant water. It had snowed, making the way even more difficult. In places, hawthorn trees grew. Sometimes she saw a deeper, clearer pool of water, but mostly it was reeds and muck and thousands of birds Pony didn't recognize wheeling into skies boiling with clouds. It smelled of rotting vegetation under the snow. Foul, foul place—just right for a witch, Pony thought wretchedly. Why had she come here? What did she hope to gain? The contrast between this misery, which she had sought, and the feeling of being filled to overflowing with life and well-being that she had run from as she galloped away from the circle of stones, was almost too much to be borne. She shook herself and turned her eyes once more to the fen.

Trekking across it, from one safe path to another when each finally petered out, took careful planning. She looked across the incredibly flat landscape to find some other hump, sometimes disguised in trees. She would always go first, being the lightest, to test the footing. She was quickly soaked and caked with freezing mud.

It happened on the second day. Dun Mare strayed from the path that Pony had tested at such great cost. She was old and had no foal to shepherd. A grunt of surprise was her only noise, that and the sounds of splashing that made Pony whirl. She found Dun Mare thrashing in shallow water, her hind end slowly sinking into the muck. The horse's rolling white eyes and flaring nostrils showing red told everything. White Stallion whinnied. He put one foot in the water and then the other, testing ground that would not hold him, but quickly slid back on his haunches to security with a scream of frustration.

Pony's throat closed. She should never have brought Herd to this evil place. They belonged on downland slopes where grass grew for grazing and a horse could run in the clean wind. "Come on," she shouted as Dun Mare tried to pull herself out. But her front legs could find no purchase. Her struggles only made the sinking worse. Mud and water splashed over the horse and ran in rivulets down her back. Pony watched the struggle in horror. What could she do? She waded out as far as she could, until the mud gave under her. It was no use. The mare was too big for her to pull out by herself. She had no rope. She had never had time for them or for the dominion over horses that they signified— but she could have used one now. Though even three or four ropes tied to other horses might not have been enough to pull Dun Mare free.

First Mare's whinny split the air. The other horses sidled nervously up on the lime ridge, not sure where to step, where to run in this horrid place where every step held danger.

Finally the old mare got tired. Her breath came in heaving gasps. Her coat was lathered where it wasn't muddied. "Come on, Dun Mare," Pony whispered. "Try." But she knew it was no use. The old mare knew it, too. She stood

197

there, her hind end now almost submerged, her nostrils blowing. Soon it would be over.

Pony turned to White Stallion. "Go," she yelled hoarsely, her face contorted in anger and guilt. "They do not belong here." His eyes rolled. He could not possibly hear her when she was shouting at him. Pony closed her eyes so she couldn't see Dun Mare. She gulped against the lump in her throat, wondering how she could possibly get enough peace to practice her Gift with her gut in turmoil and her eyes leaking tears. *Mothers, give me calm,* she thought. *Please give me calm enough for just this thing, this one thing, to send them away.*

All she could feel was chaos in her breast. The need for calm made her frantic. She must act just as if she didn't need to call the Gift, as though calm were the last thing on her mind. She slumped where she stood, thigh deep in muddy water. She let her head sag on her neck. Accept. She must accept. A certain hopelessness crept into her, and with it came the sense of White Stallion, First Mare, the others, even Dun Mare. Dun Mare had accepted, even if none of the others had. Pony did not speak. She did not even think her words. She merely thought about awayness, of downland slopes and grass, even in winter.

When she opened her eyes, White Stallion was regarding her steadily with a large brown eye. Dun Mare was his mother. He tossed his head and picked his way slowly back to Herd on the plateau. When he came to First Mare, he stopped and waited for her to precede him. The mare stood her ground, staring at Pony. Pony thought about awayness, though she guessed First Mare, of all of them, had heard her clearly the first time. White Stallion flattened his ears and turned to nip the female's haunches with bared teeth, but she kicked out at him, then wheeled and shrieked, her own ears flattened as she moved out of his way. White Stallion looked as if he would challenge her for her disobedience. But she wasn't another stallion. She was First Mare.

He pushed past her and cantered up the plateau, circling round behind Herd, exhorting them. They turned and walked back along the plateau. They did not look back. Only First Mare was left. She cantered to the point on the ridge nearest Pony. There she stopped and waited.

Pony turned back to Dun Mare. Both she and First Mare would wait. It could not be long now. She struggled up out of the water to squat beside First Mare and watch what would happen here, lest some carnivore in this strange land come to take advantage of this opportunity.

The sounds of Herd diminished. Pony's tears dried in the freshening wind. Pony kept her heart silent. Her job was to wait.

It was a long time before she realized that Dun Mare wasn't sinking anymore. She pulled up her head and watched carefully. The horse stood with her haunches underwater, her breathing labored. Occasionally she thrashed a little. But she wasn't sinking.

Mothers, no! Not this!

If Dun Mare was denied the water as her end, what was left? Could Pony keep away the carnivores when night came? Or many nights? And if the carnivores could even be denied, what was then left for Dun Mare? Some slow death by starvation or freezing or . . . what? No, it could not be like that. Not for Dun Mare: part of Herd since Pony could remember, First Mare before her own partner, mother of White Stallion. Not for her was such death meant.

Meant? Meaning? *What meaning, Mothers?* Pony railed.

She felt her face wet with tears again, pushed out of her eyes from somewhere in her gut. That was her answer, though it frightened her in some corner of herself. So she shut that corner and looked around, dazed. How? How could one do such a thing? No answer came. She looked down at her hands. Once they had been white. Now they were muddy; black crescents at her nails; red and cold where she could see through the mud.

Acceptance. Loss of hope. Calm. They permeated the cold air. She walked down into the black water, now still, toward Dun Mare, now still as well—except for her heaving sides, the breath coming hard from her nostrils. Pony felt the black water welling up around her knees and then her thighs. It was like the water in the lake from her dream where her mother slipped beneath the water and Pony couldn't save her.

Her mother had accepted water that last day. Pony stood still, looking at Dun Mare's dark eyes, but her own turned inward. She saw again the lake lapping at her mother's feet, the calm acceptance in her mother's dying eyes.

"This day will come to you, Pony, after you have fulfilled your destiny," her mother said from far away. "You are ten now. I wanted to wait longer." Her mother's voice was a whisper, hardly heard above the lapping of the tiny wavelets on the lake. "But my time is on me. I have finally reached the perfect calm."

"No, Mother," Pony heard herself sob, her voice not that of a child, but the voice she had now. She had not known what to fear then, but she had feared it.

Her mother did not smile, did not reassure, did not reach out to hold her and tell her things would be all right. Her mother did not shed a tear. Her calm had gone beyond those things. She simply turned and walked into the water.

Pony walked in behind her, splashing, tugging at her mother's cyrtle, crying, shouting, making as much noise and as much trouble as she could, to break through that awful calm that had been coming over her mother, slowly, for months.

It was no use. When she felt the loom weights in her mother's pouch that had always held only herbs, she knew. Pony stopped when the water got past her waist. Through her tears, she knew that she couldn't stop this. Her mother was beyond her.

She watched as her mother walked into the lake until the water was over her head.

There was no struggle.

Her mother simply disappeared, leaving Pony along with all the other troubles of the world.

* * *

She never thought about this. That was why she always had the dream about the raft, where her mother slipped away from her into the clear black depths of the lake. It was an echo of the real slipping away that occurred over years, until Pony's mother drowned herself and left her to face a destiny drilled into her soul but not her heart. That was not all her mother left. She'd also left the threat that Pony herself would breed, *must* breed, and then would drift away from living as well, until she too committed some act of suicide. That knowledge weighed Pony down, as it always did, like the stones in her mother's pouch.

Pony's heart clenched against such a destiny. And yet, now, with Dun Mare, she needed to find some of that same acceptance that had let her mother embrace death. It was what Pony most feared. But it was what Dun Mare most needed.

She waded toward Dun Mare's shoulders—the horse's front hooves maintained some small purchase in the muck and snow—and the fen's black water caressed her waist. Pony shut away her fear and called the calm to connect with Dun Mare: calm like her mother's calm, which transcended all the shrieking in the world of horse or child. Acceptance. It flooded through her, making her feel . . . heavy. How strange! She had always thought that true calm would seem like floating away on air. Staring at Dun Mare, Pony saw her calm reflected in the horse's eyes. They were dark and liquid like the water that was up almost to Pony's breasts now, to her heart. Cold. She hadn't realized she was cold before. As she listened, she heard more than Dun Mare. Vultures, a feral dog. She was again hearing carnivores. With a shudder, she remained open to Dun Mare while pressing down her own fear. She reached to touch the dark nostrils that contrasted with the horse's light coat, pushed fingers through the beast's black forelock. Acceptance. Calm. Pony let it surround her like the black water.

The horse buckled at the knees and sank slowly into the dark water. Pony closed her eyes, once, and pressed the head under. There was no resistance. Only the bubbles breaking the surface, letting go the last of hope. *I accept.* It was Dun Mare's Dread Day.

Pony and First Mare wandered along the lime plateaus, heading north. The snow melted. They picked their way across the swampy interstices. That should have been fearful, but it was not. Perhaps all fear had been used up. Or perhaps Pony was just too numb to think after what had happened with Dun Mare. Or too calm. Was her mother's fate inescapable? Yes. She had felt what it would be like in a swamp north of Ely where she had used her Gift to kill one of her Herd. Why did she continue on? If she would end in the lake, if her destiny were foretold, what matter how she used her Gift? What matter that she wasn't sure as Alfred was? She was not important. Her destiny was what her mother had told her it was: to practice the Gift, produce a girl-child, wait for the day like Dun Mare's and her mother's.

Maybe she went on because she wanted to make Dun Mare's death count for something. It was on this silly quest that Dun Mare had been lost. To turn back was a betrayal. She had already betrayed one she cared for. She had seen the betrayal in his eyes. Probably she had betrayed her mother and the Goddess as well. She could not afford another.

She and First Mare walked side by side when they could, or single file. Pony couldn't risk the extra weight of riding. There was not much to eat in the swamps. First Mare found grasses growing in among the hawthorns. The hips of the berries on the guelder rose proved edible, if sour. Mostly there were just the strappy, razor leaves of the sedge that grew everywhere. And every day it rained, or snowed with great wet flakes.

The skies only cleared as they approached a larger plateau in late afternoon of the third day. Pens and huts—perhaps a score in all—gathered where herons and cranes stalked the edges of a large pond of clear water. The rhythmic clang of a smith working sounded somewhere. Women moved about the clearing tending a large communal fire crowded with pots. As Pony approached, a group of men appeared, climbing up the plateau from the other side with spades slung over their shoulders, pushing barrows. They were muddy and there was a weary set to their shoulders, but for all that they were jovial, singing some song in raucous voices. With a shock, she realized it was a song with *Denesc* words. She had been in the Danelaw for days. But she had assumed Stowa was a Saxon village. Could the Danes have murdered Britta the witch?

It came as almost a relief when a pretty woman with blond braids looked up from poking new blocks of some black earth into the fire. She straightened, and Pony saw that she was big with child. She elbowed the woman next to her, and soon everyone was staring at Pony.

A huge man limped out of the crowd of men. "Welcome," he said. "My name is Karn."

Pony breathed. He spoke in Saxon, but she recognized the accent from someone else who spoke that way. He was Viking. He had a Viking visage, sure. The planes of his face were hard, his eyes ice blue. His light blond hair fell past his shoulders. He, too, wore it in the Saxon style, not shorn at the nape. Others in the crowd held to the Viking way. Pony's danger came home to roost in her heart like a jackdaw. No one here knew she was Epona of the Horse Vale. Her status could not protect her. "My name is Epona," she whispered.

"Your *hestr* is fine." He used the *Denesc* word for horse. His smile did not reassure her.

But she could hold only to her purpose, the purpose for which Dun Mare had been sacrificed. "I seek the witch. The red-haired one," she added, remembering Alphonse's confusion.

The big Viking nodded. "Many come for her."

Perhaps these people knew the way to the old woman. Pony only hoped it was close.

"Come in and warm yourself," the pretty, pregnant blonde invited. "My name is Hild."

Pony pressed her shoulder into First Mare's; she didn't want to leave her.

The big Viking stepped forward. "I will care for your horse."

As if she were your own, Viking? No. thought Pony, and did not move.

He pointed to where a great bay stallion was making his way through a manger of fodder in a pen on the other side of the village. "Thorn would like the company."

First Mare made the decision with her stomach. She followed the big Viking toward that full manger. It had been a long three days. Pony's own stomach had stopped growling, but the scents rising from the pots in the fire tantalized. She followed First Mare's lead.

Pony watched Hild pass her a steaming plate of stewed cresses. Hild was definitely Saxon, though Pony could hear Danish words sprinkled in her speech. "Where is this witch?" Pony asked through a full mouth. "I must speak with her." Hild's fire was welcome.

"Britta? She gathers herbs. Tonight we celebrate the repair of the dike. She will be there."

"The witch comes to town?" Pony had imagined a solitary crone hermited in the wilds.

Hild looked surprised. "She lives here."

Pony started. What village would harbor a witch. "Is she the one who sees the future?"

Hild pressed her lips together. "I will speak not of Britta." But she held out a clean cyrtle and some knitted stockings for Pony. "I have no clothing like yours, but I am much your size. This fit me before the babe gave me a belly."

Pony sighed and smiled. "That they be dry is all I require. I have not been so wet in my life, though standing naked in the rain or swimming."

Hild laughed. "You are not native to the fens, then. We may not be rich in silver, but we are rich in wet."

Pony took the clothing gratefully as Hild excused herself to tend the pots. She dressed and stood in the doorway of the blonde's little hut. The village prepared for a feast. Pony had not enjoyed the noise of a busy village since Chippenham and Val.

Val. The memory of him between her legs threatened to overwhelm her. And it was the limping Viking, Karn, who brought the thoughts. It was the deep rumble of his voice that went with his accented Saxon. Once the idea of a Viking leading a village where Saxon and Dane lived together would have been unthinkable. But not since Pony had seen Val in Chippenham. She pushed her thoughts away and let the sound of clanking pots, the crush of voices, soothe her. What about the mysterious witch who lived in a village? That was proper fodder for her thoughts.

Her eyes were drawn to Karn. He had changed his muddy clothing and, as the dusk closed in, he was hauling stones from the fire in a great iron cauldron to a tiny hut a quarter the size of a normal house. Trip after trip he made. He closed up the only window of the hut with solid shutters. Then he turned a wheel on a frame near the side of the little dwelling, and a gate rose. Water sluiced through a channel and right into the hut. Why would you let water into your house?

As she watched, Karn straightened and his eyes were caught. His face lit from within. A smile flitted across his lips and then was half-suppressed. "Britta!" he called, striding forcefully across the bustle of the common area in spite of his limp. Pony's gaze jerked across the flood of activity, looking among the whirl of color and movement for . . .

There. A slight woman in her prime, her hair a red halo shot through with one single streak of white. Her face lit, too, and she strode forward as well as she could with a baby in one arm and the other holding a large basket brimming with flowers and weeds. Most startling of all, at her side trotted a great black dog, wolflike and thickly furred.

"Wife," the Viking boomed. She was his wife? They met not many feet from where Pony stood. Karn took Britta's basket from her. She moved the babe to her other arm.

"You sound as though you were calling hogs," the surprising witch objected, her face half-serious. The dog barked a greeting and capered about.

"*Ja,*" he said, taking her into the shelter of his arm. "Hogs and wives are much the same."

She leaned her head into his chest. "Don't say another word. You will make me angry."

"Odin preserve me from that," he joked. And his smile so softened the hard lines of his face that Pony could only wonder at the transformation. "Perhaps a bath will help your mood. The stones are heated and ready."

"Ahh, you know the way to my heart, Viking." The young woman sighed.

As Pony watched, Karn drew his wife toward the tiny hut. Steam leaked from its one closed shutter. "That is not the only thing I know my way into," he murmured. "Shall we leave the child with Hild?"

She smiled slyly at him. "Are you proposing to join my bath, tired as we both are?"

"Hmmm." Their voices were growing distant to Pony. "There are other times."

"You may join me if you will." Britta looked Karen up and down. "You could use a bath."

"And I have news of a visitor."

That was the last Pony heard. She watched the red-haired woman hand her baby to Hild. The witch could not be more than twenty-eight, and she was married to a Viking with whom she seemed besotted. And she had a child. This did not seem like a woman who could foretell destiny. Pony felt a sigh of disappointment flow through her. Her journey was in vain. Dun Mare had died for naught. Tears welled inside her, but they would not be loosed.

Her next impulse was to flee. But she and First Mare were too tired, too hungry. They must depend upon the generosity of this village for a day or two at least. She hoped that when she left, she would leave with First Mare; the Viking had seemed to covet her. Yet, no pen such as the one Pony had seen would ever hold First Mare against her will. That was a comfort.

As the Saxon and Danish folk of Stowa made their way to the central hall, Hild came to get her. "The color looks well on you, Epona," she said of the golden ocher cyrtle.

"Thonc to thu," she replied, "for lending it." And then they went to the feast.

It turned out to be the most frustrating of Pony's life. Not that the town did not welcome her. She met Hild's very Viking husband, Jael, with his shaven nape and long braids covering his ears. Hild's father, Walther, was the smith, a wise man with huge corded forearms. There were Snurri and Frel, Frel's wife Syffa and a Viking called Bjorn the Bear-Hearted, who looked like his namesake. Food was passed and songs were sung, some in Saxon, some in Norse, and one, about the razing of the faesten at Thetford, in a strange mixture of the two.

They talked about their day and how the dike had been rebuilt. Babies cried and were rocked. Pony had never seen the life of a village up close. Everyone seemed to know so much about each other. They asked about her, where she was from, what she did. None had been to the Downland, but they understood shepherds, so they all nodded when she said she had a herd of horses there. Still, the interaction was uncomfortable. Especially when all she wanted was to talk to the witch. But Britta and Karn sat in a corner as far away from her as possible, the woman glancing up nervously at Pony from time to time. They whispered together, Karn soothing as he put his arm around her shoulders.

Britta unbuckled the brooch of her cyrtle at one shoulder and pulled it down to nurse her child. It fascinated Pony. She herself would be doing that shortly. How did one know what to do? She had never seen a child up close. She looked at her own belly and wondered that she did not already see a swelling. It had been four months now. Still, she did not know anything about the breeding cycle. Perhaps she could ask Hild.

The feasting drew to a close without so much as an invitation to state her case privately. Pony realized she would have to speak in front of all. "Britta," she asked at last, across at least five people. "I must speak with you, if you are the Witch of the Fens, as Father Alphonse said."

Karn held his wife and the babe closer. "You have no need to do this," he whispered to her.

Britta looked reluctant and a little sad as she handed the babe to him. Then she beckoned, rising, and led the way out of the hall. She and Pony went through the dark and cold night, into a smaller hut, where Britta blew up the fire in the firebox.

"Many come for answers," she said as the coals puffed into red life, echoing her fiery hair. "I have so few to give them." She turned from where she crouched and motioned Pony to sit upon a bench. "Did Alphonse send you to me?"

Pony shook her head, swallowing. Was this really the witch who brought a faesten down? "I only asked directions of him. It was Alfred of Wessex who told me of your powers."

Britta sat on a corner of the bedbox. "Dear Alfred. Does he still think I am a saint?"

Pony nodded. Hope leapt into her throat. Britta knew Alfred. Surprising as it was, the woman was indeed the Witch of the Fens. "You told him his destiny. I want to ask you about mine."

The witch sighed. "I did not set out to tell him his destiny. Did he tell you that?"

Pony shook her head. What did Britta mean?

"I saw his destiny in the fire that burned most of his body. I healed him when he was as one dead." Her voice was hard. "But I did not mean to do that either." She looked up at Pony seriously. "The power does what it wants, not what I want. Something healed him, the world healed him through me, and I saw how it would be with him and with all of us down through the ages into future times. I didn't mean to see. I didn't ask to see."

Pony felt her world contract. "You mean you cannot see about me?"

"No. The visions come when they will. I can open myself to the will of the world, and sometimes something happens

. . . but sometimes not. The visions cannot be called."

Pony fought for calm. All this way for nothing. Dun Mare's death for nothing.

Britta reached out a hand and took Pony's as though she understood. "Is knowing your destiny so important? Our destiny is all the same: to live, to love, to bear children and to die."

"But Alfred is so sure about the future that he knows what he must do. I want that sureness, too," Pony whispered hoarsely.

"Perhaps Alfred was always sure. He has the confidence of men who are remarkable. Perhaps the vision of his future is only partly right. That has happened many times. I never know until what has been foretold comes to pass, exactly what each vision means. And Alfred's vision didn't say what he should do each day."

"Then how will I know how to use my Gift?" Pony almost wailed. "Alfred says I should follow him and use it for the greater good. My Mothers call me to remain what I am, what they were. I almost lost my way entirely with a barbarian on Samhain night. My Gift is becoming frightening. Tell me how to save my Gift, how to use it. That is what I want."

"At least you are sure of that. Of what you are." Britta smiled, regret in her eyes. "Tell me."

Pony was taken aback. She had never been asked to explain herself. Except by Val. And even then she couldn't tell him, could only take him to the circle of her mothers. "I am female. I am the last of the Ones who worship the Mother."

"And who is the Mother?"

"She who brought forth the World," Pony answered, surprised that this witch who saw the future of all would not know. "Her symbol is the Great Fecund Mare, big with foal."

"Ah. You worship the world's tendency to life. I understand." Britta pressed Pony's hand. "Now tell me about the Gift."

"I listen," Pony said, shrugging. "If I gather calm inside

myself, I can hear the animals. Well, the ones who eat plants. Horses, birds, hares and such." She would tell what the Gift should be, not what it was turning into of late. "I live under the sign of the White Chalk Horse with my herd, where my mother and her mothers have lived from the beginning of time, serving the Great Mother. People come to me, to learn the Language of Touch and partner with my horses. I am breeding a girl-child to continue the tradition of my mothers."

"That all sounds wonderful," Britta whispered in the flicker of the flames. "You have your horses. You will have a family. You know which gods you serve. You listen to the way of the world, a lesson it took me many years to learn. It seems your destiny is clear. I myself would love to be so certain." She pressed Pony's hand. Pony had never felt such caring emanating from another. Her mother had never pressed her hand thus. But the woman did not truly understand.

"Yet it isn't clear." Pony gathered herself. "I thought it would be after I got myself breeding with Alfred."

"Alfred is the father of your child? But that is perfect." Surprise colored Britta's voice.

"He is just to the purpose, comely and of good stock. He will sire a good girl-child for the Goddess. And I knew he wouldn't stay with me."

Britta's brows drew together. "You don't sound like you love him."

"Mother said you can't afford entanglement."

Britta raised her brows.

"It interferes with the calm you need to listen," Pony explained. "He came just in time. My Gift was fading because I had delayed so long obeying."

Britta examined her intently. "And why did you delay?"

Pony swallowed. "I was afraid—am afraid," she corrected, "of what happened to my mother after she had me. Still, I did what I must." She raised her chin as though there was some reason to be defiant. "I did it to save the Gift."

Even though the Gift had not been saved. Not entirely. Not yet.

"What happened to your mother?" Britta asked, her voice a whisper in the glowing dark.

Tears welled in Pony's eyes. She had never said it aloud. She only said it now on the desperate chance that this woman could help her, that she was lying about not being able to call the visions. Had she not called the earth to shake and bring down a faesten? "My mother . . . drifted away from living until . . ." Pony swallowed. "When I was ten, she put stones in her gyrdle and walked into a lake." The old depression dragged at her.

Britta took an audible breath. Then she said, "I know what it is to feel abandoned." She reached for Pony's hand again. There it was, that feeling that Britta, whom Pony had known for only hours, cared more for her than her mother ever had. "Perhaps that is why it is difficult for you to love the one you choose to get you with child?" Her suggestion was gentle.

"No," Pony shook her head. "That is just the way. But . . . I don't want to drift away from life like my mother. Should I use the Gift to further Alfred's cause? Would that bind me to living? It means leaving the Vale of the White Horse, and I can't imagine doing that. Though of course I did, when the Viking took me. And then it was all spoiled. I couldn't go back. I got confused."

Britta sat up, smiled. "Confused over a Viking?" She chuckled. "That I understand."

"It was not the Viking." Pony shook her head. "Well, it was, since I . . . I don't know what came over me. It was after I was breeding, too. I hope it did not harm the babe. It was only that it was Samhain night."

Britta shook her head. "It did not harm your child." She smiled. "So you have come to me to be sure what to do about your Gift, about the Viking and Alfred."

Pony nodded, her eyes full. *Tell me my future. You know. I can see it in your eyes.*

"It is odd, since I have no sureness myself. I don't know

211

whether I am witch or saint, and Alfred notwithstanding, neither does anyone else. The magic or the grace—call it what you will—comes as it chooses, and says things I don't wish to hear. Sometimes I heal, but more often those who come are disappointed and revile me. They call me an imposter. Karn wants to protect me from that. But there is no protection to be had in this world. That is one of the few things I do know." She leaned forward, examining Pony's face. "I think we are required in this life to engage the world. What that means in its particulars for you, I cannot say. I think that you must listen to the world, embrace its direction."

"Listening is the one thing I can do." Pony was relieved.

Britta smiled. "But you don't listen to *all* the world. There are other things you shut out. Like carnivores. You hear only prey animals, those who run to live."

Devastation lodged like rocks in Pony's lungs. "I think that may be changing."

Britta raised her brows.

Pony swallowed. "I heard . . . a carnivore some time ago. A hawk. I know it is some strange perversion of the Gift. It has not happened again, thank the Mothers." But hadn't it? Hadn't she heard carnivores whispering in the background when she reached out to Dun Mare?

Britta searched Pony's face. "Perhaps it should happen again. We must listen even to the things that frighten us, Epona." The woman's voice was soaked in some emotion Pony couldn't fathom, and she turned her intensity to the glowing coals. "We must embrace everything, even those parts of our gifts that are confusing. If we close one eye, we may think we see our path more clearly. Most people go through life like that: with half vision. But it is left to a few, gift or curse, to open both eyes, to hear with both ears, to understand with a full heart. When you open yourself, you realize the need for confusion."

Pony *was* confused. "I . . . I am not sure I know your meaning."

Britta leaned forward, her face fierce under her flaming

hair. "My gift was frightening. I wanted to control it. I wanted to know everything. But such power cannot be controlled. I don't *know* anything for sure. But now I understand that." The witch cocked her head. "Karn confused me at first, too," she added. "What I felt for him frightened me. Yet in the end, he was the reason for all I did. When I listened to my heart, I felt the tug of the world and the direction it wanted to go."

"But it is my heart that is most uncertain," Pony protested. "I am feeling tugged in so many directions that I can only stand and shake."

Britta leaned forward to stir the fire with a stick and smiled. Suddenly she froze. Sparks flickered upward in the dark around her. Her eyes were big, unblinking, luminescent.

"Britta?" Fear flashed along Pony's spine. The witch was as still as stone.

Britta shuddered and gasped, as if she had not breathed for many minutes. Horror crossed her eyes. She covered her mouth with one hand and her breast heaved.

"What is it?" Pony cried, looking into the fire. Nothing but coals glowed in the firebox.

Britta turned and examined her, her eyes roving slowly over Pony's face. "I was wrong," she whispered. "It will happen more slowly than I thought." A half-chuckle sounded desperate, not relieved. "Alfred will be so disappointed. And you. . . . you! I should have known the instant you said you worshiped the Great Mother. She will have her way, oldest of the earth's incarnations." She began to laugh, deep in her throat, until her voice caught. "The earth has its way with all of us."

"Tell me," Pony commanded with all the consequence of being the last of her kind.

Britta's eyes darted around the darkened hut. "Tell you? Tell you what? It is for you to tell me, to tell us *all* how it will be."

Pony felt as though she had been slapped. "But I know nothing."

"Nothing? Everything? It is the same." Britta took another breath and stood looking down at her. "Go to Alfred. He will have need of you. After that . . . it is less clear. You are incomplete. Without . . . something more, you cannot do what you were meant to do."

Pony hung on to the words. Britta frightened her. But she knew now where she must go. "What must I do to be complete?" she cried.

"You will know when the time comes, I think."

Pony felt unsure. She reached for Britta's hand, craving the strength and the caring she had found there. "Not enough," she sobbed. "Not enough."

The witch's face softened. "Gifts, whether of seeing or of listening are hard. You know that. They tell only part of the story. Sometimes in trying to tell all, I end in telling lies. Stay and rest here. This hut is for your use. We keep it for visitors who seek out Karn." She smiled. "He is lord of the Fenland from the Ouse to the Little Cam."

"I will leave tomorrow," Pony said, though confusion still reigned in her heart. "But what must I do with Alfred? How am I part of his destiny?"

"I know not. But I know you are part of something larger. And that your way will be hard."

Pony's shoulders collapsed under the weight of Britta's words. "You can tell me nothing more?" But Pony already knew that the red-haired witch could not, or would not, point the way. "I did not mean to seem . . . ungrateful for your help," she added after a moment.

"I am used to disappointing." Britta seemed to sag as she walked out into the wet night.

Chapter Fourteen

Val glanced to the open gates of Chippenham's fortress for the thousandth time since midday. They were empty, of course. He and his men had returned yesterday, and since he had sent Harald at first light the man could not return before dark. It was seven leagues to the Vale and back. And if he stayed to speak with her, if she was away finding better grazing for her herd in winter, if she had gone to Alfred, if . . . a thousand ifs. If darkness overtook Harald too far from Chippenham, he would sleep rough along the road. Val pushed a sharpening stone along Bloodletter's blade. He was weak for sending Harald. But he had at least enough strength to refuse to run to Pony himself.

Sun broke through an opening in the clouds and beams of radiance shot down to crown the hills to the east with light. Val could imagine the White Chalk Horse shining out across Pony's Vale: a beacon, calling him. He set his teeth. More like a warning beacon of one of the lighthouses the Romans had built on every coast to warn of rocks that would tear up their ships. He must heed the warning, lest his heart be torn up, too.

Behind him, Elbert came out of the great hall. The priest had taken over the task of teaching Saxon to the *Danir*. Val dipped some oil from the wooden bowl at his side and dribbled it along Bloodletter's blade, glancing only once toward the gate.

"I hope Harald is back today," Elbert said.

Val grunted an assent he hoped concealed how much he wanted that as well.

"Una's father plans for Thor'sday, and two days is hardly enough to prepare him." Val could feel the priest's stare.

"What preparation does he need for bedding a wench?" he asked roughly.

"Ah, you forget the price for her hand," Elbert reminded. "You said you would consent."

Val snorted. "The dunking. *Ja,* I told him I would do it were I in his place."

"Was that a lie?"

Val shrugged. "Who is to know until the moment it is asked?" He continued sharpening his blade; the certain knowledge that he would never be asked to convert for love making his strokes fierce. He concentrated on the sword and the oil and the stone to fend off Elbert's questioning eyes. He watched the muscles in his own forearms bunch as he pushed the stone along the blade.

He was concentrating so, he almost missed Harald's arrival. It was only the pounding of horse's hooves that jerked his head up. Harald's mount rocked back on his haunches and skidded to a stop. Val was up in an instant, stone and sword clattering to the ground. He strode out into the yard. Harald dismounted, shaking his head.

"What, man?" Val shouted, breaking into a run.

"She's gone." Harald gasped, bending over, hands on knees, to catch his breath.

"Gone?" Val motioned for another to take the lathered horse. "Gone?"

"Hut is empty. No horses."

"They graze off a ways," Val said, exasperated. "Did you not ask the people nearby?"

"I did," Harald said, straightening.

Val wanted to shake him. "What, then?"

"The shepherds said she left a month ago with the horses. She went north."

Val searched the young man's eyes and saw pity there. He nodded brusquely and turned. Father Elbert hovered behind him. Val pushed past. "No matter," he said. He wanted to cover his longing, but his voice was husky in his own ears. He cleared his throat. "We do not need her at the council." He could feel the other two following him as he walked. "We could not get her horses, but if she goes north she is not for Alfred." The black doorway of the great hall yawned before him. He thrust himself through it. "No matter."

Pony was determined to leave Stowa this morning, but first she had to find a way to get off her knees and get her head out of the bucket at the foot of the bedbox. This had been going on since the night of the vision. This vomiting. But she could not tarry here. Britta had come forth with no further pronouncements. She said only that the way was confused, that there would be treachery, and that she thought Alfred needed Pony's help. But she did not sound sure.

Pony was still throwing up when Britta poked her head into the hut. The witch hurried to her side. "Ah, again?" She soaked a cloth in water from the jar by the door and called for Hild. When the blonde came, between them they got Pony back onto the furs of her bedbox. Britta held the wet cloth to her forehead and Hild fed her bits of bread to hold her stomach together.

Pony squinted up at them. "I am not sure I want a girl-child if this is the price."

"Mine lasted but a month," Hild reassured her. "And I cannot think why yours only started now."

"A month?" Pony protested, appalled.

"I suffered not at all," Britta soothed. "Eat bread before you rise each morning."

Pony sat up. "I am better. The bread helped." She struggled out of the furs and picked up the pack the women had made her, and her cloak. "I must away, and Karn is my best guide."

"Aye," Britta agreed. "He is for Ely to lead the Council that gathers monthly. He may even keep you dry." She smiled. "He and Thorn know the way well."

The day was bright blue and crispy cold outside the hut. Pony's stomach rolled in response to the harsh light. She shoved another hunk of bread into her mouth. The strappy leaves of surrounding sedge sparkled with water droplets from last night's rains. First Mare stood quietly in the common area next to Karn and Thorn. The big Viking held his own horse's reins in one hand and a black ball of fur in the other. As Pony approached, he held it out.

She stared at the bright black pieces of flint the ball of fur claimed as eyes, and the tiny pink tongue that lolled from a panting mouth lined with white slivery teeth.

"Take him," Britta urged. "He is a gift from Karn and from me."

Pony turned to stare blankly at her. "A gift for me?"

Britta smiled. "He is a son of Fenris. We think you should have a protector."

Pony knew it was only half the truth. "But he is a carnivore," she whispered. He was a betrayal of her heritage. The image of wolves tearing at the carcass of a horse who had been her friend churned in her belly.

Britta nodded slyly. "We think you need a carnivore. You need not be afraid."

"Why, you lie, my wife," Karn rumbled, still holding out the pup. "His teeth are like needles. That in itself be something to fear." As if on cue, the pup began to gnaw meditatively on Karn's thumb. Karn held it up to view and grinned.

Curse these two kind people! They had fed her and sheltered her for a sen'night. Britta had advised her on pregnancy and the care of babes when she found Pony's mother had told her nothing. Karn and Thorn had taken her riding with First Mare to show her the dike and the Fenland, of which he was strangely proud for a Viking who had not even been born here. They had, in short, made it impossible for her to refuse this gift she could absolutely not accept.

She sighed, feeling trapped. "I suppose it is not old enough to run beside us."

Karn shook his head, his eyes alight, and held out a sling he had made. "Put this around your neck. When he tires he will be content to sleep against the beating of your heart."

"If he wets me . . ." Pony threatened as she reached for the furry ball. Then she remembered herself. *"Thonc to thu."* She sounded a little terse, and tried to fix that. "What is his name?"

"You will name him," Britta said. The witch watched as Pony knotted the sling and tucked the pup inside.

"Will he grow to look like a wolf?" Pony asked.

"Aye, all Fenris's pups look just like him—male and female alike."

Pony called First Mare to the stump of a fen oak and mounted, glanced at her burden. What had she gotten herself into? She was stuck; carnivore or no, she could not abandon such a baby. No doubt Karn and Britta counted on that. She had wanted the predictions of a witch. She had come away with no other direction than that she should go to Alfred. And now she was cursed with a carnivore puppy. All in all a bad bargain.

Karn mounted Thorn using straps hung from that great horse's saddle, and saluted his wife. "Three days," he promised. "No more." Pony wondered whether the straps helped him balance since his hip was weak. They were a good, idea.

"I am sorry I could not tell you more," Britta whispered to Pony.

Pony shrugged, though hopelessness rose inside her. Karn and she turned out of the village, waving to those she had come to know in the last week. She called to Hild for luck with her coming babe, then she and Karn were away. She did not speak, and neither did he. First Mare followed Thorn across the lime plateaus. The unnamed puppy rested against her heart, but its warmth was not soothing. She would to Alfred. How could she not? But otherwise she was no wiser than before. Her Gift was taking some strange turn that frightened her. She still did not know what had come over her on Samhain night, or why she felt so distant now from the Vale and the way she had thought her life would go. With luck Alfred would accept her when she told him his "saint" had told her to follow him. But what if he sent her away?

She stared at Karn's broad back ahead of her. Val was a little shorter and bulkier through the shoulders. Karn's hair was blonder and straighter. Still, like Val, he was a Viking lord of this land where Saxon and Dane dwelt together. A tugging inside her was ruthlessly surpressed. Still, she could not help her questions.

"Karn," she called, urging First Mare into a trot. He turned. She cleared her throat. "Have you ever . . . ?" How could she ask it? "Uh, do you attend councils with other *jarls?*"

Karn grinned. "Only when I must. Guthrum leaves me alone. He does not trust my wife. The tales of the fortress at Thetford serve me well."

"So . . . so you would not know the men he trusts to hold other parts of his kingdom." She felt the color rise into her face until it was as warm as the pup against her breast.

"I have sat in the *thing* you speak of." He lifted his brows.

Pony stuttered to a stop, the burning in her face increasing.

Karn turned to look ahead. "You are from the downland. I have never seen the *jarl* who holds your Vale." He stole a glance to Pony. "But I have heard tell of him. Valgar, is he not?"

Pony's throat closed. She could not speak, but she managed a curt nod.

"He is a fearsome fighter, so they say. They call him Valgar the Beast." Karn looked as though he thought that was something to recommend a Viking. Pony was appalled. Val was known as a fierce predator even among Vikings! "That

Guthrum chose him to lead was surprising to many—but that wily old devil always knows what he is doing."

"He didn't seem like a beast." *No, she chided herself. That revealed too much.* "Why did it surprise people?"

Karn shrugged. "He has been gone many years and, well, with his past . . ."

Yes. This was what Pony wanted to know. "Why did he go away?"

Karn slipped a glance her way, obviously uncertain.

She must reassure him. "He said he had broken the *law* of the Danes," she prodded.

Karn's brows relaxed in relief. "If he told you that much, there is not much more to tell. He killed his father when he was but a young man." Pony felt her heart drop into her belly. "Which meant none felt they could trust him. If he knew not the way to the first loyalty a man owes, his family, how could he be counted on in *any* way? He had no choice but to go."

Val had killed his *father?* The world seemed to recede. Pony could hardly hear Karn. What kind of a man could kill his own father? An image flashed into her mind, blocking out the bright cold day, of her raising a stone above her mother's head, ready to bludgeon the woman to death. She shuddered in revulsion—or was it fear? No, no, she could never do such a thing. She felt betrayed. Val was not the man she'd thought. Not at all. He truly *was* Valgar the Beast.

"He showed himself in Cent last spring," Karn continued. "Guthrum said he was *berserkr* when he killed his father, that his years of exile were payment for the deed. No one liked to say Guthrum nay." He glanced again at Pony. "You have met him. Was Guthrum right to trust him?"

Pony shrugged and would not meet the other Viking's eyes. "How would one such as I know?" Suddenly she was certain of nothing. It was as if something had been ripped from her, something she didn't even know she'd had. Karn still looked at her. She could feel it. So she couldn't leave it at that. "He . . . he seems a just man. But," she added, "who can know when he will go mad again?"

They walked many steps in quiet. Finally, Karn said, "We *Danir* prize a man who is consumed by the spirit of animals in a battle. Who knows where such battles may take place? It could as well be in one's heart, in one's family, as on the battlefield."

Pony snorted. A man's battle was not with his father, just as her own was not with her mother. A dry sough of breath escaped her lips. A tiny voice inside wondered if that was true. She wished she had never asked after Val.

Karn and Ely were left behind, and thankfully. The big Viking had remained the whole journey a painful reminder of the subject Pony tried desperately to put from her mind. How could a man who had killed his own father fill her thoughts? But Val did. Since Ely, she had turned her attention to looking for Herd. The Gift had grown stronger. Twice she had listened for them. The second time, she had heard, weakly, an owl searching for prey in the night. She'd cut off the connection. Herd was lost, and her Gift had become too frightening to use.

She would retrace her steps to the White Chalk Horse. Surely she would find Herd along the way. But the Vale could be only a brief stop on her journey to Alfred. Maybe in giving him her Gift, by joining his cause, she would find the young king completed her, as Britta had predicted. Maybe that would bring everything back to how it should be. Of course, he might refuse to acknowledge her baby as his own, in spite of his little priest and his plan. Then her journey would be a cruel joke. But what choice was there? Her home was spoiled by her uncertainty. She could not return to Chippenham, not with what she knew about Val. Not after Samhain night. Going to Alfred was all that was left to her.

Pony and First Mare wended their way across the frozen meadows. Her pup gamboled alongside as they walked. It was early morning. Frost turned the grass to sharp iron spikes that struck cold into the travelers' bones. But the dullness that had lodged inside Pony since her mother's death did not lift. Whenever she thought about the completeness she had found with Val, the dullness turned to the ache of . . . of what? Regret? There was nothing to regret, she told herself sternly time after time. But still her thoughts turned, and still the ache came back.

On the twelfth day after the turn of the year, the weather became foul. Pony and First Mare bent their heads into the punishing sleet along the narrow path. The last traveler they passed had said there was a village ahead somewhere. Surely they must be drawing near it.

Pony was not listening at all; she was thinking about her soaked cloak, and smelling the wet dog fur at her breast. A frightened whinny pierced the twilight. Reverberation of hoofbeats pounded up through the soil and First Mare's joints into Pony's body. First Mare shied and pricked her ears, then whinnied in return. Pony whirled with the horse to survey the darkening landscape around them, blinking against the driving sleet. Despite what she felt, she could see nothing but black amid the forest to their left. She thought she remembered a stream off to the right.

Fear! Screaming, shrieking terror drenched her until she gasped with the force of it. Behind the fear came a whispering chorus of cunning. Stone-hearted, calculating intensity rustled about her, then seeped inside. Pony felt the fear rise.

Out of the black, slick trees a horse the color of darkness raced, nostrils flaring, breath pounding in its chest to match the rhythm of its hooves. Pony stared at it, its fear washing over her. But fear could not suppress the hissing wall of another intensity that seeped into her. She looked with cold eyes at the horse. *Close now. We are close. Leaders racing, low to the ground, no sound, no growl. Pack circling, ready. Soon it is ours. Blood racing but focus absolute. We move as one, think as one, hunt, as one. We are Pack.*

"No!" Pony screamed, tearing at her dripping hair as the wolves appeared out of nowhere like wraiths. There were a dozen of them, some racing fast after the black horse that thundered toward her; some circled wide to cut off all escape. "No!" she shrieked, trying to banish their hard lust for the kill out of her heart. "I will not!" she screamed. "*YOU* will not!"

The black horse almost ran into First Mare, who lurched away, herself an instant from galloping into the night, instinct overwhelming all. But she and Pony dared not run. The wolves would be on them in a moment then. *Hold,* Pony told First Mare with her legs. "Whoa," she said aloud to the black horse. Young Black! she realized, as he blew and sidled. Her gut screamed at her to run. But that way lay death. The wolves would chase them down.

She sat straight on her nervous mare and glared at the wolves. They broke into a trot and circled warily. Pony pushed her urge to run into a corner of her gut. The sleet turned to rain, slapping with the wind against the sides of the horses. The wolves blinked against it. Darkness seeped from the ground. One wolf stood in front of the others. His eyes were yellow-brown, his mouth open, panting. His teeth gleamed in the failing light. The sense of Pack washed over Pony, the need to kill for food, the rightness of hunting together, the frustration at a meal that might be lost.

He is mine, Pony thought. She worked on thinking only, *mine.*

The leader's head hung low between his shoulders. One of the others whined. First Mare trembled. Young Black was snorting in returning frenzy. He reared and pawed the air. The lead wolf growled once more, then ducked his head and turned away. Before Pony could come truly to her senses, the others had melted off into the rain and the night.

Pony breathed—and realized she had been holding her breath for what, hours? Seconds? How long had that confrontation taken? Her own little black carnivore pushed his head out of her cloak. Pony urged First Mare forward into a trot down the path. Young Black was only too glad to follow. Pony felt distant from herself, as though she stood on some cliff and looked down where two horses and a rider trotted along a narrow path in the driving rain.

It had happened. She had heard carnivores again. And she had pretended to be one of them. They had believed her. A shudder raced up her spine. Tears melted onto her rain-wet cheeks. Had she only pretended? She hoped to the Mothers that she had.

Osrick watched Alfred speak to the gathered farmers and ceorls in Muchelney, about two leagues from the sixteen acres of Wessex that Saxons still controlled. Surrounded by swamp, the little rise that held their camp was mean enough. But it was also protection for them in winter. He had never ventured forth with Alfred to recruit in the countryside, but now he watched with hooded eyes as the young king moved among these peasants, greeted them, asked after crops and children. He spat on the ground. These were not people worthy of thegn's notice.

"How long have you been without an eorl?" Alfred asked the leader of the band, a great bear of a man.

"Nigh on eight months."

Alfred examined the company's faces. "And this is not a hardship for you?"

The crowd grew wary, shuffling from foot to foot. They did not know Alfred, and did not like to answer one way or another. Alfred let loose his smile. He clapped the leader's beefy shoulder. "Did he take too much for himself and the king? Was it constant war that ground you down?"

The man nodded, relieved. Surprised to find that Alfred understood. "They took all we had for fighting, always the fighting."

Alfred nodded sympathetically. "Only with peace can we till our fields and raise our children. There is but one problem." He shook his head sadly. "We must fight once more to earn that peace." He looked up and his eyes lost focus. "When the Seven Kingdoms have thrown off the Viking yolk, they will become One Kingdom. Then the crops will support their planters, not the war."

"The Danes in Chippenham take a tenth part from us, not half," a voice from the rear piped.

"Aye, and others follow their lead," another called.

Osrick saw Alfred glance around. "*We* will take only a tenth when we have no wars to drain our coffers," he answered. "But these foreigners perpetuate the wars. We will banish them." Then the young king's eyes lit with realization. "And our army will *pay* for what we need." His voice rose as he said it, so that all might hear.

Pay? What army paid for what they took? Osrick wondered. But a shout rose from the assembled crowd.

Alfred smiled and nodded. "Join us when we rise from our damp dream at Athelney and surge out to make the island one and fight for the last peace!" Then the young, sovereign moved among his people as they cheered. But how would he pay for an army? Osrick wondered.

When at last Alfred made his way back to Osrick's side, he still wore a beaming smile for the crowd. But he whispered, "Now we must make good our promise, dear Osrick."

"Where will we get enough silver to pay for an army?" Osrick asked.

The king glanced up at him, a pious look in his eyes. "The church is the only source for that much silver," he whispered. "Go see our friend the Bishop of Sherborne. He will support our cause."

Alfred waved one last time to the crowd. The man was a genius. The church had all the silver in the world. And Alfred had asked Osrick to retrieve it! He would turn this to advantage. How, though? "Your word is my command, my King."

Alfred looked at him for a moment, speculating. "Is it, Osrick?" Then he turned and walked out of the village on the narrow muddy track that was its road.

Ignoring that, Osrick called after him: "I will to Sherborne!"

* * *

After the breakup of the council, Val walked up to the fortress beside Father Elbert. "They judged well tonight," the priest said. The night was clear and not so cold as it had been. Both men's boots squelched with every step in the melting snow. Guthrum would soon bring a gathering of *jarls* for a great Danish council at Chippenham. He would be pleased at what he saw here.

"Soon they will not need a leader for their meeting. It will become a true *thing*." He looked down at the priest almost fondly. He had grown to trust this son of Osrick. "Will you take mead with me? A fire would warm our bones in this damp. Does this island never dry?"

The gates of the fortress loomed. Elbert wisely did not defend his island's weather. "You have never asked to break bread with me. What, is your friend Harald busy?"

Val chuckled. "*Ja.* Very busy. When a man turns to wenches, he has no time for mead."

"Not to any wench," Elbert corrected. "He is newly married in the eyes of God. Una seems to agree with him."

Entering the great hall, they called to a serving woman to bring drinks. Val swung off his cloak and sat near the roaring fire. "This fire will have me sweating soon," he said after a moment. He pushed up the sleeves of his flax shirt.

Elbert sat next to him and took the mead horn proffered by a Saxon girl. He nodded at Val's arm. "Your burn has healed well. 'Twas a bad one."

Val grunted assent. A girl with purple-blue eyes had rubbed his arm to save his hand.

"How did you burn it?"

Val gulped his mead. "Harald held a torch to it, a test of my loyalty to Guthrum."

"What?" Elbert's face contracted. "What king would require such a test?"

Val waved his horn in dismissal. "You would not understand, priest. Harald challenged my right to hold the downland. Guthrum set him to prove if I was fit to do so."

"He could have . . . Thank Jesu and his Mother that Guthrum called a halt."

"He didn't. Harald's courage failed him." Val took another swig. "He was young."

"You could have done this to another?" Elbert stared at him in the flickering light.

"Of course." Val looked away. Could he? If the man were as strong as he was, perhaps. But if the man was younger or weaker, like Harald himself?

"I see." Elbert sat back on his bench. He sipped from his horn in meditation. "Harald did this to you and yet he is your boon companion—a puppy at your heels oft as not, and you encourage it. I had thought your gods were most implacable, yet this is a clear sign of forgiveness."

Val was stung into a retort. "He was young," he repeated. His words ran ahead of his thoughts. "The gods do not even see such small things, why should I? Do you say it is a sign of weakness that I let him live?" He sighed, and all the old shame washed over him.

"Do *you* think it is?" the priest asked.

"*Ja*, perhaps," Val answered, looking Elbert in the eye. "I should have killed him at the first chance. Those who hurt you are enemies. Enemies must be destroyed."

Elbert mused, "No wonder you consider the way of Jesu weak. What is Christianity if not the belief in forgiveness? Jesu forgives us all. Can we do less?" He shook his head.

"The gods never forgive. Odin sees all with his one eye. Thor's hammer will not be stayed." Val hoped his voice was hard.

"Yet they did not kill Harald."

"That was up to me. I failed."

"Did Harald not repent of hurting you? I have seen him take great care with your burn."

Val nodded. That was true.

"When the sinner repents he is worthy of forgiveness. The Bible tells us so in Jeremiah."

Valgar snapped, "Your religion is full of rules." In that, though, it was like to Danish *law*. "I was weak to let him live. I will no doubt *repent* some time that I did."

"When Jesu forgives us, we must forgive ourselves. Only then can we find peace."

Val snorted. "The world is not a place of peace, Priest. There is no room for forgiveness in it, or for a weak religion."

"Someday there will be, if each of us finds forgiveness in our heart. That is why I follow Him. Imagine your most secret crime—" Val started and glanced up from his horn. Could this priest know? "—Then know that Jesu knows it and has already forgiven you." Elbert smiled. His smile held peace. Val felt envy wash through him, quickly followed by anger.

"You are a poor substitute for Harald," he barked, standing and draining his meads. "I am for my bedbox." He flung the horn on the trestle table on his way to his own quarters.

Chapter Fifteen

Pony and First Mare stopped in water nearly up to First Mare's hocks. Young Black turned to see why. The unnamed pup bounded in and out of the water, his long black fur sodden and dripping. Unlike the fens, here the footing was fairly stable underneath the brackish marshland. Beech trees still grew up through the pools of water littered with sodden leaves, and guelder rose and young saplings choked the way. Perhaps it was their roots that gave the footing stability.

The long journey back from the fenland had taken its toll. Pony's cyrtle was wet and dirty, as was the one in her pack. She no longer cared. Her hair hung in limp strings around her face. She didn't even run her hands through it to keep it out of her eyes. What was the point? She had forgotten what she wanted, why she and the horses and the dog slogged on, as they had always done, always would do. The numbness wasn't the same as quiet, though, as peace, but her heart no longer fluttered with regret for Herd. She sometimes wondered if they had abandoned her because they suspected she had become half-carnivore herself, but those thoughts were distant. Her heart did not thump in fear of what she might hear if she listened; she just did not listen anymore. All those feelings were gone, buried under fatigue and the voice that whispered it was no use to continue.

The one good thing was that the feeling of completeness she had felt in the arms of a Viking had faded too. The regret was still there, but it had to make its way through the numbness now, and that was a hard thing to do.

Standing in the water, she put both hands to her back and arched, trying to ease her muscles. As the days warmed, her belly grew. How long had she been looking for Alfred? It must be two full cycles of the moon. Was it April? Eight months, more or less, since the night in her hut when the oat cakes had burned and she had lain with Alfred. She wondered how she would bear another month of this distended state. She did not vomit every morning anymore, but her stomach was stretched and huge and she could feel movement inside it. Another being lived inside her, one she could not control. And she could not go back. She would have this child, whether she wanted or not. Yet how could something that made her stomach so large, so tight, come out between her legs? She had never seen a human birth, just foals. She sighed. Foals were even larger, and they made it out of their mother's belly. It would be so for her. She ran her hand along First Mare's side. The horse, too, had begun to show her girth—impregnated as she was by Slepnir. She was still safe to ride, but in the coming months Pony would be forced to walk. Already Pony did for most of the day. She stroked slowly the mare's elegant neck.

"Do not blame me," Pony whispered. "You *would* accept that barbarian horse when you refused White Stallion for three years and more." Thinking about Samhain night was not good. The regret welled into longing and pierced her numbness. For a brief moment she wondered why she was trying to find Alfred when what she wanted was in Chippenham. She and First Mare had too many things in common.

She sighed. "Come. That farmer in Athelney seemed sure Alfred is here somewhere."

They splashed on. Pony's cyrtle tugged at her legs, but the water was shallower here. There was a rise ahead. Would Alfred not be on higher ground? She and First Mare struggled on until the ground was only muddy. As it rose beneath them the pup began to bark. The horses' ears swiveled. Their heads lifted. Pony went as still as she could. Something was out there. Men!

They crashed through the lacy bushes: twelve men led by a face she had forgotten she might see here, where Alfred might be hiding. Osrick's hard eyes narrowed as he came out of the newly verdant underbrush. The sound of swords being unsheathed penetrated the cracking of branches. The panting breath of the group shushed in and out behind the pup's frantic barking. More of the men brandished weapons. They seemed as surprised as she was.

"Quiet," Pony told the pup before he annoyed these hardened warriors into slashing at him. He barked once more, defiantly, then circled to her side.

"So," Osrick called, as he took in her swelling belly. "What would a *goddess* be doing in a swamp like this?" He made the word sound like a slur on her character and all her Mothers' before her.

Pony drew herself up, which made her belly protrude the more. "I come to find Alfred."

"And if Alfred doesn't want to be found by you?" Osrick sneered.

"Let him decide for himself." Could he prevent her from seeing the king?

The hemlock dropwart bushes rustled once again behind Osrick. Several of the men to the rear of the half-circle whirled. But it was only the little priest who emerged, the cleric who had acted as a witness to the getting of her girl-child. "That is a good idea," he said softly. It was just as if a half-dozen swords were not brandished in his direction.

"I am sure Alfred would want the opportunity."

Osrick looked disgusted and turned on his heel. "Come ahead," he snarled.

Pony trailed after him warily up the hill. The pup stalked at her side and the two horses followed. Pony's mind was whirling. If Alfred sent her away, she would have come all this distance for naught. She had nothing left to contribute to his cause, did she? Not when she refused to use her Gift.

The young king paced in front of a makeshift hut of beech branches laid over with boughs. Around the clearing in the horse chestnut trees and beeches at the top of the hill were perhaps a dozen other huts and tents. Men turned a deer on a spit above a fire in a central clearing. Some oiled weapons. She must not forget that though these men were Saxon, they were predators as well. One stitched a jerkin with awl and gut thread. Alfred himself looked leaner than when Pony had seen him last, but he still glowed with energy. She had found him! But what would he do when he saw her? What would his expression say?

The grin that broke his face would have lighted her hut more surely than a fire. "Epona!" he shouted and strode forward, his glance taking in her figure, her horses and her dog. "Aahhh. We did good work, did we not, Asser?"

"You did, my king."

Pony glanced around and saw Osrick's sour look harden into something more. "This is yours?" the thegn asked without respect or circumspection.

Alfred's smile glowed out again. He nodded. "With witnesses. Come, Epona," he added, putting his arm around her shoulders. "Sit you by the fire. You look exhausted. I sent Asser to look for you when you did not arrive yesterday."

He had known she was coming? She was surprised at that but, drawn by the fire, she sat and pulled her cloak around her. "Do you have fodder for my horses?" she asked. "There was naught but ragged robin and some meadowsweet to graze on in the marsh."

"Aye." He motioned to one of Osrick's party. "Take care

of her horses, and bring some meat from that stag for the dog."

Pony called to her horses: "Go with him, First Mare, Young Black." "He will give you grass." The steeds obediently trailed after the soldier. Several men glanced at each other around the circle.

Alfred squatted beside Pony, looking most unking-like. "Will you eat with us?"

She shrugged. "Anything other than meat would be most welcome."

Alfred gestured to another man, who turned and scurried off. "I had forgot. But that can be arranged."

Osrick hovered on the other side of the fire, glaring at Pony, chewing on his mustaches and scratching his beard. "You say you sent Asser after her, my king?" he asked. His voice was tight.

"I heard she asked after me, two nights ago when I was recruiting souls for our army in Burrowbridge." He grinned again at her. "Jesu, but I am glad you are here! What brought you?"

"Britta said I should come."

Alfred beamed. "Britta! She knew you would be important to my destiny."

Pony looked at him apologetically. She might as well set forth her failures. "If you want help for your cause, you will be disappointed." She took a breath. "My Gift isn't working." Better to tell him that than that she refused to use it. "And my Herd is missing, so there are no horses."

"Well . . ." Alfred's smile softened. "Your Gift is a victim of your condition. It will surely return once the babe is born. And you still have the Language of Touch. You can gentle another herd."

Osrick turned and stalked away. Alfred looked over, surprised. "Ah, Osrick prepares to leave for Sherborne. We seek resources from the church to pay our armies and buy them food in the coming battle with Guthrum. If we pay for what we take, the locals will not resent our efforts to reclaim the land from the Viking barbarians." He settled into a sitting position and took a plate of vegetables and a bowl of porridge from the soldier who brought them. "Hmm, parsnips, leeks, porridge—all the things my men have learned to hate over the winter."

"They are most welcome to me," Pony said, taking the plate and the bowl when he held them out. The soldier handed her a great sharp knife and a wooden spoon. *"Thonc to thu,"* she said.

The pup got his share, too, and wolfed it down in three quick snaps.

"We are doing rather better," Alfred noted. "We are gathering men to our cause."

Pony looked around doubtfully at the tiny tattered camp as she ate.

"We do not mass our armies yet," Alfred said with a laugh. "We wait until the best moment, then will march north to take Guthrum by surprise. My spies say his *jarls* gather at Chippenham. Osrick must be quick about his mission. We must intercept Guthrum before he takes Winchester."

"You trust Osrick to collect your silver?" Pony asked, spoon halted halfway to her mouth.

Alfred shrugged. "We will see armies will not fight for the cause alone. They need more inducement. We must bend to the ways of the world. Your Viking jarl at Chippenham—what is his name? Val? He taught me that."

Pony's stomach dropped at the mention of Val's name. Alfred did not seem to notice the flush she could feel creeping up her neck, but ran on. "You see? I take the best ideas where I find them. I will use even you to advantage of the cause."

"But . . ."

"I know, I know. No Gift." He sat forward eagerly. "But you are known everywhere. The word that the Horse Priestess was looking for me spread to every ear. When people see you are attached to our cause, and that the Church supports it, too, who will not feel the call?" He glanced to her belly. "And you bring certain proof that you have chosen me to be the king. These old beliefs linger long after Jesu has claimed hearts and minds. Your support of my cause is but another way to lure adherents. How can anyone not fight for Angleland when Jesu and the old gods converge in their endorsement of my kingship?" He ended on a triumphant note and glanced around his circle of hardened warriors.

Pony watched each speculate and finally nod, one by one. Even the little priest smiled at her and nodded. "We are both symbols of our religion," he addressed Pony. "Thus, we are bigger than the strength of our bodies or even the power of our words."

"You mean you want me just to *be* here?" she asked, incredulous.

Alfred nodded. "You bear my child."

He claimed her babe. He wanted her. Pony sighed, and a tension so deep inside her that she had not known it was there released itself into air that promised spring on a hill above a swamp in southern Wessex. Perhaps this was where she belonged.

Osrick mounted his horse and motioned the six men behind him toward the path that Alfred had ordered built three quarters of the way through the swamp with stones and earth. Invisible from the outside, it made their way in and out not quite so onerous. He wheeled his horse and leaned down to speak to a soldier still standing on the ground.

"Watch her, Raedwald," he said. "She is a danger to us. If she bears a male, Alfred could declare him heir. Her belly gives her his ear, and she will certain pour poison about me into it."

"What action should I take?" Raedwald asked.

"Do nothing until I return. I have an idea that will make me Bishop of Sherborne. Then he will not be able to cut me out, no matter what the witch says. I shall expect a full report."

He whirled his horse then and trotted down the path, leaving Raedwald rubbing his beard nervously in his wake.

Osrick knew he had not much time to solidify his position, and he must do that before he could make Epona pay for what she had done to him, for what she was.

Pony and her charges had rested for a week, watching Alfred preparing for the coming battle. Young Black and First Mare worked on covering their ribs by making their way through copious amounts of hay. The carnivorous pup showed his nature by begging meat from anyone who would throw him a scrap. In unwary moments, Pony could feel his satisfaction at each tasty morsel. Only she herself was not content. A week had not confirmed her hope that she belonged here. Alfred had been welcoming. He made clear her value to the cause. The men treated her with the deference due Alfred's incarnation of a goddess. But none of it mattered. Herd was lost to her. The peace of her Vale, replete with the spirits of her Mothers, was lost. She dared not practice her Gift for fear of hearing carnivores. Sometimes she heard mournful music and wondered at it before she realized that she herself was humming. It was the half-remembered music of a flute played during baths on Thorsday. It seemed a portent of her unease. She did not feel complete, as Britta had said she must be to do whatever it was she was destined. So Why had Britta even sent her here?

Alfred was a whirlwind of activity. He went openly off the little rise each day and she went with him. They canvassed the countryside for weapons and food on the promise of later payment. She saw Alfred's effect on his people close up. Frowns disappeared and reluctance turned to devotion within the space of moments. The young king was a lodestone and all who came near him pointed in his direction. Which made Pony feel only forlorn. He did not need her help. What could she do for a man like this? Perhaps she could warn him of Osrick. He was sure Osrick would come back with the riches of Sherborne's bishop and give them to the cause. Pony thought Osrick would be just the kind to take everything for himself. But when she tried to speak of this to Alfred, he smiled and told her to wait and see.

Yesterday Borogand and a huge force had arrived and camped by the River Parrett. Today, Alfred brought her to meet him and his eorls as though she were a talisman. She was surprised to find that Borogand, too, found her presence an omen of good luck. What had she to do with fighting? What did the Great Mother want with corpses? Did the Fecund Mare care who ruled this island? Alfred and Borogand thought She did.

Pony walked beside Alfred up the packed dirt path through the marshy ground. Pup gamboled at her side. It was spring and he was a young animal bursting with energy. He dashed up to her, bowed and yapped. She could not help but smile. She picked up a stick. But before she could throw it, he grabbed an end and tugged. They struggled back and forth, him growling and her laughing as Alfred watched, amused. Finally she pulled it away.

"Aha!" she shrieked and threw it down the path. Pup raced away into the distance. Pony gasped and placed a hand on her belly, laughing. "He is just like you, Alfred. Too much energy."

Around them, the swamp burgeoned with pale green shoots, the beeches and the hawthorn trees crowding in among the riot of rosebay and great willowherb. Life returned, just as life stirred within her belly. Her stomach rolled with a small kick.

"I am a dog?" Alfred grinned. Pup came prancing back, and worried Alfred into throwing his stick. The path opened on the hillside clearing of the camp. First Mare and Young Black came trotting up. First Mare pushed her nose in Pony's shoulder in greeting, then ran her lips into Pony's hand, snuffling in pleasure. But Young Black went to Alfred.

Pony was surprised.

"Ho, boy," the young king said, holding out his hand. "I've nothing for you." Young Black snorted and nodded his head, then touched Alfred's hand and mumbled at it with his strong lips.

"He likes you," Pony suggested.

Alfred ran his hand up over the black arch of the stallion's thick neck. A ball of dark fur floated out on the breeze. The horses were shedding their winter coats. "I like him," Alfred murmured, patting the horse.

Pony swallowed. She was about to lose the last of Herd. Worse yet, she was about to give him away. But she had little choice. "You should be partners. Will you spare an hour of your precious time each day to learn the Language of Touch?"

Alfred turned expressive blue eyes on her, searching her face. He smiled. Not the infectious grin she had come to know, not the magnetic, confident beaming light he turned upon his confederates, but a tender, intimate smile. "*Thonc to thu,*" he said softly. "I will."

"He is yours then," Pony said lightly. "I give him. Never break your covenant with him."

Alfred turned to Young Black and scratched the hard forehead underneath the white, irregular star. He knew that much about horses. "He is a wonderful gift I shall try to deserve."

"What does the King of all Angleland not deserve?" Pony asked herself as much as him. "You are a light in the midst of darkness." And it was true. Was he not more intelligent than any other? Was he not brave? Did he not care for his men, serve his God? He was all that, and in consequence he was a better man than she had ever known. More, he was the father of her babe. She ran her hand over her distended belly. Now that she had given him Young Black, they were all she had now; her babe and First Mare. She stared at Alfred's blond head as he stroked Young Black's neck. So different. Straight hair, not waving. Blond, not light brown. Blue eyes, not gray like shifting clouds. Slighter, more wiry in build. But at least Alfred did not confuse her. He did not have a past that made him a beast. Could she stay with him, if he would have her?

A thundering on the path behind them interrupted these most difficult thoughts. Pony and Alfred turned abruptly as Osrick galloped into view, followed by other. The triumphant gleam in the man's eyes told of his success. One of the others led an extra horse, burdened with an oddly wrapped load.

"My king," Osrick hailed. "I come with gifts from the Bishop of Sherborne." He threw himself off his horse. His party was bespattered with mud, their horses lathered.

Alfred strode to greet him, each grasping the other's forearm. "How does the Bishop?"

Osrick went to untie the awkward burden from the packhorse's back. "Alas, his gift is posthumous. He gave you his blessing, but he became ill and died the next morning."

"What?" Alfred gasped. "The bishop is dead? But he invested my brother as king. I have known him this score of years and more."

Osrick pulled at the ropes. The pack leaked a silver chalice chased in gold and set with winking red stones. A golden candlestick bounced into the dirt. He said: "His generosity lives after him."

Alfred ran his hands through his hair. "The bishop, dead?"

"But your cause goes forward, my king," Osrick assured. He had a gold-embroidered altar cloth slung over one shoulder and a heavy silver offering bowl under his left arm. "There is enough here to feed an army for months if we are careful traders."

"I do not belittle your effort, Osrick. It is only. . . . May his soul rest in peace."

"I'm sure it will." Osrick glanced at Pony. His look was hard. "His place must not go unfilled. The stability of a church devoted to your cause will be most helpful. I have some ideas."

"Come, then, and tell them to me." Alfred turned back toward his hut, constructed of poles with the bark still on them and covered with branches like a leafy bower. "Did the bishop show signs of illness?" he asked. "Was it really so sudden?" The two men then went to sit next to the fire that burned in front of Alfred's hut, and Pony could no longer hear them. She could but see Alfred shaking his head sadly, Osrick's sly eyes.

Osrick was planning something. The men laid out the oilcloth that bound the treasure on the ground, and set out the cache. Jewels, a Bible bound in tooled leather and encrusted with gems, bowls and chalices, small golden bells and beads of amber and jet. It was a treasure trove. Alfred would have his war. But what would Osrick have?

He watched Alfred from someplace where his brain calculated even as he smiled and clapped his king on the shoulder. "You have your army, Alfred. And you can pay these miserable ceorls for food to feed it." The king leaned against a beech tree whose giant white-barked bole told of great age, watched the camp prepare for the coming night. Men stirred pots, sharpened swords, talked and diced. A haunch of venison filled the air with the smell of succulent cooked flesh. The air was cold, though the afternoon had promised spring, so most stayed close to the fires. The bitch priestess was off caring for her horses, the damned dog of hers cavorting at her heels. Now was his chance.

The younger man looked up at Osrick with guileless eyes. "You are a true servant of the cause. The battle draws near—will you to Cornwall and see if Trevellyan joins us?"

"Aye, my king, Osrick said." I am yours to command. Have you thought of what will happen when the battle is won?"

Alfred's eyes turned inward. "I think of nothing else, my friend," he said. Squatting, he held his hands to the warmth of the nearby flames. "Winchester, my capital, shall be a center of learning and religion as well as of the state. I will write a history of this land after the battle is done."

Alfred was talking of writing books? Osrick narrowed his eyes. Perhaps the king was more than simply odd. Maybe he was mad. Osrick gathered himself. It would be good for his own purposes if the king *was* daft. It would make it easier to control the workings of the kingdom from behind the throne. But for now Osrick had need of Alfred's focus. "I speak of the running of the country."

The king came to himself. "What? What is your meaning?"

"Only this, my king." He leaned in closer. "When the battle is won, you will distribute lands to those who fought with you."

Alfred nodded. "Fear not, you will be rewarded for the true value of your service."

"But have you not thought what value to the land might be got with a friend of Alfred in the Church?" There. He had said it. Would his little trout rise to the bait?

"I *have* friends in the Church. Asser is like my brother."

Osrick shook his head, trying not to be impatient. "You know that the Bishop of Cent sides with the Franks against us. And the Bishop of Eork seems quite content to be ruled by the Danes. You need a friend to your kingship. One who can raise money from the faithful for your cause, as I did today. One who can rise in . . ." He almost said power. "In influence within the Church and lead the others into your fold as well as into God's."

Alfred rubbed his beard. "What you say has merit. Much change is necessary in the Church. Just teaching priests to read again will require fortitude and a believer in the effort."

"Yes, exactly." Osrick nodded. "I believe in the need for priests to read Latin."

"And I want to translate the Bible into Saxon," Alfred said, the light of his dreams gleaming once more in his eyes. "Priests must teach God's words in a language the people understand."

Ridiculous, but useful. "Exactly," Osrick agreed. "Let me do this for you, my King."

"*You?*"

"Make me Bishop of Sherborne." Osrick's ambition welled in his throat. "I can never fill the boots of he who crowned your brother king, yet I will be a stalwart servant of your cause."

"You have not trained for the Church," Alfred said doubtfully. "Do you read?"

Osrick was taken aback, if only for a moment. He had not realized that Alfred would think that being bishop required any special talent or effort. "I learned religion at my mother's knee. My son is in holy orders. A man need not read to support others in the learning of it."

Alfred's mouth turned down. Osrick realized his mistake. "But I wish to learn this reading, myself. Would you deny your truest servant the way to salvation?" And in that question Osrick knew he had won.

Alfred's face softened. "Of course not, friend. I shall name you Bishop of Sherborne the moment it is in my power to do so." He clapped Osrick on the back. "Asser will teach you your letters, that the words of the Bible may live in your heart and on your lips."

Osrick ducked his head as though in humility. "My king, I am grateful for your generosity, but more for your trust. I will prove a steadfast ally to your cause." He paused for effect. "Would that all around you were so dedicated to your ideas."

"What? What do you mean?"

Osrick feigned surprise. "You do not know?" He shook his head. "It is not my place . . ."

"A loyal subject informs his king of aught that affects his cause." Alfred drew himself up.

Osrick bit his lip, then sighed in resignation. "The girl, Alfred. It is the girl."

"What do you mean? Epona lends her presence. She would lend her Gift if she could."

"You have only her word that she cannot. She does not love Jesu. You know that."

Alfred nodded. He gave Osrick a penetrating look. "But many of my subjects believe more in her gods than in mine. It will not further my cause to despise them by despising her."

Osrick felt the shifting sand beneath his feet and took another tack. "I do not say you should despise her. I only

243

wonder whether she truly supports your cause."

Alfred took a haunch of meat brought by Raedwald and passed it to Osrick before he took one for himself. *"Thonc to thu,"* he said to the other man. "She supports my cause, Osrick. She even bears my child."

Osrick did not try to instill doubt on that point, not yet. "That does not necessarily follow, my lord. Men have heard her speak of the Vikings as though they were welcome as rulers."

Alfred frowned. "I, too, admire their *law*. They are fair. And Jesu teaches us not to hate, Osrick. I only seek to throw them out of a land that is not theirs."

Osrick backed off. He had planted the seed. It was enough. He watched as the girl came back to the fire, the black wolf pup nipping at her heels. "I ask only that you be on guard."

Alfred watched the girl as well. A tiny crease grew between his brows. Then he shook himself and laughed. "Your concern becomes you, Osrick. But you are wrong about Epona. You will see." He tore into his venison.

Osrick smiled. *I will see.*

Chapter Sixteen

Valgar searched the faces around the hall in Chippenham, their features made harsh by the flicker of the firelight and the glow of the lamps against the wall. Some laughed, some were more serious, like Egill of the watchful eyes, and the limping one from the swampland, Karn. They, at least, thought this latest threat from the Saxons was not a light matter. Val kept his own council, and turned to Guthrum whose voice boomed over the raucous crowd.

"They gather in the south," the *konnungr* growled.

"They are but tattered remnants of an army." Ragnor, son of Guthrum, snorted. "Their king a boy with no experience at winning battles. He has tasted only the bitterness of loss."

Guthrum shook his head. The gray locks over his ears trembled. "What say the spies?"

One named Skapti grunted in response. "The lion pennant of Borogand flutters, mad with wind, over his hundreds. They seek the support of the Cornish eorl from the End of Lands."

Guthrum nodded. "Trevellyan." Egill and Karn exchanged looks.

Ragnor shrugged. "So let us now crush them as though in Fafnir's coils. Let their blood brightly flow before their hopes are raised."

"They bide in a swamp where none can approach. Borogand's legions surround them. Others wait to rise in support. If we attack, we may not achieve Alfred's bones."

"And if we achieve not his bones, then he raises another army," Guthrum muttered, downing a gulp of mead. "This man could coax the dead to follow him. He has Loki's tongue."

"Have you thought to treat with him?" the one called Karn asked. Val had been surprised, when this *jarl* of the Fens leapt down from his magnificent horse today, to see that he was but half a warrior. He limped, and Val thought he detected a stiff shoulder. Still, Guthrum seemed to rate him above even Ragnor or Egill. And a wily warrior like Guthrum would not welcome a cripple unless there was another value there.

"Treat with him?" Ragnor asked, incredulous. Guthrum raised his chin toward Karn that he might continue.

Karn leaned forward, hands on the leathers covering his thighs. "One who holds the minds of the people is not easily defeated. Carve the island up, while we have advantage."

"We would abase ourselves to this *boy* on the advice of one who is *haltr?*" Ragnor cried. Scorn drenched his voice. Murmurs coursed around the circle. "Why not trample the black and yellow of the Raven pennant in the mud? Let the gods take us before we so shame ourselves."

Karn sucked in air as though to ward off anger. "Peace secures our holdings, *Konnungr*," he said to Guthrum. "And the first step to peace is to treat with this enemy who will raise army after army against us. Treat with him now while he is yet unsure of his strength against us."

Ragnor thrust himself up to standing. "You council peace?"

Karn's voice was calm, though Val suspected that calm was hard-bought. "I do."

Guthrum chewed his lips. Val glanced around. The circle

was still undecided. Ragnor was displaying his usual impetuous temper. It was what made Guthrum unsure of his heir. Ragnor's faith in total war created support for Karn's idea, though that was not his intent. Egill sat back against the wall, his eyes mere slits, waiting. He did not want to show where lay his thoughts.

"The land is rich, the island larger even than our homeland," Val found himself calling out. Karn glanced at him. Guthrum gave him his attention, a look of speculation in his eyes. Val cleared his throat. "Our forces are spread thin to hold it. Better we hold securely what we have taken than that we lose all trying to gain all."

His words provoked more muttering. Ragnor shook his head in disgust and threw himself back into his seat. Val hoped his face did not redden. The heat of the fire had taken residence there.

Guthrum chewed his mustaches, saying nothing. Finally, he raised his gray eyes to the circle. "I care not to share this island with a stripling Saxon lad. We will press home our advantage. But we will not hunt out this Alfred in the fastness of his swamp. Let him ready himself. We will present ourselves at a place propitious for battle, and he will come to meet us. Then will we vanquish his puny force, like the minions of Thor we are. The raven pennant will wave in the winds of this island from the rocky north to the End of Lands." He stood.

The decision was made. Val could feel his face was still red. He likely seemed disloyal to propose compromise, to side with Karn. What had come over him? Was he not Valgar the Beast, ready for any battle that came? He had likely just undermined any trust his fellow *Danir* might have in him.

Guthrum strode out of the hall. As he went, the man threw an arm around Karn's great shoulders. The *Jarl* of the Fens towered over him. "Does your witch wife yet beguile you, rider of horses?" he growled. Guthrum must have some soft spot in his heart for this man, Val thought. They acted as though they had just agreed.

"It is her Saxon ways, First *Jarl*." Karn was suppressing a smile.

"You must tell me of these Saxon ways," the old man grunted.

Karn shook his head and laughed. "Not I, Hammer of Thor. Let some Saxon wench teach you. Have you news of Ivar the Boneless?"

"He has conquered most of the Frankish northlands, so say the winds. He misses your wise council, though. Mayhap we can ally with him to crush this Alfred, if our first sally fails."

Val trailed after the others, apart. He doubted Guthrum would forgive him as the *Jarl* forgave Karn. He also wondered that Guthrum admitted they might not prevail upon first chance. But as host to his king and the Danish *jarls,* he was responsible for their lodging. Sucking in his unease, he stepped forward and guided them to the smaller halls around the common area where they would spread their blankets for the night. There Karn hung back, until he was the last. Val gestured to the final Saxon hall, its thatched roof and wattle walls speaking of warmth for the night, as much as the glow of the fire within. The winds were yet piercing, though it was April and spring. "May your sleep be untroubled," Val said. He nodded and turned to go.

"Stay, Valgar the Beast."

Val turned back. He dared not be seen talking with the only other of Guthrum's *jarls* who stood for peace, lest any think they plotted against their king's decision. What did Karn want?

"Stay and speak with me." When Val did not move, the big man raised his brows. "I may have news of one you know."

His mother or his sister? He wondered if he could bear news of his brothers. "Have you been recently to Danmork?" he asked, ducking under the lintel of the doorway.

Karn shook his head and pulled a stool toward the firebox. "Not in many years. No, this was a white-haired girl with purple eyes. She rode a bay mare."

Val had been dragging a stool forward himself, but at this he froze. Slowly he straightened. His gaze darted over the other man's face, fear and hope warring in his breast. "Pony?" he breathed. Could it be?

Karn's mouth twisted. "She called herself Epona."

Val realized that using her secret name betrayed her in a way and, worse, betrayed his feeling for her. He wanted to run from the hut—but he wanted to stay even more. He cleared his throat as he sat on his stool. "Where did you meet her?" he asked, as lightly as he could.

"She came to see whether my wife, Britta, could tell her destiny."

Val swallowed. Pony had been so sure of her destiny that she'd ridden away without looking back when she thought he was a challenge to it. What did her journey to a seer mean? "And did she find the knowledge she sought?"

Karn smiled and stretched his shoulders. "Britta's visions are unpredictable. That is her trial. She saw the future, but not Epona's."

"Ahh." Val was not sure whether he was disappointed or not. Would Karn's witch wife have told Pony that her destiny could not include a Viking? He doubted it. Britta apparently included a Dane in her own destiny. Had Epona heard something that made her wend her way back to the Vale of the White Horse, or to Chippenham?

Val saw Karn glance at him. He tried to make his face impassive. "She asked after you," the other Viking said.

Val blinked rapidly but kept his gaze fixed on the fire. "Oh?" He dared not say more.

Karn nodded. "Wanted to know all about you. I could not tell her much, of course."

Val felt his throat close. Karn would know only what all *Danir* knew about Valgar the Beast. He looked up and saw that Karn had told her. "How did she take it?" It didn't matter what Karn thought now. It only mattered what Pony thought.

Karn glanced away. "Saxons do not know Norse courage and what forms it may take."

Which said it all. The one secret he had managed to keep from her was his no more. Now she would despise him just as all *Danir* did. Val hardened himself, starting with the emptiness in his belly and moving up to his mouth and his eyes. "Killing your father is not courage."

There was a silence neither seemed inclined to break. Val wondered if he could leave the hut without cracking the careful shell he had constructed. Before he could decide, Karn changed the subject. "They say you rule by binding *Danir* and Saxon together."

"Not much choice if there is to be a future here."

"It is a hard way." Karn sat back and sighed. "Just when I think we all pull the cart in the same direction, the old resentments come out. You should have seen the smallness when our dike broke this winter. In both Dane and Saxon!" He mimicked a whining voice. " 'His land is flooded, not mine,' or, 'Why should my oxen haul the peat?' " He shook his head. "I almost used my sword to gather the work crew."

Val could not help but soften. "And you did not? I might have."

"I think not. You have started councils, have you not?"

"Cripples though they are." What had he said? Would Karn think that a snipe against his limp?

He seemed not to. "They will learn to walk and then to run, as I did. Or in my case, I learned to ride a horse into battle, since my hip was not to be mended."

The man seemed at peace with his condition. Val wondered if he himself could be so sanguine if he were *haltr*. "Epona rides horses like that, as if they are one with her." He had not meant to say that. But his thoughts kept coming back to Pony whether he willed them or no.

Karn nodded. "I have never seen the like."

Val tried to master his lips so they wouldn't smile in remembrance. He tried, too, to stop himself from asking the next question. It was no use. "Where did she go when she left you?"

Karn shook his head. "Britta told her to go to Alfred—though she was not certain how to find him."

Val felt his stomach drop. To Alfred?

Karn hesitated. "Her Gift was troubling her and she refused to use it. She was not easy in her soul. And she was looking for her horses."

"They were not with her?" Val came to himself. He tried not to think of Pony with Alfred.

"Only her mare. I offered to help her search, but she insisted only she could find them. I should have stayed with her, but I was promised to the council at Ely. She would not wait."

Pony had lost her herd? She would be frantic. Valgar wanted to leap onto Slepnir's back and go to her. But she had gone to Alfred. And she would not welcome one who had committed a crime to scar the soul and earn the hatred of his fellows. His shoulders slumped. He could not help her now. He could never help her.

Karn eyed him. "She is much like my Britta in some ways—and in some ways *not* like. Britta has a temper. She is like a fire that blazes in the night sky, shooting sparks into the darkness. Epona . . . Epona is like still water. Yet she boils like a hot spring underneath the quiet surface. They share a connection with a world I cannot see."

Val looked at his hands. "You bridged the gap between yourself and your wife."

Karn nodded slowly. "At great cost." He chuckled, remembering.

Val rose. He could not listen to this anymore. Karn rose with him and said, "I would I were on my way back to Stowa this very instant, instead of biding here on a fool's errand to give Guthrum every scrap of land he can hoard." He shrugged. "Our cause is not best served with his plan. Maybe Egill will come out against it."

Val did not say that he agreed. He felt disloyal for even continuing to question Guthrum's plan in the privacy of his own thoughts. The fact that he had spoken out against it in front of others would only confirm their idea that he could not be trusted. Egill was too wary to chance contradicting

Guthrum openly. So Val nodded but he did not speak. Instead, he ducked out the doorway into the night.

Pony watched warily as Osrick rode into camp. He came out of the morning mist that rose from the swamp like a wraith taking shape from insubstantial air, and his men shadowed into life behind, their horses blowing. He had gone to seek the support of the legendary leader of the old ones who'd been here before the Saxons. Long ago they had retreated beyond the western mountains, beyond the moors in the south, and it was to the south that Osrick had gone to find Trevellyan. It had been a peaceful week without him. Pony had regained much of her strength after the long journey here to Wessex. But now she snapped her fingers for the pup and knelt to gather him to her breast lest he be trampled by the horses pounding up the path.

Osrick shook his head as Alfred stood to meet him. "No luck, my king," he said. He swung his leg over his saddle and almost fell to the ground. All the horses were sweated and blowing.

"He will not come?" Alfred asked.

"I could not find him!" Frustration filled Osrick's voice. "I asked everywhere. I stated my mission. None would tell me where his stronghold lay, or where he was."

Alfred clapped him on the shoulder. "There is no love betwixt Saxon and Celt, my friend. I worried he would refuse you."

"If he had refused me, I could bear it!" They walked toward Alfred's hut. "I think he is a legend only."

"Oh, he refused you," Alfred reassured him.

Pony felt First Mare come up behind her and nudge her shoulder. Anticipation hung in the thick air. Once, such a gesture would have been a signal for her to *listen*, but she dared not listen now. Still, the trembling expectation of . . . something drew her head around toward where the morning sun would be if she could see it. She rose slowly, hearing the noise of the camp around her. Osrick's voice complained somewhere. Pup rose, too. He had grown tall enough that she could stroke him as she stood beside her. Her hand moved of its own volition to his head. A horse. She heard a horse. Not the horses of Osrick's men being led to their fodder. Not First Mare, behind her. Another horse. First Mare nudged her more urgently.

The figure on horseback moved in through the rising mist, dark against the light behind him. Sunlight strained through the fog until he was haloed by incandescence. He looked like a god come to earth, or a spirit come to claim some living victim. He held his lance upright. His horse whinnied. The camp froze and turned to look.

"Wessex," the figure boomed. Shadowed soldiers loomed rank on rank behind him. Or were they only trees?

Behind her, a voice spoke clearly, unafraid. "I am Alfred. Who are you, rider?"

There was no answer. The figure did not move. Asser crossed himself. The fog boiled, lit from within, until Pony wasn't sure the figure was real at all. Then the silhouetted horse walked forward, snorting—not toward Alfred, but toward her. The rider's features took shape. It was a fierce old man, his hair a white nimbus around beetling eyebrows. His mouth was a cruel slit in his lined face. He was dressed for battle in leather and chain mail.

First Mare shrieked at the rider's horse as he approached. Pony stared up at the grim visage that examined her, with its eyes that lingered on her face then moved to her belly.

"Ah," he said as his mount reached out to touch Pony with his nose. "It is you."

She looked into those old, fierce eyes and recognized the Old Ones, the ones before the Saxons. They had known her Mothers. Once the Druids were their priests. They understood that the Great Fecund Mare was older than they could comprehend. They stood in the long line of her worshipers, knowing they were not the first, afraid they were the last. "Yes," she answered simply.

All waited. The old man dipped his head in deference to her, his eyes moving over her belly. "You are here with him?

253

It is his?" he asked, nodding at Alfred but not looking at him.

"Yes."

He turned to Alfred and surveyed him with eyes blued by age. "You should have sent *her*, Alfred. It would have saved time and trouble."

"A girl?" Osrick asked between gritted teeth. "He sent his second in command."

The figure ignored him. "If she has chosen you, I am with you." His mount sidled under him as he gathered the reins. "When do you move against the barbarians?"

"Two weeks, no more."

"We will be here." Then the horse and rider turned their backs and melted into the mist.

Pony watched the Old One disappear as though he had never been. His legions melted away as well. She turned to look at Alfred, to see if he shared her delusion. Osrick stood glowering behind the young king. Asser stood by his side looking bemused.

"I think that was Trevellyan," the priest murmured.

Alfred turned to Pony and gave a chuckle only slightly nervous. "I think we are lucky he respects our incarnation of the Goddess, else he might have sided with the barbarians against us." His laugh gained confidence. "It has been four centuries since his folk retreated before us to the corners of the island, yet to him it was surely yesterday."

Pony shook her head. Here was yet another person, the Old One, who seemed surer of her importance than she herself was. "In the scheme of things, it was yesterday," she snapped. The mist was lifting now, but all trace of the fierce old warrior was gone. No army was revealed, awaiting his beck and call. Here was only the small tattered camp and the newly leafed trees, and the Saxon men muttering at what they had seen. The pressure of all the years of her Mothers' worship at the altar of the Great Mother, pushed at Pony. This man had known her just by looking at her. Knew what she was, what she should do. Why did she not know herself?

Chapter Seventeen

Pony watched the men saddle their horses, pack carts with supplies, push swords, slithering, into their scabbards. The camp was alive with tension that seemed to whirl out from Alfred's person. Now was the time. The battle must be joined, their sanctuary abandoned at last. Pony felt the sheet lightning of anticipation filling the air around her until she could hardly breathe or think. This was the opposite of the quiet she needed. She crouched off to the side, the pup's now gangly body clutched to her as he whined and tried to wriggle away. She could not let him go or he would be off with the men. He was a carnivore. He would not be dismayed by the prospect of soldiers lusting for the blood of their enemies. Which gave her pause. She should let him go. It would be good riddance to such a disturbance in her life. What was he to her? If he was hurt in the melee, what of it? Still, she held him tightly to her swollen breasts and her distended belly.

Young Black pranced proudly under his new master. Alfred had been diligent about learning the Language of

Touch; Pony had to give him that. They had spent many hours together teaching Alfred to direct Young Black with weight shifts and gentle touches—much to Osrick's dismay. Osrick glowered now on his mount beside his king. The carts began to roll, the clattering horde moving toward the path, and the great army gathered in the countryside beyond the swamp. Even Asser was mounted on a small sturdy horse native to the moors. They were going to hunt down Vikings. Alfred was going to fulfill his destiny. That should have made her glad. But Pony could think only of a flute stilled forever and gray eyes gone flat with death. There was no peace for her here for many reasons. This did *not* feel right.

Pony dreaded being left behind alone. Her babe would be due shortly. Fear shuddered through her. What had she expected? If she had been home in the Vale, she would have birthed her girl alone. What was so different here? She clutched her pup tighter, as though that would ward off any answers. In the Vale the spirit of her Mothers would be with her, guiding her. Herd would have been around, with her. But here, in this wet place filled with men who ate meat and bore weapons, there was no connection with her past. She had abandoned her Mothers and all their beliefs when she had followed Alfred and so sacrificed their solace and their aid, her Gift and her Herd.

Alfred and Young Black skittered toward her. The young king turned a smile on her made more brilliant by the joy of being released from the swamp to engage his destiny. "Epona," he said. "Does your mare grow too big to ride? I can get you a pony."

Pony felt her eyes widen and her stomach roll. "I am not going with you, Alfred. This is your destiny, not mine." Yet in her heart she felt a tugging she could not explain. Was it to Alfred? Or was the tug she felt to something else?

Alfred straightened, frowning. "My destiny includes you too now, Epona. You must come with us. Trevellyan joined us only because of you. The troops must see you. You and Asser will help us gather our forces along the way."

"Into battle? Me?" She had never seen a battle, but she imagined it would be no different than the wolves tearing at a carcass. She could not endure the pain, the blood. There would be no peace for her with Alfred, either in battle or in the glowing anticipation of his conquest. "I cannot." Yet something told her that she must be there.

Alfred turned and motioned to a soldier. "Raedwald! Get a cob horse for our priestess." He turned again to Pony. "I cannot leave you here for our enemies to find."

Raedwald brought a flea-bitten gray, shorter and less fine than First Mare, toward her. Pony rose, backing away. Her pup barked and capered into the crowd of horses and men. "Pup!" she called, but he was gone. Panic whirled in her breast. She looked wildly around, until Alfred reached down from his perch on Young Black and grabbed her hand. She jerked her gaze to his face, shaking her head. But inside her mind, she heard Britta's voice: *"Go to Alfred. He will have need of you. After that it is less clear. . . ."*

"Our destiny is shared," the king said softly, rubbing his thumb over the back of her hand. "Come meet your destiny."

She looked into his blue eyes and saw that sureness she wanted so much for herself. Her breathing slowed. He was certain of her destiny as well as his. How strange. How . . . comforting.

He nodded slowly as his smile grew.

She nodded in return, took a breath and let Raedwald help her sit with both legs on one side of the gray's bare back. She pulled the skirts of her cyrtle over her calves and settled herself.

Alfred cantered to the path ahead. The chaos of milling horses and men began to sort itself into a line behind him. Asser fell in beside Pony. First Mare whinnied and followed. They were off. She would follow Alfred's destiny into battle.

"They are on the move!"

Val jerked up from his game of *hneftafl* with Karn, knocking a piece from the board. Karn's men turned from wagering on the outcome of the contest. The mud-splattered man who shouted heaved himself off his blowing horse almost before the animal had skittered to a stop. The yard of the Chippenham fortress was crowded now with *Danir* gathered from Anglia, as far south as Cent and as far north as Jorvik, to meet Alfred's coming challenge. They camped outside the gates even to the meadow where Pony's herd once grazed.

Val and Karn looked at each other. Val could see his own dread, his own determination, reflected in the other man's eyes. They strode after Harald, who was already approaching the scout.

"Where and how many?" Harald shouted above the din.

Behind him, Guthrum came to the door of the hall.

"Beyond counting," the scout gasped as someone took the reins of his lathered horse. "They are come as far as Shaftsbury and press on toward Warminster."

"Is the Celt with them?" Guthrum's voice boomed over his men's excited muttering and the slapping of thighs and backs. His *Danir* were eager to be on the move. They didn't realize how close the Saxons were. Val knew they were not far from Pony's stone circle.

A silence fell. "*Ja.*" The scout nodded, chest still heaving. "Cornwall has brought his forces. I saw the lion flag of Borogand. There are Centish troops, too."

Guthrum nodded. His gray eyes swept the yard. "Prepare," he shouted. "We march tomorrow." He turned and stepped inside as the yard erupted in activity.

Val had been afraid that Alfred would succeed in allying with the Celt. Trevellyan's numbers and the legendary fierceness of his fighting men made the outcome of the imminent clash less certain. Guthrum had counted on the ancient enmity between Celt and Saxon to keep Trevellyan at home; apparently that had not happened.

To control where they met the Saxon hordes, Guthrum had sent riders to scout locations of best advantage. They had eventually chosen a site Val suggested, one he'd passed on his way back from the Vale with Pony. Gently rolling hills at a place called Eddington were edged with a steep slope, almost sheer, to the valley below. The only way in was through a narrow gorge—which would make attackers vulnerable. They needed to get there quickly. Val glanced out the open gates to the undulating camps beyond. He would want to leave today if he were Guthrum, but the *Danir* were not ready. Many had only just arrived.

"Are they close?" Karn's voice sounded at his side.

"*Ja*," Val said. "And if they have chosen that same ground, they may get there first."

Both believed, without either speaking, that Guthrum should have treated with Alfred while he could. It was left to the man called Jael, who had come with Karn from the fens, to define their problem for them aloud. "I hope this fight is worth Danish blood," the man grumbled. "Hild is home with a new babe. I leave my wife to be protected from brigands and Saxon marauders by my Saxon friends." He shook his head. "It is a strange world."

Val nodded. He had no woman to protect, but he understood. Most of these *Danir* had gone *vikingr* to make their fortune—and somewhere in their journey, the land had grabbed their most secret dreams and sprouted in them like grass in spring. These men had oxen and wives and pigs and children, now, halls and stables to bind them; not Guthrum and his need to rule the island, but neighbors, new families and crops. Would one of their own ruling the whole island change their lives? If Alfred won, what could he do to them? Could he make them all go home?

Val sighed. Alfred could do damage. He could put Osrick back in charge of Chippenham, with enough men to continue stealing from his people. Osrick could kill all the *Danir* he saw, at war or at peace. Would the people in Chippenham stand by for that, with Harald wed to Una and a dozen others courting? Val looked ahead and saw an endless series of battles, no matter who won at Eddington. Valhalla was here on earth, with less feasting and no hope of change. The bleakness of that vision weighed on his shoulders. He looked up at Karn and saw a similar speculation.

But it did not matter. Here was a test of their loyalty. And Val, for one, would not refuse the call. He could not. His loyalty was all that was left to him.

Both men squared their shoulders. Valgar pounded Karn on the back, not in jubilation but resignation. Without another word, they split to organize their men.

As Val opened his mouth to shout to Harald, a horrible thought intruded. He stopped in the middle of the surrounding tumult, looking around like a trapped animal. *Pony!* Pony had gone to Alfred to help with that king's cause. Did that mean she would be coming to Eddington, too? No, of course not. He swung into action again. "Harald, gather the men by the stable in the back!" he called. Alfred would not endanger her by bringing her to a battleground. That should have relieved him, but it only meant that he would never see her again. "Elbert! Organize our supplies in the carts," he yelled to the priest. Val's body seemed to move by rote, because he had practiced what he must do in preparation for battle for more years than he cared to count. Let those years stand him in good stead now, for they were all that was left to him.

Osrick dug his spurs into the side of his horse and cantered ahead to where Alfred rode flanked by his whore priestess and the stupid little priest. This was getting worse and worse. Since the Celt had joined them, Alfred had begun publicly to show her preference. Men whispered that she had great powers, that she would use them for the cause. The Celts spoke of her with great deference as a Druidess who had some special connection to the unseen world. And the fact that she was breeding with Alfred's child without benefit of wedlock seemed to bother no one, not even Asser, that stalwart of the Church who had been tormenting Osrick with learning letters for almost a month now. Bah! Osrick thought as he jerked his horse up just behind Alfred's. Apparently goddesses were excused from rites like marriage.

There was no room on the narrow road for him to ride abreast of his king, as Asser and Epona did. He seethed as he settled in beside Raedwald. They had been riding hard for two days. It had rained as they crossed the Salisbury Plain, and while it was May warm, the constant damp made every piece of leather Osrick wore chafe at his skin. He was tired. They were *all* tired—except maybe Alfred, who did not ever seem fatigued.

Pony's influence on the king was growing greater than Osrick's own. She was probably spreading poison about him into Alfred's ears at every turn—and Alfred was easy enough to influence when he was not paying attention. That had been his plan if Alfred—no *when* Alfred—brought off this miracle and won back the island: Osrick would manipulate the youth behind the scenes. He himself could never have raised the army winding out behind them like some giant dragon's tail until it disappeared into the distance; it took Alfred's intensity, his dream, his sureness and beauty. Those were what created the faithful. But Alfred's incandescence was his weakness, too. When he was dreaming of tomorrow, he forgot about today. Which left room for Osrick's machinations. But not if the bitch priestess was around. Not if she drew Alfred's attention to his plan.

Also, if someone didn't do something about her, Epona's bastard might well be declared Alfred's heir. Even if the child was a girl, of which the whore seemed so sure, she could be contracted to wed the son of Cent, riding behind them at the head of his troops, or any other man with an army at his back, and Osrick would have competition. Or maybe Alfred would hold back contracting his bastard to watch his allies fight for the chance to bind their destiny to his. No, that was too devious for Alfred. But it didn't matter; men would come to the child's mother for influence, not to Osrick. His power would be nil. The palm of his sword hand itched and couldn't be scratched.

"Eddington is the perfect place to meet them," Alfred was saying to Epona, who looked gray with fatigue. "If we occupy the rolling land before it falls away to the Salisbury Plain, they must approach by way of the gorge. It will control their attack, and we them, in consequence."

Osrick inserted himself into the conversation. "How is it you know of this place?" He couldn't believe that Alfred was sharing strategy with a girl and a priest rather than him.

The king turned in his saddle. "Oh, it's you, Osrick." Even that sounded dismissive. "You forget I was born at Wantage. I roamed all over this part of the country when I was a growing lad with a fast horse and a restless mind. When I saw the lay of the land at Eddington, I was but twelve summers, I think. But I knew it for what it was even then, and played out battles in my mind for hours there, rolling on the grass in the summer sun."

"So you come back to your childhood dreams to realize your destiny," Asser said. "I must remember that for my record."

Alfred laughed apologetically. "Asser wants to tell the history of my life."

"Is it not usual to wait until one is dead to sing one's songs?" Osrick asked sullenly.

"No songs. I will write it in a book," the priest said proudly. "It will not be forgotten, or changed in future times."

Osrick bit back the word *useless,* remembering the value Alfred put on writing and reading. "Books burn," he warned, his words clipped. "Memories are surer."

"For a while," Asser agreed. "But if the books are cared for, they will last when all who sang the song are dead, or when all those who sing have forgotten a song's meaning."

"I will build you a library, Asser," Alfred pledged with a laugh, "for all the books you write. Perhaps I, too, will write a story—about Epona, and how she lent us courage in the Battle of Eddington."

How could Alfred have the energy to laugh so? How could he give Epona the credit for the coming battle before it even occurred? Osrick gritted his teeth and resolved to do something about the bitch priestess. He was not a man to sit idly by and watch his best chance at power be snatched away—especially not by a girl who needed only purple eyes to ensnare a king.

*   *   *

Slepnir sidled nervously as Val brought him to stand beside
Karn's bay, Thorn. The *jarls* circled around Guthrum to
hear his assessment of the situation. Their army seethed at
their back, undulating across the plain in the early morning
mist. The weather was warm, a day for gathering new bud-
ded flowers with a maid. But not today. Above them, up
the almost sheer face of the hills, the Saxon army waited.
The *Danir* were not close enough to be in arrow or javelin
range. Still they could see one man, his bare head gleaming
blond, sitting a big black horse beneath a fluttering dragon
pennant. It was Alfred, and he stood at the edge of the
precipice and dared them to come up the gorge.

"The worst has happened." Guthrum glared around the
circle. "But we may yet come out whole, Thor willing." His
piercing gaze stopped on Val's face. "How lays the land to
the north?"

"A river winds through steep hills behind the battleground." Val's voice was steady.

Guthrum nodded. "The gods give us a way that is hard.
But Odin's eye of wisdom will show us how to prevail. Baldur's heart will stand with us, Dane-proud at the end of the
day." He looked around the circle. "Half will camp here.
Half will again divide and circle through these hills from
each side. We will crack this Saxon army like an oyster with
Thor's hammer."

Each knew the losses would be heavy with such a strategy. All also knew that there was no other way to win the
day, if winning could be got of it. Val fit his bronze helmet
around his ears until the cold metal of the nosepiece slid
into place. "Let me take the left circle, First *Jarl*."

Guthrum nodded. "And Karn, you are the right. Ragnor,
Egill and the others, stay here with me. Choose your quarters," he said to Val and Karn, motioning to the men behind
him.

They nodded and turned their horses. It would take them
most of the morning to get 'round behind the army. And the
Saxons would see their strategy. The hills would offer good
places for ambush. Danish blood would be spilt. Val only
hoped he could make the Saxons pay a price for that blood.

This distraction would draw off defenders and give Guthrum a chance at taking the gorge—the only answer was to pour men up at it and hope for the best.

Val wheeled to face Karn. There was a question he had wanted to ask. "Guthrum says you ride your horse into battle, Karn. That is an advantage. Your leather straps give balance?"

Karn nodded, grinning. "Others could use them. Men on horses would be powerful for the *Danir*. But Guthrum thinks I do this only because my hip is torn."

Val nodded. "He clings to the old way. I will look for you today. May you end standing." Karn held out his arm in salute, then cantered away.

Val looked up at the Saxon king, blond and gleaming in the morning sun. On one side of him, a man in a brown robe like Elbert's sat a small horse. A priest at the head of an army? Then Val's eyes picked out the figure that graced Alfred's other side. It had a halo of white hair. He swallowed, his mouth suddenly dry. Could it be? She did not ride her bay mare, but a small, stocky gray horse. He could not even be sure the figure was female, let alone see whether her eyes were purple blue. But he did not have to. His heart told him it was Pony. Confused emotion washed over him. She sat at Alfred's side, not his. But how could the man bring her into a battle such as this was like to be? His breath came faster in his chest and his heart thumped against his ribs as he recognized the answer. Alfred used her as a weapon, just as Val had done, to show that her gods favored his cause.

It did not mean he would endanger her. The battle was not to be joined until afternoon, perhaps even late afternoon. There was time for her to get to safety. Val swallowed again and turned Slepnir toward the Danish forces splitting into quarters. He dared not let thoughts of Pony distract him. They might get him killed—or worse, endanger his men. His duty was clear, his loyalty crucial against these dire odds. Those were enough for him to think about. "Harald," he shouted. "Stay by my side today. We will fight together. Perhaps I can even the score with you again."

Chapter Eighteen

Pony and Asser sat their cobby moorland horses at the top of a rolling rise to the east of what would be the battle proper. First Mare grazed nearby. Asser held a rope tied to the pup's collar. Alfred had placed them where all Saxons could see them: symbols of the gods' support.

The day was fine. The rolling meadow ahead should have been filled only with a grazing herd, buzzing insects and the smell of green renewal. It should have been quiet here. But Pony shuddered. The meadow was anything but peaceful. It writhed with men whose bodies were bound in hardened leather and chain link shirts, preparing for the coming battle. They wore brass conical helmets and carried swords or axs, lances, bows and knives. The midafternoon sun glinted off a thousand unnatural surfaces, blinding her. The day was cut with shouts above the threatening rumble of male voices. She could make out no words. She needn't try. Everything all seethed with the violence that would soon erupt. Blood would flow. The sky would soon push back echoes of pain and rage.

Death shuddered in the air. What sense was any of this? Her breath came fast. Alfred's dragon pennant fluttered, gold on bloodred, near the edge of the gorge where they expected the Vikings to advance. Was she here to help Alfred regain the island from the Danes? She did not know. But had she bartered the peace of her Vale for this?

She glared around, running her fingers through her hair. Val would soon be fighting here among these men, Valgar the Beast, who had killed his own father. She had seen his Viking forces divide themselves. Now Guthrum waited for those troops to gain their places to attack. This was Val's world, his way. It was a way she would never understand.

Asser put his hand on her forearm. She glanced down, surprised at the warm touch.

"You cannot stop it or change it," he said, his eyes pitying. "Our fate is to watch."

"To what purpose?" she almost wailed. "If Alfred wins, will the Vikings just go home? If the Vikings prevail, will the warring cease?" She shook her head.

"No. There will be other battles." He patted her forearm and sat back in his saddle. "One fights for right, for one's God, for one's way of life. And those are bought at a price, my dear."

"I don't believe it," Pony whispered. But she wasn't sure. She wanted the Vale of the White Horse, and Herd, and quiet. But there was no Herd, and she had never been further from quiet. Maybe this *was* the way of the world. It was just a world from which her mother had tried to shield her. She should have listened to her mother.

A shout rolled through the army, starting from beneath the dragon pennant. The Vikings must be advancing. Off to her left, Saxon soldiers surged into the shadowy wood at the rear of the battle lines to fight a second front. Pony turned her cob's head. She had to get out of this place.

Asser stayed her. "There is nowhere to go," he yelled over the shouting. "You are safe from the Danes only here, where all can see you."

Pony searched his eyes, looking for another answer. She

received none. Glancing fearfully back toward the mass of men, she saw they sprouted gleaming weapons like a hedgehog. She could not bear to see this thing that would happen, but she would see it. And she had some awful premonition that it would change her forever.

The fighting, when it started, held her transfixed. The shouting seemed to still. She could see individual drops of blood flung out from killing blows. Mouths writhed with death. Bodies reverberated in her belly as they hit the ground. All moved slowly, an anarchy of horrifying images without sound. Pony tried to breathe. It was all she could do.

Val and Harald burst from the trees into the bright light of the meadowland, swords swinging. Val's throat was hoarse from yelling, but he yelled anyway, the fever of battle boiling in his blood. His voice was lost in the shouting around him, the clang of metal on metal, the thud of ax against shield. The rolling meadow was alive with Saxon and Dane, indistinguishable except for the shape of their shields, hacking at each other and screaming their defiance. All strategy was gone now. Those Danes under Val and Karn who'd survived the push up from the river through the trees now met the waiting rear line of the Saxons head-on.

Val slashed to the right with Bloodletter as the first of the enemy rushed his ragged line of *Danir*. A young boy, no more than fifteen, met his fate as Bloodletter bit into his neck. He was replaced by two others. Val used his shield to bash at the shoulder of a Saxon on his right, even as Bloodletter found another's belly. He heaved up with both sword and shield and his foes fell backward. In their space he stepped ahead. Harald was at his left, hacking forward, too. His men were tired in their bones and in their minds. Sword and shield were battle-heavy. But Val expected that. He had felt it what, a hundred times before? Harald might be more surprised. Val shouted encouragement to his young friend, then kicked the sword hand of a lunging Saxon that Harald might skewer him before he himself was pierced.

Harald's face was bloodied, maybe with his own gore. Val's shoulder was slashed—thank the chain mail not very deep. He hammered at a Saxon's face with his sword hilt when the man got too close to use the blade. The Saxon fell back. Bloodletter followed.

"The line," Val shouted to his men. "Keep the line!" Only by standing shoulder-to-shoulder in their thinning ranks could they hope to stay alive. Did Guthrum yet prevail? Val spared a glance to see the raven flag fluttering above the fray. It seemed a league distant. The battle surged down the hill as Val's *Danir* gained momentum. How long could they hold out? They were fierce fighters, but the Saxons outnumbered them. He did not want to know by how much. Slash a long-bearded one. Defend against the swing of an ax. Push forward, grunting with effort as the fighting stalled in a ditch. Slice up between a pair of Saxon legs. Sever a neck exposed and watch the head topple at an unnatural angle until the next body pushed forward, until the next thud against your shield reverberated up your arm.

The Danish line pushed forward a little out of the ditch, up a rise. They were off to the right of the main battle. Good. They could turn and have the advantage of height, perhaps contain the enemy between his men and Karn's.

Val broke through to the top of the rise. Trees crowded the edges, but in front of the trees a horse stood, its rider looking out over the battle. A cobby horse, a gray. Its rider had a halo of white-blond hair. The din of battle receded in his ears. All movement slowed. Before him, Epona sat, holding the reins of another little riderless horse with a dog tied to its saddle. A very pregnant bay mare stood nearby. Val's eyes returned to the woman as iron to a lodestone.

Pony. He drank her in. Wait! What was that silhouette against the trees?

Movement captured his eye. Chain mail winked with sunlight. A warrior lunged forward, sword raised, toward Pony. Saxon or Dane, it didn't matter. Rage closed off all thought. Val's legs pumped without command. The muscles in his arms, aching a moment before, now bunched with new strength to raise Bloodletter high. His vision narrowed to the spot where the warrior would be in the next second. He heard Pony's shriek only dimly.

He lunged, and Bloodletter was met with the other's sword blade at the last second. The clash of metal echoed in him, shutting out all other sounds. He and his foe pushed away, strength equal. For two steps they circled, then Val screamed a challenge and attacked again. Light flashed as their swords caught the fading sun. Val threw himself against the man's shield even as Bloodletter pushed the other's sword aside. His foe went down. Val raised Bloodletter for the kill, but the man kicked out at his feet, throwing him off balance. He stumbled back, and that alone saved him from the worst of a thrust at his thigh. Doubling over, he saw his enemy scramble up and raise his sword. Val recovered. He swung his sword out, quick if not powerful, and nicked a forearm. He and the other circled again, more careful now. Val's bloodlust was fading. He could hear the battle once again. That was good. A trumpet blared. A shout rose of many men. Val spared a glance to the field below and saw the raven pennant fall.

The end! The *Danir* had surrendered. Val turned back to his enemy. He could see, now, that the markings on the hilt of the man's sword were unlike the ribbon dragon that adorned Bloodletter in good Danish style. His helmet had the rounded eye holes that were more Saxon than Dane, and Val saw the eyes inside flick to Pony. He cared not if the raven had fallen; this Saxon would not hurt her. He closed again, slashing. They parried and hacked at each other, both exhausted, both unwilling to call halt.

Pony was yelling something at them. It didn't matter. The sound of the battle behind him subsided under the insistence of the trumpet. He and his foe continued.

Finally, two Saxons came up and held his attacker, even as Harald and a Dane stayed Val's own arm. "Valgar," Harald shouted at him. "It is over." He struggled against them.

"Val." Pony's voice was drenched in emotion. He turned. The dog had been barking all during the struggle, he realized. He saw her bulging form astride her horse. His breath came in little gasps. There was not enough air left in the meadow to fill his lungs. He pulled at his helmet. Was the child in her belly his, from the night at the circle of stones?

The hands that held him dropped. They could feel the change in him. He stepped forward, tossing his helmet on the ground. He could not speak. He just walked to her knee and looked into eyes he had thought he would never see again. He would drown in those eyes, lose himself and all he stood for.

She shook her head, answering the unasked question. "Alfred's. It has always been Alfred's." Her voice cracked. Her face wore an expression he could not read.

"What of Samhain?" he whispered through a throat suddenly too narrow to breathe.

"A mistake." Her eyes were purple liquid overflowing onto her cheeks. She looked ashamed. She was surely ashamed of having been with him after what Karn had told her.

Val blinked, and blinked again. He clenched Bloodletter's hilt as though he could squeeze out all feeling, and stepped back from her knee. With a wrench he turned away from the revulsion he knew she must feel. She had chosen Alfred time and time again.

Osrick was taking off his helmet. Through some kind of haze Val made the connection: Why had Osrick been trying to kill Pony? Did they not both serve Alfred? Bitterness ate its way through the haze. He knew Pony had given herself to Alfred from the first. It just hadn't seemed enough to dash his hopes until he saw her big with Alfred's child. Of course, his crime surely revolted her. How could it not? She was lost to him, more surely, more painfully, than if he had never seen her again. He ran his hands through hair soaked with sweat.

"Give up your weapons," one of the Saxons ordered. "You Danes are done today."

Val looked down at Bloodletter, his companion through many campaigns. It had been made especially by the smiths in Novograd to a Norse design. He had never been forced to give it up. He had never lost in battle. He tossed the beautiful weapon onto the pile with the others, and the clang dispelled the last of the haze from his brain. One part of his life was finished, here, on this hilltop. He had to find the will to go on.

Pony knew her senses were dulled by blood and pain and overwhelming sound. She could not seem to think about the battle that had consumed her with revulsion only moments before. She did not know why Osrick was here, or how Val had appeared out of the confusion; she could think only of the pain she saw in those gray eyes and the fact that she had caused it. How could a beast look so? Why did a carnivore care that the child she carried was not his? They were not questions she could answer. She could not think why she wanted to try.

Val was giving up his weapon. The sword she had so admired clanged on the other Viking steel. The pile of blades looked like a child's game of pick-up sticks. The set of Val's shoulders registered his defeat. His hair was matted to his head with sweat. Blood smeared the chain mail on his right shoulder and stained the leather on his left thigh. Pony wanted to heave her bulk off her horse and run to him. Ah, her bulk! That fact lay between them. She sat up straighter. That and the fact that he was a sworn enemy of her king. That and his killing nature. That and the fact that her daughter might be powerful in her own right some day, if Alfred owned to her. That and the fact that she was of the land invaded, and he was the invader.

Asser returned from where he had gone to haul a young Saxon not yet dead to the safety of the rise. In the end, he had not been content as a watcher either. "Epona," he called, easing his burden to the turf. "Let us get back to Alfred. We have served our purpose here. The day is won."

Was it? Pony watched Osrick gesture with his sword, annoyance in his expression. He hated her enough to try to kill her, in spite of Alfred. Val and Harald and four or five others were herded off toward the flats, where Vikings were being gathered together. Val did not look her way. He squared his shoulders and she saw his face turn stony.

Pony wasn't at all sure the day had been won.

She ducked into the door flap of the huge tent pitched at the edge of the precipice for Alfred's use. Torches lighted the interior, and the air was close with many men. Alfred held council at the far end of a raised dais with Osrick, Borogand, Trevellyan the Celt and certain others. All around men ate and drank, standing if they could not sit. She was unsure what to do. No one here knew that Osrick had tried to kill her today, not even Asser. Only Val knew, and he was not like to confirm her story. She could not tell Alfred; Osrick would just deny it. She felt fragile and vulnerable, her mind fluttering like a wounded bird. Osrick would try again. Best she stay near Alfred if she could.

She had spent the last hours wandering uselessly among the dead and dying, watching Viking bodies stripped of valuables and thrown onto a pyre for burning, or Saxons laid out for burial in accordance with the tenets of their faith. The dead were washed and wrapped in a simple winding cloth if they were Christians. Those who sought Valhalla received a burial fully dressed for war with shield and sword and ax. It was hard work, and the captured Vikings were pressed to dig the graves and throw their fellows on the pyre. Saxons handled the Saxon bodies, that they might receive all the respect due them. She hoped that all the bodies were retrieved, for she could hear the beat of vulture wings overhead, the hissing whispers of carnivores and scavengers who did not care whether their prey was living or dead circling the edges of the field.

She had looked constantly for a Viking with gray eyes and thick curling hair. She could only hope she would see him dragging bodies across the field, not being dragged. But Val was nowhere to be found. Which was as well. The emotion that had washed over her when she realized that the fighting men were Osrick and Val refused to leave entirely.

272

Val had fought to save her life. Now he realized that the babe she carried belonged to Alfred. Would he fight to save her still? Regret sluiced over her. It was but one more bit of confusion and loss laid up on a pile of the same, at any moment ready to fuel a conflagration in her soul.

She had avoided the hospital tent entirely, repelled by the screams of the wounded. Asser was likely there, blessing those his God had failed that day. Behind her she felt more than saw a flare of light, and turned in the doorway to see a Viking pyre catch in a gush of flame. It would burn for days. She wondered if she could bear it.

The pyre pushed her inside the tent proper. She was the only woman there. Men turned and nodded to her in deference. She skittered along the path that opened before her, trying to keep ahead of their tribute. They believed the day was theirs due in some part to her intervention with the gods—but she wanted to claim no part of what had happened today.

"Epona," Alfred called, standing and waving her over to the dais. "Join us. Have you taken sustenance?" The black-furred pup that lolled at his feet leapt up and careered over to her, nudging her hand for petting.

Pony shook her head. Her gorge rose at the thought. She knelt to let the pup lick her face and ears. His warmth was a comfort to her. Alfred motioned to a young soldier pressed into duty serving food. "Get our horse priestess some cakes if we have them, or flatbread, and some cabbage stew." The soldier retreated in martial discipline to do his king's bidding.

Alfred put his arm protectively around Pony's shoulders and guided her to her seat in the circle of rough stools. She hesitated. She wanted to be nowhere near Osrick. But how could she refuse this place of honor? "We were just discussing our next steps," the king said. He stood behind her and glanced around the circle. "We could use the perspective of the gods, could we not?"

There were several sour looks, Osrick's among them, but Trevellyan the Celt smiled. He was seated on Pony's right.

"Her presence alone revives us," the old man said, nodding. "It was her influence today that tilted the battle our way."

"And Alfred's strategy." Asser took Epona's plate from the returned soldier and passed it to her.

"Aye, that was fine, but *Epona* brought us victory. . . ." The old Celt glowered.

Alfred raised his hands, chuckling. "Enough. Perhaps it was my strategy to have her at the battle, that in saving herself, she would save us as well."

Trevellyan looked with approval on Alfred. "You are not as young as you look."

Osrick turned the conversation from Epona and Alfred's clever strategy, obviously annoyed. "I say we execute every Viking of importance, down to the first rank of command. It is the only way to break the back of this invasion."

After all the killing this day, Osrick contemplated more? And in executions, not fair combat? Alfred, who worshiped a god of forgiveness, would not condone such a plan. The young king paced around the circle like a beast full of coiled energy, even after waging war all day. There was not a scratch on him from the conflict, though Pony knew he had fought in the thick of the battle. Was it any wonder that he was sure of his destiny and becoming king of all Angleland?

"Perhaps that *is* the only way to break them," Alfred said, a crease disfiguring his brow. "Still, can Jesu bless a killing when there is no combat?" He puzzled over the problem and began to pace again.

Pony's protest withered in her throat. She knew nothing of war, wanted to know nothing. Her words could not influence the course of it here in this circle of fearsome men.

Asser's face was a mask made ruddy by the torchlight. "Jesu would not kill his enemies," he said. All in the circle turned toward him. "He would bind them to his heart and show them mercy."

Alfred stroked his beard. "If we tell them to withdraw . . ." But he did not seem certain.

"They will not leave the island, not when they still control the east." The Celt's words carried weight. His own people had not given up; they'd retreated and held what they could of the west.

Osrick leaned forward and took a rib of slaughtered pig that had been roasted in the fires outside the tent. All watched as he ripped at the meat on the bone with his teeth, and juice dribbled into his beard. His teeth ground rhythmically. When at last he swallowed, he looked around the circle. "Strength is what they understand, these barbarians," he proposed. "If we buy them off with Danegeld, do they show us mercy for our restraint? No. They come again the next year and ask twice as much, or threaten war. They will never rest until they have the whole."

"Even if they quit Wessex," Alfred mused, "I cannot let them have the east—neither Anglia, Cent or Northumbria. My destiny is to rule the island. It has been foretold."

Pony saw how it would go. The king's belief in his destiny would draw him toward Osrick's plan in spite of his religious qualms. But did Valgar the Beast deserve death? She did not know. She only knew she could not live if she stood by and watched a sword thrust in his belly. The vision of steel and flesh twisted in her gut.

"Alfred," she cried. All turned in her direction. She looked around, confused. What could she say against his belief in destiny, his desire to erase an enemy? Words stuck in her throat. What would Britta say, in her place? But what Britta would say had nothing to do with why she did not want Alfred revenging himself on all Vikings. Time. She needed time to think. "Should you not bring them here to confront these men you condemn? It is the kingly way."

Alfred's brows raised in surprise. Asser actually smiled. The old Celt nodded in sage agreement, and Osrick glowered at her. Alfred turned slowly toward the sentries at the door. "Go. Bring Guthrum and his *jarls,* that we may judge them," he said. His voice was strong, but there was a thoughtful quality there that gave Pony hope.

Osrick filled with protest the time until the Vikings arrived. He put forth his plan in more detail. But there was a feeling in the circle that smothered words. At last Guthrum ducked into the tent looking every inch the vanquished king. Parts of his grizzled locks were braided and entwined with amber beads; they hung on a chest covered with chain mail that glinted in the torchlight. About his shoulders was a woolen cape dyed indigo, with worked embroidered bands and a wolf skin at its neck. His boots were leather most supple, and the empty sheath for his sword was worked silver, its belt studded with cabochon jewels that bespoke a rich weapon, now absent. Behind him, his *jarls* stood with straight shoulders despite wounds and fatigue. Karn was there, his ice-blue eyes watchful; and one Pony craved the sight of more; Val. He limped but a little, and she was glad to see his wounds were not more serious. But, after a sweep of the room, his eyes focused resolutely on Alfred and would not meet her own.

Guthrum nodded to the circle. "The gods favored you this day, Alfred," he said in Danish. He was a king talking as if to an equal, not a conqueror. He glanced to Val, who translated.

"You are come to hear your fate," Alfred said. He did not seem as sure as before. Pony began to hope. How could she widen the crack in his resolve? Val murmured each translation in Guthrum's ears.

She called out; "Will you kill them now, my king, as Osrick asks, or will you wait until the morrow? Will you wield the sword yourself, or simply watch it done?" Make it hard for him, she thought. Let him imagine the act against the tenets of his God.

Guthrum's eyes jerked to Alfred, then hooded themselves. Tension vibrated in the air.

"Kill them, or they will prove the backbone of a new rebellion," Osrick pressed.

Alfred looked less certain than ever. "Let them send us to Valhalla, father," a young hothead Dane seethed. Pony translated for Alfred.

Another standing behind his king spoke. "There is no Valhalla unless we die in combat, Ragnor. I wager there is another way."

"Then let us die like warriors, in single combat, Egill."
Ragnor had his eye on Osrick. "I make my challenge to these
coward Saxon curs."

Guthrum turned but half his attention to his son, and
shook his head to silence him.

Pony spoke with all the weight of the Goddess she could
muster. "Kill them and you ensure that you will have to fight
every other Norseman to the death before he surrenders."
Pony said, glancing at Osrick. "They are your protection
against their fellows."

Alfred looked at her with cocked head, speculating. "Let
it be in some sense up to them. Will you yield the island,
Guthrum, king of Danes?"

Guthrum considered. From what Pony had learned from
Valgar the Danes seemed always practical: extracting the
blackmail of Danegeld rather than provoking a fight, if they
could; trading rather than taking if that was easier; taking
when that was easier too. They had surrendered today. That
meant they wanted to live to fight another day, did it not?
Pony held her breath.

"What care you for the east? "Guthrum asked slowly." It
does not your bidding whether I yield it or no. I yield you
Wessex, and the western Celtic lands."

Pony saw her way. Alfred must be practical, too. "Alfred,
with peace you will have time for all your plans. Churches
and reading and standing armies and ships—nothing happens without peace."

"They will never *keep* the peace," Osrick hissed. "Unless
it is the peace of the grave. They are greedy for the whole
island."

"So let us not be like them, greedy." Asser followed
Pony's lead.

"But the whole land is my destiny," Alfred protested.

"Sooner or later," she agreed. "Yet who knows *when* your
destiny is to be achieved? Mayhap, if you push too early,
you risk losing all." This, this felt right, somehow. Britta
had said it would happen more slowly than she had at first
predicted and Alfred would be disappointed. Was he *not*

meant to prevail here? "Bring a map, draw a line of peace."

"Even if I were to show mercy," Alfred began, rounding on Pony, "there is no guarantee Guthrum would stay behind any line we set."

"Pull him close, my king." Pony almost whispered, coming to Alfred's shoulder and facing the Vikings. "Baptize him in your faith, stand godfather to his sons. Bind him to you with hostages. Make him vow to your god—he will understand that."

Pony saw Alfred make his decision. His shoulders relaxed just slightly as he considered the path ahead.

Osrick went red in the face. He knew his plan was lost. "Something of more substance must be pledged," he sputtered. His eyes grew sly.

Alfred nodded. Pony breathed in relief. "I will have maps sent from Winchester," the King of Wessex said and Pony could hear authority in his voice once more. "We will draw a line. Then we will repair to the sacred river Axe. There we will conduct the ceremony which will bind us, Guthrum, and our families, one to another, and to our word. You will provide the first among your trusted men as hostages against the peace. We will pledge our progeny to marriage. Thus we live on one island with two kingdoms."

Guthrum set his teeth. Karn whispered in one ear and Val in the other. Only Pony understood enough Danish to know they were telling him he had no choice. "Better half an island than death," the one called Egill said. "Your offspring will rule the whole island."

Val nodded in agreement and whispered again. Of course his would be the influence of reason. It did not fit the image of a carnivore, but so it was with him.

Ragnor protested. He must be Guthrum's son, the one slated to inherit.

Guthrum silenced him. The Viking king sucked in air as though he could inhale resolve, then nodded. "I agree."

"He will look at your map," Val said in Saxon.

Alfred nodded. Pony thought he looked relieved. He had not liked Osrick's plan of executions, really. He was a moral man, by the light of his religion. "Take them to a tent and treat them with respect," he said to the room at large. The two sentries at the door-flap moved to do his bidding.

Thus allowed, the party of Danes turned on their heels and marched proudly out. Pony's confusion did not abate. Val might despise her. She half-despised herself. But at the least he lived. That was something good that had come of her siding with Alfred. She suspected that some part of her destiny had been served today.

Chapter Nineteen

The blue of May had warmed into June. Pony sat on First Mare at the edge of the River Axe at Wedmore, where the river rushed out of the Cheddar Gorge and spread itself lazily across the meadows. It was shallow here, perfect for the ceremony.

Pony's fine white cyrtle covered her stomach, but she was uncomfortable all the time. She could not sleep or hold her water. The babe kicked at her from the inside, and her belly was so huge she could no longer see her feet. Her breasts were swollen. The lithe practitioner of the Language of Touch was a dream she could barely remember. She *must* give birth any day now, surely. But each day came and went. At least she would not be alone when the time came.

On the contrary, she was in the middle of a crowd of men. Alfred was dressed in his finest blue wool cloak with silver workings at the end of elbow-length sleeves. He sat Young Black looking every inch the king, surrounded by his eorls, also in their brightest finery. The Danes were also turned out well. Her gaze skipped over Guthrum, Harald, Guthrum's son, over Egill—the architect, along with Alfred, of the treaty—and even the imposing figure of Karn, to rest upon the broad shoulders of Valgar the Beast. His curling hair gleamed brown. She was glad he didn't shave the nape. The arms encircled by his silver bands were massive, the thighs under his leather breeches bunched as he strode forward behind Guthrum. Why could she not refrain from looking at him? It was most annoying. Her eyes sought him out at every turn, even as his eyes avoided her and her distended belly. That had not changed a whit in the last weeks.

Asser and Osrick's son Elbert bound up their robes and stepped into the shallow water, preparing for the baptism. Vikings, perhaps even a hundred of them, lined the shores waiting to be baptized. Pony felt huge and useless. Alfred had wanted her to be here; she was to start the ritual with words he had given her. But while she was glad the ceremony was a baptism rather than an execution, she could not feel a part of it. She had helped Alfred to find a way to peace. That had felt right. But she felt no more complete now than she had before that deed. She did not belong here. She did not belong in her Vale anymore than she had yesterday. The loss of Herd left a hollow place right up under her breastbone. She was cast out into the world, without a destiny, without a place of comfort, no connection to the gods or anyone who cared for her.

With a start, she realized the truth of that. Alfred did not truly care for her. He had put her in the way of battle with her child, even knowing the child was his! They might have been killed, by Danes or by Osrick. They very nearly *were* killed—and all for Alfred's destiny, his ambition. He did not love her. She reached instinctively for First Mare's warm hide. She had never wanted his love, she told herself fiercely. She had wanted his seed, and she had that.

But that had been when she knew who she was. Back then, she'd been her mother's daughter. Now all was lost. She had betrayed her mother, betrayed the only destiny she understood in search of . . . of what? She straightened on First Mare's back. Not Alfred's love. Not that.

* * *

Val stood with hands clasped behind him at Guthrum's side. His translations gave him precedence even over Ragnor, Guthrum's son. Both he and Egill galled the heir. But all Vikings were galled today. Guthrum might bend to practicality, but he still considered it a day of shame. He would be baptized in the Christ cult, along with his men. Guthrum did not care that he gave up Odin and Thor and Baldur and Loki—but that he renounced his dream of ruling the whole island.

Val translated Pony's welcome and Alfred's words of brotherhood. Chippenham was lost to him now. It sat on Alfred's side of the line they had drawn on the map. Val would return to the east with Guthrum, but he did not know if he would have a place there. That land was already parceled out. What use was his skill treating with enemies or fighting when there were no lands to conquer? How could he prove his value to Guthrum now?

"Guthrum," Alfred said solemnly. "I call on you to swear by your old gods, your allegience to the new."

Guthrum took a breath, then glanced once at Egill, who nodded. "By the one wise eye of Odin, by the tricks of Loki, by the tears of Baldur, do I embrace Jesu and his father. May the Hammer of Thor strike me dead if I betray them."

How strange a pronouncement of loyalty, Pony thought. But Alfred was a crafty king. The swearing by the old gods had been carefully negotiated.

Guthrum loosed his cloak and walked into the water, the first to be dunked. "Holy father," Elbert began. He pushed the *Konnungr's* head under the water.

Karn had already declared that he would not be dunked; he would not be disloyal to his gods. Val looked at him now in wonder. Karn watched, stone-faced, as his king betrayed something he himself would not. Karn's loyalty to Guthrum's decisions was only as strong as his belief in their rectitude. But the real wonder was that Guthrum accepted it. The *Konnungr* had only nodded, and told the gathered Danes that any might follow Karn's lead.

The Viking leader came up sputtering. A very un-solemn cheer went up around the edge of the stream. Alfred waded into the water and clapped Guthrum on the back. "My brother in Christ!" he said. Guthrum did not need translation.

"Ja," Guthrum said, dripping. *"Broder in vaather."*

"Water?" Alfred asked, then burst into a series of chuckles. "Aye, brothers in water." Laughter rolled over the assembled host.

Val did not join in. Egill strode into the water with a purpose born of long hours of bargaining. Egill took the dunking to seal their agreement, no more, not because he believed. But it was Karn's decision that disturbed Val. This day had brought a clear choice: to be disloyal to one's gods or to one's king. One could not have it both ways. For Karn, his gods had come before his king.

What did Val believe? Ah, there was the trap. For the *Kristr* cult was seductive. A god who forgave you? An afterlife that promised more than endless battles and feasting and whoring? It promised the renewal of a man's spirit. It was a richer way, this *Kristr* cult. But it was also meant for the weak, men who could not live with their deeds, who needed forgiveness, whose souls were not courageous enough to battle on, even until the certain destruction of Ragnorok.

He could not truly embrace such a religion. Forgiveness was not for him. Pony had showed that to him clearly three weeks ago, on the rise at Eddington, her face disfigured with revulsion for his crime. Still, the ways of the old religion had grown stale. Valhalla was no enticement for him. The gods, if they existed, were indifferent. Why should he not be indifferent, too?

Elbert motioned to him, smiling, so Val waded into the stream. It didn't matter. If neither religion called to him, he might as well choose loyalty to Guthrum. The water was cold around his thighs. He pushed on as it chilled his genitals and caressed his waist. The little priest called Asser stood in the river to his chest. Under his chin, he held a book bound with leather. Val could see the thin sheets of sheep's hide tanned almost to translucency covered with the strange and complicated curving runes of the Saxon church. "*In nomini Patri, spiritu sanctu—*" the little monk read as Elbert pushed Val's head down. Val felt the cold water penetrate his ears, his eyes. Elbert kept his head under water as they finished their prayer. Just when his lungs had started to protest, Val felt the hand removed from his head and he surged up, gasping. As the water drained away, his eyes came to rest on Pony, sitting on her pregnant mare, a picture of fertility, staring back at him. She was sure of her religion. And she now had her girl-child. She had no further need of men. A cheer went up. Alfred grabbed his elbow and pulled him from the water.

"You are reborn," the Saxon king said. "Salvation is yours." Val pulled his gaze away from Pony's purple eyes and examined the brown ones of the father of her baby. He didn't feel saved at all.

All afternoon, Val watched impassively as the line of *Danir* marched into the water. Pony sat on First Mare to his left, both hers and the horse's swelling bellies overshadowing the new Christians with an older reverence for a more primal world. He did not look at her. She was proof that there was no forgiveness, as this new religion pretended. He still paid for his crime, with her disapproval added to his own shame. She had chosen Alfred. She thought the night of Samhain a failure, not a triumph. All that was left to him was his loyalty to his people. That was the last shred of his dignity he might save. Perhaps they were revolted by his crime, as Pony was, but they would respect his sword, his devotion, his strength. He could *make* them respect that.

When the last Viking dripped in Jesu's service, Alfred turned to Guthrum. "Now will I be godfather to your sons. I will stand their protector in time of need and give them in marriage at your direction. They shall have gifts of me, of land and goods and chattel, that they may know their bond with me and all my kin. And by these acts shall you know that this peace will be kept."

"Let me give over five of my *jarls,* King of Saxons, to be peace-bound—that if *Danir* break the truce, then may you kill them in a manner of your choice," Guthrum said formally.

"They shall be honored guests, accorded every hospitality." Alfred bowed.

Val thought not a moment. Here was his chance to prove his loyalty in a way that meant more than just converting from one religion that did not hold him to another he did not believe in. "Let me be among the number of those you pledge for surety, First *Jarl.*"

Guthrum nodded. Val glanced to Karn, but he shook his head. "I am for Stowa and Britta," he murmured. "There my loyalty must lie." Val tried to hide his disappointment.

"Let me stand as your pledge," Harald cried to Guthrum.

Val glanced to Svenn and saw that he would take this opportunity to advance inside the Danish ranks, not risk spending a year or years in confinement. *Years?* Val's belly rolled. To what had he committed? Surely Guthrum would not leave him hostage to Alfred forever. . . .

Three other Danes stepped forward to make good Guthrum's bond.

Alfred nodded, flashing a brilliant smile. "Thank you for your trust."

Val whispered the translation, and Guthrum grunted his assent.

Val noticed that Osrick loomed behind Alfred, and that his eyes were hooded even as he smiled. "Let me show our Danish guests the hospitality of Sherborne, my king," he suggested.

"Well said, Osrick." Alfred clapped him on the back. "Our newly consecrated bishop."

What? Would he be hostage to Osrick? Val pressed his lips together. His eager commitment had been half-informed. What were the terms? How long? And with Osrick? Why not with Alfred? Perhaps the Saxon king did not want Danes in his capital to spy upon him.

Guthrum didn't seem to have any qualms. He nodded to Alfred and motioned the hostages to go. Val spun on his heel, seething. He had no wish to join the feasting that would take place this night. He only hoped he was not a goat of Osrick's making, or Alfred's, or even Guthrum's. Would Guthrum, who wanted the entire island, be content behind the lines of this agreement? If he was not, if he attacked, his hostages were forfeit.

Pony watched the horses carrying Val and Harald and the three other Danes splash through the River Axe and ride into the dawn accompanied by Osrick and his score-and-a-half of men. Groaning, she pushed her fists into her back to ease her weight, uneasy with the situation, irritable with her discomfort. Why had Osrick volunteered to house the hostages? What could she do about it?

Guthrum's army prepared to depart for the east, to occupy the former outlines of the Danelaw. They had lost many men here, but so had Alfred lost men in years of battle and yet risen again to victory. Would the Danes not rise again as well?

Chippenham would revert to Osrick. The people there would not be happy. Should she tell Alfred? Could she even catch his attention, with all the plans spinning in his head now that the peace was won? He had been up all night talking of them. She must get him to focus on Chippenham. The downs had prospered under Valgar. Alfred could learn from that.

Herself, Pony would go with Alfred to Winchester. She had no illusions that he would take her to wife—nor did she want that—but he would be protection for her girl-child, as being the bastard daughter of the King of Wessex might not be safe. Not with Osrick in Alfred's confidence; not when he controlled the Vale. When she was sure the Vale was safe from Osrick, *then* she and her daughter might return. Yet while she stayed with Alfred there was another danger. The young king had been talking about using her daughter to achieve alliances. It was a shrewd ploy, but she wanted her girl-child to be her successor, not a pawn of state.

Around her, men mounted their horses. Wagons lurched forward. Two men heaved her into the saddle of her cob. She, Epona, who had never needed a saddle, who leapt nimbly to First Mare's back, was forced to accept help. Her body was unrecognizable, an uncomfortable lump. But she would bear her child soon. She hoped after they reached Winchester, where there would be women who knew their way around the birthing chamber.

Her shape was not all that she had lost. How long had it been since she had used her Gift—months. Would she lose it entirely if she did not call upon it? What matter? It was lost to her if she was afraid to use it. The horrible weight she had felt since her mother's death settled on her shoulders. She whistled for Pup and First Mare and plodded off in Alfred's wake.

Osrick's Saxons and the five Danes marched through the town of Sherborne. It was a town like others Val had encountered on the great island: huts and workshops open to the packed earth road. But Sherborne boasted an elaborate stone church, unlike Chippenham. In its tower hung a bell, ringing now in greeting or in warning. It sat in a burial yard surrounded by a stone wall, its doors open to the devout. Beyond lay the fortress that housed the bishop's residence, and that of the men who protected the town.

The journey was uneventful. Osrick was polite, not mentioning his disappearance from Chippenham, nor goading Val or the others with their hostage state. Still, Val was uneasy. Something lay behind Osrick's sly smile. He said nothing of his misgivings to the other Danes.

Harald talked of Una, how he would miss her, wondering if he could go home for harvest. The fact that the man now considered Chippenham his home bolstered Val's determination to prove his own loyalty and stay his course, no matter how long it required.

Osrick's party approached the fortress at Sherborne openly. The fortress gates were closed against them, but Osrick himself hailed the sentries peering over the palisades. "Open the gates in the name of the new bishop," he shouted. Val knew he had sent word ahead of his appointment.

"State your name and your purpose," the sentry shouted back.

Osrick's countenance darkened. "Osrick, Bishop of Sherborne, Eorl of Chippenham."

The sentry made no move. "Why are there barbarians in your party?"

"Hostages for Guthrum." Osrick's voice tightened in anger. "If you do not open these gates, you will suffer for your insolence." The sentry's head disappeared. The gates swung open.

Val urged Slepnir through the giant archway, the other Danes following. His spine tingled as the gates swung shut behind him. A commitment was made that could not be retracted.

The central hall was richer than the one at Chippenham. It flaunted a second story, no doubt used for sleeping quarters. It was surrounded by the usual lesser halls, for soldiers and the clergy, and outbuildings for livestock and the business of providing for its occupants. Osrick's party halted in front of the grand hall as a flurry of priests hastily assembled in greeting.

"Your Eminence." A stout fellow bowed. The ranks behind him raggedly followed suit.

Osrick turned to the soldiers also assembling. "See that my men are suitably housed," he said. He motioned to Raedwald, who peeled off with others. Which left Val and the Danes alone with him. Osrick turned back to the priest. "If you could provide for my guests and I as well . . ."

A stuttering murmur passed through the priests as they scurried and fluttered about. Osrick smiled indulgently at

Val, as though to apologize for his new retainers. Val did not smile in return, but Osrick did not seem to notice. The Danes were given quarters upstairs with a room to themselves, basins to wash in and promises of mead and food to come. It was unheard-of luxury. Osrick departed for a tour of his new demesne.

The promises were kept. A feast was laid before them. Osrick ordered wenches from the town. Neither Harald nor Val availed themselves, though the other Danes indulged. Much mead was drunk. Joviality abounded. But Val saw the watchfulness of Osrick that the others did not seem to mark. He longed for the weight of Bloodletter swinging at his side. When at last the sleepy Danes retired, each to their room, Val grew uneasier. Was it luxury or separation Osrick offered? He sat upright in his bedbox, awake but weaponless, and stared out into the night.

He did not realize sleep had claimed him until the door to his quarters burst open. Val pushed himself up, grabbing for a sword that wasn't there. The room filled with Saxons. Raedwald was first among them. In an instant they were upon him. He swung fists, since they were all he had. The connection with a jaw shivered up his arm. His own head snapped back. A fist found his belly. Arms reached for him. There were too many! He kicked at his nearest assailant, on his right, catching the Saxon between the legs. As that one doubled over, one of his fellows pushed him aside and rushed in, wielding a staff. He laid it again and again over Val's shoulders. The sheer weight of his attackers toppled Val to his bedbox. He lay struggling, pinned under them.

As they lay in a panting, heaving mass, one Saxon cried, "Thank Jesu the others did not struggle so." They heaved him up and jerked his wrists behind him, which Raedwald proceeded to bind with a sturdy strip of leather.

"I might have known Osrick has no honor," Val gasped.

"He serves his king better than his king commands," Raedwald responded. He shoved Val toward the door. Down the stairs, out through the now empty hall and across the yard. The gates were open. Ahead, he could see another party of Saxons shoving someone, no doubt one of his brother hostages, down toward the stone church.

Osrick grinned in its wooden doorway. As Val watched Harald dragged inside. "What treachery is this?" he growled. "When Guthrum finds Alfred has no honor—"

Osrick's bellowing laugh grated against Val's ears. Inside, the church nave was dark except for candles lit on the altar. It was not large like the church in Cent. It looked as though it had been looted, for it boasted only plain wooden candlesticks and an altar cloth embroidered but of plain fabric. There were no bowls, no platters of silver. Val feared for an instant that the altar was their destination, that he'd become some sacrifice for the Christian god who had condemned his own son to bloodthirsty death. But already the Saxons were pushing Harald down a series of stone steps ahead, almost hidden in the darkness to the right of the entry. Ah, Val had heard that some Christians stored their dead aboveground in the bowels of their churches.

Raedwald held a candle aloft as he pushed Val ahead of him. The darkness on the steps retreated but slowly. Val stumbled down. Osrick's dribbling chuckles echoed after him. The stone floor leveled out. The candles held by the group around Harald flickered ahead. They thrust Harald through a small rounded doorway designed only for corpses and slammed the heavy wooden door shut. A row of such doors retreated down the aisle. One maw of darkness yet yawned. His captors thrust Val through the opening. He stumbled to his knees and over onto his side as the door slammed shut. All light vanished.

Osrick could not do this! Val and the others were pledges against Guthrum's peace! But Osrick *could* do it. He had done it. They were captive without protection now. A shout of rage rumbled out of Val's belly and strained his throat. As its echo died away against the stone, he could hear, dimly retreating, Osrick's laughter.

Chapter Twenty

Val listened to the sound of boots on stone as they approached the door. His hands were numb, swelling; the leather binding them bit into his flesh. He was hoarse from shouting to his fellow *Danir*. They could hear each other through the stone and thick timber if they shouted, and so he knew they were as outraged as he was. He'd tried to give them comfort. Harald, especially. He'd heard the younger man's voice falter as he shouted brave words. And Val's knowledge that he himself was somehow responsible for the others made him feel all the more helpless. It was like it had been with his brothers: He had never been able to protect them either. Val tried to fight the feeling that he was spiraling down into some nightmare of inevitability. Osrick knew no limits, just like his father. And the darkness, the fear of others who depended on him, felt too familiar.

The boots stopped in front of his door. Val scrambled to sit. A crack opened on candlelight. If it was day, no daylight penetrated to this crypt. Raedwald and another ducked through the short portal and to each side of the door in the narrow cell meant for corpses, not living creatures. They carried stout cudgels. Osrick, beyond, lifted a candle and stood blocking the entry.

"Well, Viking. How do you like our accommodations?" His hated chuckle followed.

"Where is your gain from this?" Val asked.

"Apart from seeing you kneel instead of issue rules for the eorl of Chippenham to follow?"

Val watched him warily. Revenge was surely part of this. But Osrick risked much. "If Guthrum finds that his hostages are treated badly—"

"Oh!" Osrick rolled his eyes in mock horror. "And how would he find out? You would have to escape and tell him." He looked around and shrugged. "Not much chance of that."

"He will send emissaries to check us. . . ." Val threatened without hope. He knew that the peace rankled Guthrum, who wanted in his heart of hearts to rule the entire island. And since he wanted war, he could not care about hostages who would be forfeit if he attacked.

"Guthrum will be busy defending sorties against his underbelly in Cent. And when he breaks the peace, I will kill you and no one will ever know how you were treated." Osrick lounged against the stone wall opposite Val. "However, if he is slow to rouse himself to war, perhaps I shall invite him to Sherborne for a guided tour of your accommodations. He will break the peace. Alfred will have no choice but to engage, and in the end, all the island will belong to Alfred and, through Alfred, me. While he builds churches and translates Bibles, I will pull the strings of church and state." Triumphant laughter gurgled in his throat.

There would be no help from Guthrum, or from Alfred, Val agreed.

"In the meantime," Osrick continued, "for however long the peace lasts, you are my guests." He peered at Val. "How careless of us. Unbind his hands, Raedwald. There is no pleasure in having him die from rot too soon."

"Eorl," Raedwald protested. "I mean, Your Eminence. I dare not untie a man such as he."

Impatience crossed Osrick's features. "Must I do everything? Render him pliant first."

A confused look was replaced by a gap-toothed grin when Raedwald understood. He motioned to his companion guard and hefted his stout cudgel. Val rolled to the side, that his shoulders might take the blows rather than head or ribs, but that did not help much when Raedwald began kicking him as well. After a while he did not feel anything anymore. Only the part outside himself looked on—until even that part closed its eyes.

Val blinked his eyes open on darkness. At first he was not sure he'd succeeded. Someone was coughing, faintly. It had a wet sound. Val's body began to bleat at him. His head ached mightily. His shoulders, his ribs, his thighs. Was there any place that did not give him pain? Stone; he was lying on uneven stone. Groaning, he propped himself up on one elbow. The coughing came again. Was it he who was coughing? No. No, it wasn't him, he was sure. He could barely breathe. He raised himself to sitting. That was definitely his groan. It was loud against the stone.

His hands were free. Blood circulated in them. He must have been unconscious for a long time, else they would be hurting as the blood came back. He remembered now: Osrick, Saxons, cudgels. He hated the helplessness that circled in his gut, waiting to leap out at him and make him despise himself instead of them. In the dark, he touched his body. His leather breeches had protected his thighs, but his shirt was torn in many places. Bruises, cuts, no broken bones. Not yet. But the Saxons would come back.

They had not bothered to take his armband; they were after larger gain than his paltry silver. But they had taken his flute. Why something so poor as a flute and not his armband? he wondered. But he could guess the answer. The flute might have given him solace. They did not know that the music had gone along with Pony, and so it did not matter that they took it. He was only surprised he had kept it for so long.

A wet cough sounded again in his ears, faintly. He dragged himself to the wall he shared with Harald's cell and pressed his ear to the stone. "Harald," he shouted. There was no answer. "Harald, can you hear me?" A scraping sounded, then a weak voice.

"Valgar?" The cough was clearer now. It faded to a groan.

"Harald." No answer. "Harald!" The meaning of the wet cough rushed through Val like a wave through rocks at the shore.

"Valgar, I . . ."

"Can you breathe?" he yelled. The cough sounded again.

"Not well," Harald said. His voice was weaker.

"Save your strength," Val shouted. "We will get them to take you where you can heal."

Harald's chuckle gurgled into another cough. Val wanted to reassure him that the Saxons could not want him dead, but he bit his words back. What did the Saxons care if one of them died? Osrick had made his plan clear enough: All roads led to death for the Danes. Perhaps Harald, choking on the blood seeping into his punctured lung, was the luckiest of the five. He would go quickly. It might be a long road for them until they could share his fate. And it was Val's fault. The strands of thread the Norns wove into his fate were closing tight around his throat.

Pony heaved herself out of her bedbox only by rolling her legs to the wooden floor and pushing with all her might. She had not closed her eyes all night, she could swear. This room in Alfred's hall at Winchester was sumptuous, its walls hung with tapestries, the coverlet on the bedbox filled with goose down. The bowl for her private needs was not wooden, but fired and painted. The young king had done everything he could to give her comfort. But she was far from comfortable. It had been a whole cycle of the moon since the baptism at Wedmore, and still she swelled. The skin across her belly was so tight she felt she would burst.

The child moved within her constantly, it seemed. Pony felt possessed by spirits. She could not sleep. She could barely climb the stairs to this cozy apartment. She had to relieve herself a dozen times a day. Riding was lost to her. She wanted her body back! Surely she was long past her time. Waiting for the pains to begin had been torture. She was afraid of this thing that would happen to her. Yet it was the only way forward. She could not go on as she was.

The pup took his cue from her and yawned as he got to his feet. He had grown more than gangly. He looked like his joints were not quite tightly bound. His ears were too big for his head, and as first his front legs grew and then his back legs, he seemed to be running either uphill or down. She held out her hand and he trotted over, tongue lolling, to receive the petting he felt was his due. She did not need the Gift to see his bright black eyes willing her to get him some breakfast. She pushed herself to standing. "I will let you out. We are both in need of relief." She opened the door and he skittered down the stairs eagerly and out through the hall downstairs. He would be back for breakfast.

As she turned into the room to find her chamber pot, she counted up the months since Alfred had spent himself inside her. The number was the same as always. She chose a cyrtle to wear. Alfred had ordered that she have finely embroidered clothing. The tiny buckles that bound the sleeves of her shift were edged with silver, her soft boots of the finest leather. But she would trade all for her leather breeches, a flaxen shirt and a body that would fit into them.

Thank the Mother that Alfred was distracted with his plans. If he had given her his company, he might have noticed that Pony was long overdue. But she was sure that Asser could count. She had seen him staring at her only yesterday.

Was there something wrong with her? She knew naught of birthing, but how she felt could *not* be right. A midwife or a wet nurse, she needed to find someone who could tell her why the babe would not come. She imagined herself swelling until she burst in a fount of blood and gut. "Not good for birthing," she could hear her mother say, frowning at her small hips. Pony looked down. She couldn't even see her hips at this point. Fear shuddered through her as she imagined her daughter fighting her way out of her belly or suffocating when she could not.

All was going wrong. She had to find someone who could give her a potion to bring on the babe.

The red-faced woman leaned her ear into Pony's distended stomach, listening, while Pony held her breath. As she could not ask Alfred or Asser or any of the other men, Pony had sent for the midwife using the attendant girl Alfred had assigned, then she had banished her from the room. She wanted no witness to this examination. "Can you give me a potion to start the baby coming?" she asked, though she was unsure whether she wanted the dreadful event to begin.

Shaking her head, the woman heaved her bulk upright and smoothed her brown cyrtle over a belly more formless but not much smaller than Pony's. "No, I cannot." She frowned.

"But how am I to get it out of me?" Pony whispered, shocked. She wanted nothing more in the world than to have this pregnancy over.

"The usual way, I expect." The midwife cackled.

"What do you mean?"

"I mean, your babe is not ready to come out. The bun is not yet baked."

"But . . ." Pony protested, her mind racing. "It has been nine months and more."

The woman put her beefy fists on her hips. "You still have at least another month."

"I cannot get any bigger than this," Pony protested. "You must be mistaken."

The woman chuckled again. "This is your first." It wasn't a question. "You know nothing. See how high you carry your belly? It will get bigger, until your navel pops out the wrong way and your skin is tight like the head of a drum.

Then it will drop down before you spit out your child. I have seen women far bigger than you. It only feels big because you are slight of build."

"My mother said my hips were not wide enough," Pony murmured, dread shuddering through her. "Can the child come out?" The visions of alternatives flashed in her mind.

The midwife cocked her head and looked at Pony. "I think we will not have to cut it out."

Pony bit her lip. This was more horrible than she could name. Not only because she could not bear another month. Still there was one more question. "How will I know it is coming?"

"You mean, besides the pain?" the woman asked. "Well, your water will break."

"Like urinating?"

The woman shook her head, smiling. "You will know when it comes."

"So, gentle mother . . ." Pony used the term of respect, but she drew herself up and let the voices of her own Mothers echo through her own voice. "My time continues. The child of a goddess and a king takes longer 'to bake,' as you say."

The woman gave a sly look and nodded, then took herself out of the room. Only when she was gone did Pony breathe. She'd thought she was only a month late. Now it looked as though she had another month to go. She did not need to count, but she counted just the same.

Samhain! The worst had happened. Alfred, whom she had chosen because he was a beautiful king, because she did not care for him, was not the father. The daughter in her belly was the product of the wild chaos of Samhain, in the place of her Mothers, with a barbarian Viking invader. He was strong, and comely enough to father her child. But he was a barbarian foreigner. He was more a carnivore than ever Alfred was. Worse, he went against everything Pony's mother had advised. Pony had bred with him because she wanted, in the madness of Samhain, to be with him more than she wanted to obey her destiny. He had made her feel complete as she never had. Ever since that night he had possessed her body, and, if truth be told, her mind.

She put her fist to her mouth as tears welled in her eyes. What had her disobedience, her wild desire, wrought? She was hurtling toward a fate she could not divine, let alone control. The ordered descent of generations at the Vale of the White Horse, practicing the Gift and worshiping the Great Mother, would be broken and scattered. The consequences were unforeseeable, but Pony was sure they would be bad.

Chapter Twenty-one

Val huddled in the corner of his stone cell, clutching his knees, his face buried in his arms. The sounds were what still tormented him, more than the belly cramps from the spoiled bread and water they were given to eat, or the pain from the repeated beatings. Over and over again in his mind he heard the strangled gasp that must have been Harald's last. The silence afterward echoed louder than the din of battle, until he filled it with shouting protests and finally his own strangled, impotent sobbing. The thud of the door next to his, the coarse jesting of the Saxon guards as they divided up Harald's silver neckbands and the brooch that held his cloak, the terrible scraping sound as they dragged Harald out: all repeated in his mind. He lifted his head and began to bang it back on the stones. He could not stop for long. The pain of it kept the memories from echoing in his mind, at least for a while.

My fault. Harald was my responsibility. He was too young to know what he committed. He volunteered because I did, thinking I would protect him—as I did in our first battle with Alfred, as I did in the battle at Eddington. In forgiving him, I bound him to me. I became responsible. I betrayed him to his death. The endless round of self-recrimination was harder to bear even than the recalled sounds of Harald's death.

Harald would not be the last to die, either. Val could not hear the others now that Harald's empty cell stood between them, but if they were starved much longer, Osrick's guards would soon carry them out feet first, too. Those others would not be willing to go to the lengths Val was to stretch out such a miserable existence just to spite their captors.

The rhythmic thud of his head against the wall beat back thought. His blood was warm and sticky as it trickled down his neck. His rhythm was interrupted by the sound of foot-steps on the stone stairs. He stopped to listen. There were five of them. Three paused outside his cell door first, as they always did, though normally there were only two; the others went on down the line of cells. The door creaked open and candlelight filtered into the cell.

Val raised his head. Tangled hair covered his eyes, but he saw *Osrick*. The bishop had come with his men today, no doubt to watch the beating. Osrick looked around at the foul cell: the rotted rushes, the pot full of sloshing night soil that had not been emptied in several days, the molded crust of uneaten bread in the wooden bowl. "You certainly don't take care of the quarters you have been given," he said. Then he turned to one of the others. "Raedwald, look, we must be giving him too much to eat. He left some for the rats."

Val did not tell him that he'd left some for the rats to prevent them nibbling upon his flesh and to draw them to a place where he knew their location in the dark. He had killed three thus far and eaten them in place of the bread. Their gnawed remains were concealed in the chamber pot each day. The raw meat made his gut knot. The one other Dane who had tried this method couldn't stomach it. He'd ended saying that starving was a less painful way to go. But Val didn't throw up the second rat, as he had the first. He had learned to eat them slowly. He had vowed he would not let Osrick starve him to an ignoble death with no Valkyrie for a glorious welcome into Valhalla. Much as he had once despised the prospect of feasting and fighting eternally in Valhalla, still it was better than a visit to the icy realm of Hel until the day of Ragnorok.

"Look how he hates us, Raedwald," Osrick observed. "It is there in his eyes."

Val had not seen Raedwald in some time, almost since they'd first arrived. How long ago was that? He glanced with hooded eyes to the wall and saw six groups of scratches marking each day's bowl of rancid food. He had been in this cell for six weeks.

"I must say I feel the same for him. These Vikings are stubborn." Osrick crossed his arms and leaned against the wall, looking all the while at Val. "Guthrum, for instance, refuses to break the peace. Or perhaps he hasn't noticed our raids on his fat friends who hold Cent."

Val held himself motionless. Inside he rejoiced. Guthrum refused to break the peace. He would have bet—what, his life?—that Guthrum would take the first excuse to start up the war again. But perhaps the *Konnunger* waited for reinforcements from the Northmen who had settled on the Frankish coast. Guthrum would be more careful of Alfred now, but he would also show forbearance under provocation only if there was a stratagem in it.

Osrick was about to speak again when one of the two soldiers who had passed on to other cells stuck his head back in. "The one in the end cell is dead," he said.

Val's stomach knotted. Skedir. He was too old to survive being treated thus.

Osrick shrugged. "Take him out and burn the body." He turned back in speculation to Val. "Down to three. So sad." He straightened and appeared to make a decision. "I must have pity on the rest of you." Then he stopped. "All?" He shook his head. "No, not all. Just on you, Viking." He straightened. Val did not move. "You are free to go." Then, without another word, Osrick turned on his heel. The surprised Raedwald and the others trailed after him as he left.

In the corridor, Raedwald moved to slam the door, but Osrick stayed his arm. "Did you not hear me? He is free to go. Leave the cell door open."

"But Osrick," Raedwald protested, "we can't let him go. He'll straight to Guthrum—"

"Who will break the truce, fool." Osrick turned back to Val. "You have your freedom. But if you take it, Alfred will bring an army against the Danes for your treason—he will crush them and all they love. I doubt they will be prepared. Think of the slaughter." Osrick laughed and made his way up the stone stairs. "What a pity."

"And the others?" Val heard drifting down.

"They stay."

Val stared at the open doorway. A little light leaked down the stairs, no doubt from the crack under the door at the top. He had not heard the bar for that door snick shut.

He squeezed his eyes shut against that faint shadow, less black than its surroundings. Osrick could have thought of nothing more cruel than opening his cell and setting him free. He could not leave, not without leaving all honor behind, all loyalty to his pledge to his king. It did not matter how he was treated. It did not matter that the others had died. He was pledged as hostage, and his loyalty was all he had left. He could not flee through that door and still be a Dane. He could not break the truce and bring down death on his people. One of his remaining fellows called out weakly. Val could hear him now that the door was open. "Valgar," the man said. His name was Turgi. "Can you hear?"

"*Ja,*" Val said, his voice hoarse with disuse. It had been weeks since he had spoken. "I hear."

"They, they said you could go. . . ."

He must have learned Saxon from Pony. Curse her. He did not want the others to know what had been offered him.

"Go quickly," Turgi said. "Get help. Tell Guthrum."

Val took a breath through tattered lips. "I cannot leave without breaking the truce."

"But two are dead. The Saxons have already broken the truce." The desperation in Turgi's voice raked Val's heart. The third man's cell was quiet. That was Rotan. It must mean he would shortly be leaving feet first.

"Terms are terms," Val muttered. "I will hold up the honor of the Danes."

The shriek that answered this declaration rose and fell, on and on. Turgi was exhausting himself. Val held himself tightly, trying not to think of his responsibility, now grown to horrible proportions, for what would happen here.

He thought of Pony instead. Not as he had last seen her. No, no. He would not think of that, or what it meant, or what he wanted. He thought of her riding her mare, hair a white pennant in the wind, laughing over her shoulder and challenging him to gallop to the stone circle. The shrieking faded from his ears. Eyes blue-purple, like lapis lazuli from the Nile. Skin like fine glazed milky glass from Roma. Hair the color of the moon ringed with glowing light. The way Pony rode ahead, tantalizing, all the way to the stone circle, all the way to Samhain night.

He shook his head. The shrieking of Turgi assaulted him once more. He could not think of Samhain night. That way, too, lay madness. He would never have her, never feel her body writhing under his. Her belly swelled with another's child. She had chosen Alfred. He pushed his thoughts away—away from Harald, away from Pony, away from Turgi's screaming.

Slowly, he began to thud his head against the stone wall, staring at the open door to his cell.

Pony walked in the yard of the great hall at Winchester, among milling suppliants for Alfred's time, among soldiers marching in formation, and among several most un-kinglike barnyard animals. She was on her way to visit with First Mare. Both swelling females would take a constitutional walk side by side outside the palisades as they did each day. The midwife had said it was good for her. Pup gamboled at her feet, shaking a stick enticingly. But Pony did not feel like playing. Her belly pushed out in front of her like a heavy barrel, her back ached constantly and her breasts hurt. She had always thought that the symbol of the Great Fecund Mare was graceful, life-embracing, but how wrong she had been! She had never felt less graceful. And the "renewal of life" simply made her cross.

Asser stepped up beside her. She started. Where had he come from? She had been avoiding him for weeks. "Oh!" she said. "It is you."

"Yes." He appeared thoughtful. Which was not promising. "Is there aught I can do to make you more comfortable? I am afraid Alfred has been distracted of late."

"No, nothing." Pony tried to recover some fleeting calm. "He is most generous."

"Yes. That is true is it not? I have been worrying about that." Asser clasped his hands behind his back as he strode beside her, a good hand span shorter than she was. Now he would make it clear that he could count months. Her time was near, but it had been almost eleven months since that night in her hut with Alfred. Pony did not know which way to turn. Could she just walk away? But that would hardly stop Asser's going to Alfred with his accusations. She looked away, nauseated.

"Still, your pregnancy is convenient for him," the little priest continued. "He has the preference of the last Druid priestess on the island."

Ah. She glanced at his face from the corner of her eye. He had not exposed her because he thought her pregnancy an asset to Alfred. "Is it a fair trade in your mind?"

Asser opened his mouth to answer, but a thundering clatter of horses through the main gate of the palisades interrupted him. All in the yard turned to stare. It was Borogand at the head of two score mounted men, dressed for battle.

"Where is Alfred?" Borogand shouted. "The Danes have broken the truce. They prepare for war." He threw himself from his horse.

Pony's mind jolted to a stop. The news meant only one thing to her. She cared not for the fact that the peace she had striven for with Alfred at Wedmore was broken; she cared only that Val's life would be instantly forfeit. Osrick would not even be blamed for killing him. As a hostage, death was his fate if Guthrum broke the truce.

Around her, the chaos of the yard swirled as Borogand's men dismounted. Questions were shouted. Pigs squealed and raced among the horses' hooves. Chickens squawked and fluttered. Men scurried up to hold the newcomer's mounts. Pup barked and raced in circles around Pony. Borogand strode into the great hall. Asser hurried after him.

Pony stood frozen. How long would it take them to send word to Osrick? Only so long would Val live. Slowly, she looked around the yard. Thoughts came unbidden into her brain. *Clean clothes. A pack of food.* But she could no longer ride. That meant she would need a cart. What horse to pull it?

She moved through the chaos, amazed at herself. Did she abandon the destiny Britta had foreseen for her by leaving Alfred? It did not matter. Destiny could wait. Alfred could wait. Everything could wait.

No one noticed her in the current excitement, which was good. She floated through the tumult, skimming through the portal into the hall, moving smoothly up the stairs. The pup had caught her mood. When she reached her bedchamber, she found him trotting solemnly at her heels. Very well; it would be a threesome. She packed a sack of clothing and threw her cloak over it and her arm. Reality set in. She staggered back down the stairs, light in body no more, and around to the kitchen outbuilding. There she begged flat bread and carrots and cabbage from a serving girl, and stuffed them all in her bag. A whine from the pup reminded her that he would not dine on such fare, and she grabbed some jerked meat from a sideboard before she hastened outside. Better jerked meat than forcing him to hunt like the carnivore he was.

Next it was around to the horse pen. First Mare rolled up to her, nickering for their walk. Pony examined her carefully. The horse was still two months from her own moment of birthing, and Pony could not leave her behind—she might never come back to this place. Could First Mare pull the weight of the cart, even with only Pony and her pack inside? How far? How far to Sherborne from Winchester? Seven leagues perhaps. Could they make it? More important, could they make it ahead of the runner Alfred would send? Perhaps in all the preparation for the battle, Alfred would forget. All calm left her. Would she be able to see Val, to warn him? What would he do when she told him Guthrum had broken the truce? Thoughts careened through her brain without resolution, or even order. She looked wildly around for a cart. She must go now!

The horse boy was nowhere to be seen. Pony opened the gate to the pen and First Mare pushed through. Pony shut the gate. Inside the stable, several carts tipped forward on their tongues. She raced to the smallest, lightest. First Mare caught her urgency and broke into a lumbering trot behind her. Pony had the collar and the traces on First Mare in no time. She did not bother with reins or bridle. At the last moment she saw a bucket, and she flung it into the cart with another full of oats.

"Come, Pup." Pony clambered into the seat of the cart. Her belly stirred, followed by a sharp pain. She started and bent over. What was that pain? As it subsided, she knew. Fear burned through her. Hold back, girl-child. If she stayed for a midwife, Val was forfeit, sure. She straightened. She could not live with that. That was all she knew.

"On, friend," she called. First Mare picked her way out through the chaos of the yard. Pony nodded to the sentries at the gate. They saw her leave with her horse each day. If they marked that today she used a cart, no doubt they attributed the change to her state of pregnancy. Pony could not see the end of the journey she and First Mare and the pup started; she only knew she had to go.

She heaved herself from the jolting cart in the trees outside the town as dusk closed in. It had been three days to Sherborne. Her knees nearly gave way. The pains came and went—once there had been no pains for a whole day—and they had not gotten regular, as the midwife said they would. And she had not seen anything that might be the breaking of her water. Still, Pony trembled with dread that her time would come before her task was done.

First Mare drooped in her collar. Pony unhooked it and heaved it off. "Stay and graze, friend," she whispered. First Mare did not need the instructions; she moved off, head down in the darkness. The pup moved like a shadow among shadows in the trees.

Pony had had three days to think. There was no guarantee her mission would be anything but pointless. The messenger from Alfred might already be there. Even if she was first to Sherborne, how could she convince Val to desert his role as hostage? On their way to the Circle of Stones he had said that to him duty and loyalty were all. And Osrick might find her. Her bulging belly was hard to miss. Putting herself in that man's power was not an idea she relished. And what would Alfred say when he learned where she had gone, as surely he must?

She wasn't even certain why she was trying to save a barbarian carnivore who had killed his own father. . . . Was he not deserving of whatever his fate might be at Osrick's hands? Several times she had tried to convince herself to turn back. That was the only sensible course. How could she be here, quaking in fear of giving birth alone on some wooded hill where predators might lurk? But she had not turned back, and she still was not certain why. Gray eyes, perhaps, that told of pain. Did regret redeem a crime such as Val's? Or mayhap it was the way he listened to music she could not hear, and made it sound out through his flute to touch her soul. Could one wholly bereft of goodness have such a Gift from the Mother? She sighed. More likely she still sought, against all her mother's teachings, connection to some part of herself she had never known before the night of Samhain.

Her journey certainly did not further the one instruction Britta had given her about her destiny. She had abandoned

Alfred in favor of his enemy. How could she be so lost to her obligation? To her own loyalty?

Without any answers she wended her way, Pup at her heels, past the stone church to the gates of the bishop's hall. She had to stop once as a pain doubled her over, but it passed and she staggered on. The sentries only stuck their bellies out and laughed as she ducked her head in pretended shame and hurried past. Through the gates, the yard was quiet. Most everyone had gone in to the evening meal. Yet she dared not walk boldly up to Osrick's doors, seeking admittance to speak to a hostage she knew he hated. She had to find Val on her own.

She took a breath. Her only way was through the Gift. There were those who would know where in the huge maze of rooms Val was, or where his routine was like to take him: Her first task was to find them. The constant dreadful possibility that she would hear carnivores if she tried to use her Gift had kept her from using it for these many months, but she no longer had a choice. Pup at her heels, she crept around the back to the animal pens. Would the horses know? They milled in their confinement, restless. One stood taller than the others: a chestnut stallion. She would know him anywhere. Smiling, she approached the pen. He nickered and shouldered his way through the throng.

"Slepnir," she whispered as she stroked his velvet nose. Cautiously, she focused. *For the Mother's sake, let not my pains overwhelm me now.* She pushed away her fear for Val, the fear of Osrick, fear of the coming birth, fear that she would hear carnivores. The world stepped back from her, giving her room to listen. *Ahh.* She breathed, then stilled her breath. She focused on Slepnir's liquid brown eyes. He stared back at her. A picture of Val filled her mind.

With a jerk, she came to herself, gulping. Slepnir didn't know. He hadn't seen Val for a long time. Which was strange. In the enforced idleness life as a hostage surely brought, she had imagined Val would ride out every day.

But Slepnir had an idea who might know where Val was, and it made Pony shudder. In his mind they were just the small, scurrying ones. He didn't trust them, but he didn't see them as a threat. *Why couldn't it have been the cows, or the hogs or the chickens?* Pony's shoulders sagged. *Because cows or hogs or chickens would have* told *Slepnir where Val was.*

No; the ones who knew, Slepnir could not understand. They were not plant eaters, rats. And he believed only the rats knew where Val was.

It suddenly seemed as though she had stones in her belly. Rats were both carnivores and plant eaters, both and neither. They were scavengers, lowest on the scale of life according to her mother. They ate things that nothing should eat. They had eaten the remains of Chestnut Mare. Pony had never tried to use her Gift on them. But who knew what her Gift could now do? After carnivores, might not she hear *carrion-eaters? Oh, Mothers, give me strength.*

How to begin? Find them. She looked around. The grainery. Graineries always had vermin. She crept from shed to shed until she found it and cracked open the door. A besmirched boy came round the corner of the shed and headed for the great hall. Pony went in and closed the door behind her, locking Pup outside. He wouldn't mix well with the rats. Inside, in the dark, among the wooden bins overflowing with grain, she heard the small, scrabbling sounds they made. A shudder coursed through her. But Pony held her breath, closed her eyes and searched for calm. An impression of dozens of small bright eyes and twitching noses almost overwhelmed her. There were *lots* of rats here. Fear bulged in her throat and cut off sensation. She almost closed herself off. Breathing hard, she pushed at the fear and opened once again. Breath jerked through her and was stilled. A need to be busy with the getting of food flushed through her. Grain was good. The rotting vegetable pile outside the kitchens was a possibility. But best was the haunch of meat with morsels yet left after the dogs were called away. Hiding, always hiding—that was important. Dart here, searching. Dart there. We go everywhere.

Pony did not allow the shudder. She simply thought of

309

Val. Immediately a pulse of energy swept through the darkness around her. Warning! Cold stones and dark. Damp, as if something were buried in the earth. Dark should be good for hiding. But there was death in the air among the cold stones and the darkness. Warning! Do not go near *that* one!

Pony shivered into her own awareness once again. Chittering echoed around her, and then silence. Her Gift had descended yet another step on some ladder she dreaded. She could hear carrion-eaters. Revulsion churned in her, but she could not afford such vain regret. What had the rats told her? That Val was dead? The sense of death where he was was overwhelming. She stumbled out of the grainery into the twilight. She could not think about death. She *would* not think.

Where? Where would there be damp stone and darkness? The two-storied hall was wooden. A cistern? She cast about but didn't see one. Out through the still-open gates in the palisades, the stone tower of the church rose through the dusk.

There. It had to be the church, which was built of stones. She started forward; then she realized that, if she found Val and convinced him to leave this place, he would need a mount. She whirled and returned to Slepnir's pen. "Whoa, boy," she soothed as she let him out. Then he and Pup followed her down toward the gates and the sentries.

"Halloa," one of the men called. "Where are you taking that horse?"

"He's breeding our mare," Pony called without stopping. "My husband says it is time."

"Your husband would know obviously when to get a breeding done," the second guard joked. He looked at her pregnant stomach.

"Wait," the first called uncertainly.

Pony did not stop. "I'll have him back before the mead is poured."

Her seeming confidence outweighed their uncertainty. She, Pup and Slepnir strode down toward the church. By the time she reached it, her heart was thumping in her throat. Was this where Val was? The wooden door opened at her touch, its beaten-metal latch unfastened.

"Hello," she called into the dim flicker of candles at the distant altar. The only answer was the hollow echo from empty recesses of the stone nave. The priests apparently ate dinner at the great hall. There was also no sign of Val. What would Val be doing here, anyway? Had his baptism turned him devout? She doubted that. Could the rats have been mistaken?

Off to her right the dark abyss of a stairwell drew her eye. Stairs down? Down to what? Ahh . . . crypts. Had she not heard that some newer churches were built with crypts in the Frankish style? Those would be damp if they were underground. The rats thought Val was here—she was sure of it, now. They thought he was dead. Was he buried below? Her heart clenched. She strode to the altar and grabbed a candle, trying not to think. She went to the staircase. Not halfway down, a miasma of rotting meat and night soil, dank and mold, rose to meet her. What would she see at the bottom?

Her candle revealed a hallway with wooden doors opening off it. Only the first was open. Trembling with the fear the rats had imparted, Pony took several hesitating steps. In front of the open door she wavered. All was darkness. She raised her candle, but it illuminated little. Was there a darker smudge on the wavering shadows there in the corner? She held her hand to cover her nose and pushed forward.

A slumping figure in the corner flickered into view. The rats were right! Curled in the molding straw, the body before her eyes was surely dead. Half-naked, with dirty, caked hair and ribs like the teeth of a harrow, the body was covered with black scabs and dark red, congealed gouges. The smell of rotting meat mingled with the stench from a wooden bucket in the corner. Dumbly, Pony noted the half-eaten carcass of some small animal. A rat?

The horror of it all seemed to toll inside her like the bell in the tower of this foul church. Osrick had done this. Honored hostage? What honor had Osrick? Had Alfred known of this, Val's death? Her hand moved to her cheek of its own accord and wiped away tears that burst forth, unstoppable. How would she live, now Val did not?

His head raised. Pony started. Then she ran to him, called his name. She choked, kneeling beside him. Her hands fluttered about like uncertain birds, afraid to touch him. His eyes squinted up at her.

"Pony?" he croaked.

She sucked in her breath. "Oh, Val. . . ." He was not dead! Which meant that life began to move again. Her brain began to churn. "We must get you out of here. Guthrum has attacked. Where are the others?" She glanced over her shoulder, remembering closed doors along the hall.

"Dead." His voice was the creak of an unused hinge. "I made them die."

"Harald?" Pony's heart sank.

"He was the first."

"Osrick." It must have been Osrick, no matter what Val said. And the villain might come down the stairs at any moment. She grabbed Val's hand. "Can you stand? There is a flight of stairs . . ."

He shook his head, almost imperceptibly. Weakly, he tugged away. "I will not go."

Pony pressed her lips together. What had she expected? Grimly, she glanced at the open door. She turned back to Val, taking in the horrible beatings he had gotten, the carcass of the rat, his protruding ribs. "Oh, yes, you will," she breathed. She looked around. Once she would have recoiled from the only solution that occurred to her. But she lunged from the room, feeling in the gyrdle under her belly for her small knife.

It was the work of moments to trundle up the stairs, grab a heavy wooden candlestick from the altar and stand awkwardly on a bench to cut a length of rope from the bell in the tower—a nice, long piece that had been coiled on the floor. Cutting it, she peered into the night, expecting soldiers to descend upon the church in ranks, but saw and heard only the muted indications of a village at dinner. Outside, she formed a loop in the rope and cast it over Slepnir's neck. She walked him into the cavernous church. His hooves thundered against the stone, but he did not shy or resist. Perhaps he felt the presence of his partner below. Then she took the other end down the stairs.

She returned to Val's cell, where her nerve nearly failed her. She had never hit beast nor man, even in anger. She was not angry now, except with Osrick. But as Val roused himself in protest, she trembled above him, then brought the candlestick down on his crown.

He went limp. *Oh, Mothers, I have finished what Osrick started.* But he would not have wished to . . . She knelt and put her fingers to his throat. His flesh pulsed against her fingers. Now came her trial. She bent to grab one foot, still booted. Could she drag him to the stairs, so very pregnant as she was? She put her back into it, grunting, and he moved a bit. She stood and gasped. The stairway seemed a league away. She bent again.

When she finally made the stairs with her limp burden, with fumbling hands she looped the rope under his arms and made an untidy knot. Slepnir tugged, making it difficult, but somehow she heaved Val over near the door. She struggled up the stairs herself.

"Now, boy," she whispered. She pictured Val being pulled up the stairs, and Slepnir understood. He stepped back toward the open door as she pushed against his chest. The rope strained against Val's weight. Pup nosed the trembling hemp. Back and back Slepnir stepped, through the open door now, the rope halting, straining, then halting as Val no doubt bumped up the steps. At last she saw him slide into the doorway. Pup raced back and forth between them eagerly. Yes! They had done it. She hurried to the nearby wood where she had left First Mare and brought the cart. She tilted it; shortened the rope; threaded that through the back and over the seat; then positioned Slepnir in front of the cart and urged him forward. Val was hauled up and in. It was done. Fastening the leather buckles, Pony harnessed Slepnir to the cart. He would pull while First Mare walked. Had the stallion ever stood in harness?

Pony heaved her bulk into the plank seat. She shushed Pup, who had caught her sense of urgency and begun barking. Sparing a glance toward the lighted hall inside the faesten walls behind her, she clucked to the huge chestnut horse. It was all she could do not to urge Slepnir to a gallop. She wanted to be far away when Osrick discovered his hostage had been stolen.

A messenger, splattered with mud, hurried into the hall where Osrick broke his fast.

"My Lord Bishop," he began, bowing low.

"What is it?" Osrick would have been angry at the interruption, but the man's gasping meant it was something important.

"Guthrum broke the peace!" The messenger panted, stood. "Alfred bids you join him at Winchester. They march to meet the Viking and blast his kind from the island forever."

The satisfaction glowing in Osrick's gut lit his smile. "So Guthrum moves at last." He stood and flung his empty mead horn upon the trestle table. He glanced to Raedwald, who lifted his in a toast. Osrick nodded. His man and his soldiers had done well. He turned back to the messengers. "Rest, herald of these tidings, then away to Alfred with our firm commitment. We will join him at Winchester before the moon gains a belly once more."

He and Raedwald began bantering plans back and forth while the messenger was led toward food and a bed. Then Osrick thought of something. "Raedwald," he hissed. "Bring our lone remaining hostage. He must pay for his king's treachery—here, in front of us all." He'd almost forgotten. Anticipation rippled through his loins. The end would not come quickly for Valgar the Beast: He would see to that.

Raedwald was back shortly, breathless. "Tell me not that he's died," Osrick complained.

Raedwald shook his head. "Gone," he breathed.

"Gone?" Osrick leapt to his feet. For a stunned moment he stared at Raedwald. Then he pushed past. "I'll see this for myself." Raedwald and several others followed him out the gates and down toward the church.

Yet Osrick knew what he would find. Raedwald would be right. The reality of it had begun to soak in. Had he misjudged the Viking? He had wagered much on the fact that Valgar would not choose escape. Racing down the stairs, he held his torch high. He came into an empty cell. It looked very much as if he had lost the wager.

"He cannot have gone far in his condition," he said calmly. "Search the village."

Chapter Twenty-two

Beneath the great elms interspersed with more graceful birches Pony heaved her bulk off the cart and stumbled to the spongy forest floor. There had been no sleep this night, just hurried driving and a growing feeling that she was abandoning Alfred and her destiny. She pushed it down, too tired for any such thought. Below, the River Stour rushed on its way to the sea. The early morning sun shafted through the tree trunks. Kingfishers flashed brilliant blue above. Collared doves made a soft burring sound.

Surely no one would look for her and Val here. She had driven the cart half a league around a bend in the river from the place where the narrow track forded at a shallow crossing. In any case, she could not go farther; she'd had another pain not half an hour ago, more wrenching than the others.

First Mare walked down to the river to drink, Pup trotting at the horse's heels. Pony was thirsty, too, but she would wait. She unbuckled Slepnir from the harness. He followed First Mare. In the back of the cart Val was stirring. She let down the back. He glared at her dully. In the morning light the damage to his body was even more horrifying.

Wiping the dismay from her face, she refused to let it be replaced by pity. "You no doubt wish to thank me for saving your life," she lied. "You will have more strength for it after we drink and wash. Can you get yourself to the river? It is but a step."

He pushed himself to hands and knees, and hung his head between his shoulders. "What did you hit me with?" he growled through cracked lips.

"A candlestick." She was not proud of it.

It seemed the act of a predator. What was she turning into? He crawled to the edge of the cart and sat heavily. "Better you killed me than dishonored me," he muttered. Pushing himself off the edge of the cart, he found his legs buckled and fell to his knees.

Pony crouched beside him and pulled his arm over her shoulder. He smelled of his cell, yet the stink was not what sent shocks through her body. She pushed herself erect, stumbled forward with both her own weight and his. "Talk of honor later. Now, just get to the river."

They staggered down the gentle slope. Pup greeted them happily, his fur soaked. They waded into the shallows where the horses stood, still gulping, occasionally raising their heads to swivel their ears and sift the wind with their noses. Val slid to his knees and drank direct from the river. Pony cupped her hands and sipped, crouching, her cyrtle floating out about her. She splashed her face before she rose, then went to get her pack from the cart. Though she had left in haste, she had packed much of what they would need. She pulled out soap and the single blanket she had brought. The soap was perfumed with Frankish lavender, a luxury from Alfred. What would the man say if he knew she had saved his hostage from death?

She stumbled back down the slope. Val looked up at her resentfully from under dripping locks. His shirt was in shreds across his shoulders, the marks of Osrick's hospitality beneath. He was too weak to wash his wounds, so she would do it for him. "You will fester unless your wounds are cleaned." She dipped the soap in the water and rubbed up a lather.

"Torturer," he grunted.

It *was* torture. But he bore it. She ripped off the shreds of his shirt, cleaned his wounds and even soaped his hair. At his nape it was caked with old blood, and near his temple with the sticky result of her assault. She ended by pulling off his boots and averting her eyes while he fumbled at the leather thongs binding his breeches. Throwing him the soap, she caught glimpses of the bruised flesh of his naked legs. He lay in the shallows, soaping what he could. Likely he didn't even hear the soft grunting sounds of effort he made. When he was done, she pocketed the soap and held up the blanket. He struggled to his knees.

Somehow they made it back up the slope. She lay him in the soft leaves and moss under a huge elm tree. She wanted to give him food, but his eyes closed almost instantly in sleep. She longed to join him there. But she had seen raspberry bushes nearby, and the bright yellow of sulfur mushrooms, "chickens of the wood," and she went to collect them.

Later, letting the sweet juice drip down her throat from the summer berries, she watched Val breathe. There had been another pain, a serious one, as she had picked the berries. Her time was so near! Where could she go to have her babe? To Alfred? Not with Val in tow. Besides, Winchester was three days away. Fear bubbled up inside her. Could she just present herself to strangers at some farmhouse? Better that than having the child alone. But who would take in a woman who was about to give birth?

She forced her thoughts away from fear. No one was going anywhere right now. Val slept as one dead. Pony fed Pup one of her pieces of jerked meat, while she herself nibbled the yellow mushroom she'd gathered. A man like Val was used to eating meat. Whether she liked it or not, that was part of who he was. Would he not need meat to regain his strength?

She resolved to save the rest of the jerked meat for Val, what little there was left. Pup held his piece between his paws as he gnawed at it. What of Pup? Did he know how to hunt? She doubted it. He had been taken from his mother young, and he had had only Pony for an example since. A fine example she was for a carnivore. . . . Both he and Val needed meat.

Pony's stomach turned as she realized what she must do. She had seen it often enough. The Mothers knew she had freed enough frightened animals from them. But could she set a trap? Her mind fluttered in protest. Kill? Could she kill an animal so that those she cared about could eat? Her mind whirled in protest and horror. What was she becoming?

And yet she did care for these two carnivores, Val and Pup. She reached out to stroke the dog's black fur. The little beast had wormed his way into her heart. He was so eager to see what wonders the world held. Was it his fault that he was a predator? And if not his, whose? Her thoughts strayed into territory she knew was dangerous. If the Mothers connected to the earth and all its denizens, were they less connected to predators than prey?

You do not listen to carnivores. Britta's words echoed in Pony's ears. The witch had said that Pony heard only half the world. Ah, but now Pony *could* hear carnivores, frightening as that was—the eagle and the wolves and the rats. Perhaps all the world was open to her, if she would but listen. Every fiber in her body wanted to reject that blood-lust she'd felt from the wolves, that longing after carrion of the rats. And yet . . . was Pup evil? Was Val a bad man because he ate meat? She cared about him, too. There was no use denying that, not when she had crossed nearly thirty leagues to save him. She'd gone even though she knew he would not want to be saved. She had never banished Samhain night. It had lived within her, waiting to pounce when she pulled Val out of the cart, or helped him up the slope. Anytime she touched his flesh, Samhain was there, waiting. Her mother would have told her that what she felt for Val was wrong for one such as she.

Perhaps it was. But perhaps not.

The echo of those words reverberated down her spine. Implied in them was rebellion. First she had questioned her destiny, perhaps abandoned it. Now she wondered if what her mother had taught her was wrong. Yet could not what happened on Samhain be the work of the Mother, too? It had seemed so right, so inevitable. It gave her such completion. The night had demanded what they'd done together. . . .

She looked at Val, his face drawn and bruised but softened by sleep. Now was not the time to sort things out: she was too tired, too confused. Pulling a long thread from the frayed hem of her cyrtle, she began to sharpen a stick with her knife. She would set a trap.

Her fatigue overcame her determination as the morning warmed. She dozed fitfully until she was wakened by another pain. She clenched double, gasping, before it passed. Only slowly did she unbend, controlling her breathing, to look around. Pup was nowhere in sight. Slepnir and First Mare stood quietly among the trees, lipping at some grasses. Val had pushed himself up against the bole of the elm with the blanket clutched tightly around him. He was chewing on a piece of jerky. His hair had dried in soft brown waves over his shoulders. The scrapes on his cheekbones had crusted almost to black. Blue-black shadows lived under his eyes—but gray intelligence still shone in them.

"What trick of Loki induced you on such a fool's errand when you are so close to your time?" he asked derisively. "Birthing Alfred's brat is your only reprieve from the penalty for freeing a forfeited hostage. You should do it in his sight."

Pony bit her lips against a shout of protest. What would she say? Complain that he did not value her sacrifice? That it was not Alfred's child anyway? Val was apparently not good at counting. Or perhaps he had lost track of time, locked in his crypt.

Val tore with his teeth at the jerky. "Did you plan that I endure the scorn of the *Danir* when they discover my disloyalty?"

"Better shamed than dead," she muttered, pulling herself to sitting.

"*No.*" The bitterness, the regret that drenched his voice invested that one word with the eloquence of sagas.

"Will they not forgive you when they see your ribs and your scars?" She felt her anger rising in her throat. "Is there no limit to what you must endure for this thing called honor?"

The bleak look in his eyes said there was not. And his eyes had always held some measure of that pain, from the first moment she saw him. Perhaps, in his mind the torture he had suffered willingly was payment for his crime against his father. She pushed herself up and handed him her cloth full of raspberries. He shook his head.

"Ah. You are not worth even the enjoyment of summer fruit," she remarked, and tossed him a parsnip. "Perhaps this will be bitter. That should suit you." He tossed the parsnip back.

She wanted to shriek. To be reviled for trying to save him was unbearable, when the effort had cost her so much. "So, you are trying to demonstrate your loyalty, past all reason, because you want them to forgive the fact that you killed your father." She hoped her words shocked him.

His eyes snapped up to hers in anger. Which was better. But he mastered the emotion and closed them slowly. "There is no forgiveness. If I am trusted to do my duty, that is enough."

"No. I think you want their forgiveness," she continued. "I suspect that is because you are skipping the step where you forgive yourself."

He did not deign to answer that. "You sound like Elbert, with all this talk of forgiveness."

"I suppose I do. You took the dunking. Is forgiveness not now the teaching of your faith?"

"I took that vow because my king required it of me. It does not change what I believe."

"Ah. You adhere to Odin and Thor."

"Only when they adhere to me. . . . Which is never." His voice was full of bile.

Pony ached for him. He had solace from neither the old gods nor his new ones. Yet how different was that from her own situation? Did the Mothers give her any solace? Did she herself understand what was required of her? Even the small part she did understand, she had betrayed. She had left Alfred, abandoned her destiny of helping him. "Perhaps you underestimate the power of your new gods," she said in quiet consolation.

Val's eyes strayed to her sharpened stick, the green thread and the bucket. "A . . . trap?"

Pony pressed her lips together. "Well, if you keep eating all Pup's jerky, he will have nothing to eat—and he is too young to hunt on his own."

Val's gazed moved over her face, questioning. He said nothing but nodded, and reached for his boots and breeches. Pony looked away. She only looked back when she heard him stagger to his feet. He stumbled into the woods, the materials for the trap in hand.

"Let me," she called, heaving herself up. "I will set it."

"You would do it badly," he cast back without looking. "And I want rabbit for breakfast."

When he returned, he was exhausted and collapsed against the bole, eyes closed. Pony had another contraction, one he could not notice since she bit her teeth against any sound of pain. With fear fluttering at the edge of her mind, she realized that the pains were coming more regularly and strong. There would be no time to get to a farmhouse if she didn't leave right away. But if she was exhausted, so was Val. She couldn't leave him here. And who knew where the nearest farmhouse was? She'd heard stories of women who drowned in their own blood in childbirth, or could not pass the babe because they were too small and so they died. She ran her hands over the immensity of her gigantic belly.

What could be bigger than what she carried? Glancing around, she realized she could well die in these woods.

Though it was July, the night would be cool. Pony stumbled up, while she could, to gather firewood. The pain was on her before she could return with her first load. Still, it passed and she straightened, sweating, and went out again. Building a fire, she crouched and struck her flint. The plume of smoke was soon a crackling blaze. Kneeling before it, with hands outstretched to the warmth, a pain grabbed and shook her. She cried out and collapsed to the leaves, clutching her belly.

"Pony," Val gasped as he crawled across to her. "It is time?"

She opened her eyes to see his clear gray eyes perusing her. His hand cradled her neck, his thumb rubbed her cheek. She looked down as she realized that her cyrtle was soaked. What? Where had all that water come from? She raised frightened eyes to Val's face.

"What is it?" he asked.

"I think my water broke. The babe cannot be far behind." Her voice trembled.

Val's expression said he was as frightened as she. "We must get you to a woman. . . ." He looked around, as though making plans. Pony contracted in another pain.

"I . . . I think it is too late," she gasped when she could straighten. "They come faster."

"Is this not sudden?" Val's tone was almost accusing.

Pony raised herself on one elbow. "I have been having pains off and on since I left Winchester," she said crossly. "Which does not seem sudden."

Val looked around the little camp as though some solution to their dilemma would pop out. Pup approached to nose Pony tentatively, as though asking what was wrong. First Mare lifted her head in interest from where she and Slepnir pulled at some forest ferns. The horse's great girth belied the fact that she was still two months from dropping her own foal.

Pony pulled herself up to sitting as her breathing slowed.

323

"I know naught about birthing," Val warned. "That is for women."

"And I know naught about dying in the woods trying to pass this girl-child," Pony almost hissed. "The Mother has left neither of us choices here." She drew herself toward the crotch of huge elm roots that had supported Val so recently, then collapsed against them.

Val squared his shoulders and set his jaw. He unwrapped the blanket from his shoulders. "Lie on this," he ordered gruffly. "You cannot drop your babe in last year's leaves." Together, he weak, she ungainly, they got her on the blanket.

The pains were so close and so much worse: the next contraction came almost immediately and wrenched a cry from Pony's throat. Val knelt beside her, chafing her wrist helplessly.

Around them, the day was dying. She had heard tell that it took many hours of slow increase to birth. This did seem sudden. "Mayhap it was the jolting of the cart," she whispered, as though to reassure herself that things were normal.

"Water," Val declared. "We need water." He stood.

"A bucket," Pony murmured. "There's a bucket in the cart."

Val wiped Pony's sweating forehead with the damp cloth torn from her cyrtle. He was a warrior, a mercenary fighter for the czars, pillager of towns from Paris to Constantinople. What did he know of pregnant women? All he knew were the stories of women rotting from within, babes deformed or killed by being pulled out wrong. He had no desire to save Alfred's brat. But he could not bear it if Pony died because she had only him in this lonely wood, because she had thrown away all caution and stolen him from Osrick. He should be dead by now. But perhaps he'd lived so Pony would not be alone. He had no idea what to do, and apparently neither did she.

* * *

He had stumbled down to the river in the fading light, then returned and fumbled through the pack she brought. There were clean shifts and a clean cyrtle inside, but he'd chosen to hope that she would need those later, in fierce defiance of the despair in his heart. So he'd used this bit of the crytle she wore. He had been watching her suffer for many hours now, occasionally wiping her brow. The night noises of the wood only intermittently echoed over her harsh breathing or her cries of pain. Outside the circle of firelight, he could feel how alone they were. There was no help around for leagues. The sky had begun to lighten, almost imperceptibly, across the river.

As suddenly and as fiercely as the contractions had come on, they had not led to an immediate birth. Pony's great belly, covered only with the thin linen of her shift, rippled and strained with the forces of life, but no babe appeared. She was so tiny. How could she pass this great thing out between her legs? What if she did not pass it? What if she just went on and on with the contractions and pains until her heart burst? She was tiring; that was clear. She had been tired when all this started. Val had never felt so helpless in his life. His sword arm was useless against such an enemy. His strength meant nothing.

"Val?" Her voice was nothing but a whisper.

"Save your strength," he counseled gruffly.

"No. I want you to promise something."

Val did not want to hear this. "I promise only to slap your girl's backside at her birth."

Pony shook her head, her breathing shallow. "No. Promise now before another pain. I want you to take my knife and cut out my baby, if I cannot . . ." She looked at him steadily.

"You can. Births are like this." He felt his heart clench and stutter. He would not do as she asked.

"They are not like *this*. You must promise."

"I will not kill you to save Alfred's baby. Any baby," he amended. No accusations now.

"I am dead anyway, if it comes to that," she breathed,

then could speak no more as another pain took her. Her screams echoed against the silent trees.

Val groaned in frustration and despair. She couldn't even clench against the pain anymore, just lay there and let it wash over her. He wiped his arm across his forehead. The babe *must* be near! He gently lifted up her shift, his lips pulled back against his teeth in a grimace of self-loathing. What he knew of a woman's parts had nothing to do with what came out, only what went in. It seemed a fatal flaw now. In the flickering light of the fire, he could see something. Her opening was larger than he ever would have believed possible—but it was not large enough. So close! Could he reach in and grab the child without killing her? He would gladly sacrifice the child for the mother, but he did not know if it would work! He only knew her strength was waning. He sat back on his haunches. If she went unconscious, was the only solution her knife?

"What do you see?" she asked, so weak he could barely hear.

"I know not," he answered. "I see . . . something."

She raised her hand. He scooted up to her and mopped her brow. "The knife. It is time. Save my girl-child," she begged. He shook his head, his face beginning to contort with the inevitability of her plan. "She is why I was born," she continued, but he had to lean in to hear. "My mother said so. If she lives, *I* have lived."

Val gritted his teeth. "No." The rebellion rose within him. There was nothing he could do. But *she* could.

"Forgive me," she breathed.

"Noooo." It was a hoarse cry torn from him. "I do not forgive you, Pony!" He pulled her shift up around her waist, not sparing a glance for whether the babe was there or not. He took her shoulders and half-lifted her. "I want you alive!" Her eyes were limpid with resignation. "Do you hear me? You have not tried." His elbow touching her belly told him another contraction was coming on. "Push that baby out, Pony," he threatened. "I do not forgive you if you do not try."

"Too late . . ."

"Not too late." He squeezed her. She gasped as the contraction came on. *"Try!* Push it out, Pony." She stared at him, a cry beginning in her throat. *"Push!"* He saw a fleeting question, then the gritting of her teeth. Her breath came raggedly. "I give you my strength," he shouted into her rising wail. "I push with you. We are *berserker,* animal together." He saw her clench almost double, and he held her up by her shoulders, and they screamed together, until her shriek spiraled up even higher and she collapsed in his arms.

She was dead! He had killed her after all. He laid her down. "Pony, Pony," he whispered, looking frantically at her. He pushed open an eyelid and saw only white. Unconscious! All right. Take the babe. He would grab it. It was her only chance. He scrambled to her open knees.

Half a baby lay exposed, bloody, on the blanket. What? She had done it! He hesitated only a moment, at the hugeness of his own hands and their calluses, before he circled them gently around the babe's tiny torso and gave a tentative tug. The infant slipped free as though gliding on ice. Where was all its resistance now? Licking his lips, Val tasted salt as he laid the babe on its back. Tears.

Wait! It was not dead. He could see it moving weakly. But breathing? He had made Pony only one promise. He held up the babe with both hands. The cord still connected it to its mother. One had to hit the backside; even he knew that much. He grabbed its tiny feet and held it upside down. How could you smack a thing so small? But it wasn't crying. Pony would not forgive him if he let it die after all her effort. He smacked it once—received a cough only, so tiny it did not seem real. He slapped again. Nothing. Panic rising in his breast, Val laid the babe down. It opened its mouth, but no sound came. He put a finger in the tiny orifice to clear its throat, scooped out mucus. Was that the problem?

A lusty scream said that it was. Val breathed again and sat back on his haunches. *A baby!* He looked again, registering the child fully for the first time. He glanced at Pony, uncertain, and saw her eyes open a slit. "Pony . . ." Suddenly he was so tired, he was not sure he could speak.

"My baby," she said, holding out her hand weakly toward it.

He gathered up the bloody thing and realized he had another task. Slowly he picked up the knife he had laid down and cut the cord, then knotted it as close to the baby as he could; there would be time for a better job later. Raising his brows, he picked up the baby by the torso and lifted it gingerly to Pony. What would she say? She gathered it, gory as it was, to her breast.

"My girl, my girl-child. Shall you be Epona, too, as we all are?" she cooed softly.

"Pony . . ." But her gasp told Val she had noticed.

"A . . . a boy?" The shock was plain. "I . . . I cannot have had a male-child!" She spoke as though the concept was blasphemy. "We always have girls . . ." She trailed off. "Take it!" she commanded, though her voice was weak. She held it out, stiff-armed. "Take it away!"

Val chewed his lip. "He will die without you," he muttered. "You do not want that."

The horror in her eyes as she tried to comprehend was painful to watch. In the end she was too weak to hold the child out, and let him lay across her breasts. Tears welled in her eyes. "This is *your* fault," she gasped. "All your fault."

"What, because I was here?" Val was incensed. After all he had done, even though he wanted no part of such women's work? "Blame Alfred!"

Pony's tears overflowed. "Oh, can you not count?" she asked fiercely. "It is yours. Get me something to wrap him in."

Chapter Twenty-three

Exhaustion made it hard to even lift her eyelids, but Pony woke to tiny, raw and desperate cries. Pup came over and sniffed with interest at the noisy bundle in her arms. Would it not stop crying? Pony jiggled the bundle tentatively, but the wailing continued. She struggled into a more upright position. Midafternoon sunlight slanted through the forest canopy, lighting Val, who was pushing up on one elbow near the smoldering ruins of the fire. First Mare and Slepnir stood in the river, drinking. They all looked so at ease.

For Pony, nothing was right. How could her babe be a boy? She had birthed a carnivore? That was what her mother had called all males. This was what came of her transgression against all her mothers' teachings on that Samhain night. This was her fault. All her fault.

What was she to do with him? She pulled apart the cloth in which Val had wrapped the child, to look at his tiny, wizened face. He was ugly—there was nothing else that could be said of him. Was he deformed in some way? Neither she nor Val looked like this!

Val. He had been appalled by her confession. The look on his face had been easily identified. He had said nothing in response, only adjured her to rest and collapsed by the fire, but he no more wanted this product of Samhain than she did. Weight descended upon her shoulders once again. It was the weight she had fought against in seeking out Britta, in following Alfred, even in telling Val to follow her to the Circle of Stones. She could not escape it. It was the weight of her mother's death, the weight of the inevitability of her own future. She had resisted her mothers' destiny and she was punished today. Her Gift was polluted, her baby was a carnivore, Val was lost. *All* was lost.

Tears captured by the corners of her mouth were of a salty taste that made her want to gag. Could she try again to heed her mother's teaching? Could she have a girl-child yet? But how could she ever lie with another man after Val?

Pup nosed in and licked the babe's tiny face. What was he doing? The thing would never stop its infernal crying if he bothered it. She made as if to push him away—but, miraculously, the infant's crying stopped. He hiccuped once, then made a sound more like a cough, though it was so small it sounded like something else altogether. Pup sat back, pleased with himself.

Val appeared over her, his torso bare and still marked by Osrick's cruelty. He looked stronger than he had yesterday, though he was still thin, and circles still darkened his eyes. She did not meet his gaze but chuffed in disgust. "We are a pair, both weak as kittens." She did not acknowledge the child.

Valgar looked down at Pony, her face streaked with tears, holding the babe she had made plain she did not want. *His* baby. Even now he could not help but be amazed by the reality of it. But he had counted. It was July, by the sun. If it had been Alfred's baby, she would have been breeding eleven months, for he had kept her by his side between the day he had vanquished Alfred's troops and the night of Samhain. The boy was his.

330

Pony should be his as well. He let that thought flower in his chest. It was what he had wanted in his heart these many months. He had denied it because Pony had cantered away the morning after Samhain, an echo of many betrayals he had known, but Pony had claimed his thoughts and heart and would not be banished. A longing for stability and a home had driven him back to his people from the steppes of the Russias, but he wanted nothing more than to cradle this woman and their baby against his chest, to wander back to the Vale of the White Horse to till the land, raise horses and children with her. But it could never be.

"Are you going to feed that baby?" he growled. "Or listen to it cry?"

Her face went from accusing to uncertainty. "Is that why it cries?"

"Yes, if its belly is as empty as ours." He looked about. "You feed it. I will find a way to feed us." He reached for the knife and went off to see if their trap had borne fruit. Glancing back, he saw Pony undo the brooch that held up her cyrtle, then pull down the neck of her shift. She looked dismayed, even frightened, but she would feed the baby.

The trap was empty, but the bait was still in place so he left it and made a second plan. A willow near the river provided the pole he required. He cut at the joint and snapped it off, then sat and began to plane the end to a point with vicious strokes of his blade. He would take Pony and the child wherever they wanted to go. He owed her that much. And she wanted no more than that from him. She would abandon him again just like his family after he had saved their lives. They had turned their hearts to stone against him, just like his people. And now Pony blamed him for this "disaster." She'd wanted no entanglements. She had said she looked for a father for her babe who would not be part of her life. Now this.

He could not be a part of her life anyway; his loyalty was owed to Guthrum. He sliced at the green pole without seeing, his gut clenching as though it sucked at a stone. What to do? Guthrum would expect him to be dead. It mattered not that the *Konnungr* had broken his bond under provocation from Osrick; Val's duty was to Guthrum, and he had violated troth. And had his duty not been to Harald and the others, too? It was his fault they were dead, killed in a way that would deny them forever even the glory of Valhalla. Paltry as that seemed to him, the reward might have been everything to them. His head wanted to split.

Two loyalties were not possible. One must take precedence. But which? Duty to his king or to his men? He stabbed his knife into a tree trunk with a grunt of pain. It was a new version of the old question. Duty to the strong, or duty to the weak? Loyalty to father or to brother? He could not answer. All he knew was that he had chosen loyalty to Guthrum, and that was what was left to him. His dream of living in the Vale with Pony was impossible. Even had she wanted it, such a life could not be his. Not as a respectable Dane. He had forfeited all such hopes the day he killed his father.

Valgar realized with a start that he had trimmed a good six inches from his pole. He pulled the knife from where it trembled in the tree trunk and stuck it into the thongs that bound his breeches. Hefting his pole, he stood. Weak he was, but he would provide for Pony. She needed meat, to build her strength and produce milk for the child. She would not like that. But perhaps she could start with fish. Fish was not the same as meat, was it? He started toward the river, upstream of the place where the horses drank. *Let the fish be slow today.*

His thoughts circled back to his dilemma. He could not walk into Guthrum's camp. The man would have to kill him, since Val had deprived Alfred of the opportunity. His only choice seemed to be to disappear back to the Russias— yet that barren life felt impossible. The certainty shuddered through him: he could not go back. Which meant all choices led to the same end. He looked inside and accepted that. Very well. But first he would feed Pony.

He stood still in the shallows, arm raised, the dappled afternoon light glinting off the river's surface. There! They hovered in the water, tails moving just enough to keep them in place over the pebbles of the riverbed. Dinner, if he was quick enough, his hand sufficiently steady. He stabbed his sharpened pole down through the water. It came up dripping but empty. Again and again he waited then plunged, and at last a fish flapped at the end of his pole, skewered.

Now he knew what to do. It would take more courage than facing down the Mongol hordes.

Pony watched Val struggle up from the river with three fish perhaps two spans of her hand in length impaled on his willow pole. She adjusted the baby at her breast. Thank the Mothers it knew how to suck and that her milk was flowing. Though why she should care about such an ugly baby, and a boy at that, she could not say. She held it awkwardly. What was her mother thinking to have left her without any knowledge of how to care for a baby? Britta's words and Hild's seemed distant and unreal.

Britta. What would Britta say she should do? Her destiny lay in shreds. Pony had no girl-child to continue the line of her Mothers. Britta had said she should go to Alfred. But it was too late for the one thing Alfred should take from her, the impulse to peace. Even now he marched on Guthrum, bent on making the entire island his own. And why not? Hadn't Britta seen the whole island united under him? Hadn't it been Pony's role to be Alfred's talisman for victory? Would it be, still? She could not face another battle where she encouraged men to spend their lives in such meaningless waste. . . .

No, she could not go to Alfred at all. What would he say if Asser encouraged him to think about her baby's heritage? Yet . . . where else was there? This boy-child was also the final blow to her returning to the life she'd known in the Vale. He was a symbol of all her frailty, her betrayal of her heritage. She looked down at the tiny face, the fingernails . . . so perfect and so small. She touched the fingers, gently. So small, so helpless, just as Pup had been. Pup was a carnivore. She had learned to accept him, even to care for him, though it cost her to admit it. Could she learn to care for this small carnivore as well, even though he was a betrayal of all she had been raised to believe? Pup hovered, occasionally touching the baby with his nose. Pony clutched the dog in the crook of her other arm and buried her face in his fur.

Val strode up, scowling, and silently began to make a fire. He cared not that the child was his. Which was just what she wanted. She had no need of a man in her life. That much of her mother's teaching she could heed. The sooner he moved on, the better. Pony found herself drifting, each breath an effort of will almost too much. A man she did not want, a baby who was a shocking disappointment, and no way back to the life she understood. The prospect numbed her, and the familiar weight descended.

Val laid the charred fish on a flat stone, along with a piece of flat bread, and carried it to Pony. "Here," he said gruffly, crouching to set it beside her. He pushed the dog away. Pony was rewrapping the baby, now that it had fed.

"I do not eat meat." She wrinkled her nose in distaste.

Val stood, considering. "You need meat to make milk."

"Mayhap I care not whether I make milk." Her voice was dull. She laid the bundle down beside her and struggled up. He moved instinctively to help, but she pushed him away.

"You are not strong enough . . ." He began.

"I want to wash. I feel unclean." Stumbling to where the soap she had used to wash him lay on a stone near the fire to dry, she scooped it up.

He wanted to follow her, but the disgust in her eyes and her listless manner held him back. He knew what she was feeling. The emptiness inside was powerful. Yet he could not let her go down the road he himself had chosen. She must care for the babe.

After a moment he scooped the sleeping bundle up from where she'd left it and grabbed a charred fish. He stood with his back to the trunk of a young elm, close to the water. He could not let her bathe alone when she was so weak; she might stumble and drown. Scraping the succulent flesh from the spotted brown trout, he rocked the baby and watched Pony strip and huddle into the river. She did not even glance over to see if he looked.

He did look. The white of her flesh and the blond of her hair were stark against the dark ripples of the river. He remembered her on Samhain, a wild force of the gods outlined against the stones by the wash of moonlight. His eyes saw the looseness in her belly before the water rose over it, but all he could think was that she was the most beautiful thing he had ever seen. Together, they had made new life.

He tossed away the skeleton of the trout and pulled back the babe's blanket. Already the child was less wrinkled. Its head was covered with wisps of pale hair; pale lashes brushed tiny cheeks less mottled and red than yesterday. Why did women say that a baby looked like one person or another? They looked only like other babies, as far as Val saw.

He glanced up to find Pony coming out of the water. Her breasts were full and dripping water, her hair hanging wet over her shoulders. She reached for her shift and cyrtle. Before he knew it, he was walking down the slope, hand outstretched to help her. Tears, not river water, coursed down her cheeks. Her eyes were red and accusing. She slapped away his hand.

"This is your fault," she choked. "I have nothing now— not even who I am." She clutched her clothing to her and pushed past, shoulders shaking. He turned, anger growing inside him.

"And can I not say the same?" he shouted after her. "You strip me of my last honor and yet accuse me? I rue the day I took you from the Vale." He turned away.

"No more than I," she yelled at his back.

Val strode down to the river. In the crook of his arm, the baby began to cry. Pup came up out of nowhere, nosing at him anxiously. He set the baby down. What was he to do with it? Pony was nowhere in sight. She had probably left him. He glanced to the cart and saw it still there. He strode down to the river, leaving the baby in the shade of the willow. Pup standing over him protectively.

Let her leave. I do not care. The feeling made him press his lips together.

Osrick bowed his head to his king as he dismounted. His troop behind him did the same. The faesten at Winchester was the largest in Wessex, as befitted Alfred's capital, and it was filled with the din of preparation for war. "My king," he shouted over the noise. "What others have arrived?"

He concealed his frustration. Of course he wanted to be here at Alfred's side to claim the glory of defeating the Viking horde at last—but he'd wanted to discover the whereabouts of his escaped hostage, too. They had searched the village that night to no avail. While some readied for the journey, he had sent other men into the surrounding woods . . . without result. Valgar had made good his escape. They'd found his chestnut stallion missing. But it was worse than that—

"Borogand has already arrived. We expect Trevellyan on the morrow," Alfred called, interrupting Osrick's thoughts. The young king grinned. "Guthrum will taste all our swords." His eyes were lit with anticipation of battle. The little priest, Asser, appeared out of nowhere at Alfred's side. He was becoming the king's shadow.

Osrick slapped the dust from his leathers, gathering his wits to ask what had been burning in him ever since Sherborne. He'd questioned the guards at the gates about who'd taken the chestnut stallion out, and he was suspicious, but he dared not ask outright. "How does this child of yours?"

Alfred frowned. He took Osrick's arm and led him to the grand hall. Asser trailed behind. "Epona's babe? I know not. She disappeared just as the babe was due."

It was true! Osrick hardly believed it possible. The guards had said a very pregnant woman with white-blond hair had taken the chestnut stallion. The anger that had been growing in his belly for three days churned into his throat. He tossed his helmet onto a table in a smaller room where Al-

fred took a seat, and raised his hand to a serving girl for
mead.

"I know where she is, or was," he growled. "She helped
the Viking, Valgar, escape before I could execute him."

"Epona?" Alfred took the first proffered horn of mead.
"Why would she do that?"

Sly satisfaction in what he was about to relay partly covered the rage that boiled inside him. "Can you not think of
a reason?" he asked, trying to mask his contempt. "If she
was still swelling three days hence, then her babe cannot be
from the night you had Asser witness. It would have been
eleven months and more."

"Oh," Alfred said. He gulped from his horn and glanced
at Asser. "That. I knew it wasn't mine. You are saying it
was Valgar's." He nodded thoughtfully. "That would make
sense. I have heard that they were much together. She could
do worse . . . couldn't she, Asser? He was a sage counselor
to Guthrum, and I liked what I heard of how he managed
his conquered lands."

"You knew this and yet you let her stay here? Fueled
speculation that it was your child?"

Alfred shrugged and grinned. "I was a little disappointed.
I would have liked to be the chosen of an incarnation of the
Goddess. . . . so I let people think it mine. All for the cause."

"You should have executed her," Osrick muttered. Alfred
was shrewder than he thought.

"Execute a goddess?" Alfred chuckled. "You have much
to learn about governing."

"She duped you!" Osrick had to convince Alfred of that
if he was to take revenge on Epona. But the king did not
seem the simple youth he had imagined, suddenly. What
else did Alfred know?

The monarch shook his head and took another gulp.
"That she did not. She said what she wanted. I said the
same. Perhaps neither got their wish, but that was not her
fault or mine."

Osrick could feel the vein in his temple throb. "At the

least, she has robbed you of your right to execute one of the hostages for Guthrum's deeds."

Alfred nodded. "True. And what of the others?"

Osrick glanced away. He could feel the king looking at him, and Asser. "They are dead."

Alfred rose. "Then four-fifths of my rights have been honored. I must settle for that."

Pony came back into camp sometime near dusk. She could hear the baby crying from a hundred yards away. All her anger, her tears, her emotion had run dry, left her beached on the shore of her calamity. Not looking at Val, who crouched by the fire turning the spitted carcass of a rabbit, she sat on the blanket next to Pup. The dog panted happily over the baby, who burbled at him in return. Pony made no move to pick it up. It wanted feeding.

Val rose and came to stand above her, holding out a haunch from the rabbit. He said nothing. Pony's body screamed at her to eat. But the smell of the dripping meat turned her stomach. She covered her mouth and shook her head. Val set his lips and turned away—but he came back with the charred fish from that afternoon and silently offered it. His adjuration that she must eat meat to make milk rang in her ears.

Pony sighed. At least the fish did not make her stomach clench. What did it matter whether she adhered to her mother's command not to be a carnivore? She heard carnivores and scavengers. She had bit at Val as though she were a predator. She had birthed a male child. What other tenet of her mother's teachings had she not already broken? She took the fish. Val did not stay to gloat that she had given in, but turned back to the fire.

Pup's nose appeared from nowhere. His bright eyes said clearly that he would be glad to eat the fish if she did not. She elbowed him aside. The baby cried, but it did not grate on her nerves—she was so numb she had no nerves left. She picked at the white flesh with her fingers and put some flakes in her mouth. After the first impulse to gag, she got hold of her stomach and chewed away, refusing to register the taste. After resolutely cleaning most of the flesh from the fish's bones, she tossed the carcass aside, and Pup bounded after it.

Very well, she would do what she must. She was tired of thinking, simply *tired*. Undoing the baby's wrappings, she removed its cloth, soaked as it was with urine and worse. Then she wrapped the child in a new cloth from those cut from her cyrtle yesterday, and undid her brooch to let the child feed. All as required.

When the baby was done, Pony lay back against the bole of the elm and pulled the blanket up around her. Val sat crouched in front of the fire, facing away. She decided to rest, if just for a moment.

The raft bobbled on the dark, translucent lake, the water sloshing over its uneven poles. The moon was full, like Samhain night, casting an eerie glow that made the ripples glisten all along their sinuous length. Pony was slipping off the raft, slipping into the water. She had always thought this lake sinister somehow. But it wasn't. It was cool and comforting, all-enveloping, its soft caress a promise of peace. And it was quiet. The only sound was the lapping of the tiny wavelets of its great black expanse. She held on with one hand to the pole that formed the edge of the raft and slipped into the waters. It would be so easy to let go.

Boots appeared. Soggy leather boots. And, beside them, four legs covered with wet black fur. Where had they all come from? She hadn't noticed. The raft dipped. She could have let go then, as the pole jerked under her hand. But instead she looked up. Val leaned over her, holding out a callused hand. In the crook of his other arm he held a bundle. The legs beside him were those of Pup. The dog yapped at her, disturbing the gentle, quiet caress of the water. The bundle began to wail. Val called out: "Pony! Grab my hand!" His voice seemed far away over the lake, but it was coming closer. All this noise! She wanted quiet, the quiet of the water. Her mother was somewhere below, waiting for her.

With a sigh, she let go of the raft. It drifted away from her. The sounds of the baby crying, and Pup barking, and Val calling to her, faded as the water closed over her head. She watched the moon, shining whitely down, as she sank into the transparent blackness of the water.

Pony woke with a start and a stifled scream, her arms clawing as though to pull herself up through endless water even though heavy wet garments dragged her down. Gasping, she registered her surroundings. Pup was staring at her, whining. Val lay near the fire for warmth. He stirred in his sleep. Only the baby at her side was quiet.

The dream! She'd had the dream again. And this time it was more frightening than it had ever been. She needed no interpreter to tell her what it meant. She lay trembling for a long moment. When she finally noticed that Pup was still concerned, she held out an arm to him, and he came over and curled next to her. After a while the baby started making soft, wet noises with his mouth and she held him to her breast to feed.

It took some time before she was able to fall back asleep.

When Pony next woke, steam rose from the damp leaves on the forest floor. The metallic blue ripples of the river babbled by just beyond the trees. Val was already up and about. He was buckling Slepnir into the harness of the cart, the pack of their belongings neatly tied at his feet. He was leaving. That was obvious. Pony did not rise, but let the particularity of the scene seep into her. Slepnir's shoulder muscles rippled under his copper-colored hide as he nervously stepped from foot to foot—just like Val's muscles glided under the skin of his back as he fastened the harness. The Viking's wounds were puckering as they moved; his scabs showing dark against his tanned skin.

First Mare moved up to stand beside Slepnir, her bulk impossible on such graceful, slender legs. Pony could clearly hear her soft nicker and the affection for Slepnir behind it. She heard Pup's excitement as he ran to show Val something he held in his mouth. *Prey*. She felt the dog's triumph at his first kill, a rabbit. Her mind sloshed out into the woods around her. She could sense shrews and wood tits, a snake slithering by looking for an unsuspecting animal for dinner. She felt his satisfaction when he found one of the shrews. A badger poked out of his burrow somewhere nearby and decided to take a constitutional. A congress of crows feasted on a carcass somewhere nearby. Everything was there for her to hear—herbivores, carnivores, scavengers. She could hear them all, everything but Val and the baby.

Strange that those made most like her were most closed to her. But it had always been thus. What was suddenly different was how open she felt to the world at large. The tumult she had felt yesterday was not gone, precisely. Rather it had taken its rightful place. There was a place in the world for tumult, for noise and emotion and hearts that beat until you could not hear anything else. Just as there was a place for those who ate meat, and even those who ate carrion.

She would not let the dream become her, or herself become the dream. That was the only thing of which she could be sure. She must engage with the world. That was what her dream had told her. Engage or suffer her mother's fate. And it was up to her. She could extend her hand and grasp those who reached for her, or let go of the raft. Her mother had chosen to let go. But Pony need not do the same. That was not what the Great Mother required. Had it not been Her who reached out for Pony on Samhain, that most sacred of Her nights and given her Val? Was what happened in Her circle of stones on Her most sacred night not true and right in the Goddess's eyes? How could it be else? It was Pony who had been trying to dictate to the Mother what would happen in her life, instead of listening to what the Mother told her of life and the world.

Her own mother was wrong. The chant of the Great Mother did not include the adjuration against carnivores. It did not say one should be alone. Those were her mother's additions and they were wrong. Could carnivores exist without the Mother's will that they exist? Did not even scavengers have their place in the Mother's scheme of things?

Tears coursed down Pony's cheeks. They were the Great Mother's tears—fulfilling, completing, with the completeness of a realization. All her life Pony had been afraid of carnivores, of men, of those that were not like her. And the Great Mother had shown her the way by tugging her toward Val, by granting her a boy-child. Even Britta, giving her Pup and telling her she needed to listen to carnivores, was part of the Great Mother's will. Pony had pushed away everything her mother had told her was frightening. That was where lay all her confusion. She had abandoned Val. She had even felt revulsion for her own child, and his. Yet the Great Mother showed her the way, even still.

Pony smiled through tears and drew back into herself, away from the senses of others. A breath. How magical! The world had carnivores, and male babies, and Vikings. Ahhh! That was another way she wanted to engage with the world, with all the Great Mother had given her, with Viking and babies. She thought lazily of Alfred, far away somewhere, bent upon battles. Was Britta wrong, too? What had he to do with her? As the image of golden hair and his dazzling smile circled in her mind's eye, she felt a tug. A tug? She had not felt the tug of Alfred in many weeks.

Val turned and saw that she had wakened. He set his mouth and stalked over to her, a piece of jerky in his hand. As he drew close, he examined her face warily. "You look better."

"I feel better."

He cleared his throat. "I must go to Alfred. I will take you where you would before I go."

She looked at him, thinking. Yes. She understood why he would go. She understood what was in his heart; the confusion, the resolution on a course he knew would end in death. She also realized that somehow, Britta was still right. She herself felt the tug of the world toward the young king. Her way also lay with him. "I, too, go to Alfred." It was the only choice if she was to avoid the black water of the lake. She held out her hand to Val. She could not help but soften as she looked at him. So stern, so determined, unable to forgive himself for what he had done. He could not forgive himself his nature. He did not know that she had forgiven him.

He took her hand, but instead of letting him pull her up, she pulled him down. He glanced at her cautiously, then sat cross-legged beside her. She realized she might well be making a terrible mistake. But the time to avoid such dangers was past. When he handed her the jerky, she turned it over, looking at it. It was a strip of an animal's haunch, dried. How many times had that revolted her? She broke off a piece and tossed it to Pup, then broke off another for herself. The rest she handed back to Val. She could not quite bring herself to look at him as she did. Perhaps it was just as well. It gave him some privacy for a reaction to the question forming on her lips, in her heart.

"Why did you kill your father?"

The words hung in the remaining plumes of morning mist as though she had screamed not whispered them. No answer came—for so long she thought he might just stand and leave without ever speaking. She didn't want that. But she didn't want to take the question back, either.

She heard him suck in his breath and chanced a glance at his face. Pain filled not only his gray eyes but the lines around his mouth. He pressed his lips together as though that could deny their softness. He wasn't seeing her. "What was his name?" she prodded.

"Thorvald. He was a hard man." He shook his head. "More than hard. He was a monster." Val looked up and out at the river beyond the trees. The sun had banished all the mist. "When the mead was on him, or when he wanted to show how hard he was to men who were his betters . . ." He trailed off. "My mother grew smaller each year they shared. I was the oldest boy. I watched him cow her. I watched him make my brothers into shadows, or make them cruel just like him, if they were bigger than their adversary. I tried to take his anger on myself. I could stand the blows." He looked up at her for the first time. "I was a stout lad even then."

She nodded, keeping all judgment, all sympathy, from her eyes.

It was a moment before he could go on. He had to clear his throat. Even so, his voice was hoarse. "I was to marry. Hers was a good family. I thought I loved her. She brought a dowry of land. Which meant freedom from him. When he saw that I would soon escape, the ice we stood on began to melt. He seemed to choose my youngest brother, the smallest of us, more frequently for his beatings. How could I protect him, when I would soon be gone?"

Val swallowed. His hands picked the jerky into feathery strips. He looked up again, his lips twisting, his eyes hard. He took another breath. "He beat my youngest brother to death on the day before my marriage. I let it happen." The words were torn from him. Silence followed. As though he'd explained all.

"You mean you stood by and watched?"

"No. I was away, drinking with my friends."

She felt something like remorse fill her. "On the night before your wedding. That sounds like something young men do."

"But I knew. I knew the danger!" he hissed.

"Then . . . ?" She wanted him to relate the whole story.

"I came home. He was drunk. Erik was a bloody mess on the floor. My mother crouched in the corner. My other brothers were nowhere to be found." The words poured from him now. "He was laughing and drinking. And I could see in his eyes that he dared me to leave, that he would kill them all, one by one, because I was not afraid of him and he had only them with which to threaten me. So I took the ax for chopping wood—it was not even a weapon, not elegant, not made for killing—and I cleaved his skull."

"And freed your family—"

He grunted and tossed his jerky to Pup, who sat attentively about a yard away. "My mother never spoke to me again. My wife-to-be unplighted her troth. The *jarl* of our free *soke* completed any shame by stripping me of the rights of first son and telling me that I might never return to *Danmork*. They deserted me, all of them. And why not? I deserved their scorn. I had done what no son should do." He looked sick.

"I think your *jarl* should have completed the job for you years before," Pony snapped indignantly. She saw now how she must have hurt him when, in her own confusion, she had abandoned him after Samhain. The realization coursed through her, leaving her wondering if it was the closest she could come to hearing another human. That was why Harald's death had so wounded Val. Harald was an echo of his youngest brother.

So now he would go back to Alfred to fulfill his role as hostage, even if it meant that Alfred and Osrick would kill him. He would do it just to prove he was a loyal Dane, to make up for the fact that he had not been loyal to a father who had not deserved loyalty. He was letting go of the raft. She could see the water closing over his eyes.

Well, Alfred wouldn't kill him, not if she could help it. But . . . how much influence with Alfred would she have after she had freed his hostage, and her baby was not his? She sighed.

"Is this what you wanted to know?" Val's voice was husky with raw emotion.

"Yes," Pony answered. But that was not the whole truth. "No. After I have heard your story, I want to know why you are ashamed of such an act of bravery and sacrifice."

"It was an act of cowardice." Val's contradiction held the same dullness hers had held yesterday.

Pony nodded, thinking. "I know you feel that way. But Karn does not." Val looked up, squinting. "He thinks you were *'berserkr'*. Is that the right word? He thinks you were fearless in battle against a foe who was stronger than you, not only in muscle, but because he was your father." She saw him consider what she was saying. "He used his position of power against you—while you defended the weak."

Val shook his head. "It has always been a fault of mine."

"Elbert and Asser would not think it a fault. Their God values those who defend the weak."

"They believe in forgiveness, too." Val waved his hand, dismissive.

"I believe in that more all the time," she said. "I forgive Pup that he is a carnivore. I forgive you that you killed your father. Elbert forgives you. Karn forgives you. Guthrum must forgive you, else why would he trust you? Can you not accept that? Can you not forgive yourself?"

He simply looked at her. She knew what he was thinking, but there had to be some way to get at him. How could she make him confront the terrible choices his stony beliefs demanded? "If you should not defend the weak, then you must forgive yourself Harald's death." She smoothed her cyrtle over her thighs. "In doing your duty, you chose not to defend him. A hard lesson in loyalty, but one you must believe in."

His shoulders sagged. "Your words are wily. But you know Harald's death cannot be forgiven."

"You cannot have it both ways!"

"Do you forgive yourself for Samhain?" he growled. "Do you forgive that you had a boy-child, instead of the girl you wanted?"

She sucked in air. He was difficult. "Not entirely," she admitted. "Not yet. But I am trying." She touched his shoulder. The shock of hot flesh against her palm shot through her. She willed herself not to tremble as she mustered a smile. "Our way is hard, Valgar the Beast. Is there *no* comfort to be had?" And suddenly she realized, with some surprise, that only Val could give the solace she required.

He put his arm around her and leaned his forehead against hers. She hoped he did not notice her tiny gasp. All he said was, "Let us to Alfred, both of us, and make what way we can."

She nodded and brushed her cheek against his scratchy bearded one. "Let us to Alfred." She could not deny the pull that had come upon her earlier, but it was a good thing that Val would go with her. What could she expect from the future? What was her true destiny? What did the Mother demand, and what would be the result? As she gathered up the child, and Val heaved the pack into the cart, she knew she must think of one thing: a way to protect Val from his strange brand of honor.

Chapter Twenty-four

Valgar trudged beside the cart; Pony sat on the seat board and nursed her baby. *Their* baby. He pushed his thoughts away from that.

They should be making faster progress. Slepnir and First Mare moved slowly in the heat of late July, and at this rate, he and Pony would not reach Alfred before the final engagement with the *Danir*. Once Guthrum prevailed, Val's sacrifice would be too late. His honor would not be reclaimed; he would be despised by his fellows forever.

They were just east of Ashford, following the great South Downs Road, jostled by carts and horses, oxen and men whose backs were bent almost double with their goods. At every stop they got word of the Saxon armies just ahead moving east. The first skirmish had taken place at Horsham, the next at Crowborough. Each time, Guthrum had retreated before the battle could be fully engaged.

Val knew what his *Konnungr* was doing; he was only amazed that Alfred did not. Guthrum was leading his Saxon foes, tricking them. Word was Alfred's army was bigger than the Danes', and Guthrum was no fool. He was surely heading for the seaside, where reinforcements from the Northmen across the channel would catch Alfred in a vise. Guthrum would go to that fortress on the white cliffs overlooking the sea. The ones who'd built the roads had left a stone lighthouse there, its tower a good signal for allies.

Val pushed his fingers through his hair. He was sweating, but he did not remove his shirt. It had been more than two weeks, but still the bruises and the scabs on his body would attract attention. He must remain in this garment, one they had bought with hack silver he had made from his silver armband. It had been this hot when first he had met Pony. The memory, the wonder of feeling her moist palms rubbing the muscles of his arm, he would take to his grave. But that was the problem: Val *was* intent upon going to his grave, sacrificing himself to Guthrum's violation of his word, and his own honor. He owed Guthrum. He owed for Harald's life.

Yet, as he had traveled with Pony this fortnight, the two of them had grown only more comfortable together. And that had made him unhappy. He had been eating as though he were a starving man—which was true, as it happened— growing stronger day by day. But with the return of strength, his traitorous loins began to tug at him whenever he let his eyes linger upon her. The baby undermined his purpose, too. He held it when Pony got down from the cart, or when she relieved herself, or sometimes when she ate. It had gotten to look more human. In fact, sometimes he could see a little likeness around its mouth to its mother's. Pony had remarked only last night that she thought the child was getting rather more attractive. Though she had said that it had the cleft of Val's chin, Val could not see it.

What are you thinking? he asked himself in disgust. Even now, she lured him toward life and living—but he could not go, because he was already dead. He glanced up toward her, the bleakness of his soul leaking into the air around him until he was certain she would feel it.

She looked over at him and smiled. "It is too hot to walk. Will you not ride in the cart?"

Why did she have to smile like that, so softly? He shook his head.

"You are not strong yet." She glanced at Slepnir, and Val stopped walking. "Ride," she urged.

He did not want to ride. The narrow driver's seat placed his hip against Pony's. Her arm would brush his. He shook his head and walked on. But had to say something. "You seem content." And she did. She fairly glowed these last few days.

"Almost," she agreed. Slepnir walked forward again.

"What has changed?" He hardly dared ask. But something had come over Pony since those first grim days after the birth.

"Ahhhh!" She breathed, looking up into the blue sky, strewn with shredded clouds, faint white and high. "Everything happens all around us. I can feel it. We are on our way toward it. Everything is on its way toward . . ."

"Toward what?"

She shrugged and laughed. "I do not know. Britta said I could do what must be done only when I was complete. She said I would know what could complete me when the time came. I know part, but still . . . that time is not yet, I think."

Val turned back to the road. The fact that Pony was so full of life cut at him, an ax to his purpose. He could not allow himself too close to her and her radiant purple eyes. He would not ask what part she knew completed her.

"Val."

"Ja," he said. He did not look at her.

"I have something for you. I bought it in Ashford." She held out a wooden flute like the bone one Osrick had taken at Sherborne. It sent shivers of blackness around the edges of his vision.

"I was waiting for the right time to give it to you. Perhaps there is no right time." She scooted to the far side of the cart seat. "Come, play me a song to pass the time."

What could he do? The call of the flute was physical. The

cart stopped. Val found himself sitting beside her, handling the instrument. His hands were sweating. The flute was well made, the wood native. Yew, he thought. Polished. The holes were drilled carefully and cleaned. It would give a different sound than bone, softer but no less true. He lifted it to his lips. He had no other choice. His breath gave it life. He tested the scale, then let it drop to his lap and sat, staring.

"Play. Play the music you hear," she whispered.

He stroked the flute's length, lifted it. The notes that came to him were surprising: mournful, haunted, searching. He closed his eyes and let the music take him. It became his breath and his breath became the melody. His tongue caressed the mouth hole, controlled its release. Pony's shoulder pressed against him, and the urgency mingled with loss that he felt was expressed in song. When at last he finished and the notes died away, he opened his eyes. The music still seemed to hang in the summer air. It was the first he had played since she left him. A man saluted as he walked past the cart. A woman with a gaggle of geese called out in appreciation.

"That was amazing," Pony whispered. "Your Gift surely must sustain you."

It did. He felt cleaner, lighter. He stuck the flute in his boot. What harm to keep it? He would not refuse the gift.

Pup bounded out of the tall weeds at the side of the road, his fur laced with leaves and the petals of summer flowers. He had been chasing rabbits, who seemed to be everywhere. Pony beckoned to him. The dog scrambled up in the back of the cart and stood with his front paws on the back of the seat. His tongue found its way through her hair to her ear. She laughed and shuddered. "Pup, you rogue!"

"Does he not deserve a better name?" Val asked, his voice still uncertain from the emotion conjured by the flute. He dared not ask why she did not name their baby. Mayhap she could start with the dog.

"He is Pup. Like First Mare." She looked up, curious. "What would *you* name him?"

"Loki," he answered, almost without thinking. "He is a trickster."

"Loki . . . I shall consider that."

Perhaps she would name her dog Loki, to remember Val when he was dead. The thought gave him no comfort. He fingered the top of the flute that stuck out of his boot. How much was honor worth? Where did his loyalty lie? He cursed himself for even thinking such thoughts. They were born of the music. He must not play again.

"We are close, now." Val pointed as the cart lurched over the crest of a hill. Pony could see a stone tower in the distance. "The lighthouse." The structure was perhaps a league away. Most of the rolling ground in between was filled with armies. Alfred and Guthrum were found.

Pony urged Slepnir forward. She felt strong. The mourning for the loss of Herd was over. She did not worry that Alfred would not accept her. She did not even worry that she had birthed a boy-child. That was all as it should be. Everything was coming together. In some ways, she felt that the weight of her mother's teachings, of her mother's death, had all been lifted from her. She would do things for the world. The sadness she had felt since she was ten, except when she was with Herd, or on Samhain night, had washed away. She could breathe again. The swell of thoughts around her cascaded over her like a tide. She embraced that tide. Her Gift was back, more powerful than ever, since she had accepted the full range of the Great Mother's energy. The whisper of wolves, the bleat of roes in rut, the hiss of snakes and the rustle of rabbits and voles and field mice: all blended into a song that sounded remarkably like a chorus of flutes. She did not know what she would do for Alfred and his cause—but she would do what was right, in the right time. She was not yet sure that the tug toward Alfred and the amazing affinity she felt for Val were opposites. What was opposed, when the Great Mother could embrace both carnivores and plant-eaters?

The only thing not right was Val. If he did not share her

exultation, nothing could be complete. She could not erase his pain. He would not sacrifice himself, she would see to that. Yet, if he did not himself choose to live, the life in his body would mean nothing.

"To Alfred?" she asked.

"To Alfred," he agreed.

She focused on the red dragon pennant of Wessex fluttering in the breeze, identifying the forces ranged down the hills directly ahead. Guthrum's raven waved over a slightly smaller force, arrayed before the gates of the great faesten surrounding the lighthouse. As Val and Pony wove their way among the Saxon troops, men surged around their cart.

"Viking!" one soldier shouted and pointed.

"He was one of the hostages!" another cried.

"Why is he alive?" The first man spit at Val, and another. Val's jaw worked as he wiped his cheek. Saxons surged around him and Pony, their faces working with hatred.

"You *will not touch him.*" Pony's voice surprised even herself. It held all the sureness of her Mothers, all the strength she had found in the last days. The Saxons stepped back a pace. "By the Great Fecund Mare, I swear that the one who harms this man will be a eunuch by nightfall. This is the will of the Mother." Several glanced to the rotund figure of First Mare. The baby wailed.

"The Goddess . . ."

"She holds Alfred's child!"

By the time Pony and Val reached the flag of Wessex, they had collected an honor guard. Alfred squatted, bent over a plan of the faesten, writ on a vellum sheet. Osrick stood behind him and Asser on the other side. In back, a half-circle of eorls and warriors in full battle dress assembled.

Alfred glanced up and grinned. "Epona! You belong here. I fulfill Britta's vision today."

"Yes, I belong here," Pony returned quietly. She set the baby in the back of the cart and clambered down next to Val. Osrick's brows were drawn together, his eyes dark with hatred.

"I see you bring back what you stole," he sneered. Then to Val: "Were you too cowardly to meet your fate?"

Val wore a dogged look. "She had no right to free me. I am come to fulfill my bond."

Osrick hissed into Alfred's ear, his hand on his swordhilt. "Let me complete my duty."

Alfred stood and eyed his ally. "Your eagerness for blood will soon be slaked." He turned to Val. "She could not free you against your will, Viking. Have you simply changed your mind?"

"I had to hit him over the head with a candlestick, my King," Pony explained. She was so sure of herself, she smiled. Why was she so sure? This should be the worst moment of her life. She had no idea what would happen here. But whatever happened would be right.

Osrick grunted in disbelief. "More like he hid behind her belly to escape."

Val's fists clenched at his side. In a moment he would lunge for the other man.

Pony lost her smile. She turned to Alfred. "Do you not ask where I found him, liege?" Her voice grew hard. "Was he in a place of honored comfort as befits the hostage of one king to another? Or was he beaten, starved, his comrades dead, in the crypt of a stone church with moldering straw and rats for company?"

"You imprisoned him?" Alfred turned on his man with narrowed eyes. "That is not honor."

"She lies." Osrick managed a laugh. "I did not keep him locked up."

"True. That was the worst punishment of all. He stayed in that foul cell with the door open, for honor's sake, no matter your cruelty. And you!" She rounded on Alfred. "Did you consider whom you trusted with your hostages? Did you watch over them with the care required? You were too busy with your dreams of glory to pay attention to the execution of your will. Do you know what Osrick does in your name? Do you care to know? He harried Guthrum until he saw the peace broken. Your secret wish to engage the Danes has been fulfilled." Alfred's face went white. Pony was fairly certain no one had ever spoken to him thus.

"I ask no quarter, Saxon king," Val protested, glaring at Pony. "I fulfill my vow."

"I treated the hostages as you would yourself, Alfred," Osrick countered. "And there was raiding on both sides constantly along the border. This witch has no proof of what she says."

Alfred looked relieved—and that infuriated Pony. She welcomed rage as she had never done before. Whirling to Val, before he could protest, she jerked the neck of his shirt as hard as she could. It ripped in her hands, exposing his muscled shoulders and chest. The underlying gouges were crusted with scabs, the bruises mottled gray and green. But they told a story. Val stared at Pony in horror for a moment before he pulled up his shirt. Silence fell. Pony glared around the circle. "I have proof at least that the hostages were not treated well." There was no relief on Alfred's face now. A wash of shame flickered there, then was gone. Osrick's eyes darted to his king. Asser wore his usual thoughtful look.

"What right have you?" Val growled at Pony. He stepped forward and bowed his head before Alfred. "Do your will, Saxon."

The young king drew himself up and took a deep breath. "Go fight for the Raven, Viking. I give you safe passage." When Val shook his head, his frustration clear, Alfred added, "I will send a note by my hand telling that you served honorably." Asser whispered in his ear. Alfred nodded. "I had forgot. Your people read runes and we write them not. Asser will be my messenger."

What? This was not what Pony had imagined. She did not want Val to fight for Guthrum, but to stay here, with her. In her haze of optimism about fulfilling the will of the Great Mother, she had not considered the possibilities. She turned anguished eyes to Val. For a moment, her anguish was echoed there. Then she saw his eyes accept and harden.

He would go do his duty and leave her here. Was this what serving destiny meant?

He nodded once to Alfred, and to Asser and strode off to unharness Slepnir.

Pony whirled on Alfred, emotions churning in her gut. "And what of Osrick?"

Alfred shot the man a look of scorn. Osrick's eyes widened, as though he had never expected such a glare. Then Pony had the satisfaction of seeing the surprise replaced by fear. "He will bear watching," Alfred agreed, as though Osrick were not there. "More closely than I have done. But today I need him. If he serves well, he may earn a chance to serve again."

Was there to be no retribution for Osrick's crimes? Pony looked around wildly. Something was wrong. She clutched her throat as though that would help her breathe. Val swung up onto Slepnir and, after Asser mounted his little cob, he straightened his shoulders to ride toward the forces massed in front of the faesten on the cliff. The Viking line there rippled. A big man with long gray hair rode out of the gates on a white horse and moved along to.

White Stallion! Pony could feel it was he! Others on horseback followed their leader. Pony glanced about and saw horses hitched to Danish carts. Herd! Herd had been captured by Vikings! First Mare, behind her, let out a shrieking whinny. She knew it was Herd as well. Things were converging here, repeating. What should she do? How was she meant to help Alfred to the destiny Britta had seen for him? And what of Herd and Val and her baby? They seemed even more important than Alfred and Guthrum, suddenly, though she knew it was wrong to feel so.

Alfred buckled on his swordbelt. Osrick and the eorls melted away, moving to their troops. Quivering energy signaled imminent battle. It rolled through the thousands on the field, aching to be released.

Pony remembered Val squaring his shoulders. She blinked. Destiny. Destiny was important here. But not in the small way she had thought of destiny before. She had to find the way. "How can I help you?" she asked Alfred, tearing her eyes from the chestnut stallion wending its way between the armies.

Alfred grinned, pleased by her support. "Take your mare and your baby to the rise. Watch over our effort today and bring the blessing of your Great Mother to our cause." He turned up her chin. "I know the child is not mine, but they do not," he whispered. He glanced to the field below. He straightened and spoke for all to hear. "Though we may not need your help. We outnumber the Danes two to one. Angleland will soon be mine and the Vikings banished to their homeland."

Pony searched his face. Wrong. Somehow *all* of this was wrong. "I . . ." She did not know what she could say. *Why* was it wrong? "You should not fight today," she finally blurted.

He laughed. "You urged me to peace once, Epona. But now it is too late to draw back. Blood will spill today, Saxon and Viking—and in the end, one man will rule the island." He turned and began shouting orders. The warriors in his line presented their shields and readied themselves.

Pony heard shouted *Denesc* as the two armies drew closer together. A flock of carrion crows circled up into the air from somewhere. She could feel their anticipation of the coming feast. Pony's eyes followed them as they rose, then focused on the sea behind them.

"Look!" she shouted, pointing. Heads turned to follow her finger.

Just visible in the distance, coursing in toward shore, was a lithe and evil-looking Viking ship, its oars rhythmic, the yellow circles of shields lining its flanks. The red striped sail belled in the breeze. Behind it another dozen ships emerged out of the haze. More appeared even as she watched. Alfred stood frozen for a single moment, then dissolved into action.

"Move into battle, before the Nor'men can join the fray!" he yelled. "It is our only chance." He leapt onto Young Black and began to make his way up and down the lines, towering above his men where all could see him. "This day is ours. Embrace our destiny!" he shouted.

Pony snatched her baby from the cart and clutched it to her breast. Pup nosed nervously at her side, and First Mare sidled over to breathe on her neck. They were trying to tell her something. Everything was trying to tell her something. Where was all her sureness now? Why couldn't she hear them? What was getting in her way?

Alfred lifted his sword. It glinted in the sunlight. All watched for his signal. His red cloak refolded itself over his chain mail, blown by the breeze that brought the Viking ships closer. The sword descended. "For Angleland!"

Alfred's cry echoed through his surging troops. Huge men pushed past Pony at a run. The army across the valley surged forward under the raven pennant. Where was Val? She strained to see. Where was the chestnut stallion? The only riders were Alfred on Young Black and the Viking she guessed was Guthrum on White Stallion: everyone else had dismounted to fight on foot. The lines met and shattered into the chaos of swinging swords and axs. Men fell. The heaving mass of flesh and metal swallowed them.

Soon Pony was standing alone at the rear of the battle. Her baby began to wail. Pony stood rooted to the ground. She had no wish to stand on the rise and encourage this carnage. Was this what Britta had predicted of her? She could not believe it. Everything felt wrong. The tug to Alfred that had been her lodestone for the last days was gone. She knew nothing, felt nothing. Britta had said she must be complete; then she would know what to do. But how could she find any peace, any fulfillment, with all the clanking of swords and shrieking of men?

All sound fell away. Pony saw the flashes of metal, the divots of turf, the blood. She saw everything, but it was silent. A realization came to her: She had known what she needed to be complete since the morning after her last dream of the River Stour. It had seemed secondary to the tug of Alfred, less her destiny. She'd been wrong. That made her smile.

Sound welled up around her once again. She looked around for the rise. She could not take her baby into battle, but that was where she herself was going. Rushing to the top of the rise, she laid her baby in the grass. "Take care of him," she whispered to First Mare and Pup. The dog looked up solemnly at her and sat down. He would not leave her child, would protect it as long as breath was in his body. First Mare ranged her bulk behind them, nostrils sifting the air, ears pricked forward. She, too, would guard.

Pony turned back to the battle and pressed down her fear. She moved into it. At its center reared Young Black, wild-eyed, his saddle empty. A flash of red beside him said Alfred had dismounted to fight. Pony walked toward them. Around her swords cut, axs swung. She pushed a man aside and scurried around others. Men grunted with effort and howled in battle rage. Boots churned the turf to mud. Chain mail scraped her. She could not tell Viking from Saxon; they were all the same: pointed helmets, hardened leather, chain mail for some, wooden shields, sweating, grimy skin, beards and clenched teeth and blood. The smell of blood assaulted her like the chaotic sound. She shrank from a pair of giants hacking at each other, and put her shoulder into a broad back so that she might press ahead.

Young Black loomed up before her, his master's red cloak flashing by his side. Alfred had promised not to bring the horse into battle—but he betrayed his promises in favor of what he thought was destiny. The young monarch hacked at an enemy, then glanced up. "Epona!" He lunged forward and pulled her toward him, even as his sword found the gut of a man behind her. "Get on the horse!" He didn't protest that she shouldn't be there. Instead, he shoved her up on Young Black's back and turned back to the melee.

Young Black sidled and reared. "Shh," Pony whispered, though she could not hear herself in the din. The great horse quieted. Around her, as far as she could see, death flowered in bloody blossoms. The red of Alfred's cloak, the red of blood, all the red stood out starkly against leather and steel. And Pony knew why she was here.

*   *   *

Val shoved Asser in the direction of the fortress gates. "Stay away from the fighting!"

Asser nodded. "Go! I will be fine."

Val saluted the little priest. The man had courage, to put himself in the way of *Danir* on the verge of battle. He had just played Guthrum like a flute, telling of Val's courage, Alfred's acknowledgment of his honor, then reminding Guthrum of the forgiveness on which his new religion depended. This *Kristr* cult had its uses: The *konnungr*, on his great white horse, had not killed either Asser or Val. Now Val joined the rear of his countrymen's lines, unease growing in his belly. This fight suddenly did not seem his fight. Guthrum's desire to rule the whole island seemed petty.

Even as he wondered what to do, the Saxon army surged forward. They were trying to finish off the Danes before the reinforcements arrived. All around Val, the Viking troops gave a battle yell and lunged forward. Only one man shoved the wrong way: Svenn.

Val swallowed. Would the man condemn him, seeing that he had escaped his fate as a hostage? But Svenn grinned and tossed a sword at him, and a round red shield. "We might as well have the good of your arm," he yelled.

Val grinned in return. Then the two of them pressed around and forward to join the Chippenham contingent in the fray. Soon Val was locked in chaos, blood, sweat and mud. He fought toward Guthrum's white stallion—slash and shove with the shield, step forward. The blood should have been singing in his veins, the lust of battle infusing him with strength, but there was no magic transformation into *berserkr*. Val felt himself flagging as he and Svenn finally stepped up behind Guthrum. He was still too weak for battle. He might well die here after all. A Saxon poniard found his side and opened it. Guthrum was besieged on all sides. Val and Svenn redoubled their efforts. They had to hold until the dragon ships could unload reinforcements and those warriors could climb the cliffs to join them. Then would Alfred and his Saxons be crushed like those delicacies they called walnuts.

Why did that make Val feel only despair?

His shoulder touched the haunch of Guthrum's white stallion. His leader's voice echoed over the fray. "Hold the line," the *konnungr* yelled. "*Berserkrs*, all! The Nor'men come to our side."

Val did not hear. The warm hide of the squealing white horse pressed against his shoulder, the muscles beneath hard. This was one of Pony's horses! The stallion of her herd. Val felt that in the hide. The battle receded around him. He heard it from a distance. A sword glinted in the sun nearby, and he turned his head slowly toward it. His arm moved of its own volition to parry a cut at his shoulder. The glinting sword ahead swung again, this time across the white stallion's neck. Blood showered forth.

Val felt the spatters hit his face like blows. The stallion shrieked. The sound drew itself out and scraped Val's nerves. The horse reared, its chest blanketed in red. Guthrum slipped off, down to the side. Svenn stepped up to protect his king from the Saxons all around. Val watched the stallion's legs buckle, and it went down among many slashing Saxon blades. *Pony's stallion!* Val looked up across the vale to the rise above the fray. A black horse there reared. Pony sat astride it.

Waves of sound and motion crashed over Val as the battle engulfed him once again. Why had Alfred brought Pony to the center of this bloodbath? Everyone could see her, sitting so high. She would be killed like the white horse beside him who'd spent its blood on the earth and gasped his last. Rage shuddered through him. He turned away from Svenn and Guthrum, trained his eyes on Pony and raised his sword. If Alfred would not protect her, by the Gods, he would. He purposely let the *berserkr* rage that had so frightened him once well up and command his body. A yell exploded from his gut. When something you loved was at stake, all you had, including your rage, had to be mustered to protect it. Everything around him seemed to speed up. He slashed a

Saxon face and shoved the corpse aside. Rushing forward, he cut left and right, banged at his enemies with his shield, dug in with his heels and kept moving down the hill—across the stream bed, toward the black horse and Pony.

Pony felt White Stallion's death in her belly. This was her fault, because this was all wrong, and she might know what would make her complete, but she could not think how to put things right—not in the middle of a battle with all this shrieking. The Saxon line pushed away from her, engulfing the Danes. Pony shrieked herself. White Stallion was dead!

In all the confusion, her gaze was caught by one point in the Saxon line that was giving way. The momentum of the entire battle focused there. She saw waving hair drenched in sweat without a helmet, a grimace that made features almost unrecognizable as their owner hacked at those around him.

Val. He raised his head. She knew he saw her. *Yes.* Nothing more. Simply yes. It echoed inside her. She knew what she must do. Only she could right the world, and it started here. With Val. Without thinking, she urged Young Black forward into the fray.

Val cut toward her, his eyes glancing up at every step. Around him Saxons fell. Danes pushed up into the space he created. Pony should have been afraid. She should have looked for Alfred, whose destiny she was supposed to serve. Instead, she had eyes only for Val. The dissonance of battle receded. She could think. But she did not need to. She pushed toward her Viking, knowing, as clearly as she had ever known anything, that he pushed toward her.

They came together in what, for Pony, was total silence. He looked up at her and his eyes lost their crazy battle fever. She looked down at him and smiled. Calmness welled inside her, cascading over both of them; the surrounding battle did not matter. Pony actually saw a Dane behind Val push up and raise his blade. She glanced away from Val's eyes, curious. The Dane's blade flashed. Young Black lurched to the side. A line of red appeared in Pony's white shift, across her thigh. Val swung around, his sword following. She could not hear the scream, but his mouth was a rictus of rage. He cut his countryman down where he stood.

Val's shoulder pressed against her knee, and he turned to defend her.

The touch, shoulder to knee, brought a current that rippled across the very air and made Pony complete. She could not live without Val, or he without her. She could not live hearing only prey, not predators. She held up her arms and threw back her head. The teachings of her mother dropped away. The spirit of the Great Mother surged up through Pony, and the joy of wholeness was so exquisite it seemed another kind of pain. The presence of countless other entities echoed around her. Drifting up, her eyes found birds flapping in from the sea. She turned. They rushed out of the woods in waves. Thousands of birds, millions, more than she had ever seen. Vultures sailed above fluttering sparrows. The blue of jays clashed with the rust of robins' breasts. Had she called them? They swirled over the battlefield.

Pony looked down at Val, slashing and killing everyone who came near her. He seemed oblivious of the birds. Danes pressed him more closely now. They thought he was a traitor now that he had turned to protect her. She wondered at that. Did they not know he fought for the world today? She looked up again toward the wood. From the trees, foxes darted. Stags and their does stepped out in stately disapproval. Pony felt them in her mind; carnivores, plant eaters, scavengers, all of them. Badgers and wolves, eagles, voles, a wave of animals of all kinds converged on the battle. Those warriors at the edge of the army turned, startled. She could feel their fear. Her gaze was drawn back to her protector. She saw recognition bloom in his eyes. Pony turned to find Osrick raising his sword behind her—

But then Val was there, beside her, countering Osrick. Blows flurried between them.

Osrick's hatred surged around Pony, but it could not break her calm. Birds now darkened the sky. She looked to the sea. The back of some giant beast heaved a Viking ship out of the water. The sea was bright, silvered with flashing fish scales. The Norseman flotilla was under siege. Oars snapped against the hide of whales. Hulls were crushed by the slap of huge flukes. An impossibly long tentacle raised from the water and twined itself in the mast of one ship, pulled it. Men cascaded into the water.

The living pulse of the world sang through Pony, strong and sure. Animals were everywhere, pushing in toward the center of the battle. Around the field, combat stilled as men realized a miracle engulfed them. Pony's Herd cantered through the stilling melee to join First Mare upon the rise behind her. A sound began. It welled into a roar. Birds cawed, rabbits shrieked, wolves yipped their hunting victory. Men cried out in fear, all thought of battle gone. Many fell to earth, covering their heads against the sound of the earth raging against them.

Osrick and Val stepped back from each other. Osrick pressed his palms against his ears. Val looked around, then up at Pony, hand stilled, eyes calm. It grew as night, the darkness alive with flapping wings. He stretched out a hand. She gripped it, felt the slick of sweat and blood. She raised her head to a sky full of living things and sucked in air.

She saw it—saw it all as Britta must have seen it—through Val's touch. Poor Alfred. Poor Guthrum. Neither could be allowed to prevail today. The world needed Saxon and Dane to share the island a little longer. And she saw something closer to her heart, something wonderful and terrible about her baby. She breathed and took in the will of the world.

She looked down at Val and knew what had made this moment possible. She gripped his bloody hand and craned around behind her. Alfred stood, transfixed. Osrick cowered on his knees. Animals stalked among them, lowing, shrieking, cooing. The predators and prey of the animal kingdom had declared a truce. No man dared raise a hand against them, they were so many. Their numbers stretched into the distance. They must have come from all over the island. They must have been coming for days, awaiting the moment when Pony and Val would join and touch. Slowly they circled.

The silence, when it came, fell like a blow. All the animal cries stopped at once. The beasts stood, frozen. Birds descended from the sky to settle over all. An old stag stood before Pony, his antlers festooned with sparrows. Wolves slunk in around the stags' feet to surround Young Black and those surrounding him. Warriors across the field glanced around in horror, not daring to move. Yet Pony could see that some had also grown calm: those who yet knew how to listen to the Goddess and her world.

"Guthrum," Pony called into the silence. He was only yards away. "Alfred."

The two kings mustered themselves at her command. Both were indomitable men, but wariness bordering on fear lurked in their eyes. They made their way gingerly toward her, among the wolves, eagles, stoats and oxen. Svenn and Egill stepped up next to Guthrum, and Osrick scrambled beside Alfred. Osrick looked frightened. He should.

"There will be no more battle between you today, or any other day," Pony called, her voice clear. It carried across the field, though she did not shout. "The world will not allow it."

"The Goddess speaks," she heard men mutter.

"Saxon and Dane will live together." She turned to Alfred. "Was that not ordained the day Britta brought the faesten down at Thetford? You must not continue to deny her vision."

"My destiny . . ." Alfred began.

Pony sighed. "She was wrong to tell you specifics. She knew it, when I saw her. It is the timing of the thing. This all *starts* with you. But it is your progeny, your daughter's sons who will rule. You are the catalyst to a new world. Go get you a daughter but pay attention to the world around you, not just to conquest."

She turned to Guthrum. "The Danelaw is yours. Be content, or you will end with nothing. Trust the strong hearts among you, not the fruit of your loins, to make your name after." She glanced to his son, then to Egill and Svenn. "The gift you are given is the new religion you share with Alfred. Spread it among your fellows. It will sustain them in times to come."

"The Goddess urges us to worship Jesu?" Alfred asked, ducking his head in deference.

Pony smiled. "She is everywhere—in the new religion, in the old. We will understand Her if we listen for Her, wherever She is. That is all She asks."

"What can you tell us of—"

Pony cut him off with a raised hand and shook her head. "I can tell you no more. Listen with your heart." She glanced at Val. His hand moved to her knee. "That is the only answer."

Osrick lifted his head. More hatred burned in his eyes than ever. He did not feel the healing message of the Goddess. "Your dream is gone, Osrick." Her pronouncement was like a slap. His knuckles tightened on his sword hilt. He raised the weapon's point, his lips pulling back.

"And I blame you, both of you," he hissed at Pony and Val.

"Blame yourself, forgive yourself and move on to be a better man. . . ." Pony's whisper echoed uncannily across the field. She exuded the calm of the strong, sure animals all around.

It could not reach him. He lunged forward—his blade met by Val's.

The two men leaned in, muscle to muscle, steel to steel, eye to eye. But Val's eyes were calm where Osrick's were wild with fury. No one made a move to stop their struggle. Guthrum and Alfred glanced about themselves but knew not what taking action would portend. In the end, they did nothing.

Then the ground began to move. It wriggled. The stag, the wolves, all stood still and silent; but a chittering only too familiar to Pony filled the air. Rats. Rats swarmed in among them. Guthrum picked up his feet, eyes wild. Svenn, beside him, shuddered and made as if to stab with his sword any who came close. Only Osrick and Val did not take notice. They stood, still locked together, sword to sword.

"Be still," Pony commanded. "The world will have its way. You cannot change it."

The rats surged around the combatants' feet. Val glanced down. But the rats were not for him. They climbed up Osrick's legs. The Saxon shrieked and pushed away from Val. They enveloped him in a moment. Fat gray bodies, long ropy tails—there were hundreds of them. Osrick pulled back, brushed them away. Some fell, only to be replaced by more. Pony saw the gleam of white teeth. The first stains of red were small. Osrick screamed. Men retreated from his thrashing figure, alive with rats, gnawing and squeaking. He did not look human anymore. Red seeped everywhere. His face disappeared entirely. Even his screams were muffled as he fell to the ground.

Pony looked on, strangely detached. This was an execution, for effect. Had she called these rats? Perhaps. But this, too, was part of life. Like herbivores and carnivores, predators and prey. He who lived in violence would find his end in violence. Below her, Val stepped forward, chest heaving, and plunged his sword into the writhing figure. Mercifully, it stilled. The wave of rats subsided as it had come, through the legs of the larger animals.

Val leaned on his sword with both hands, staring at the bloodied mass of flesh that was left behind. The entire battlefield was still, though full to overflowing with living things.

"You do not repent. I do not forgive you," Val muttered. "But I have mercy on you."

He tore his gaze from the ravaged carcass to see Elbert, pain creasing his face, staring at his father's corpse.

The young priest crossed himself. "I forgive you, father. Now may you find forgiveness in more exalted places." He took the forgotten Saxon pennant, rampant gold lion on red, and drew it over his father's corpse.

Around them, the beasts began to move. Men kept still,

afraid. The birds circled back into the sky. Air rushed through their feathers in a muffled roar. This time they circled out like a whirlpool, expanding until they disappeared into the distance. Beasts melted back to the wood. Cattle wandered off to their grazing. Bears sank to all fours and lumbered away. Skunks and river otters and mice flowed away, off around the silent men. Pony looked out to the sea and saw the silver tide of fish recede. Men floated in the water where several ships had been sunk. The sea itself heaved with the presence of great water beasts, then sloshed free as they submerged.

Men turned to each other, eyes wide. Muttering rolled over the battlefield that was strewn with dead but empty now of animals. What had they seen? Had it been real?

Asser picked his way forward. "Was this a miracle?" Alfred asked his priest.

"Oh, yes." "The man seemed dazed. I shall write of—"

"No." Pony interrupted. She smiled. "You are meant to tell of Alfred's life, as a lesson to others. Would anyone believe what you say of Alfred if you tell what happened here today?"

Asser tapped his chin. Alfred clapped Guthrum on the back, his brows raised. They glanced together toward Pony, awe and fear writ on their countenances. Guthrum shrugged to cover the fact that he had no choice, then both men turned together toward the faesten.

Val put a hand on Young Black's bridle. "Let Elbert tend your wound," he said to Pony. She saw that red soaked her shift. Her thigh hurt. Then she realized something else.

"I must get back to my baby." She looked around, disoriented.

Val nodded and led Young Black toward the rise. The sun slanted low. They stepped over what was left of Osrick under Alfred's pennant. Around them, men helped up the groaning wounded, gathered weapons from the fallen, whispered together over what had happened here. The joy of battle no longer sang in their blood. What was left was the task of living.

Even before they reached the rise, Pony knew that First Mare and Pup were not there. Panic rose in her breast. "Where is the baby?" she cried. The ground was trodden to mush with a thousand prints of hoof and pad. There was no sign her baby and her friends had ever been there.

Fear appeared in Val's eyes, too. "Stay here. I will search for them."

"Where could they be?" Pony scanned the dark shadows in the trees behind the hill. "My baby! Who could have taken him?" In an instant, she realized just how much he meant to her, how she had come to care for him in spite of her earlier fears. Now, even her love for him was dwarfed by his importance. He would be unique in all the world, and she had lost him!

Val spun, taking in the wood, the battlefield. Then he pointed. "There!" Out across the meadow to the east was the little farm they had passed on the way in. The hut and the lean-to stable glowed where the late afternoon sun hit them. He started off at a run. Pony urged Young Black forward. Val flagged before the horse. "Go!" He waved Pony on. Young Black broke into a canter.

A great stag guarded the curved road to the lean-to stable. Hope burbled in Pony's chest as she cantered past the abandoned farmers' hut. There could only be one reason for the stag. The wolves that slunk in the shadows gave her pause for only a moment. She was grateful now for their fierce ways to protect her defenseless babe—there were good things to come of the predator. She slid from Young Black's back. Rats and badgers, cows and hawks—all gathered at a respectful distance. She stumbled around the corner of the stable to the open side.

Calm suffused her. Standing in the straw, First Mare nosed softly at a foal folded at her feet, its copper coat still wet, its wide brown eyes blinking at the new world around it. The afterbirth, red and blue-veined, was lumped in a corner. It was a healthy foal, if somewhat early. Slepnir snorted at her from a post just outside. Pup curled protectively around her own baby. Its tiny hands waved at nothing. She knelt, her tears flowing unchecked, and picked up the bundle, wet and smudged with dirt. How had he got here? She heard pounding feet and looked up to see Val.

"Is he well?" he asked, gasping as he stopped short.

Pony nodded and looked down at her boy-child. "There is a legend in which the child of the Goddess is lost. Sometimes it is told as twins," she murmured. "And the child is found in the stable of a mare newly foaled." She looked up at First Mare, then surveyed the foal. "You have done well, friend. He is beautiful." She turned to Slepnir. "And you! He has your coat."

Val fell to his knees beside her. His jerkin was streaked with blood where he had been wounded. His eyes showed exhaustion. "You have done well, too, Pony." He stretched a finger to the babe, who clasped it strongly. "Is he really the child of your Goddess?"

Pony lifted a shoulder and smiled. "He is ours. Who can say who else was with us in that circle of stones?" She looked down at her babe. "He will be special. I saw that when I saw what Britta saw of the way of the world. The first boy-child born to our line: He will do great things."

Val nodded. "He has your Gift. I think he hears Pup."

Pony stroked the dog's soft black head. "I hear Pup, too. And it does not seem so terrible." Peace filled her. This was right. "I will call Pup Loki. It is a good name."

Val sat back on his haunches. Behind him, Herd wandered up among the other animal witnesses. Several horses came to hang over Pony and breathe at her in welcome. Val stroked a random flank. "We will bury White Stallion with great honor." His voice was pained.

She shook her head to ward off the image of White Stallion's life draining out, crimson spurts over his white chest. "Perhaps Young Black can take his place. Herd needs a stallion." She looked up to see First Mare nose over to Slepnir and nibble at his withers. Two others turned and exchanged breath with the stallion. Pony raised her brows. "I am wrong. They will have Slepnir." That seemed right, too. She glanced at Val and saw him watching her, uneasy.

She did not like that look. He should be at peace as well. Could he not feel the rightness filling this stable? If Slepnir belonged here, so must he.

He glanced down the hill to where shadows lengthened across the battlefield, still alive with men carting off their dead. When he turned back, his face had hardened around the mouth. "Where does the Goddess wish to go, now that her destiny is hers once more?"

She could hardly believe what she saw in his face. "You think to go back to Guthrum."

His eyes were masked entirely. "It is either Guthrum, if he can forget that I slew *Danir* today, or back to the shores of the Volga to fight for the czars."

Could he not feel what was right? Was he afraid he was not worthy of it, or was he afraid that what was right would betray him, as his family had? Pony did not try to push down the tumult. She used its swell to fuel her words. "Do not give in to confusion, Valgar Thorvaldsson. You felt what was right today. We were drawn together whether we would or no, and when we touched, the world spoke to us, through us. You heard it. It sounded like your flute. You cannot deny the world's music."

"That music is not for me but for you," he whispered.

"Ah, and we are back to the fact that you will not forgive yourself enough to allow peace into your life." Her anger flowered. She would *not* let him do this thing, what she had once done to herself. "You took pity today on Osrick, yet you spare none for yourself."

"I did not forgive Osrick. Forgiveness is weak." Finality echoed in his voice. But the crease of pain between his eyes said he was not yet lost.

"So, be weak!" she hissed. "At least once in a while." She wondered what else she could say to him. "Britta told me I could not be whole as long as I refused to hear the ones who kill for meat. They frightened me. That I might be like them frightened me. I understood the weaker ones who ran away, the hiding ones, the prey. I did not want to hear the strong." She put a hand on his shoulder and felt him flinch at her touch. That was good. He felt the burning just as she did. "Well, you are the opposite. You are afraid that you will feel something beyond the strength and ruthlessness of a carnivore, the need to devour. You are afraid that makes you weak."

"It *does* make me weak," he protested, angry. "And more than strong. I lost control. I forgot the *law* of Danes, I was *berserkr*."

"Strong and weak together is more than either alone. You hate yourself for this *berserkr*. You hate that you are soft with those who are weaker. But together they make you more than any other man."

"*I* abandoned my first loyalty to my father, though I knew it was the way to dishonor."

"This is an argument you have said many times, but can you really believe it? Was it not your loyalty to your brothers and your mother that made you sacrifice yourself to save them? Is that loyalty less important than the one to your father?" She cast about for words that might serve her. "You dared not listen to the weaker ones for fear of the tumult it will unleash in you. But the tumult of embracing what you fear is what frees you, makes you *whole*. You were strong for your brothers. Forgive yourself for your strength."

"I should have saved Harald." His voice was bleak.

"Ah remember, Val—you cannot have it both ways. You were strong for your brothers. You sacrificed yourself for them against the *law* of your land. But in Harald's case, you made yourself serve your *law* above your friend. And he made his own choice. Must you blame yourself there, too?"

He shook his head, as though to keep her words away. "I must do something for Una." Then he shrugged in disgust or despair. "What can take the place of a husband?"

"Send her to Britta and Karn in Stowa. They will care for her." Pony felt the sureness surge. "Britta will make sure she finds a new life."

"Karn, *ja*." He was thinking about the other Viking who

had bridged to a life beyond the only world he knew. She could see it in his eyes.

So she pressed her advantage. "Embrace what you fear about yourself, Valgar the Beast. You are no beast at all. Forgive yourself for owning weakness and strength together. The very emotions you consider weak are strong in another's eyes." She ordered. She cajoled. "Does not Father Elbert think forgiveness shows strength? The world demands that you forgive yourself. Your new religion requires it." Her hand threaded up through his beard to cup his cheek. His eyes were full. "*I* demand it."

"Mayhaps I believe more in this *Kristr* than I thought." His voice was thick.

"You are more than Viking, Val, more than carnivore. You always have been. That is why Guthrum chose you, why the elders of Chippenham followed you, why Harald loved you." She did not add the final tribute, the one that she could not lay at his feet until she knew that he could reach to pick it up.

He looked thoughtful as he rubbed his cheek against her hand. "There is more than Viking in the world."

"More than loyalty?"

He shook his head. "No. But mayhap loyalty can be to more than one. It is hard."

She smiled. "But real. These choices are hard but real. The rules my mother gave me were too simple. They were but part of the truth. Can you not see that the rules of your father and his before him were not enough?"

Val took a breath and blew it out, not even able to answer. But she knew she had him.

"You felt whole today, as I did." She raised her brows. He wanted so much to yield, yet some part still believed that yielding would destroy him. Ah. It was the fear that any act of loyalty or courage would be betrayed. "Admit at least that you felt whole when we touched and the world spoke through us."

"*Ja,*" he whispered, swallowing. "And when I saw you kneel among your animals, with the baby at your breast."

She nodded, not daring to let any trace of a smile show. "Our baby." She let the tiny fist grasp her finger. "We cannot know whether the Goddess will abandon us," she whispered, "if we have the courage to choose her way of wholeness. But we can refuse to abandon each other." There. She had dared to promise.

Val's eyes strayed to First Mare and her foal and then to Slepnir guarding them. "I chose today, as he has." He looked at her with wonderment. "Why do I yet harry the question? It has been answered. I fought for you today, not for Guthrum. I am yours, for as long as you will have me. I have been yours since the night at the stones."

Pony nodded. She dared say no more. Val had the courage to declare his choice. But she felt most keenly that she was the one who had galloped away on the morning after Samhain. It was for her to give a sign that she would not abandon him. She looked at the baby. Spittal burbled at his lips. "What is your youngest brother's name?" she asked softly. "I have forgot."

He looked startled. "Erik."

"This boy shall be Erik Valgarsson." She adjusted the child's wool blanket.

Val reached to take the tiny bundle from her. He peered at the tiny face, its chin now most distinctly cleft. "Not much of a name for the son of a Goddess. But it will do." He gathered Pony into his other arm. The dull pain in her thigh receded as his lips brushed her hair. The feel of his hard body under his shirt made her loins ache.

"You once said the soil in the Vale was good," she ventured after a moment. There was silence above her.

"The Vale is not in the Danelaw, but part of Alfred's land."

She nodded. "Alfred will have need of an eorl for Chippenham, now that Osrick is dead. He will be looking for ways to keep peace with the Danes." She chuckled. "The folk in Chippenham will not oppose a Dane in the *faesten*. Especially you, as you have many friends there."

"Friendr." He paused to think. Their baby gave a watery

sneeze. He jogged it gently on his hip. "Family. Land." First
Mare nickered at her foal and shoved it gently with her nose.
It struggled up on spindly legs, and she pushed it toward
her swollen teats.

"Home." Pony took Erik and set him next to Loki. "This
begins a new time. Alfred will open many doors. Our son
will open others." When she turned to Val, she saw his eyes
alight with what burned in her own loins. His mouth curved
up ever so slightly on one side.

"Can we ourselves, not open certain doors?"

"I warn you, Valgar the Beast, I want more than just a
father for my child."

"What more could a woman want?" he asked, pretending
innocence.

She put her arms around his neck and pressed her breasts
against him. The throbbing in her was part of the tumult
she now welcomed. "I want a man for my bed, a companion
in my old age. I want someone to tell me their secrets."

Val shrugged, as if he had no choice. "How many men
can say they bed a goddess?" His lips brushed her throat.

"Only one. But we goddesses expect the world. We must
be bedded frequently."

"So do beasts expect," Valgar returned.

All else was lost in kisses. The hay was redolent of summer, the breath of the animals around them comforting. The
coming night would be warm. All was as it should be.

HIGH PRAISE FOR SUSAN SQUIRES!

DANEGELD
*2001 Golden Heart Award Winner
*HOLT Medallion Winner

"An outstanding debut novel that takes some risks and succeeds. Susan Squires gives us a gritty, complex love story that is as engrossing as it is endearing."

—*The Romance Reader*

"Readers, throw away any preconceived notions you might have of a pretty medieval romance. *Danegeld* is unique. If we let this wonderful, original book fall by the wayside, we will be stuck with cookie-cutter books and will have only ourselves to blame."

—*All About Romance*

"A competent and well-thought-out historical novel, with just a bit of magic thrown in for delicious spice. Brava, Ms. Squires!"

—*Old Book Barn Gazette*

"The author distinguishes herself and her work from the bulk of the genre."

—*The Historical Novels Review*

SACRAMENT

"Be prepared for a very different vampire story, a wholly original new take on the old legends."

—*The Romance Readers Connection*

"With its complicated plot twists, deep passion and very dark pleasures, *Sacrament* should delight those seeking a romance that's out of the ordinary."

—*Romantic Times*

"A beautifully written romance novel, full of twists and turns, depth of emotion, and vivid characters."

—*Romance and Friends*